Body of a Girl

Leah Stewart

VIKING

VIKING
Published by the Penguin Group
Penguin Putnam Inc., 375 Hudson Street,
New York, New York 10014, U.S.A.
Penguin Books Ltd, 27 Wrights Lane, London W8 5TZ, England
Penguin Books Australia Ltd, Ringwood, Victoria, Australia
Penguin Books Canada Ltd, 10 Alcorn Avenue,
Toronto, Ontario, Canada M4V 3B2
Penguin Books (N.Z.) Ltd, 182–190 Wairau Road,
Auckland 10, New Zealand

Penguin Books Ltd, Registered Offices:
Harmondsworth, Middlesex, England

First published in 2000 by Viking Penguin,
a member of Penguin Putnam Inc.

1   3   5   7   9   10   8   6   4   2

PUBLISHER'S NOTE
This is a work of fiction. Names, characters, places, and incidents
either are the product of the author's imagination or are used
fictitiously, and any resemblance to actual persons, living or dead,
events, or locales is entirely coincidental.

LIBRARY OF CONGRESS CATALOGING IN PUBLICATION DATA
Stewart, Leah, date.
Body of a girl / Leah Stewart.
p.   cm.
ISBN 0-670-89164-9
I. Women journalists—Tennessee—Memphis—Fiction.
2. Memphis (Tenn.)—Fiction.   I. Title.
PS3569. T465258 B64   2000
813'.54—dc21   99-055518

This book is printed on acid-free paper.
(∞)

Printed in the United States of America
Set in New Caledonia
Designed by Betty Lew

For Matt

Acknowledgments

Thanks to my agent, Gordon Kato, and my editor, Carolyn Carlson, for their good advice and faith in this book.

For counsel on everything from police procedure to Memphis geography, thanks to Zack McMillin, Steve Hall, Cletus Oliver, and Dr. Wendy Gunther. I couldn't have written this book without Angie Craig.

Many thanks to my teachers, A. Manette Ansay, Charles Baxter, and Nicholas Delbanco. I am grateful for the support of Wyatt Prunty, Cheri Peters, and the staff of the Sewanee Writers' Conference, and also to Norma Diala at the Harvard Graduate School of Education, for giving me a job while I wrote this book.

For love and encouragement, thanks go to my family, particularly Susan and Skip Francies, Cameron Stewart, Gordon Stewart, and Julie Finch. I am also grateful to my friends and readers Carolyn Ebbitt, Caroline Kim, Surrena Goldsmith, Leigh Anne Couch, Terry Joffe, Shivika Asthana, Nina Reid, and especially my coach, Elwood Reid.

1

This has been a summer of murders. Memphis is so hot people move like they're wearing something heavier than their skin. I can't help but feel that these things are connected. I can't put this in the stories I write. It's not fact. It's not *true,* in the way we mean true at the newspaper, which is that we got someone else to say it.

There are reporters at this newspaper whose whole job it is to interview zoo workers about new baby animals. One guy wrote a three-part series about how to avoid the lunch rush at the fast-food drive-thru. I'm the one the cops like to show photographs of raped and beaten women, looking at me out of the corner of their eyes to see if I can take it. "Okay," I always say, when I think I've looked at them long enough. "I see." I work the police beat. Murders are my responsibility.

It's cloudy this morning, and so humid I'm sweating just standing still. Here and there patches of light shine through the clouds, as though someone poked holes in my jar so I could breathe. On the ground not three feet from me is the body of a young woman, white, my age. Steam rises from the dirt all around her, and when I look down I can see it coming up between my feet. I'm trying to get it straight in my head, how I'll describe this scene in the paper, how to make it simple, clinical, how to explain that what looked like smoke was only rainwater evaporating in the terrible heat. But all I can think is *My God, my God.*

She is curled up. Her hands are bound in front of her, her wrists wrapped round and round with what looks like white string. Her white T-shirt is patched red with blood. From the waist down she is naked, tire marks slashed across her skin. On one foot she wears a sandal; the other is bare. She is lying among tire tracks in a patch of sandy ground, and around her tufts of wild grass and dandelions push up through the dirt. She knew that car was coming. I would ball myself up like that, trying to disappear.

This is not where I'm supposed to be. Normally I'd arrive at the scene after the crowd had gathered, and I'd stand behind the yellow tape, with the rest of the press, the crying neighbors, the mamas with babies on their hips leaning in to get a look, lucky to catch a glimpse of the body bag when they brought it out. Today I was about to pull into the newspaper parking lot when I heard it over the police scanner—DOA, at the park, less than two miles away. I followed a police cruiser to the site and stopped my car next to it. When I got out, the uniformed cop sauntered over to me and asked me what I thought I was doing. I said I was press and he looked me up and down. "You want to look," he said. "Go ahead and look." He's not supposed to do that, but maybe he thought I would faint and give him a story to tell his buddies. So I kept my face blank, and I walked right up to the dead girl and didn't say a word. The cop watched me, and shrugged, disappointed. "Stay out of the way," he said.

I've learned to stomach the photographs they show me, but now I know it's nothing like being so close you could lean down and touch that dead, dead skin.

I flip open my notebook. This is the first time I haven't had to wait for the cops and the medical examiner to give me a secondhand version of the crime scene. Faced with the real thing, I realize I don't know where to look, what details I'll even be allowed to print. The body lies near the river, not far from the park entrance, where the ticket booths were during the two festivals in May, one for barbecue, one for blues. Whoever dumped the body made no attempt to hide it, or to drag it to the water, only yards away.

Around us, cars arrive, their tires kicking up dust. Doors shut, and the rumble of male voices grows louder. Somebody shouts. I don't even turn my head to look, scrawling words in my notebook.

The feet are small and narrow, with tiny pink toenails.

The exposed legs are slender, with just the hint of muscle beneath the skin. There's a little scab near one ankle, as though she nicked herself shaving.

A white T-shirt is pushed up above the curve of the hips to reveal a pale stomach, the edge of a belly button. On the shirt I can barely make out the letters "MUS." Something about the lettering is familiar, and then I realize why. It's the Beale Street Music Festival T-shirt from last year. I have the same one at home in my closet. I wonder if the shirt is what made her killer think of bringing her here.

Her fingers are clenched, the nails painted the same delicate shade as her toes.

Her head is curled in toward her chest. The hair draped across her ruined face is long and dark, clotted with blood, powdered with dust.

Someone bumps me, passing by, and still I don't look. I barely feel it. It's like we are alone here, the dead girl and me, two sides of a coin.

From the ground in front of her face, steam rises, almost like breath.

I lift my hand to write and see that it's shaking. I watch as though those trembling fingers aren't even mine. The body beyond slips in and out of focus as I wait for my fingers to steady. When they do I grip my pen tightly and write in my notebook: *T-shirt*.

This is just my job.

The crime tape has gone up and detectives are arriving. I know they won't want to see me here. I haven't been on the beat long enough to have the contacts other reporters have, and I don't want

to antagonize any of the cops. I take another look at her before I
turn away. A few steps from the body, I can't help but look again. I
turn around, walking backward. A cop stands over her, obscuring
my view. I can still see her bare white legs, her tiny feet.

"Hey," someone calls out. "Get the hell back." I turn and see a
cop striding toward me. I think his name is Detective Buchanan.
He's young enough to still look a little sick at the sight of the corpse.
"What do you think you're doing?"

"I'm sorry," I say. "The tape wasn't up yet. I didn't realize how
close I was."

"The body should've given you a clue," he says.

"I'm so sorry," I say again, flashing him a smile, wondering if he's
lead detective. "I'll be more careful next time."

He stares at me a second. "Getting to you, isn't it," he says. "You
look sick."

"So do you," I say, and he snorts. "Do you have a positive ID?"

"I can't tell you anything," he says. "You know the routine; when
the lieutenant gets here, he'll talk to the press."

"Come on," I say. "Give me something. Off the record."

He just shakes his head, and waves me away.

Behind the yellow tape I watch the rest of the press arrive. The
TV stations park their vans so close the cops have to squeeze in and
out of the scene. People shout. The satellite towers go up, and the
reporters line up in front of the tape. The cops stare at us from the
other side. It reminds me of the Civil War reenactments my father
used to drag me to as a child, the two lines approaching each other,
volleying fire. If this were a neighborhood, I'd be canvassing the
crowd, looking for somebody who knew the victim, somebody to tell
me she'd been fighting with her boyfriend, somebody to tell me
she'd heard the boyfriend hit her, she'd heard the dead girl ran
around on him. But here there's nothing to do but wait for the lieutenant, watching the cops' backs as they bend and stand, cluster and
part. Detective Buchanan passes by again, frowning. I can't remember where I saw him before, which crime it was.

Off to the right I can make out the taller buildings of downtown, the red letters on the roof of the Peabody Hotel. Somewhere past that, the glass panes of the Pyramid are glinting in the sun. Nearby is Beale Street, its strip of garish bars and souvenir shops isolated among warehouses and parking lots, as if it had been constructed as a movie set and allowed to stand. A hill rises on one side of the fairgrounds, dotted with the houses of rich people and local celebrities. I squint at the houses, trying to judge the distance. They're too far away for the residents to have seen anything.

This is my job, to give you all the details right up front, what time it was, where and how it happened, so you can use them to determine whether it could have been you. *I'd never go there alone at night,* you think, putting the paper down beside your cup of coffee after you read the headline and maybe the lead. It's my job to keep you reading past that first paragraph, to make you see it like I do, what it is possible for your body to look like, how easily you could be destroyed.

A cop in uniform stands in front of me, turning his head from side to side. It's his job to keep the media and the curious out of the way. His white hair is damp with sweat, and the skin of his neck droops over the too tight collar of his shirt. He takes a handkerchief from his pocket and mops at his face and neck. Then he says something about a little white girl.

"What?" I say.

"Heard she's a pretty little white girl," he says, leaning toward me.

"It'd be hard to say if she's pretty," I say.

"D'you see her?" He's surprised when I nod. "Are you the one that found her?"

"No," I say. "I just saw her. Do you know who found her?"

My notebook is in my hand, but I keep it closed. If he's going to tell me something, I don't want to scare him off.

He doesn't answer the question. He says, "That'll give you nightmares."

"I don't have nightmares," I say. He looks skeptical, but it's the truth. Lately I dream in words. My dreams aren't movies, with images and sound. Instead I watch them scroll past like a story typed out on a computer, like when you play a video game so long that you still see the figures moving even with your eyes closed.

The cop leans in like he's going to tell me something, then he sees the notebook in my hand and stops cold. "You a reporter?"

I say yes, wishing I'd kept the notebook in my bag. You never know what casual comment you might be able to use.

"Big story for you, ain't it," he says. "White girl killed, probably raped. Not the usual black-on-black killing we get here. This girl's young. Innocent."

"Nobody's innocent," I say. "There's always something."

He laughs. "That's nice thinking for a little gal like you," he says. "You sound like a cop."

Here we go again. I say, "We cover a lot of the same territory." Detective Buchanan comes up behind the cop and says something I can't hear. The cop nods, then moves a foot to the right and doesn't speak to me anymore. Now it comes to me where I saw the detective before. He was the officer in charge three weeks ago, when four men carrying semiautomatic rifles kicked down a couple's door in the middle of the night, mistaking it for a crack house. They raped the wife in front of her husband, then shot them both. Their toddler hid under the bed until the men left, and when the police arrived they found her sleeping, curled up against her dead father's chest with her thumb in her mouth. My roommate, Hannah, says, how can you write about these things?

Verb follows subject, I say. Object follows verb.

Lieutenant Nash keeps taking his jacket off and putting it back on, torn between his need to look professional and his need for relief from the unbearable heat. He's a large man, and his round dark face is shiny with sweat. When he takes off his jacket his white shirt clings wetly to his back, though I can see that he's wearing an undershirt. I'm right behind him, close enough to touch that back, and around me is the rest of the press. We follow him as he makes his way around the perimeter of the crime scene, all of us looking around for someone who might tell us more, who might tell us something no other reporter knows.

Nash, the official spokesman for this case, has told us nothing I didn't already know. I wrote it down in my notebook anyway: *dead girl, white, mid-20s, no ID yet, no cause of death yet, no suspects yet*. So far I barely have who, what, when, where, and how, let alone why, which is what everybody wants to know anyway, like they want to know why that athlete got AIDS, why the neighbor's husband left her, why that house burned down and all the children in it died. They want to know, what made them choose this girl over another, over me? I find the reasons for them.

"Any idea when you might have an ID?" I ask Nash.

He looks exasperated. "By the end of the day," he says. "We'll call you at the end of the day."

That does me no good. By the end of the day, I'll have no time to track down anyone who might know her, my story will be nothing but her name and no one will read it because they'll have gotten all their information from the evening news. "Thank you," I say, and smile prettily at him. A reporter from Channel 7 jostles against me and I resist the urge to elbow her in her pink-suited side. Instead I drop out of the pack and drift back toward the tape to watch the activity around the body. I can't see anything until they all part to let the body bag through.

I swear I must be feeling faint from the heat. When they bring the body bag out, that plastic shimmers beautifully, like water under the sun.

In the police station, it's always cold, even now in the middle of June. The furniture looks as though it hasn't been replaced since the '70s. Twenty years ago, the chairs were bright orange, and maybe when they were new they made the place look cheerful, but now they're just tacky, part of the general drab-and-dirt atmosphere. The interview room in homicide is white, with files spilling everywhere on the rows of metal desks. I'm sitting on a file, because it was in the chair when I went to sit down, and I couldn't see anywhere on Sergeant Morris's desk to put it.

Morris is saying, "I'm not supposed to tell you anything." On Saturdays he brings in barbecue for everyone, even me, and tells me stories from his decades on the force. Right now he holds a photograph, up and away from me.

"Just give me her name, please," I say, looking at his name tag, which I can't stop reading over and over. I don't know if they call those things they wear name tags. It seems like they should have some more official term, like breastplate. "Please."

"I don't know," he says. "The brass is cracking down."

I look at my watch. "Please, Sergeant. You know I never quote you," I say. "I won't print anything without confirmation. Please. I'm on deadline."

"I hate to think about you on a story like this," he says. "A nice little girl like you."

On the streets all over Memphis, I see cops whose muscles are thick under tight uniforms. They stride in twos or threes down the street like a posse in a Western movie, eyes scanning back and forth, their whole bodies heavy with assurance. I never talk to these cops. My cops are always fat and old and grimly sad. They have thick southern accents and call me "little lady." There are female cops, too. The female cops never talk to me.

Morris fingers some papers on his desk. I lean in closer. He's about to give up the name. I can feel it.

"Had a little girl killed a couple days ago," he says. "Guy shot a revolver in the air, bullet came down, hit her."

I nod. I already wrote that story.

"You know what really bugs me?" he says. "On TV? When they

take a revolver and put a silencer on it." He shakes his head. "A silencer doesn't work on a revolver."

My leg starts to jiggle, impatience slamming through my body. "Sergeant . . . ," I start.

"And bodies?" he says. "They don't float. When you're dead . . ." He mimes a shooting, pointing an imaginary gun at me and jerking it back. "You're dead, you sink to the bottom like a rock. Watch when they shoot somebody on TV. They fall into a swimming pool and they just float like a cork."

"Yes," I say. I've heard all of this before. I know if I listen long enough, he'll have to give me something in return.

"Olivia," Morris says. "Does your mother know what you do for a living?"

"She knows I'm a reporter." I hold my pen ready.

"But does she know what you report? Does she know her little girl is crawling around crime scenes?"

"Do you have an ID?" I say.

"You saw the body?" he asks, and when I nod, he shakes his head. "I don't know why you have to look at things like that."

"The other detectives like to show me homicides," I say. "They get a kick out of it."

"Because you're a girl," he says.

"So how come you don't want me to see them?"

"Because you're a girl," he says, and a slow grin spreads across his face.

"I can't win," I say, and I'm surprised by how grim it comes out sounding when I meant to be joking. "Who was she?" I say. "Tell me about her. I need to know."

He hesitates, shaking the photograph like a sugar packet between two fingers, then finally he gives it to me. It's not the crime scene photo I expected. In the picture, a young woman stands holding a beer in one hand, an expression of exaggerated surprise on her face, eyebrows up, mouth open, laughing. A guy in a baseball cap is kissing her cheek. She has shiny dark hair that falls to her shoulders, green eyes, a large mouth. It takes me a moment to understand that this is the girl whose crumpled body I stood over this morning.

Morris tells me that her friends reported her missing this morning, after looking for her since late Saturday night, when she didn't show up to meet them. Neighbors saw her car parked out in front of the apartment building, instead of around back in the lot, so the cops think she must have run in to get something, and somebody got her when she came back out. She worked in the outpatient clinic at the Madison Medical Center. Her name was Allison Avery.

I'm looking for something in her face, some detail, that will tell me who she was. She laughs up at me. She could be any girl who went to my college, any girl I pass between stores at the mall.

Morris reaches out to take the picture back. "Good luck," he says.

"Can I keep this?" I ask, holding on to the picture.

"No," he says. "But I'll let you make a photocopy." He looks from the photo in my hand to my face. "You look a little like her," he says. "Same hair color. Same shape to the face." In the air he traces the curve of my cheek.

"She was prettier," I say. I drop the picture on his desk. He doesn't contradict me, just picks the photo up and stares at it. "What about the car?" I say.

Morris shakes his head. "Haven't found it yet."

"You got any thoughts on this?"

He frowns.

"Point me in the right direction," I say.

He sighs, hunched over his desk. "How long you been doing this? Months?"

"Three," I say.

He nods. "Long enough to know," he says. "Nine times out of ten, girl dead like this, it had something to do with sex. You know that. She turned him down, slept around on him, whatever. If it's a stranger, maybe he raped her and got carried away, or scared she'd identify him after."

"What's your guess here?"

"None of this is for the paper?" He waits for me to nod, then says, "I'd say the way she was found, outside, some stranger grabbed her, drove around trying to figure out what to do with her. Boyfriend kills you, it's usually at home. He shoots you or beats you to death. Now, could be a premeditated thing, or could be she was out someplace with a guy she knew and he brought her there." He hunches down lower, his voice heavy with exhaustion. "You know," he says again. "We're gonna be looking for any boyfriends, any exes, trying to figure out where she was those missing hours between when she left work and when the neighbors saw her car."

This is all he knows. "Thanks," I say. "I really appreciate it."

He stares at the picture, rubbing the back of his neck with one hand. He says, "She was just your age."

Outside the interview room, I sit and make a list in my notebook. *Get family. Go to workplace. Call Peggy. Where's the car? Boyfriend? Cause of death? Call medical examiner. Get milk. Deposit check. Do dishes. Call Mom.* It's not a list I need to make, but it passes the time. I'm hoping to catch the family coming out after they talk to the cops. They're easy to identify because they're always crying. I draw a series of little flowers across the bottom of the page, thinking about the dead girl's body. When I close my eyes it's not the image that I see. It's the words I wrote in my notebook—*T-shirt, string, blood.*

I've been a full-time reporter for three years, and I can't remember half of what I learned in college, but these words are growing in me like weeds. It's been three months since they put me on the police beat. All summer I've had photographs of dead bodies fanned across my desk, buried under stacks of paper until I come across them looking for something else. It's not these pictures that appear in my dreams, but the words I used to describe them.

Again and again I check my watch, every second putting me

closer to deadline. After a long time the flowers on my notebook page have overtaken the list, and I'm thinking this may be a lost cause when a couple walks out clinging to each other. The man has obviously been crying, the woman has the look of someone who's just been slapped, and her cheeks are red, the rest of her face white as paper. I'm certain these are the girl's parents. I stand up slowly. The trick is to make it sound like you're giving them some kind of opportunity, and never, never ask how they feel—that's for television reporters. Refer to the victim in the present tense, say nothing directly about her being dead, ask whether she has a boyfriend, because more often than not it turns out to be him. Be polite. Be apologetic.

"I'm very sorry to bother you," I say, "but I wanted to talk to you about your daughter."

"Are you a reporter?" the woman asks.

"Yes, ma'am." I'm staring at her face. She looks familiar. I can't place her.

"We can't talk to you right now," she says. Her voice breaks, but she doesn't move to find a tissue, or bury her face in her hands or her husband's shoulder. Instead she stares angrily at me, even while tears start down her cheeks. I notice that her husband doesn't comfort her. His eyes never move from her to me, as though as long as he doesn't look at me, I'm not here.

"I know this is difficult," I say. "I'm sorry."

"Difficult?" she says. "What do you know about it?"

It's a conversation I've had so many times I feel like I'm watching it from outside, like something on a television drama. There's only so many ways you can say these things, only so many ways they can respond. *What was she like*, I'll say. *She was our daughter*, they'll say. *We loved her.* Some people are eager to talk, grateful for your desire to listen. Some, like this woman, have to be coaxed.

"Ma'am," I say as gently as I can, "I just want to write about Allison's life."

"If she weren't dead," she says, "you wouldn't give a shit about her life."

They turn their backs on me and walk away. I listen to the sound of their footsteps receding, then I glance at my list and put a line through *Get family*. I rummage through my bag for my car keys. *Go to workplace* is next.

"She's just a nice, nice person," the receptionist at the Madison Medical Center keeps saying. Tears are starting in her eyes. "Just the nicest person in the world." She has also told me that Allison was a nursing tech in the clinic, that she had a big smile and was good with patients. I resist the urge to drum my fingers on her desk.

One thing I know, people hardly ever say anything about someone that couldn't be said about anyone. I don't know if this is because lately the people I talk to are almost always talking about someone who's dead, and therefore immediately becomes a nice girl, a great guy, a loving mother, a generous friend. I'm beginning to think it's because this is how people see each other, as members of these sad generic categories. Allison Avery, Nice Girl.

The receptionist tells me Allison was friends with Angela Schultz, one of the nurses in the clinic. She directs me down the hall to the third door on my right.

"Thank you," I say. "You've been very helpful." She never even asked me who I was. People don't, in general. If you ask them a question, they answer it.

Before I tell her, Angela Schultz doesn't know her friend is dead, and the way her eyes empty and her face drains of color when I say it, I think for a moment her heart has stopped.

Angela is one of the friends who was supposed to meet Allison Saturday night, so from her I learn that Allison had some errands to run after work and then was going home to change and drop off her groceries. She was supposed to be at the Lizard Lounge at nine. I write that down, *Lizard Lounge,* and sit staring at the words. I've been there, with my boyfriend, David.

"How long did you wait before you called her?" I ask Angela.

"Half an hour," she says. "Allison was always late." At midnight, after calling Allison's house, her parents' house, and another friend's house, Angela called the police. That's all she knows, and she's choking as she talks, so it takes me a long time to get her to say it. Angela is another version of the girl I saw in the picture this morning, her hair dark and sleek and pulled back from her face, her features even and unremarkably pretty. She is made up in the manner of a respectable southern girl, light foundation, peach lipstick, muted eyeshadow, and mascara that's now smudged around her wet eyes.

This won't be the last time today I'll bring this news to some unsuspecting friend or relative. It's exhausting, my throat tightening with the grief of someone I don't know, for someone I've never met.

When you're told something terrible about someone you don't know—your cousin says her sister-in-law is dying of cancer—you have a moment of anxiety about what to say. Maybe you've met the woman once, and for a moment you really do feel bad, but in the end you're just going to say, "That's awful," and let some silence pass before you talk about something else. When you're a reporter, you're always talking to strangers who have just had something terrible happen to them. In college, I interviewed a famous journalist for the school paper. "In Vietnam, the rivers were thick with bodies," he said. "Either you had the stomach for it or you didn't."

I have the stomach for it.

If I didn't I couldn't sit here listening to Angela Schultz talk while the image of her friend's dead body rises in front of me, as real as this live woman's face. "That's all I know," she is saying, her hands covering her eyes as she begins to rock back and forth in her chair. "Oh God. Not Allison. Oh God. Oh God." I write in my notebook: *all she knows.* She lifts her face, ghoulish now with black streams of mascara tears, her lipstick half chewed off. "Are you sure it was her? Are you absolutely sure? Did you see the body?"

I hesitate. Then I nod. "It was her. I'm sorry." She wails and drops her head again. The room is a typical examining room, chair, rolling stool, someone's diploma framed on the wall. Altogether sterile, except for a vase of lilies tucked in the corner of the counter, near the sink, and a framed photograph nearby on the wall. I go over for a closer look while behind me Angela's wails quiet into sobs. It's a staff photo. Allison and Angela smile on either side of a tall man in a white lab coat who must be one of the clinic doctors.

I'm glad I've seen these pictures of the dead girl's face, and not the eight-year-old senior yearbook shot they'll probably run on the front page. If you die young, they always pull out those high school pictures. No one really looks like that—the false smile, the cocked head, the hands folded awkwardly against the cheek.

Next to the picture, you'll see my byline. Then the copy. The victim was twenty-four years old. She was a nursing technician from a middle-class family, and she had just moved into her own apartment in Midtown a year ago. Saturday night, she worked late at the office, went to the grocery store for a few things, and drove to her apartment. She was late to meet friends at a Midtown bar, so she parked her car on the street in front of the building, instead of behind the building in the lot. When she came back out, hurrying, maybe checking her watch, someone grabbed her. What happened next is not entirely clear. I'm guessing that they'll tell me someone drove her in her own car to Tom Lee Park, raped her, beat her, and killed her finally by running her over.

Her name was Allison Avery. She was a nice girl.

I turn from the picture. Angela is folded in on herself, not making a sound. I go toward her and let my hand hover over her shoulder, not quite close enough to touch. My voice low, I ask her if Allison was seeing anyone, if she had been on a date lately, if anyone had shown any interest in her.

She shakes her head, not looking up.

"She didn't have a boyfriend?"

Angela lifts her face. She says no with such finality, her eyes so deliberately fixed on mine, I'm certain she is lying.

"There was no one?"

"No," she says again. We stare at each other for a moment. Then she returns her head to her knees. I stand looking at her bent neck, the wisps of hair escaping from her bun. Who could Allison's boyfriend be, that her best friend would keep him a secret, even after death?

A man comes hurrying in, like the answer to a question. I recognize him from the picture on the wall. He steps between us and scoops Angela up into a standing position and into his arms, as easily as lifting a baby. He is startlingly handsome, between thirty-five and forty, with a strong jaw and dark hair lightly touched with gray. He wears a wedding ring. "Is it true?" he asks me.

"I'm afraid so, sir," I say.

Angela shudders and presses her face to his chest. She's going to leave black smudges all over his straw-colored linen jacket. "I'm so sorry," he whispers. "Poor girl." I wonder which of them he means.

When I ask, Dr. Gregerson tells me what I expected, that Allison was a hard worker, a good worker, a nice girl. She used to bring in flowers for the office, unasked, which is, finally, a detail I can use. She liked carnations, because they last a long time, but every once in a while she brought in lilies because, she said, they were too beautiful to resist. "There, in the vase," he says. "Those are hers."

Straightening up, out of his embrace, Angela carefully pulls her loosened hair back into place. Her sobbing has slowed into an occasional hiccup and she seems oddly calm, her eyes glazed over. Over her shoulder I see the doctor noticing the black and tan traces of mascara and foundation on his jacket. I'm staring at his face, eyes narrowed, looking for signs of grief. He brushes at the streaks of makeup, frowning, then catches my eye and drops his hand, embarrassed. After a moment he lifts the same hand and squeezes Angela's shoulder.

"Angela," I say gently, brushing my fingertips lightly against her forearm, "do you have a picture of Allison I could borrow?" I move to indicate the framed photo on the wall, though I'd prefer to have a shot of the girl alone. I open my mouth to give the speech about why we need a picture—personalize the crime, make it visceral—but Angela just nods, reaching numbly for a red purse and extracting a wallet. She flips it open to one of those plastic picture holders and slips a small photo from its casing. She says nothing when she hands it to me. "Thank you so much," I say. I look down, and there it is, the high school yearbook photo, teased hair framing the dead girl's carefully made-up face, some boy's class ring heavy on the hand beneath her chin.

Angela is saying that if I really want to write about Allison I should know she had a secret ambition. She wanted to be a singer in a rock and roll band.

"She's too practical to give up her job for it," Angela says. "She had gigs around here sometimes." When I nod, she goes on. "That was what she really loved. If you saw her up there, you knew right away, the way that big voice came pouring out her little body, it just washed you away. That was her. That was who she was." She tells me Allison's voice made your heart ache—it was the sound of longing, just hanging in the air. It moved you, she says. You couldn't help but cry. And now she's crying too hard to say any more, but that is enough.

It was the truth, what I said to Allison's mother. What you want to write about is someone's life, even if her death is the reason you're writing about her at all. Allison Avery has slipped out of her category, and I come out of what used to be her office scribbling in my notebook, circling *lilies*, underlining *rock & roll*, crossing out *nice girl, nice girl, nice girl,* all down the page.

2

My next stop is Allison's apartment building. It's a tall wide building, fairly new. I park my car in front of it, just like she did, and stand in the parking lot trying to imagine what it would feel like to have a stranger grab me from behind, whether I would scream, or freeze, or elbow him in the groin like the heroine in an action movie. Everything seems clear and sharp in the bright sunlight. The front of the girl's building is perfectly landscaped and it's impossible to imagine anything bad happening here.

Inside, I stand outside the door to her apartment, listening for sounds that would indicate the police were still inside. Nothing. Maybe they've already been and gone. It's just a white door like all the others on the hall. Slowly, I try the doorknob. Locked. Below the brass apartment number Allison hung a drawing of the New York skyline, sketched in bright streaks of pink and purple on a deep black background. With my finger I trace the brass 13, a good number for a girl with such terrible luck.

The building is quiet and my footsteps make no noise on the beige carpet in the hall. I rap briskly on the doors around Allison's. Two apartments down, I hear someone coming to the door. It opens partway and a woman peers out at me. "Excuse me, ma'am," I say. "I'm sorry to bother you. I'm from the newspaper, and I wondered if I might ask you a few questions."

The door opens all the way. A short woman with slack brown hair and glasses stands blinking at me. She is so skinny her skin stretches away from her mouth like fabric pulled tight on a frame. "Is this about the girl in thirteen?" she says.

"Allison Avery?" I ask.

She frowns. "I told the police everything I know."

I take a guess. "About the car?"

With an aggrieved sigh, she says, "I saw it out front around ten. Next time I looked it was gone."

"Do you know what time that was, ma'am?"

"Right after the news," she says.

I write that down. "Your window looks out on the front of the building?"

"The bedroom window," she says. "But you can't come in."

"That's fine, ma'am," I say. "I just wondered if you might've noticed anyone you didn't recognize out front last night."

"I already told the police I didn't," she says. "How many times do I have to go through this?" She peers at my notebook. "Is this going to go in the paper?"

"Maybe," I say. I get her name—Joan Bracken—and ask her how well she knows the dead girl.

"I've had to go over and ask her to turn her music down." She looks down the hall toward the apartment as though she expects the radio to come blasting on. "I've had to ask her more than once."

I make a sympathetic noise, and she goes on, "Once I asked her to water my plants while I was gone for the week. This was before I knew what she was like. She stole from me. She said she didn't, but I know it was her. She had a key to my apartment!" She shakes her head. "She played innocent, but I'm not a fool."

"I'm sorry to hear about that, ma'am. Can you tell me what she took?"

"A pink angora sweater," she says. "And some shell earrings. They were from the Philippines. My brother sent them to me. He's in the air force."

Looking at what she's wearing now—a long denim skirt, a garish

T-shirt with raised plastic letters spelling out the name of a country singer, and dangling silver earrings in the shape of a knife and fork—I'd have to guess those earrings were not something the girl would bother to steal. "I'm sure they were lovely," I say. "Did you report this to the police?"

She snorts. "Why would they believe me? That pretty girl would have made her big eyes at them and said she didn't do it." The way she says "pretty girl," I can tell she means "slut."

"That's a shame," I say. "It's terrible to be taken advantage of." I give her a sympathetic smile.

She crosses her arms across her chest and narrows her eyes.

"Would you have recognized anyone Allison knew?" I ask. "A boyfriend?"

"There's always boys coming and going from her place," she says. "I saw one of them a couple nights ago. Noticed him because I heard him yelling. I looked out in the hall and saw him kicking her door. Then he left." She sniffs.

I keep my voice even. "What did he look like?"

"Just some boy," she says. "How am I supposed to tell them all apart?"

"Was he tall, short, dark-haired?"

"I don't know. I just looked out for a second. I didn't want him coming after me." She shakes her head while I list the things she might have noticed—clothing, glasses, facial hair. "Facial hair," she repeats, letting her head come to a stop. "He had one of those . . ." She plucks at her chin. "One of those little beards."

"Goatee?"

"Goatee." She nods briskly and puts her hand on the doorknob. "Now, I've told you all I know."

"Thank you, ma'am," I say. "One more thing, if you don't mind. What kind of car did she drive?"

"A blue 1993 Honda Civic." She smiles for the first time. "I know cars," she says, stepping back inside. I say, "Thank you," to her closed door and listen to the deadbolt click into place.

In apartment 17 I find a young blond woman with a Mississippi accent and two small children. Cartoons blare from the television in the living room as she stands at the door shifting the weight of her sleeping baby from hip to hip. Her white T-shirt is marked with green and orange stains, but she wears a perfect coat of pink lipstick. I tell her I'm from the paper, that I was wondering if she knew the woman in apartment 13. She says sure, she knows Allison. Allison baby-sits for her from time to time. She's good with kids. A nice girl.

"You're friends?" I ask, and she nods.

"It's weird, though, you know," she says with a laugh. "She's older than I am, but the way she comes and goes, while I'm home with these two, it makes me feel about a million years old."

"How old are you?"

"Twenty-two," she says.

"You are young," I say, and then a crash sounds from inside the apartment and a loud wail starts up. She looks around as though searching for somewhere to set down the baby.

"Can I hold him for you?" I ask.

"Oh, thanks," she says, thrusting him at me and turning to jog down the hall. He is heavy and hot and moist all over. I hold him up and press my cheek against his warm soft head. "Come on in," the mother shouts from inside. The child's howling goes on and on. The baby only opens and closes his eyes like a dreamer and snuggles into my chest. I pass through a gallery of family photographs into the living room, where the girl is bent over her wailing child, an overturned plant on the floor beside him. "You're okay, you're okay," she is murmuring over and over, stroking his hair. The little boy's cries trail off into sniffs and hiccups and his mother scoops him up and stands. We face each other, arms full of her children.

"He was more scared than hurt," she says. "Weren't you, pumpkin?" The little boy stares at me. I cross my eyes at him and he smiles.

"Two boys," I remark.

"Yes," she says. "And less than a year apart, Lord help me."

I'm trying to imagine that this is my life, my face in a cloud of white tulle in the bridal picture on the wall, my eyes painted to look wide and hopeful, my pink mouth smiling that sweet and eager smile. My arms began to ache from the weight of the baby. I ask her the boys' names—Nathan and Parker—and her own—Lisa—and what her husband does, where she's from, what brought her to Memphis. By the time I bring up Allison again, we're sitting in her living room with Nathan playing on the floor at her feet, two cups of coffee on the table and the baby still in my arms. Though Lisa offered to take him back, she seemed relieved when I said I liked holding him, and to my eyes her whole body looks lighter with no children hanging on. She hasn't spoken to the police, and says she must have been napping when they came by, because, Lord knows, she's always at home. I've told too many people already today that Allison is dead, so I've just said that she's missing. She says again and again, "I do hope they find her. She's a sweet girl."

I ask her if they ever go out together, if she knows any of Allison's friends or boyfriends. She's met Angela, but never any of the boyfriends, and she knows nothing about an angry man outside Allison's door. Joan Bracken, she says, is an old busybody.

"What do you and Allison usually talk about?" I ask.

"Oh, you know, if she should call a boy she hadn't heard from in a couple of days, if it sounded like he liked her. The usual sort of thing. Sex. Whether to, you know." She looks at her children. "It's hard to know what to say. You see where it got me." She laughs.

"You mean Allison is waiting for marriage?"

"I don't know for sure," she says. "I know she goes to church regularly. She's a good girl. I do hope they find her."

"Can you think of anything else that might be important?" I ask her. "Anything about an angry boyfriend?"

She shakes her head. "I never saw anyone angry at her. All the boyfriends, it sounded like they really liked her."

"Do you know her family?"

"I've never met them, no, but I know who her mother is."

I pause. I must have missed something. "Who is she?"

"Oh, you don't know? She runs the children's hospital. Or maybe she doesn't run it, but she's some kind of bigwig there. She was in those ads they ran in the paper, remember?"

"That's right," I say almost to myself. "I knew I recognized her." I jiggle my knee, excited. This gives me a much better chance of making the front page. I make a note to check the paper's library for clips on the mother.

I ask Lisa to call me if she thinks of anything else, and when I leave she waves good-bye to me from the door, baby in her arms, like I'm an old friend who dropped by for a visit. "I hope to see you again," she calls.

"Yes," I say, and for a moment I do feel that we're friends, that I might call her to ask what she thinks of my boyfriend, David, whether he's the one. The feeling is gone by the time I get to the end of the hall.

We're not friends. This is just my usual rhythm, slipping in and out of all these strangers' lives.

The newsroom is like an outsized classroom, long and rectangular, with row upon row of tan metal desks and, at the front of the room, the glass-walled offices of editors. The outside wall is top to bottom windows. I almost never look out. All that's there is the street, and my desk is on the opposite side of the room. In the far corner a cluster of desks forms the features department, a part of the room I rarely enter. I walk to my desk past people leaning into computer screens, vertical lines appearing between their eyes, people murmuring into telephone headsets, fingers flying over keyboards, people spreading today's papers out on their desks, looking for their names. Some people wear suits, some wear short-sleeved shirts and casual pants, depending on what they cover and whether they need to impress anyone. Me, I wear suits to look older. I say hi to one of the metro editors, and he nods, dreadlocks bouncing against the back of his neck. I pass a reporter who sits constantly chewing sunflower seeds, whistling under his breath. I exchange a sympathetic glance with the reporter whose desk is next to his, a chain-smoking nervous woman who covers education and goes everywhere with a fanny pack around her waist. She rolls her eyes and sighs. All of the women in news are either borderline anorexic or plumping up from too much late-night pizza and after-deadline beer. I'm still hovering somewhere in the middle.

At my desk I run a search on Cynthia Avery, the dead girl's mother. I skim a few articles that quote her, many about fundraising, one a feature piece about her, the joys and trials of caring for terribly sick children. I write down one of her quotes. "We do our best to be of comfort to the families. There's nothing harder than losing a child."

I pick up the phone. I don't usually call the family first, because it's easier to hang up than to avoid someone who's at your door. But since the direct approach didn't work at the police station, I dial the number and get the girl's mother on the phone. I never gave her my name, so she doesn't have to know it's me again.

"I'm terribly sorry to bother you, Dr. Avery," I say. "I'm calling because I want to tell the city about your daughter. I understand from talking to her co-workers that she was a very gifted singer."

She makes a choking sound and hangs up.

I count to ten and call back. Often someone much calmer answers the phone the second time. The phone just rings and rings. From his desk next to mine, Evan Fitzpatrick is pretending not to watch me. I've known Evan since we were both summer interns here in college. He is always here when I get here in the morning; he is always when I leave at night. Once a week or so he brings in clippings from *The New York Times* or *The Boston Globe* that he wants me to read. "This guy really knows his stuff," he'll say. "Look how he works the background information into the lead." I can't call him on Sundays, because he is making his way through three or four

Sunday newspapers and will speak sharply to me on the phone. He is the only reporter I've ever known who writes other reporters fan letters. Evan believes in The Truth; he takes on a story like a mission from God. He never has to stop and wonder what he's doing on someone's doorstep, because he carries the answer around like a cross on a chain—the public's right to know. Evan makes me feel ashamed any time I have doubts, the way my Southern Baptist high school boyfriend made me feel ashamed for not wanting to go to church.

"I hear you're working on the girl's murder," he says when I put the phone down. I pick it up again and dial the weather report. "Phone call," I mouth at him. I don't want to talk about this yet.

"I'll wait." He crosses his arms and stares at me.

I pretend to take notes, then I realize how ridiculous that is, since I haven't said a word into the phone, so I hang up. "What?" I say.

"What's the scoop?"

"Nothing," I say. "They know nothing." Evan loves words like "scoop." When he gets depressed he goes home and watches *All the President's Men*, and it restores his faith. I watched it once with him, and when it was over I said, "But then what happened?"

"What do you mean?" Evan said. "You saw what happened. They got the story."

"Too bad you don't get stories like that all the time," I said. "That story was really important."

"Every story is important to somebody," Evan said.

Now he rummages under his desk, to reappear after a moment with a torn and dirty magazine, cheaply printed on white paper. "Look at this," he says.

I reach for it, but he pulls it back. "Look with your eyes, not with your hands," he says in a schoolboy's taunting voice. "It's a Satanist magazine."

"So?"

"Don't you get it?" he says, paging slowly through the magazine. "I found it in that kid's trash."

"What kid?"

"The one they suspect of killing that ten-year-old in Arkansas. You know about it?"

"Of course I know about it. I wrote the first story, remember?" I glare at him. "So you dug through his trash?"

"It paid off," he says. "This is front page."

"You're frightening me," I say, only half joking.

"Hey," he says. "I have to write something." He seems hurt, and he puts the magazine away and doesn't talk to me anymore.

That's one reason why we're so eager for news, because when it's not there we have to manufacture it, and that's no easy task. When I was still a general assignment reporter, I spent one Sunday afternoon at the Mississippi River Museum asking people why they were there. "We wanted to do something touristy and tacky," one girl said. "It was this or Graceland, and I've been to Graceland before."

"I haven't," her boyfriend said.

"He hasn't," she said. "But I have."

Then I went back to the office and made a story out of this. When I wrote it, it said, essentially, that a few people were at the museum. The headline in the paper said MISSISSIPPI RIVER MUSEUM COULD BE IN TROUBLE; LACKS VISITORS.

Peggy, one of the metro editors, leans over me, both palms flat on my desk. "How's that story coming, kid?" she asks. Peggy is black, with close-cropped hair and a few dark freckles on her cheeks. She is my favorite editor, because she never changes a lead without showing it to me first. She is also the smartest, and so the hardest to fool. I'm leaning toward leaving the girl's parents alone now. I know she won't go for that, and I need her behind this story. For this, I want better than the front of Metro, where local crime goes unless it's particularly sensational.

"Peggy," I begin, leaning forward and lowering my voice, "I think this could go front page."

"Do you now?" She laughs, rocking back a little. "Why's that?"

"Young girl, brutal killing, probably sexual, and she's got prominent parents."

"I don't know, kid," Peggy says, pulling a list from her pocket.
"We've got competition today. See what else you can come up with."

After she goes I sit, drumming my fingers on the desk. Evan hits
me in the back of the head with a balled-up piece of paper.

"What's that for?" I say.

"Front page," he says. "You brazen hussy. What else *can* you
come up with?"

I pick up the phone to dial Sergeant Morris. "Listen and learn," I
say to Evan as the phone rings. A couple of weeks ago Morris mentioned that the city was approaching the one-hundredth-murder
mark earlier than ever this year. I'm wondering if Allison Avery
might have hit it.

"I don't know," Morris says when I ask him. "We did brisk business over the weekend. Don't know times of death yet."

"But she could be, right?" I say. "She's close."

"She could be," he says. "We're over one hundred now. For all I
know, she's the one."

I hang up the phone, writing down: *Allison Avery equals 100.* It
may not be the truth, but it's close enough to count.

At Peggy's desk, I say, "She's the hundredth murder victim in the
city this year. Earliest we've hit the mark since cops can remember."

"All right," she says, glancing up from her computer screen. "I'll
push for it."

"Thanks," I say, turning to go.

"Get the family," she calls after me. "We have to have the family
now."

The Averys live in a quiet, middle-class neighborhood of elegant
two-story brick houses and two-car garages, each a slight variation
on the last. Their lawn is neatly mowed. There's a basketball hoop in

the driveway. I stand on the porch and look at the landscaping, low clipped bushes and daffodils. Off to one side, three tall orange lilies sway a little in the breeze.

After I knock on the door, I hear slow footsteps, and then a breathing silence that tells me someone is watching me through the peephole. I try for an expression that is somewhere between a smile and a sad face, and end up, I'm sure, grimacing horribly. A moment passes, and then another, but whoever watches me from the other side of that door doesn't open it. I listen to the footsteps retreat.

I turn to go, feeling all of a sudden tired and heavy with disappointment. Here on the porch it's cool and shaded, and I'm reluctant to step back out into the heat. I lean against the banister, looking out from Allison Avery's porch at the neighborhood where she lived. It's a lot like the neighborhood where I grew up. For a moment I can hear my mother's voice, as though from the house, saying, "Don't go too far. Stay where I can see you." The sun behind me bathes the street in light. A few houses down two small children squabble over a tricycle in the driveway. Over their high angry voices I hear the slap-slap of rapid tennis shoes on pavement, and then a teenage boy comes into view, running hard, right down the middle of the street. I watch him. In a T-shirt and gym shorts, he's running as fast as he can, his long arms and legs all right angles, knees high, feet pounding on asphalt so hard every step must send a jolt through his whole body.

As he reaches the house next door, a red sports car comes flying around the corner, headed right at him. Horn blaring, it swerves wildly just in time to miss him as he jumps aside. The boy takes a few steps after it, jabbing his arm into the air and shouting, "Fuck you." The whooping of teenage voices trails after it down the street. The boy stands for a minute with his hands on his hips, his chest rising and falling rapidly. He shakes his head. "Goddamnit," he shouts. Then he turns and walks back up the street in my direction, head lowered.

When he reaches the end of the Avery's driveway he stops and bends over, hands on his thighs, breathing hard. Then he lifts his head and squints up at the windows on the second floor. I'm watching him watch the house, and I wonder who he is, whether he knew her and has heard what happened. He's an attractive kid, moving with an easy long-limbed grace. After a moment he opens the mailbox and reaches way inside. I take a step toward him, trying to see what he's doing. With the sun in his eyes, he doesn't see me. He straightens up, a pack of cigarettes and a lighter in his hand. Lighting a cigarette, he keeps his eyes trained on the house. He lifts his T-shirt and slides the pack into the waistband of his green gym shorts.

He starts walking toward me up the lawn, looking at the ground and taking deep drags on his cigarette. That's when I realize, he must be her brother, coming home. He's tall, with that unformed skinniness that boys have before their weight catches up with their height, and his hair is the rich brown of good leather, with a touch of curl around his heart-shaped face. His white T-shirt is patched with sweat, clinging to his stomach and chest.

Standing up straight, I walk down the porch steps and out onto the lawn. I don't want to startle him. "Hello," I call out. He stops short and looks up. He squints into the light, trying to make out my face. To him I must look like a dark outline against the sun. I lift my hand and wave as though I know him. He takes a quick step, and then another, his hand reaching out toward me. An expression comes over his face, of hope and astonishment, and he opens his mouth and says, "Allison?"

It is a terrible moment. How badly he must want to believe she's not dead. I take a breath but find myself speechless, and so he goes on for a few seconds thinking I am his sister. He smiles, and his eyes fill up with tears, and he is suddenly so beautiful that I can't even look at him.

I move forward, so that he can see my face. His hand drops to his side, and on his face there is a look of such stricken sorrow, as though I have just broken his heart. It's gone quickly, his mouth smoothed into a thin line and his eyes blank. Turning away, he runs his free hand through his damp hair and takes another drag of his cigarette. Then he looks at me again. "Are you one of my sister's friends?" he asks.

"No, I'm sorry, I'm not," I say, and to my astonishment my voice wavers, like I'm about to burst out crying.

"Who are you then?" he says, his voice all sharp edges.

I consider saying, "I'm at the wrong house," but I'll probably see this boy again, so I tell the truth.

He looks down at the ground. Then he drops his half-smoked cigarette and rubs it out with his toe. Slowly, he lifts his T-shirt and uses the bottom of it to wipe his damp forehead. His flat boy's stomach is bright white in the sun. "Don't you feel bad, coming here like this?" he says, dropping the shirt. "My sister's barely been dead one day."

"I do feel bad, yes," I say. Then I just stand there, my mind turning over possibilities for what to say next. After a minute I realize my mouth is hanging open, so I close it.

"I thought you were one of her friends," he says, looking me up and down. He lets his gaze linger over my breasts, as though trying to unnerve me. He must want revenge for that moment when he thought he had his sister back. "You're young to be a reporter."

"Old enough," I say. I cross my arms over my chest. "I mean, I am a reporter."

"Now I know where I've seen you before. At the Four Corners."

"That's across the street from my apartment."

He nods slowly. "I work there weekends," he says. "I'm a busboy." He looks me in the face now, studying me. "Your hair used to be longer, didn't it? About to here." He reaches out as though to touch my shoulder. "You always order the banana pudding. Once, I told you we were out and you left."

I don't recognize him. I don't know what to say. It's too late to try the "I want to tell the world about your loved one" approach on him. I don't know what's become of my professionalism. Then it clicks into place, how I should be—sympathetic, regretful, even a little ashamed. "Are your parents home?" I ask, gently, watching him take the cigarette pack from the waistband of his shorts.

"They don't want to talk to you." He slides another cigarette out and puts it in his mouth, then offers me the pack. I look at him. The cigarette dangles from his lips as he watches me with hooded eyes, playing the tough kid. I imagine him practicing this look in the mirror.

I shake my head. "I wouldn't want to talk to me either," I say. "I'm sorry about your sister." I start to go past him. He grabs my arm, then quickly drops it.

"Will you put something in the paper?" he asks. He takes the unlit cigarette from his mouth and jabs it in the air. "Whatever I say?"

"Yes."

"Here it is," he says. "My sister's dead. How do you think I feel?"

By the end of the day I know that the boy's name is Peter and that he is seventeen. I know where he goes to school, where he works, where he lives, and what he looks like. But I don't know how he feels.

The truth is nothing really terrible has ever happened to me, although before I learned to harden myself I was afraid of all kinds of things. I used to believe I would be killed by a serial killer, not someone who would just shoot you, but someone who would torture you and cut you up and scatter your body parts throughout the city. Before that, I was afraid of sharks and alligators, for the same reason, the way they chew you to pieces. Then it was death—just dying, no matter how. I couldn't even let myself think about it without getting a cold burning in my stomach and face. Until I was twenty-two, I had never been to a funeral. Now I've been to the funeral of a baby shot inside her mother's womb, the funeral of a teenager stabbed in an alley, the funerals of all manner of strangers, but I have never been to the funeral of a person I have loved.

Allison's funeral is in three days. It's my job to be there. I put it in the story, what her brother said. Peggy thinks it's a great quote. "I like the steam rising, too," she said. "Nice touch." It's running front page. Headline: CITY CLAIMS 100TH MURDER VICTIM THIS YEAR. Subhead: Daughter of Prominent Doctor Found Dead. Byline: Olivia Dale.

It's 11 P.M. Instead of leaving I'm sitting at my desk watching the second hand make its way around the clock on the wall. The newsroom is almost empty and quiet like it never is during the day, the only sounds the murmur of two editors' voices and the click the clock makes when a minute passes. I just sit here thinking about that boy, Peter. A seventeen-year-old boy hasn't shriveled me up inside like that since I was fourteen and Fred Lamar tried to feel me up on the band bus when he hadn't even kissed me yet. I played the clarinet for seven years. At my school we were called "band fags," and when someone asked me my schedule I said, English, Band, French, with the "band" said so quickly the *a* and the *d* disappeared. My mother wouldn't let me quit. She said, "Some day you'll understand it was good for you." I hate feeling ashamed of something, wishing I could quit. I'd like to live a life where that was never true.

The first edition is on the presses. I get up and go down the hall to the window overlooking the press room. The huge steel machines turn and whirr without stopping. I press my forehead to the glass, darkened by newsprint, and watch the pages fly by. While I watch, it comes back to me, the rush I get from what I do. I've stood here just like this and watched every night I've thought that a story was important, that what I had written meant lives would be changed. This is what I live for through the boredom of highway fatalities and armed robberies and endless hours of pretending to be busy at my desk, waiting for someone to commit a crime. It's like driving alone for hours on a straight Texas highway, just to see the sparkling lights of a city rise over the darkness of the plains.

The front page goes by again and again and again. That's my story there, under that big bold headline, leading off the day's news.

3

On my way out of the building, I say good night to the security guard, a plump older man with the swollen features of an alcoholic. "Be careful out there," he says jovially. I nod, my lips pressed together, gripping my keys tightly in one hand, the points jutting out between my fingers the way I learned in a college self-defense course. The newspaper building is not far from crime-ridden government housing. When the door closes behind me, I start moving as quickly as I can toward my car, which is just outside the dim light thrown by the building's lamps. My footsteps sound on the pavement, and when I'm close enough I bend down to make sure no one is beneath the car. Last month I wrote a story about three women who had their Achilles tendons slashed by a man lying in wait beneath their cars in a mall parking lot. He was never caught.

I open the door, swing my legs in and pull the door shut, locking it. I turn around. I forgot to make sure no one was crouched in the back. I'm alone. I take a deep breath and relax against the seat. The car starts and I shift smoothly into first and glide from the parking lot. There is nothing I'd like better than to go home now, but I'm scheduled to meet a midnight-shift cop named Smiley at the police station for a ride-along. Peggy suggested it as a good way to get to know the cops. "Could be a story in it," she said. "Maybe you'll get lucky."

Officer Smiley is leaning against his patrol car in the parking lot, his arms crossed over his chest. A light-skinned black man, he's the sort of cop who looks like he divides his time between his beat and the weight room, his close-cropped head a solid block on his wide, thick-veined neck. He watches me approach with the slightest movement of his eyes.

"Officer Smiley," I call out when I'm two feet from him. "I'm Olivia Dale." I go toward him with my hand held out.

He waits another beat before easing his body forward off the car and extending his own hand to grip mine. "Ma'am," he says formally.

I laugh. It's involuntary, a quick nervous burst. I'm afraid to look at him again, but when I do, he's smiling, and I suddenly realize how young he is, maybe even younger than I am.

He walks me around to the passenger side and watches me settle in against the warm black vinyl before he shuts the door. He moves around the car with the slow wide-legged walk of the muscular, and when he gets in the car it seems to sag with his weight.

"Thanks for agreeing to this," I say.

"I didn't *agree*," he says. "I was told."

"Oh," I say. "Well, thanks anyway."

He seems tense as we pull out of the parking lot and negotiate our way out of downtown, both his hands tight on the steering wheel. Then he relaxes back against the seat, dropping one hand to his leg and jerking his neck from side to side in the weight lifter's stretching motion. He hasn't said a word.

"Are you from Memphis?" I ask.

"Orange Mound," he says. "I stay there still. My family's there."

I get him talking about his background, how he left his poor neighborhood to go to college, then decided to come back to the people who raised him and do something for the community. He tells me that he really thinks he can make a difference. I nod, working up a hometown rookie cop angle in my head, just in case I need it.

"What do you think the city should be doing about crime that it's not doing now?" I ask him.

"More cops, number one. I know the mayor wants that, but nobody wants their taxes raised." He shakes his head. "Always the same thing. Nobody wants to pay for you, but everybody thinks you should be there the second they pick up their phone."

"What . . . ," I start. He holds up his hand to stop me and turns up the radio as the dispatcher's mechanical voice recites the code for domestic disturbance. He radios back and I grip the door handle as he swings the car into a U-turn. We hurtle down the street, the siren wailing our battle cry.

The house is enormous and decrepit, one of those grand old Memphis houses with half the windows boarded up, the roof caving in. It's quiet. "Stay here," Smiley says. He shuts the door and leaves me cocooned inside the stifling car. After a moment I push open my door and sit facing out. I watch him knock on the door. "Police," he calls. He leans over, trying to peer in the closest window. Then I see his body stiffen. "Hey," he yells. "Hey." He reaches for his gun and flings himself through the door into the house. A gunshot cracks the air and I am on my feet, running up the lawn. I trip over the first porch step and clamber up on my hands and knees. Inside a woman's voice is rising toward a scream. On the porch I press my face to the window.

Smiley and another man stand facing one another, each with a gun aimed at the other's face. A woman in a pink housedress, her nose dripping blood, stands rocking herself from side to side, moaning. I draw a stick-figure diagram in my notebook so I'll be able to describe this later, the room, the distance between the two men. I draw a squiggle of blood down the stick woman's face.

"Drop it," Smiley says between his teeth. The man looks wildly from side to side. Then he spots my face against the window and his eyes narrow. He raises the gun, and I drop to the floor of the porch as a bullet shatters the window, glass raining down on my back. I hear the woman screaming, and the sounds of a scuffle, and when I rise up gingerly, pieces of glass cascading down my back, the man is on the ground, Smiley's gun pressed to his head, Smiley's foot planted firmly on his back. The woman's throat is convulsing as though she's going to vomit.

"Damn," I say out loud. "I missed it." I pick up my notebook and shake off the glass. There's a smudge of red on the white paper. I look at my hand and see that my finger is bleeding. I pluck a tiny shard of glass from my skin. My heart slams against my chest like it's going to burst on through.

Officer Smiley comes out the front door, pushing the handcuffed man before him. Reciting the man's rights, Smiley looks right through me. The man stares at me as he passes, his face red and pulsing with rage. I just stand there, my notebook slack in my hand, while the woman inside keeps screaming, while Smiley walks the man to the car, puts his hand on his head and gently eases him into the backseat. He moves slowly around the car and reaches in for the radio.

Then I start moving. When I reach Smiley's side, he's putting the radio carefully back into place. "What happened?"

"What happened is you almost got shot," he says.

I wave my hand to dismiss this. "I mean, how'd you get him on the ground?"

"When he turned toward the window, I tackled him and he dropped the gun," he says.

"Why didn't you shoot him?"

"I don't know." He looks up at the house. "Shit," he says. "Can that woman scream."

"What are you going to do about her?"

"They're sending someone," he says absently.

I lean into the car and look at the prisoner through the wire mesh that divides the front seat from the back. He glares at me. "Why did you hit your wife?" I ask him.

He says nothing. A lump of chewing tobacco pushes out his lower lip, making him look like a petulant child.

"Why did you have the gun out?" I ask.

"To kill the bitch," he snarls. He turns his head to the side and spits a brown puddle onto the seat beside him.

I straighten up. Officer Smiley looks at me and shakes his head, as though to say, why did you even ask? I look down at the blood welling out of my finger in a neat little bubble. We stand together in silence until another squad car arrives, listening as the wailing goes on and on, until it just seems like part of the night, the heat, the smell of wet dirt and grass, that agonized, endless sound.

When we get out of the car at the station, Smiley says, "Am I going to see this in the paper?"

"Hero John Smiley," I say, making a headline in the air with my hand.

He laughs. "Don't say that," he says. "I'll get endless shit." He shakes my hand and goes around the car to retrieve his prisoner.

"Thanks," I say. He doesn't hear it, and I don't repeat it. I just turn away and walk back to my car.

When I get home, the house is dark. On my way through the living room I bump against the flimsy coffee table Hannah and I found out on the street and one of the stacks of magazines cascades onto the floor, scattering across a cardboard box with half a pizza still in it. I know if I went in the kitchen I would find a sink full of dirty dishes, a counter dirty with bits of food and the occasional cockroach, and an overflowing trash can surrounded by crumpled paper towels that didn't make it in. The couch is draped with clothes, some mine. I settle down among them and watch the clock on the VCR blink 12:00. I'm working on an angle in my head, thinking I can use this incident as the lead-in to a series about domestic violence in Memphis, or violence against women in general if I tie in today's dead girl. I think of making a list—*get stats, call a shelter*—

but I'm too tired to go digging through my bag for my notebook, or even to turn on the light. It seems like a million years since I stood over that dead body this morning.

I say to myself, *I could have been shot.* No matter how hard I try I can't make myself believe it.

One thing I know, when you read about what happened tonight in the paper, it will never occur to you that I was there.

4

When I open my eyes, my roommate, Hannah, is standing over me. She is wearing a black cardigan over a sleeveless pink cotton sundress that buttons up the front. She looks as though she has no idea what the season is and is trying to allow for all possibilities. "What are you doing here?" she says.

"I live here," I try to say. My tongue feels swollen inside my mouth. I sit up. "Aren't you hot?" We don't have central air, just window units in our bedrooms, and the heat is like another presence in the room. I must have fallen asleep in my clothes, my shirt soaked through and clinging to my skin.

"Why did you sleep on the couch?" Hannah sprawls beside me and turns on the television.

I look down at my rumpled skirt. "I didn't mean to."

"David called like three times last night," she says.

"What did he want?" I put my wet face in my hands and rub it vigorously.

"I don't know," she says. "He's *your* boyfriend." She says this with scorn. Hannah believes in being alone. She thinks no woman enters a relationship with a man without sacrificing something. She's afraid of men who want more than sex from her. When we're out late at night, she'll walk home by herself, because she wants everyone to believe she's afraid of nothing.

"What time is it?" I ask. "Aren't you going to work?"

"Aren't you?" she says. "It's quarter of ten."

"Oh my God." I jump up. "I'm late. Why didn't you wake me?"

"I thought you needed the sleep," Hannah says without looking at me. She is watching a music video; a very young, very undressed girl with frightening wide eyes is looking bewildered in a close-up. Her hair is straight and unwashed. She is so thin that the thrust of her lips seems violent after the deep hollows of her cheeks. "How could anyone find that attractive?" Hannah says. I notice that she doesn't change the channel.

Hannah herself is thin, though not as thin as the video girl. Her cheekbones, her collarbones make elegant lines beneath her skin, pale as soap. She's a green-eyed redhead—another reason she shouldn't be wearing pink—and her hair is a rich red-brown, cut short to her chin and smooth against her face. She dated a guy in college who used to call her "red velvet," which she hated. She is tall and in every way lovely, a fact that she steadfastly refuses to acknowledge. "Did last night go okay?" I say.

"Obviously." She leans her head back to look at me. "Don't I look okay?"

"You know what I mean. What happened to your date?"

"We had a drink, then I sent him home." She makes a face. "He was an eager puppy."

"Did he lick your face?"

"My neck, actually." She shudders. "Let's not talk about it anymore." She turns back to the screen. The video girl rolls over and over on a carpeted floor, her long white legs bony and exposed. I can see what she would look like without her skin, the shape of her skull, the enormous caverns for her eyes. It makes me feel sick. I keep watching. I'm a television junkie. I get sucked in by all those imaginary lives. I become involved in commercials. So even though I'm late for work I stand there until Hannah says, "Sit down. You're looming."

"I can't," I say. "I've got to get ready."

"So go get ready," she says.

"Are you going to want a ride to work?"

"I don't know," she says. "Are you going to hit the curb like last time?"

"Memphis woman kills roommate with couch pillow," I say. "Police say Dale, twenty-five, snapped after third bitchy comment in five minutes."

"Quote this," she says, giving me the finger. But she laughs, and gets up off the couch to give me a quick hug. "Good morning," she says.

My bedroom is strewn with clothes, on the floor beside the open closet, across the unmade bed, hanging out the open drawers of the dresser. This is why David almost never comes here. I stuff jeans and underwear back into the drawers, push them shut with my hip, and find something on the bed to wear.

When I come out of my bedroom Hannah is no longer in the living room, though the television is still blaring. I turn it off and go looking for her, slinging my bag over my shoulder. She's sitting at the kitchen table, her head bent over today's newspaper. I come up behind her and look at the paper over her shoulder. There I am, front-page lead. "I'm leaving," I say. "Do you want a ride?" Hannah is working as a temp; right now she's doing data entry at a hospital near the newspaper.

She doesn't say anything.

"Hannah?" I say. "Do you want a ride?"

"You didn't tell me you were on this story." She says it like an accusation.

"You didn't ask," I say. "Hannah, I've got to go."

She looks up. To my surprise, her eyes are filled with tears. "Olivia," she whispers. "I know this girl."

"Are you serious?" I say. I slide into the seat beside her and grab my notebook out of my bag. "How do you know her?"

She doesn't say anything, staring at me.

"How do you know her?" I repeat.

"What are you doing?" she says. "Do you think you're going to *interview* me? I just said this girl I know is dead, and you take out your notebook?"

I feel a flush creep up my cheeks. "I'm sorry," I say. "I'm sorry." Slowly I open my bag and put the notebook away. I make my voice gentle and say, "How do you know her?"

"I didn't know her well," she says. "I knew who she was. She went to my high school. I probably talked to her twice."

"It's still a shock," I say. I hesitate. Then I ask, "What was she like?"

"She was a high school girl. I don't know. She seemed okay. She was one of those girls who always had a couple of guys following her around."

"Was she the type who invites that? Or couldn't she help it?"

"I don't know," Hannah says. "Should she have helped it?"

I shrug.

"Come on," Hannah says. "Don't tell me you wouldn't be one of those girls if you could." A pink flush mottles her pale throat. "I mean," she says. "Not that you're not."

"I'm not," I say. "And I don't want to be." I turn my gaze from her face to the newspaper and read my lead. *The body of a 24-year-old Memphis woman was found yesterday in Tom Lee Park.*

Hannah sighs. "I can't believe it. That's a pretty nice neighborhood, where she lived."

"Let it be a lesson to you," I say. "Don't walk home alone."

"She wasn't walking two miles home, Olivia," Hannah says. "She was right outside her building. That's why there's no point in living in fear. You can't avoid danger."

"Maybe," I say. "But you don't have to invite it."

"You think I invite it?" She's turned toward me, her eyebrows raised.

I meet her gaze. "Sometimes."

"How did this girl invite it?" She shakes the paper at me, crumpling the girl's smiling face.

"I don't know," I say.

"You . . . don't . . . know."

"That's right." I look at my watch. "I've got to go, Hannah."

"See you later," she says without looking at me.

I push my chair back with a clatter. At the kitchen door I turn to look back at her. She leans forward over the table, her shoulders hunched in tight, running her hands over the newspaper, trying to smooth the creases from the dead girl's face. "I don't know," I say to her back. "Yet."

"The big bad reporter," Hannah says. She doesn't stop what she's doing. "I bet if you keep trying, some day you'll know everything."

On the porch I stand and take a deep breath. No one is visible on our dead-end street of duplexes and small brick houses. Everybody's blinds are down.

Our street opens onto a road with wide lanes and an arching corridor of trees, running alongside Overton Park, where the zoo is, and the art museum. When I had regular working hours, I would go running through the wooded areas, past the museum and the baseball fields and the picnic tables. When the path disappears into the woods it's like you are the only person in the world, the smack of your footsteps and the rush of your breathing the only sounds you hear. Through tall thick trees the sunlight makes dust glitter like gold shavings in the air.

Once I made the mistake of going there close to sundown, and when the light faded the whole place changed. Somewhere near I could hear a car moving far too slowly, and then I heard somebody shout. I started running like someone was chasing me, the blood pounding in my ears, and when I burst out of the woods the families had vanished from the fields and picnic tables, as though they all disappeared the instant the sun went down. I forced myself to walk calmly to the car.

Hannah and I moved to this neighborhood to be safer. We used to live on the third floor of an apartment building on Madison, across the street from a nightclub. We went there sometimes for a drink, and at night we could sit by our windows and watch the people going in and out, drunks stumbling off the curb, girls in high heels leaning against guys, their laughter echoing down the dark street. I was a general assignment reporter, covering south Memphis and DeSoto County, Mississippi. Church ground breakings, programs for inner-city youth, Graceland's battle against Elvis copyright violations. One Saturday, when the cops reporter called in sick, they sent me to the station to go through the day's reports. It wasn't the robberies, the assaults, the murders that shocked me—I had been reading my own paper. I had been hearing it every night on the evening news.

But three women had been raped the night before, one in the alley of the nightclub across the street from where I lived. It had happened at eleven o'clock, while inside the music was still playing and outside the people ambled tipsily down the street. Why hadn't I read about it in the morning paper? From our window, Hannah and I could see the part of that alley where the trash cans were. Then it disappeared into darkness.

Hannah and I knew some of the regulars by sight, and we noticed that one had stopped appearing, a middle-aged blonde with a bad dye job who wore heavy makeup and tight skirts, shirts cut short enough to expose a roll of flesh at her waist. She drank too much and leaned in close to men when she talked so that they could look down her shirt at her heavy white breasts. We thought maybe she was the one. I didn't want it to be a girl like us.

I went into work Monday and looked through a month's worth of papers, trying to find a story or even a brief about a woman being raped. I couldn't find a single one. Next I checked the weekly breakdowns of crime statistics for each Memphis neighborhood, maps that show you what to look out for on your street: car theft, breaking and entering, homicide. There was no statistic for rape, as though the terrible things that happen to women are either too shameful or too commonplace to report. Flushed with indignation, I went to the managing editor and asked him why we never ran rape stories. An hour later he was having a heated conversation with the news editor.

This is how I ended up on the police beat.

This is how I came to find myself sitting down with women like the one I interviewed last week, who was dragged off her front porch on a quiet street by a stranger with a knife. He took her in her own backyard and raped her, and she didn't fight it. She said, "I knew he might have AIDS. I thought, I can die now or I can die later." She is still waiting for her test results.

This is my city. Every morning in Memphis people eat their breakfasts over the list of crimes in the newspaper. Every summer thousands of people gather at Graceland in the terrible heat of mid-August to mourn a man who died twenty years ago. They cry as though it were yesterday.

At my desk, I spend some time on the phone, getting nowhere with the medical examiner's office. I hang up and watch Bishop ambling across the newsroom, hands in his pockets. Bishop is one of those men who always gets called by his last name, so that his first name seems to have nothing to do with him, like most people's middle names. I wouldn't even know his first name if I didn't see it in his by-line every day—it's Martin.

Bishop is white, thirty-seven, with a high forehead and straight black hair that sweeps back from the middle of his head to end just below his chin. He wears John Lennon glasses, and lets his front teeth show all the time. To work he wears khaki pants, sneakers, and short-sleeved plaid button-downs, and he always has a little note-book in the breast pocket of his shirt. He drives a Dodge Colt with no seat belts and a jagged gap where the glove compartment used to be. If you saw him on the street, you might think he was the kind of man who still lives with his mother, but he has his own apartment and a series of girlfriends, mostly career waitresses. His nonnewspaper friends are all martini drinkers who throw a party every other weekend. I've never gone to one. I don't like parties. When I asked Evan about it, he just shook his head and said, "Whew." Bishop kissed me once in the back room of a bar, near the rest rooms and the pay phone. It was a very gentle kiss; he didn't even touch me, just leaned way forward and pressed his lips to mine. "Well . . . ," I began when it was over.

"If you didn't like it, I'm sorry. I won't do it again." He touched my arm so lightly I could only just be sure that he had touched me, and then he went back to the table. The truth was, I did like it. But I was drunk, and that can explain a lot of things.

Now Bishop catches my eye and winks. I wave him over and he comes, whistling between his teeth. "Do you have a source in the ME's office?" I ask him.

He props his hip against my desk. "The streets are crawling with my sources," he says. "Can I help you with something?"

"The girl from yesterday," I say. "I'm not having any luck getting cause of death."

He straightens up, nodding. "I'll be back."

I'm watching him walk away when the phone rings. "Olivia Dale," I say, tucking the phone between my ear and my shoulder.

"Hi," a male voice says. "This is Peter."

There's a beat while I try to think who Peter is. Then I see the front-page spread across my desk and I realize. "Hi, Peter." My voice melts with concern when I ask, "How are you?"

"Um . . . . ," he says, letting his voice trail away. He sounds matter-of-fact when he says, "Have you heard anything more?"

"Not yet," I say cautiously, wondering if he's hinting at something. "I haven't been to the station yet today."

"Okay," he says.

"Have you heard anything more?"

"No," he says. "Nothing." Then he bursts out, "Not a goddamned thing!" His breathing grows labored. I say nothing, giving him a moment to compose himself. When he is silent, I say, "Peter? Did you want to talk about something?"

"I saw your article," he says. "You quoted me. It's strange . . ."

"Yes," I say. "I know." I make my voice low and smooth, like what would be my phone-sex voice if I had one, like I want to wrap this voice around him, soft and warm. "I'd like to be able to say more about your sister." I pause. I don't know what he wants, but as long as he's called I might as well get what I can. "Are you close?"

"Of course," he says. "She's my *sister*." His voice veers close to the edge of hysteria.

"You're lucky," I say gently. "Not all siblings are close."

"Do you have a sister?"

"Yes," I say, then stop, the word a lie I didn't even know I was going to tell. "I mean, no. I *am* a sister. I have a brother."

"What would he do if something happened to you?" He asks as though he really thinks I know, as though he's seeking a model for his own behavior.

"You mean, how would he feel?"

"No, no. What would he *do?* Would he sit around looking at photo albums, like my mother?" His voice drops to a whisper. "Would he go looking for the guy?"

"No, Peter, definitely not," I say. The fact is, I have no idea what my brother would do. If something happened to me, part of him would probably be saying I brought it on myself, the line of work I'm in too dangerous for a girl. "He would know to leave that to the police."

"So what would he do?" he asks again. Then, almost as if talking to himself, "I don't know what to do with myself."

"I don't know," I say. "I guess he would grieve."

"Yeah," he says. "Yeah." There's a silence. "How?"

"That's different for everyone." I venture, "It might help to talk."

"Yeah, to who. My parents are . . . I don't want to talk to my friends. I don't have a girlfriend."

"You can talk to me." I hold my breath during the silence that follows.

He says, sharply, "You'll just put it in the paper."

"That would depend."

"I'm not stupid," he says.

"Why did you call me, Peter?"

"I don't know," he says. "I shouldn't have." I hear him inhale deeply, probably lighting a cigarette, and a picture comes to me, of him looking up at the second story of his house, hiding the pack in the waistband of his shorts.

"Isn't your mother going to catch you smoking?" I ask.

He laughs bitterly. "She's got other things on her mind." He falls silent for a moment. Then he says, "Gotta go," and abruptly hangs up the phone.

I sit for a moment, looking at the receiver in my hand. "What the hell," I say.

"What?" Evan asks, looking up from his computer.

"I just had the strangest conversation." I hang up the phone. "Brother of the dead girl. Called me, asked if I had a sister, hung up."

Evan shrugs. "Crazy with grief, maybe."

"I guess," I say. "Or just crazy."

"Who's crazy?" Bishops asks, appearing at my desk.

"Nobody," I say. "What did you get?"

He drops a notebook in front of me. *CAR*, it says, in big block letters. *SKULL*.

"What's this mean?" I ask. He has written "jack-o'-lantern" in the middle of the page.

"He said the car crushed her skull like a jack-o'-lantern," Bishop says. "He asked me if I ever smashed them on Halloween."

"Did you?"

"Of course," he says. "All the boys did." I don't tell him how I cried the year the neighborhood boys smashed our jack-o'-lanterns to pieces on the front steps. Every year after that they stayed in the window. My mother never put them outside again.

I page through the rest of his notes while he narrates. They found signs of rape, semen, a few fibers. Under her fingernails they found skin. The physical evidence points to one man, though he may have had accomplices. He or they probably bound her wrists after they took her out of the trunk, after she scratched at least one of them. I read Bishop's notes on the condition of the body. Scrape marks and road burns. Bruises on the lungs and liver. Rupture of the bladder and stomach. Blood in the chest and abdomen. Rib fractures, dozens of them. Pelvic fractures. Tire tracks on the clothes and the skin.

"Looks like a stranger attack to me," Bishop says.

I say, "So they think she was alive when the car came at her."

"They know it," Bishop says. "She was badly beaten. But she was alive."

"I hope she was unconscious." I see it again, her body in fetal position, her hands to her face. I'm certain she was conscious. She heard the sound of the engine approaching, she felt the tires touch her skin, the crushing weight.

"That's the best you can hope for," Bishop says. "What an awful way to go."

I slide the photocopy of her face out from under today's newspaper on my desk. She's laughing. The boy is kissing her cheek. "Why her?" I say, tapping my pen on her face. "Why this girl?"

"She was there." Bishop shrugs. "Sometimes there is no reason. Just the wrong place at the wrong time."

"Even that's a reason," I say. "Isn't it?"

"I don't know," he says. "That's the kind of thinking that can make you crazy."

"Not having a reason makes me crazy," I say. "Fate, and all that. That makes me crazy. There is no fate. One action leads to another. There's always some reason, no matter how small. There's some reason this girl died. There has to be."

"Jesus," Bishop says. "Don't think about it, okay? You can't think about stuff like that. Some people are bad, and one of them saw this girl and took her and killed her. It's a terrible, random thing. The important thing for you now is to keep it in the paper so the police feel pressure to catch the guy who did it." He leans in and looks at the picture. "Look at her," he says. "She looks so normal."

The phone rings. I reach for it, and Bishop touches me on the shoulder and goes back to his desk. I watch him walk away, his lips moving like he's singing. "Olivia Dale," I say into the phone.

"Hey, it's Hannah." She sounds friendly, as though she's forgotten or forgiven our earlier exchange.

"Hey you," I say. I push the picture of the dead girl away. "What's up?"

"You know that guy Carl? With the weird goatee?"

"I don't."

"You know, he came to that party we had in January. He's a friend of Kathleen's. Somebody dared him to eat a whole bag of potato chips in three minutes and he did it, remember?"

"Oh yeah," I say. "Are you going out with him or something?"

"God, no," she says. "But he called me. He knew that Allison girl. I guess he went to my high school, too, though I've been racking my brain and I can't remember him from there. He saw your story in the paper."

"Did you say goatee?" I ask, paging through my notebook.

"What?" she says. "Yeah. He's got a goatee."

I'm looking at my notes from Joan Bracken. *Guy kicking door. Goatee.* "What's his last name?" I say. "Can you tell me anything else about him?"

"I've got his number," Hannah says. "That's all I know."

She gives me the number, and I thank her and tell her I'll call her later. There's a silence. I say, "Hannah? Are you there?"

After a moment she says, "It's scary, isn't it."

"What?" I say, tapping my pen on the paper where I've written Carl's number.

Hannah says, "How close she was to being one of us."

❖

Carl Fitzner lives in one of those monolithic apartment buildings that look like something out of a science fiction movie, floor upon floor of identical modern kitchenettes, thin gray wall-to-wall carpeting, and the musty scent of too many residents, not enough vacuuming. He lives on the lowest level. When he opens the door he smiles at me with tentative hope, as though I'm his blind date, and invites me in. His small, high windows look out at the ground and his neighbors' feet.

Carl is tall and plump; his face has a soft roundedness that gives him an air of bashful naïveté, despite his trendy all-black outfit and goatee. He seems nervous, and we stand awkwardly in his living room for a moment before he asks me to sit. The couch is 1970s brown velour and when I sit on it a puff of dust rises around me. Carl blushes and excuses himself, returning a moment later with a towel, which he drapes over the cushion beside me like a man laying his cloak over a puddle. I thank him and slide over onto the towel. Carl shuffles his feet on the carpet and asks me if I'd like something to drink, then disappears into the kitchen. I hear him washing glasses in there. He must not get many guests.

He returns with two glasses of water and sits on the edge of the armchair next to the couch. I warm up by making small talk about his acting ambitions, his part-time job as stage manager at the Black Horse Theater Company, people we know in common, like Kathleen, whom he knows from acting class and Hannah knows from her gym. "When I saw your name in the paper, I remembered you from your party," he says. He speaks slowly, as though everything he says has to pass through a layer of cotton in his brain, and I wonder if he's still in shock. "I called Kathleen and she gave me Hannah's number. Hannah's a nice girl." I nod, and he says, "Did you ever meet Allison?"

"Not that I remember, unless you brought her to that party," I say. "Did you?"

He shakes his head. "I came with Kathleen."

I'm relieved to hear it. I wouldn't want to know I'd shaken the hand I saw clenched, bound tight with stained white string. "So," I say. "How do you know Allison?"

"Our mothers were good friends," he says.

"Were?"

"My mother died when I was in sixth grade."

"I'm sorry," I say gently.

Carl shrugs and looks down into his water, swirling the ice cubes in the glass. He seems embarrassed to have revealed this information. He says, "Allison's mother helped me through it."

"So you and Allison grew up together?"

"We were close as kids. And then in high school we went out a couple of times, to a dance or two."

"You must have been very fond of her," I say.

He smiles wistfully. "For years I had this huge crush on her, you know? I mean, she was beautiful. You can't even imagine how beautiful."

"I've seen pictures."

"You would have had to see her in person. She practically glowed. It sounds silly, I know. But it's true."

"But you were never a couple?"

He shakes his head.

I touch him gently on the knee. "Did you want to be?"

He laughs and sighs at once. "Of course. She was always saying, 'Too bad I can't fall in love with a nice boy like you, Carl.'" He blinks, then tilts his head and drains his water glass.

I wait for him a moment, knowing that if I don't fill the silence he will.

"I loved her," he says finally, rolling his glass between his palms. "But I was only her friend."

I feel sorry for him, his lonely apartment, his motherless childhood, the way his voice cracked over the words "loved" and "only."

It's hard to picture him screaming in a hallway, kicking the dead girl's door.

I smile at him. "So you were still close friends in high school?"

"We hung out with different people, but I was over at her house a lot. We went out a couple times, like I said."

"What was she like then? Was she a cheerleader?"

"No." He looks at me oddly. I can't help it. I picture her in a short skirt, with pompoms.

He says, "She ran more with the arty crowd. You know, theater and the school paper and such. She was in the choir. She never cared for sports."

"I'm sorry to have to ask this, Carl," I say. "Was she ever into any kind of risky behavior? Drugs? Anything like that?"

"She smoked marijuana sometimes." Then he catches himself. "Please don't put that in the paper."

"Off the record," I say. "This is all off the record. I'm just trying to get a feel for what she was like, who she might have known . . ."

"I don't think anyone she knew could have done this to her."

"You'd be surprised," I say. "The killer is often a boyfriend. Or an ex-boyfriend."

"Maybe," he says. "Maybe."

"Do you know of anyone who could have been angry with her? Anyone she might have rejected?"

"She went out with a lot of guys. I don't know of one in particular who . . ." His voice trails off. He becomes very still, watching me, as though it's just occurred to him I might not be his friend.

"When was the last time you saw her?" I ask.

"A few days before it happened."

"At her apartment?"

He nods.

"And you didn't have a fight, then?"

He nods, shakes his head, then is still again, looking as if he doesn't know what to do next. He asks me if I mind if he smokes and then he takes out rolling papers and a pouch of tobacco and starts trying to roll a cigarette. "We didn't have a fight," he says. "We never fought." He licks his finger, gets bits of tobacco stuck to it, licks it again, and then sits there trying to pick tobacco off his tongue, grimacing. The rolling paper falls open and tobacco leaks out.

"Here," I say, and I roll the cigarette smooth and hand it to him. "I ask because a neighbor saw a man with a goatee leaving Allison's apartment."

"Lots of people have goatees," he says, fingering his chin.

On the coffee table is one of those fat silver Zippo lighters that people carry to draw attention to themselves. I pick it up and lean in to light the cigarette for him, putting us eye to eye over the unnecessarily large flame. "The neighbor says he seemed angry. That he kicked the door." Carl looks away. "Thanks," he says.

I watch him take a drag. He's working very hard to appear relaxed. "Must have been somebody else," he says. "Wasn't me. Definitely wasn't me."

"Any idea who it could have been?" I try to say this without sarcasm.

"Well," he says slowly. He studies the cigarette in his hand. "Allison knew a lot of people. And she did like to live dangerously." He looks up and laughs nervously. "I don't mean she had a secret life as a stripper or anything."

"What do you mean?" I ask, picking up my pen.

"She drove a little too fast, drank too much, ran with a fast crowd."

I write it down: *drank too much.*

"Some of the fellows she dated," he says. "And that Angela." He says her name like my mother says "pimple."

"What about her?" I ask, trying to picture the smooth-cheeked girl in the doctor's office. All I can see is her white coat, her ringed hand clutching at a tissue.

"She's no angel," he says. "Despite the name."

I press my lips together against the urge to laugh. In my notebook

I write: *Angela no angel?* "Do you know if either of them ever stole anything?" I'm thinking of Joan Bracken, her sweater and earrings.

Carl frowns. "I remember Angela stole from a teacher's purse once. Allison probably did it too, when we were kids. The thing about Angela, she had a boyfriend in high school, liked to play with knives. I heard he was into some unsavory business." He hesitates, then leans forward and whispers, "S and M." He doesn't need my questions anymore. He settles back in his chair and keeps talking. "He was in my gym class, and once I saw him with his shirt off. Long marks, all down his back, like whip scars."

I'm beginning to notice a habit he has of smacking his lips, like he's imagining something savory in his mouth. I sound interested, respectful, when I ask, "And Angela?"

"She dated him, didn't she? You wouldn't know it now, but she was a big-haired heavy metal chick in school, painted her fingernails black and hung out in the parking lot smoking cigarettes during lunch. When we were fourteen, Angela was at a party where this kid died from snorting butane."

"What about Allison?"

"She seemed like a normal girl," Carl says, putting the emphasis on "seemed." "But she was Angela's best friend, wasn't she?"

He goes on to tell me his low opinion of the rest of the people Allison knew. He tells me Allison wore her necklines too low, her skirts too high, laughed too loud at the jokes that boys told, spent too much time in the backseats of cars. Insinuation settles on my skin like a layer of dust. Some of it could be true, so I just keep nodding and taking notes.

"You talk like you think Allison brought it on herself."

He lets out a breath like I punched him in the stomach. "That's not what I'm saying," he splutters. He stabs out his cigarette and stares at the ashtray. Then he holds up his hands, palms facing me. "All I'm telling you," he says, "she was no Goody Two-shoes. She ran with a wild crowd. If you ask for trouble, you get trouble, right? Right?"

I don't say anything. For a moment I'm sorry to have turned him inside out, the lonely young man who laid a towel on the couch for me, and found this. This is what they all end up giving me, the bitterness, the hate, what lies underneath.

He stares at me, his defensive expression crumpling into sorrow. "You look a little like her," he says, and his eyes fill up with tears.

Sitting in my car with the windows rolled up and the doors locked I watch the light dim around the crime scene. There's no breeze and the yellow police tape is still. One end has already pulled loose from a tree, trailing on the ground. I'm smoking one of David's cigarettes, and the smoke floats in the hot thick air inside the car.

Allison Avery and I were born in the same year. I grew up like her, in a white middle-class neighborhood of two-car garages and driveway basketball hoops, with two parents and a brother, though mine is three years older and we are not close. It's surprising that, like me, she was on the school paper and in theater, that our paths didn't diverge as early as I would have thought. Before I talked to Carl, I thought Allison Avery was like the girls in my high school that you didn't have to know well to know. These girls started bleaching their hair and wearing bikinis to the swimming pool at twelve. They joined the cheerleading squad and dated football players and were voted to the Homecoming Court. They called their fathers "Daddy" and were rumored to give blow jobs at parties and drove around in red cars with big cups of orange juice topped off with their fathers' vodka. I still think Allison Avery had something in common with those girls. They looked at you and held your gaze and you knew they never thought about the consequences, even getting caught another kind of thrill. I wanted, briefly, to be like them.

I had a friend named Lydia who, despite her wealthy family, had a penchant for shoplifting. She taught me to boost makeup from the drugstore, and to jimmy her parents' liquor cabinet open and replace the vodka we drank with water. When I was thirteen, we got silly drunk and painted our faces with our stolen makeup and fell giggling off the bed. We got caught. My mother cried. I never did it again. One day I noticed Lydia had become one of those girls, her hair as shiny as a model's. After that we passed each other in the hall without saying hello, both of us embarrassed we had ever been friends. For me there have always been consequences.

If I had grown up with Allison, I think there would have been that same moment, when we averted our eyes from each other as we passed, less than a foot apart. I don't know what would have caused it. There is something that she did that I didn't, and because of that, she is dead. I am alive.

When I press the unlock button the click reverberates, and I step quickly out of the car, drop my cigarette on the ground and rub it out with the toe of my shoe. Even out here the air is so dense and wet it's like breathing liquid.

Hands in my pockets, I take a slow walk around the perimeter of the yellow tape. The place has the postapocalyptic stillness that comes when something terrible has been and gone, as though even the air has slowed like a passing car to survey the damage. I've grown familiar with these places—the rubble of a burned house, the lonely stretches of highway littered with bent metal and broken glass—places most people go by as though in slow motion, craning their heads backward for another look at what, thank God, didn't happen to them. Like tourists on a boat ride, they pass safely through the wreckage of someone else's life.

Me, I stop and take notes.

The dirt all around here is crisscrossed with tire marks—some of them made by my car, some of them made by hers. It's impossible to tell now which is which, until her tracks split off from mine, the cops', the other reporters', and veer into that cordoned-off space. There they swerve over a blood-darkened patch of dirt and pass out again, heading off, away from here, the place where Allison died.

5

The Lizard Lounge, where Angela was waiting for Allison the night she died, is the main venue in the city for small bands. I pull into the parking lot, late to meet David. The building is square and windowless, with Lizard Lounge spelled out in green neon script below a giant lizard with pulsing yellow eyes. Before I go in I stand for a moment in the hot parking lot, watching the eyes blink on and off. I hate meeting David at clubs. It's always too loud to talk, and he's only interested in the music. I don't know why he insists I come. About tonight, he said, "This band could take off, I'm not talking just local, and I think they're going to sign with us. You gotta come." David is an A&R man for a small Memphis label. He and his friends sit around smoking joints and cigarettes and talking about Stax and Big Star and seeing Al Green preach at the Full Gospel Tabernacle. Memphis, they say, will rise again. "Memphis is the pop culture Bethlehem," David likes to say, waving his beer bottle in the air. "Elvis may have been born in Mississippi, but *Memphis,*" and here he leans back in his chair, tilting so far on two legs that I always think he will fall, "Memphis is the birthplace of the King."

When I walk in the bar, the music hits me in the chest, the girl singer's baby-doll voice rising like a scream. I give my money to the bored bouncer, and while he checks my license I read the band names scrawled in red marker on a bulletin board. The Barnacles. Guys and Dolls. The bouncer hands me my ID back, taking a long suspicious look at my face. "It's really me," I say, and he waves his hand to indicate that I can go past him into the bar.

For a moment I see nothing but dark figures bobbing in unison, smoke hanging in the air from their heads to the ceiling, and I think that if Allison Avery had walked into this room on time Saturday night she would still be breathing now. I wonder if we've ever been here on the same night, bumped against each other in the crowd.

I can't even see the band over all the people, just the face and hair of the bass player, a tiny severed head bobbing in time to the beat. Then I see David, back by the bar, leaning against a stool with one foot on the rung. I stop, watching him. It's one of those moments when the world swings around and a person you've had in your bed looks like no one you've ever seen before. I'm looking at a man, back by the bar, tall and unremarkably attractive, tufts of his brown hair sticking up like he's been running his fingers through it. His hands are large and thick-veined, the fingers long and graceful. He wears a T-shirt and jeans over a lean muscled body just starting to get softer.

He's not smoking, but by the way his knee jiggles I can see he's itching for a cigarette. I think, *That's why he's stood his hair on end,* and then he's David again, my boyfriend of nearly six years.

"Good timing," he shouts when I reach his side. "They just went on."

"Sorry I'm late," I shout back.

"What?" He removes an earplug from one ear.

"Sorry I'm *late.*"

"That's okay," he shouts. "I didn't notice."

"You didn't notice?"

"You're always working," he says. "I expect you to be late." He gestures behind him at the bar, eyebrows raised, to ask if I want a drink and when I shake my head he asks me if I'm sure. Then he turns and orders himself a beer. While he's waiting he points across the bar and shouts, "Hannah's here." I follow his gaze. At first all I can see is a swarm of bobbing, oblivious faces, and then a girl with a

frozen grin that pulls her lips back so far it looks painful. She steps
aside, and I see my roommate on a tall stool, leaning her elbows on
the counter that runs behind her along the wall. She is not so much
sitting as propped, one long leg dangling off the front edge of the
stool so that her foot hovers inches from the ground. The other foot
rests on the rung. A man is standing beside her, talking and gesturing, and though she nods at something he is saying, her eyes are focused on the stage, and her head is tilted away from him. Her red
hair slides forward across her face. Even in a resting position, something about Hannah always suggests motion.

"I think that guy's in love," David says, his voice lower now, his
lips inches from my ear. "Poor bastard." David himself used to have
a crush on Hannah. I listened to him talk about it for six months before he turned his attention to me.

I watch as the man leans in close to Hannah, touching her lightly
on the knee. He says something in her ear, and she turns to look at
him, raising her eyebrows. She shakes her head slowly, and then he
says something that makes her laugh. Whatever the question was,
though, the answer is still no, and after a moment he walks away,
across the bar to the bathroom. Hannah spots me then, lifting her
hand in a wave. She slides forward off her stool and disappears into
the crowd.

I lean back against David's warm chest. Over my head he watches
the band I can't see and I watch the crowd, trying to picture the
dead girl among them, laughing with a beer in her hand as a boy
gazes at her, desire in his eyes. On my tiptoes I tilt my head back and
say David's name over and over until he hears me and takes the
earplug from one of his ears. "Do you know a girl named Allison Avery?" I shout up at him.

He frowns. "Who?"

"Allison," I say, enunciating each syllable, "Avery."

He shakes his head. "Doesn't sound familiar. Why?"

"She wanted to be a singer," I shout. "Just thought you might have heard of her." He keeps shaking his head. "Can you ask around? Maybe someone you know knows her."

"Sure," he says. "Remind me." Then he puts the earplug back in and turns his attention to the stage. The crowd parts enough so that for a moment I can see the girl up there singing, thrusting her pelvis at the microphone like a female Elvis. Then she disappears again behind the bobbing heads before me, and I come down from my tiptoes and see Hannah stepping out of the crowd. She never looks like she's pushing people aside. They part for her, like curtains on a stage. "Here she comes," David says in my ear with amusement, "Miss America." Then he raises his voice and says, "Did you make a conquest?"

Hannah rolls her eyes. "He asked me to do coke with him," she says. "I took a rain check." Then she turns to me and touches my arm. "You look tired," she says. "Hard day?"

"The usual," I say. "You're not going to, are you?"

"Do coke? No. I don't like it. It makes me feel like my heart's jumping on a trampoline. Besides," she says, grinning, "I'm already really stoned. Why taint a perfectly good downer with an upper?"

"You've done coke before?" I've known Hannah for seven years, lived with her for five, and yet she still manages to have secrets.

"A couple of times." She waves a hand vaguely. "Did you talk to that Carl guy?" she asks, and when I nod, she says, "Creepy, isn't he?"

"He had a thing for the dead girl," I say. "Classic stalker. Like that guy Hardwick in college that used to follow you home."

She shudders. "Remember when you saw his room?"

"That was awful," I say. A friend of mine lived on Hardwick's hall, and once when I was passing by I happened to glance in through his open doorway. The room was a shrine to Hannah, pictures of her all over his walls. Some of them he'd cut from the school paper or yearbook. Several were snapshots, like he'd been lurking behind bushes, snapping her picture as she laughed, or searched through her backpack, or sat talking over lunch, gesturing with her spoon. It was frightening and sad, and the worst part about it was, I was jealous. I stood there looking at Hannah, every expression of hers captured. The girl in the pictures was my friend, and yet she wasn't, because I'd never looked at her this way before, as an obsession, a symbol of unattainable perfection. She was so beautiful and remote. I couldn't help but feel it, the terrible strength of his longing for her, and I was jealous. I don't know what part of it I wanted, to long, or to be longed for.

I look at David. His eyes are on the stage.

When the set is over, and the bouncers turn on the lights, David says, "Come meet the band." I trail after him across the dance floor, through the dispersing kids looking dazed in the sudden brightness. David pushes the door to the dressing room open, and I see him framed there, walking toward one of the guys with his hand out to shake, saying, "Great set, great set." I stop and let the door swing closed. I stand with my hands in my pockets and watch two girls bump into each other, then scream, "Oh my Gawd," and dive into a frenzied hug. If I went in there, David would after a moment introduce me, and they would all say how nice it was to meet me and maybe shake my hand, and then I would stand there trying to look interested while they talked about the acoustics, and how the mix sounded, and how David thinks next time they should open with a different song. And tonight I know what I would be doing while I pretended to listen to the baby-doll singer's opinion on crowd reaction, because it's what I can't stop myself from doing when I look at every careless girl in this place.

I would be picturing her dead.

When David finally comes out I'm leaning with my eyes half closed against the wall, and he doesn't see me. He walks past me and stands looking for me, turning his head from side to side. He's muttering something under his breath, but I can't make it out. Then the singer emerges from the room, wearing a tight tank top, a miniskirt, and thigh-high boots, her bleached blond hair moussed into disarray on top of her head. She goes up behind my boyfriend and touches his arm. He turns, smiling. She stands on her tiptoes, her hand on his shoulder while she talks to him, cocking her head ever so slightly to the right. He listens intently, nodding, and then finally she stops talking and he says something back, gesturing toward the stage with his hand. She stands so close to him I can barely see through the space between them.

Finally she takes a step away from him, walking backward, and says so I can hear it, "So I'll see you later?" He nods, and she turns to go back into the dressing room. Watching her go, David spots me. Her eyes glance over me without seeing me and she disappears through the door.

David strides over, grabs my hand and shakes it a little. "Where did you go?" he says. "Do you know how embarrassing that was? I said, 'And this is my girlfriend,' and turned around and you weren't there."

"I wasn't in the mood," I say.

He stares at me. "You weren't in the mood," he repeats slowly, then he turns away from me, shaking his head. Across the bar, the same man is talking to Hannah. I catch her eye and she smiles. "Do you want a ride home?" I mouth.

She shakes her head. "I'm going to walk," she says, her voice traveling the nearly empty room.

I go over to her. "You can't walk," I say. "It's the middle of the night."

"I'll be fine, Olivia."

"Let us give you a ride. It's not safe."

She sighs. "I want to walk," she says. "I'm going now. So I'll see you tomorrow, okay?" She turns to the guy, who has been watching this exchange with wide eyes, and tells him that it was nice to meet him, and then she says good-bye to David and walks out the door. I watch her go, and I wonder if Allison Avery had that easy grace, if she took her pretty body and marched it down the streets at night.

I leave the guy standing there without a word and go to David's side. "Let's go," I say. "I want to follow her."

"She's fine, Olivia," he says.

"It's too far for her to walk."

"She walked here, didn't she?"

"I'm serious, David," I say. "It's not safe."

He sighs. "All right. Let's go."

In our two cars we go after Hannah, and when I come alongside her I roll down my window and ask her to get in. "Go away," she says, not looking at me, still walking. "Or I'll call the police." I glance in my rearview mirror and see the guy from the bar running as fast as he can down the sidewalk toward Hannah. When he catches her he grabs her arm and holds her there, breathing hard. "Are you all right?" he says, casting a suspicious glance at me. "Are these guys following you?"

Hannah laughs, the sound echoing down the quiet street. David must have had enough, because he honks his horn twice and pulls a fast U-turn. When he passes me, I see him leaning out his window waving for me to follow. I take another look at Hannah, and she, too, is waving for me to go. I swing my car around and go after him. I watch Hannah in the rearview mirror until I can't see her anymore, striding up the sidewalk like she couldn't be safer while that guy does his best to put his arm around her waist.

David lives on Mud Island. I follow him down Third past a series of dark and empty parking lots, my headlights shining on the white signs advertising $5 All Day. The cars bump over the trolley line to the Auction Street Bridge, and we are out of downtown, over the river and onto the island. We turn into David's neighborhood and pass down streets lined with houses that remind me of childhood beach vacations, the temporary homes I remember seeing squinty-eyed through the car window at night as we pulled, finally, into town. David's taillights disappear ahead of me as I slow down, looking at the houses. The buildings look lightweight, wood painted in pale yellow, the windows angled and huge, and inside ceiling fans, spider plants with their tangled shoots dangling from the hanging pots. I can't help but feel that here life isn't quite real, as though no one ever has to vacuum, the dusting and the polishing and the washing done with precision by unseen maids.

When I pull into David's driveway, he's letting his dog, Lou, out of the house. The dog stands on his hind legs, his tongue reaching for David's face, and the two of them do an awkward circular dance. Finally the dog sprawls on the ground, and David sits on the front steps. He doesn't look at me as I approach. He's rubbing Lou's stomach vigorously, one of the dog's legs flapping helplessly in the air. I sit down beside him on the steps. He takes a cigarette from a pack and lights it.

"Thought you were quitting."

"I'm working up to it," he says irritably, still annoyed with me. I lean back on my elbows. My body is heavy with exhaustion, but my mind is jumping and the music has left a high ringing in my ears.

A young redheaded woman strolls by with a large white dog. David waves, and Lou lifts his heavy head, ruffs softly, and then returns to sleeping, his barrel chest heaving as though he's just run a mile. "It must be nice to feel that safe," I say.

"This is a good neighborhood," David says. I close my eyes and open them again. The woman has passed on. The street has the cheerful misty look that comes from bright artificial lights at night, and sometimes a breeze shifts the air that sits wet and heavy on my skin.

David is quietly singing "Every Little Thing She Does Is Magic" by The Police. It's his favorite song. I know a great many facts about David: his favorite songs, his fear of heights, his statistics: twenty-seven, six feet three, and 190 pounds, give or take one or two. Hair: brown, that shade that tells you he was blond as a child. Eyes: gray. I can remember the first time I was close enough to notice that they weren't blue, as I had thought, but gray, and how that made him seem unusual, intriguing, mysterious. I can't remember how it felt to think those things about him.

"You know her?" I say.

"Hmmmm?"

"That girl who just walked past."

"The redhead? I don't know her name. I just run into her some-times when I'm out walking Lou. Lou really likes Petra."

"Who's Petra?"

"Her dog," he says. "That big white dog." A firefly blinks, inches from David's face. "You know," he says, "that was the first time I'd been to a club in at least three weeks."

"That's not like you," I say. When I first knew David, he was con-stantly searching for new and better fake IDs, not because he wanted to drink, like most of our friends, but because he wanted to go see bands. After a good show, he'd come back and tell me that he thought this band had something, his face shining, as breathless with excitement as if he were in the band himself. "Someday I'm go-ing to discover someone, Olivia," he'd say. "Someone big."

"I don't know," he says now. "If I know a band is good, that's one thing. But I haven't got time to waste on crap anymore."

"What about all those lectures you gave me?" I say. "'You have to take a chance, Olivia. You never know what you might find.'"

"Yeah, well," he says. "I get tired of coming home with my ears ringing and smoke in my clothes. Too many bands confuse loud with good, you know?" Lou rolls over on his back, paws flopping in the air, and David leans forward to rub his stomach hard. "I came home from work today and took Lou out in the yard, and the bastard ran off," he says. He thumps Lou. "You bastard."

The dog is part hound, and so stubborn and half stupid, chasing anything that moves. Every now and then I come in the room and find the two of them in a frenzy of love, Lou pinning David to the carpet, vigorously licking his face with his washcloth of a tongue. Lou and I don't really get along. "I left him out in the yard and went to the bathroom," David says. "When I came back he'd run off. I had to walk two blocks over before I found him."

"Why did you leave him in the yard?" I say. "Didn't you know he'd run off?"

"I thought he'd be okay." David shrugs, nudging the dog with his foot. "Goddamn dog," he says, grinning. "You goddamn dog."

We are silent. I'm waiting to see if he's going to ask me what I did today. David doesn't like it that I'm on the police beat. He was happier when I still wrote stories about senior citizen swimming meets and small town arguments over zoning.

"Stupid dog," he says, tugging on Lou's ear. Watching him, I find myself wrestling with an urge to provoke him.

"David," I say slowly. "You remember me asking if you knew Allison Avery?"

He nods.

"I was asking because I stood over her dead body yesterday morning. I was this close," I say. I slide a couple feet away from him and reach my arm out to touch his knee. "This close. Somebody picked her up, raped her, ran her over with her car, and left the body." He winces, lifting his cigarette to his mouth. "The rest of the day I spent talking to the people she knew, her friends, her family, and watching them cry. Some of them didn't even know before I told them what had happened to her. Last night I watched a cop stop a man from shooting his wife." I tap his knee with my finger, trying to decide how much to tell him about that man, the gun he pointed at me through the window.

He drops his cigarette and rubs it out with his foot. Then he reaches his arm around my shoulders and slides me back up against him. "I don't like to think about you around guns," he says quietly. "It scares me."

I say, "What did *you* do today? You dealt with the pretty girl singer from Guys and Dolls. You probably went out to lunch and talked about what you think of their guitar sound."

David stiffens, dropping his arm. "Well, maybe tomorrow I can arrange for some corpses at the office," he says. "Maybe then my job will be as important as yours." He picks up the pack and grabs another cigarette.

"That's not what I'm saying."

"Oh?" He lights the cigarette. "What are you saying?"

"Forget it," I say. "I'm sorry I brought it up."

Lou raises his head and looks at us, his eyebrows dancing up and down with worry. "It's okay, boy," David says, his voice low, soothing. I think about a postcard David sent me one summer, when he was on vacation with his friends. Every sentence ended with an exclamation point. The beach is gorgeous! We went swimming! I miss you! Only the "Love, David" went without one.

"I had a bad day," I say. "Let's not fight."

David nods, bringing his cigarette to his lips. I put my hand on his thigh and play imaginary piano keys. "Für Elise," the right-hand part, which is all I remember from five years of lessons. The red-headed woman walks by with her dog again, on her way home.

A radio is playing in the house across the street. By the look on David's face I can tell he's trying to hear what the song is. "Okay," he says absently. Then he smiles. He recognizes the song. He starts to play the drum part on my leg. I close my eyes and let my irritation go. The warm air wraps around me like a blanket and David's fingers dance up and down my thigh. I try to imagine us, like this forever, but I can't make it seem real.

The dog's chest rises and falls with his heavy breathing. David sings a melody without words. A breeze slips across my face. Then I say I'm going to bed.

"Okay," David says, "I'll be there in a second." I kiss him on the cheek, stand up, and go inside, where it's cool, and everything David owns is neat in its proper place.

6

There is nothing more important in this city than crime. It's always there, running its current through your body, like the high electric hum of computers and fluorescent lights.

There can't be anyone in this city who doesn't know that Allison Avery is dead, who doesn't know the way she died. It led the morning news on every channel again today. They picked up on my hundredth-victim line, showed the spot where flowers and candles and scribbled prayers now cover up the bloodstains on the ground. You all know, *this is the modern world and its dangers,* and you touch your own skulls, thinking how fragile they must be, no matter how solid they might feel beneath your hands.

I'm sitting at a round table with seven men in jackets and ties, poking powdered eggs with a fork. I'm listening to them trade stories—who was shot in what neighborhood, which stores have been robbed. This is the Concerned Citizens for a Better Memphis breakfast, where the mayor comes to address the problems that concern them, which is to say he comes to talk about crime. Waiters quietly refill our water glasses as the mayor takes his napkin from his lap and stands to approach the podium. A hush falls over the room. I reach for my notebook.

The mayor is a good-looking man, tall and strong-featured, his skin a deep, rich brown, and as he steps up to the podium I note how nicely his silver-gray suit hangs on his shoulders. When he begins to speak his voice rolls out over the room like a flag unfurling. "Ladies and gentlemen, thank you for coming here today." He takes his time, scanning the room, and for a moment his eyes rest on my face. He smiles as though he knows me, and automatically I smile back. "Let me begin by saying that I know you all love this city as much as I do, and that, loving it, you are in pain every day over the dangers that threaten it."

Dangers, I write down idly. He goes on to push his plans for revitalizing the downtown, for annexing parts of Shelby County, and then he comes to the budget, and from the budget to increasing the police force, which brings us back around to crime.

He says, leaning in close, "There is no more fundamental concern than our safety and the safety of our children. I won't stand up here and say that it won't cost money. But I want you to know that money won't be wasted. We're going to make Memphis a safer city. We are going to look the criminals in the eye, and say to them with a unified voice, 'We will fight back.'" He pauses for applause, which bursts forth as though everyone here has simply been waiting for the chance.

"You all read in the paper the terrible story about a young lady brutally killed in one of our public parks, already the hundredth murder victim in our city this year. A promising young person, daughter of an esteemed physician, working in medical care. Who knows how many lives she might herself have saved if she had been allowed to live? We've all seen too many of these stories, about people from all walks of life, young and old, black and white. We must refuse to let those deaths be in vain. We will let the tragedy of that young woman's murder drive us to strike back at those who took her life, who have taken so many of our city's young lives."

He looks at me again as he says this. I can feel his eyes on me as I copy down his words in my notebook, and I wonder if he knows that Allison Avery is mine.

❀

Afterward I wait patiently while the mayor shakes hands, and smiles, and thanks people. I page through my notes, wanting to ask for details, how many new officers, and where.

"Mayor," I say when it's my turn, "I'm Olivia Dale, from the newspaper."

"Yes, Miss Dale," he says, taking my hand. "I've been seeing your byline. You've done a fine job with that poor young woman's death. A terrible, tragic story."

"Thank you," I say, feeling a flush rise in my cheeks.

Another man approaches, and the mayor turns toward him, still holding my hand. "Charles Franklin," he greets him. "I want you to meet Olivia Dale, the young woman who has had the sorrowful task of writing about Miss Avery's death." He passes my hand to Charles Franklin, who squeezes it and says, "A tragedy. A young, innocent life cut down like that."

As the mayor turns away, Charles Franklin goes on to tell me about a story he thinks I should write, an inner-city program run by a reformed drug dealer now looking to give kids a place to go after school. I make a note of it, thinking I'll pass it on to Neighbors, and then I look around for the mayor. He's in the center of a cluster of people, with more waiting outside the circle. I give up. I'll call his office for the details.

Heading for the door, I see a man walking purposefully toward me, his hand extended. He looks at me as though he knows me, but I can't place him. I keep a smile fixed on my face, searching my mind for his name. "Miss Dale," he says when he reaches me, taking my hand. His voice is deep, his grip firm.

"Hello," I say, trying to keep the uncertainty out of my voice. "How are you?"

"I'm well, thank you," he says. He pauses, letting go of my hand. "I'm the Reverend James Freeland. You and I met last year, at the ground breaking for my new church."

"I remember," I say, relieved. I drove around in a panic for half an hour before I found the place and climbed out of my car. The rain was coming down so hard the ink ran down the pages of my notebook when I tried to take notes. All the congregation in their Sunday clothes stood huddled together under umbrellas singing "To God Be the Glory" while the women's heels sank into the mud. "Is the church finished?"

"Not yet, not yet," he says. He rocks back on his heels, as though to physically change the course of our conversation. "You know I am the president of Concerned Citizens for a Better Memphis."

"Yes," I say, though I didn't.

"As the mayor says, one of the biggest concerns for the people of this city is crime, as you yourself are well aware. I appreciated very much the article you wrote about our church, and I believe you would be interested in a meeting we're having tomorrow night."

"Reverend, I'm not sure . . . ," I start.

"Miss Dale," he says gently, looking into my eyes. "Are you or are you not concerned about crime in this city?"

"I am," I say.

"Because I believe it is just as important to write about what the people are doing to fight back as it is to write about the times when we lose."

"All right," I say. "I'll be there. But, Reverend," I call after him as he turns to go, "if a crime does occur, I'm afraid I'll have to miss the meeting."

"Then we will hope one does not," he says.

At the police station, the first news I hear is that a dog carried a woman's head onto a playground in a poor black neighborhood and dropped it at the feet of two children. "If it rains, it pours," Peggy says with a sigh when I call to tell her I'm going to the crime scene.

Driving down Vance, I pass old hotels turned into low-income housing and enormous, abandoned houses with their paint faded or flaked off, shards of glass where there should be windows. All these old Memphis houses, coming down slow, crumbling into dust. Two black women in sundresses sit on one of the porches, too hot even to fan themselves, watching their children splash in a wading pool in the yard. If I traveled the other way down Vance, I would come to the part of Midtown near the Annesdale Historic District, where rich white people sip iced tea on their wraparound porches, sitting on swings beneath the green profusion of hanging plants.

Turning into the housing projects, I hear on the scanner that the police have found the woman's body in a nearby Dumpster. This time, I know I won't get close enough to see anything, and I'm not sorry.

Each building here is like an outsized brick with doors and windows, and the whole place is just brick after dull red brick, kids sitting on the tiny porches, riding old bikes over patches of dead grass and dirt, down streets lined with beat-up and ancient cars. Getting out of the car, I see that the area around the small playground is crowded with the cops and the curious. The nearby fertilizer refinery fills the air with the smell of chemicals and manure.

I spot a cluster of people and head over to see a circle surrounding two children, a young woman standing behind them with a protective arm around each. "I'm from the paper, ma'am," I say to the woman. "Are these the children?" She nods. I ask if she's the mother—yes—and if she minds my asking them a few questions. It would be so helpful, I say, and would only take a minute of their time. She nods.

I squat in front of them. The little boy is wearing a bright yellow windbreaker and clutching a toy car close to his chest. The girl twists the bottom of her striped shirt round and round in her hands. "Can you tell me what happened?" I ask.

The smaller child is shaking and can't even look at me. He looks guilty and frightened, his eyes screwed shut as if he's flinching from punishment. His sister says, "It was bleeding," in an awed voice. "The Tuckers' dog had it in his mouth."

"What did you think when you saw it?" I ask her. She looks at me, chewing on her lip. "I know what it's like," I tell her as an image comes to me of a head rolling over blacktop, dark hair flying. "I've seen things, too."

She nods, and her face clears a little. We understand each other. "I thought it was a joke," she says. "But it was a real head." She shakes her own head. "Poor lady. Now she's dead."

"Did you know the lady?" I ask.

She nods. Her mother says, "She's from this neighborhood. Her name's Bernadette Smith." She points to a woman standing silent and expressionless inside the moving crowd. "That's her sister Janice."

The little boy suddenly bursts out, "I touched it." His voice trembles on the edge of hysteria. "I touched her *face.*" He wails, and his mother bends to scoop him up. I can imagine it, the way his little voice shook when he said he wasn't scared to touch it, the way his nervous laughter erupted into screams when he pushed his fingertips against that skin and felt it give.

"He didn't know," the little girl says. "We didn't think it was real." She wraps a protective hand around her brother's ankle. "It's okay," she says, turning her face up to his. "You didn't know." He shudders against his mother's shoulder.

The mother says, "We have got to get out of this neighborhood." I don't know if she's talking to me, her children, or herself. She hugs her little boy close. How frightening it must be to have these horrors thrust upon you. At least I choose to see the things I see.

The little girl looks at me calmly, waiting for me to say something.

"Is there anything else you can tell me?" I ask her.

She thinks for a minute. She says, "I've seen a lot of bad things. That was the worst thing I've ever seen."

Bernadette Smith's sister Janice stands with her hands in the pockets of her jeans, staring so hard at something that I involuntarily turn to follow her gaze. There's nothing to see but the street, the playground, the crowd kept back by the yellow police tape. "Ma'am," I say. "I'm terribly sorry about your loss. Would you mind if I asked a question or two about your sister?"

"Go ahead," she says.

"Do you have any idea who could have done this?"

Slowly she moves her eyes to my face, then looks away again. She shrugs. "My sister was a prostitute," she says. "She was a junkie and a prostitute, and she'd been on the streets about ten years now. I'm the one raising her kid and holding down a job. I don't know who killed her, somebody she fucked, somebody she owed money. The way she lived, something bad was bound to happen. Just a matter of when."

I write that down: *just a matter of when.* Watching the woman's face, I wonder at what point her life diverged from her sister's, so that her sister is dead, and she is alive. I ask, "What made her become a prostitute?"

Inside her pockets, Janice Smith's hands ball into fists. "Bernadette made a lot of bad choices," she says. "Ever since we were kids. I feel sorry for those two." She gestures toward the two children with her head. "Having to see that. Probably see it in their dreams."

"Did Bernadette work for someone?" I ask. "A pimp? A boyfriend? Anyone she would've been fighting with?"

"Bernadette had a lot of boyfriends," she says, putting a sneer into the word. "There's nothing I can tell you." She moves her eyes back to my face. "It was just a matter of when," she says again. "Just a matter of when."

As I walk away I turn my head to take another look. The area just inside the crime tape is thick with cops, two of them laughing together, one slapping the other on the shoulder. Passersby stop and turn their path toward the crowd, their mouths slowly coming open, shaping the words "what happened, what's going on." Felicia Fitzgerald from Channel 2 is speaking into a microphone, her brow carefully furrowed with concern as she glances down at some notes in her hand, out of view of the camera. In the midst of the crowd, unmoving, stand the mother, holding her children close, and Janice Smith, her body drawn up tight and her face hard, absorbing yet another blow.

Back in the newsroom I read my notes over and over, trying to find a quote I can use. Finally I settle on the things the little girl said, on the mother saying she had to get out of that neighborhood, on Janice Smith saying she felt sorry for the children. I add in the statement from the cops. Then I sit typing in "just a matter of when" and deleting it, once, twice, three times. Finally I leave it in and send the story to Peggy.

Later Peggy comes to my desk to ask me to edit the story to a one-inch news brief. I cut it bare. Body found. Known prostitute. Police investigating. One short paragraph is all this death is worth.

In the afternoon I write an obituary and spend some time on the phone with the highway patrol, checking fatalities. Two teenagers died last night in a drunk-driving accident. I hate to write 18 or 19 after a dead person's name. When I look at the obits, I scan them for ages. On good days everyone who died was over sixty. If the dead person is under fifty, I'll skim the obit, and if she's my age, I'll slow down and read it word for word, looking for cause of death, relieved if it says "after a long illness." Those deaths are expected and couldn't have been prevented by one less drink at the dinner table, one turn of the steering wheel.

Allison Avery's picture is propped up against my computer. The boy kisses her cheek, the beer bottle tilts in her hand. I watch her as though she's going to kiss that boy, to finish that beer, to wink at me, shape her lips around my name. Somewhere there must be a picture of me from college, looking just like this, half-drunk and flushed with giddy joy. I page through my notes and make a list. *Pretty. Hard worker. Singer. Thief. Slut. Sweet. Young. Churchgoer.*

Pothead. Drunk. Tease. I wonder what pulls these things together to make a person, if it's only skin and bone.

One page is blank except for what her brother, Peter, first said to me. I add that to the list. *Dead.*

I call Angela Schultz and ask if I can come talk to her. I tell her I've spoken to Carl Fitzner and would like to get her version of some things.

After a long pause, she says, "All right. I guess I'd better set the record straight."

Angela's apartment is sun-bright and spacious, with the walls muted shades of green and peach, and shiny hardwood floors. The carefully hung pictures, the plants, the curtains, all make me think of how little Hannah and I have done to our apartment, how temporary it still looks. We have crates stacked in the kitchen, box springs and mattresses on the floor in our bedrooms, a dead plant on the porch in a cheap plastic pot.

It's true that Angela Schultz, at home, is not the same demure girl I saw at the doctor's office. Her hair is down, falling past her breasts in a dark smooth stream. She's wearing jeans and a clingy V-neck T-shirt, her feet bare, with red toenails. I can't picture her the way Carl does, snorting butane, cracking a whip. If those things are true, I'll see it in her. What you are always bubbles up eventually, a dead body rising to the surface of a lake.

"That little shit," Angela says after I tell her a few of Carl's opinions. Then she tells me that Carl was infatuated with Allison, that she turned him down and he soured. He left a poem tacked to her door about how he used to want to cradle her like a kitten but now he could see she was no soft kitten but a vituperative snake who had bitten him and run hot poison through his veins.

"Something like that," she says, sighing. "He's not normal. Even all these years after high school, he still followed her around. He would turn up at her gigs, at places where he knew we hung out. She was much nicer about it than I would have been." She doesn't look angry anymore. Her eyes well up. I pretend not to notice, writing in my notebook: *vituperative snake.* I think of Carl's tongue, the way he darted it out, picked the tobacco off it. I write down: *not normal,* and underline it twice.

Whips? Angela says. Knives? She hauls out pictures of herself in tight jeans in high school and shows me that she painted her fingernails black. She asks, "So what?," turning the thick pages of her photo album. "Didn't you wear too much makeup in high school?" she demands. "Didn't you?"

"Of course." The truth is I can't remember when I stopped. It doesn't matter, because nothing wins a source's trust like sympathy. I have looked into a murderer's eyes and said, "I understand." It's nothing to pretend I coated my face with foundation and blue eyeshadow until I was twenty, that that could be me in the pictures, wearing jeans as tight as skin.

The front of Angela's album is decorated with cut-out felt letters spelling her initials, the name of her high school, and the year of her graduation. She tells me she decorated matching albums for herself and Allison. Purple and white, she says, running her fingers over the felt like it's braille, were their high school colors. Allison is in some of the pictures, her hair like an explosion, permed into curls, her lashes thick with mascara. There are pictures of her with boys, with beer bottles in her hands, and in one it looks as though the white object between her fingers is a joint. In another Allison is on a stage in a high school gym, leaning into a microphone with a band behind her. "You can't really see, but that's me on the drums," Angela says. "I was terrible. Allison said, 'Angela, honey, your talents lie elsewhere.' She knew how to tell you the truth without making you feel you'd been criticized."

"Is that a joint?" I ask, pointing at the photo.

"Yeah, I think so," Angela says, leaning in close.

"So Carl wasn't lying about some things," I say.

"Of course not," she says. "Allison gave great parties when her parents were out of town. We knew how to have a good time."

"And when you got older?"

She sighs. "Look, I'm sure some people would describe her as a little wild. But a lot of them would be Bible beaters like my mother."

"Mine too," I say, and she smiles.

"Allison wasn't like Carl says," she says. "She did what she wanted, that's all."

She shows me a picture of the two of them standing together in flowered dresses, squinting into the sun, arms wrapped around each other's waist. "We were just normal girls," Angela says, "me and Allison."

"What about your boyfriend?" I ask. "The whip scars?"

"Truth is, his daddy beat him. If he said it was S and M, it's because that sounded better to him than telling people his daddy whipped him in the basement when he got drunk." She shows me a picture of a slim dark-haired boy in a heavy metal T-shirt and sunglasses, a cigarette in his hand, a smile pulling at his lips. "He wanted to seem tough," Angela says, "but he was just a poor scared boy." She shuts the photo album. "People have secrets," she says sadly. "They're just not always the ones you think."

"I believe you," I say.

She leans forward and touches my knee. "Men like Carl," she says, "they have a way of making you feel dirty just for being a woman. You know what I mean?" She watches my face seriously while I nod. Then she smiles. "I'm sorry," she says. "I never offered you a drink."

Although I said it to win her over, I do believe her, because our opinions of others are built on details, Angela's felt-lettered photo album versus Carl's Zippo lighter. It's true that I left Carl feeling like he had revealed himself as the kind of man who believes a rape victim in a low-cut shirt deserved what she got.

It's also true that if I see a woman walking down the street with her breasts bouncing out the top of her shirt, I think *slut,* just like he does.

I am watching Angela's face. She cries a little, I hand her a tissue, she grows angry, I shake my head with her in disgust, she wanders into her philosophies, I murmur agreeably. I prompt. I've stopped taking notes, but I'm listening to everything she says, and the whole time I'm thinking, *Why does she trust me? I never said I wouldn't put any of this in the paper.*

According to the surveys, no one likes a reporter. No one is supposed to want to talk to me. The secret I know is that almost everyone does. They're on their guard at first, until they realize what they have in me. I'm a rare thing, a listener so interested she writes down their rambling sentences word for word. It starts slowly, with the facts. Once they get started they can't stop. One revelation tumbles after another. Because they want to be heard, they want to explain themselves, they want to be famous, because seeing their opinion in print makes it fact. And because I listen they think I am their friend.

Often they don't remember what they've said. Some of them read their words in the paper and call my editor screaming that I've gotten it all wrong. One woman insisted on coming in to hear the tape of her interview. We sat in an editor's office and listened together as her voice recited each and every word I'd put in the paper. Still she didn't believe it. "But that's not what I meant," she insisted. She pointed at me. "She knew that wasn't what I meant."

Whatever I knew or didn't, it doesn't matter what she meant. I reported what she said.

Angela says that she took Allison to an abortion clinic when they were sixteen. "I talked her into it," she says, her eyes fixed on my face. "I said she was too young. And if I hadn't . . ." She chokes up, presses her hand to her mouth. "If I hadn't, maybe she would have had it. And now, she'll never have any."

"You couldn't have known," I say. I reach over the coffee table and squeeze her hand. She squeezes back and holds on. I think of the girls I knew in high school who got pregnant. Some of them kept coming to school until they were too big to fit in the desks, and then you'd see them working at McDonald's or the 7-Eleven. The wealthier ones disappeared for a few days and returned with stories about visiting an aunt in the city. One girl left town halfway through the school year. When she was back at school in the fall she joined the cheerleading squad, as though she wanted the whole school to see her in those short skirts, shaking her pom-poms in the air. She was on the JV squad. Varsity wouldn't have her.

"I'm just glad her mother doesn't know," Angela says. "She'd be thinking there was a piece of Allison she could've kept." I remember how my own mother shook her head over those girls, said they were all careless and sinners, and some of them murderers. I never knew how she knew about them. I didn't tell her.

Angela dissolves again into gasps and sniffles. Her hand is hot and moist and my shoulder begins to ache but I hold my position. "What's her mother like?"

"I hate to say this now," she says. "But the truth is I never liked her. She looked at Allison like she wanted something from her. I always thought she was jealous of me, that she thought I wasn't good enough for Allison."

"And Peter?"

"Peter's a great kid," she says. "He idolizes Allison. You know how some younger kids, it's almost like they have a crush on their older siblings? He's like that. She's a good big sister. She takes care of him, looks out for him. Once, before he got his license, she let him drive their mother's car and he hit a parked car, did some damage. Allison took the blame. She had to pay the deductible, and she wouldn't let Peter help, said it was her fault for letting him drive." She squeezes my hand. "That's what she was like. Those things Carl told you, that's not what she was about at all."

She lets go of my hand to reach for a tissue, and I sit back, resisting the urge to rub my shoulder. "What about Allison's boyfriend?" I ask. "What's he like?"

"I already told you," she says sharply. "No boyfriend." Her hands hide her face. I don't ask again. "I'm just crying all the time," she says in a small voice. "I can't make it stop." She looks at me and I notice that her eyes are enormous and green, and that she has again blinked wet mascara onto her skin. If Hannah had just been killed, I wonder if I would still put on my makeup.

"Is it because I miss her?" she asks me, voice trembling. "Or because I'm afraid?"

"Both," I say. "It's only natural. You're grieving." I reach for her hand again.

"What happened to her, it could've been me. It could still be me." Her hand is still beneath mine, and she is not crying now. She says, "It could be you. You even . . ." She stops without saying "look a little like her," watching my face. Her voice is suddenly so firm, so cold, I lift my hand from hers and put it back in my lap. "You know that, don't you?"

Across from me on the sofa is a girl like any number of girls, pink-cheeked with blush and emotion, smooth and painted and smart enough without being too smart and pretty even in her grief. Across from her she sees a woman her age, wearing no makeup but lipstick, hair cut short, businesslike in a skirt and tailored shirt, a closed notebook beside her on the couch. We've been sitting here comfortably, talking like friends, but now as she stares at me my head whirls with the thought that neither of us has any idea what lies beneath the skin.

Then her eyes tear up again, and she puts her face in her hands. "She didn't deserve to die this way," she sobs. I watch her, my discomfort fading. I know exactly who Angela Schultz is. I could take a few details and put her in the paper for anyone to see, captured in a sentence like a moth beneath a glass.

At the door, I turn and hug her. She sags against me like her own weight is unbearable. Her body in my arms is everywhere soft, her breasts against me, the cotton of her shirt beneath my hands. She takes a trembling breath. "Thank you for listening," she says.

"You're welcome," I say. I don't say "It's what I do." "Please call me if you need to talk. Not for a story or anything. Just if you need to talk."

She pulls back, but keeps one hand on my upper arm. "Listen," she says, "I need to go over to Allison's and get some things before her mother clears it out. Would you come with me? I can't bear to go alone."

This is how easy it is. A few tissues, one hug, and this girl opens up her life and asks me in. I like her. I feel sorry for her. We could be friends, although I'm using her. If it's hard for me to tell the difference, she can't be expected to. I think about asking her why she's asking me, if she's sure, if she wouldn't rather take another friend of Allison's instead of me, a reporter.

When I joined my college paper, the news editor told me the best way to get an answer someone doesn't want to give is to close your notebook, exchange pleasantries, and then, as an aside, ask the question you really wanted to ask. Off guard, because you're standing, and smiling, and your notebook is tucked away inside your bag, the person answers. You say thank you, go out in the hall, and write it down. I think about telling her that just because I don't have my notebook out doesn't mean I'm not taking notes.

"Of course I will," I say. "When?" We make plans to meet at the building Monday morning, and she says she'll see me later. "By the way," I say, turning at the door, "who was the father?" I'm imagining a lean-muscled football player, or a dark troubled boy like the one in Angela's picture.

She looks at me blankly.

"When Allison got pregnant."

"Oh." She gives a short, bitter laugh. "I think it was her boyfriend at the time. Tommy."

I hesitate. "You *think*?"

She shrugs. "Allison was never exactly faithful. She sort of . . . scooped people up."

"Even Carl?"

"Oh, Carl. I think she went out with him once, kissed him maybe." Watching my face, she says, "You have to understand. She was special. Everyone wanted to be around her. It was like she was buzzing with something."

"Sex?"

She frowns, taking it as a criticism of her dead friend. "More than that. It was like, she wanted to *touch* everybody. Not just physically." She shakes her head. "I can't say it right." Lifting her eyes to the ceiling, she says slowly, "It was like she wanted to touch the whole world."

We stand in silence. I think, *and this death is what finally made her famous,* though I know that what this girl is talking about is not exactly fame. Then Angela drops her gaze to mine. She presses something into my hand and closes the door. I'm left standing in the hall, the picture of Allison I had been forming blurred once again, like a home movie that keeps slipping out of focus. I look down to see what she's given me. It's the photo of her and Allison in flowered dresses, their arms around each other, smiling into the sun.

I come back to twenty messages on my voice mail, three of them hang-ups, one a man who says, "Oh," in a surprised voice and then breathes heavily into the phone until the beep cuts him off, sixteen of them women telling me they know who killed Allison Avery, every one of them with the same rushed, anxious inflection in her voice.

I spend a couple of hours calling them back, all of these women giving up their fathers, their boyfriends, their ex-husbands as the murderer, their voices sharp with bitterness and fear. He hits me, they say. He hit my mother. He broke my leg. He drinks too much.

He's a thief, he's a liar, he's a drug addict. He tied me up and raped me, one woman says, and then breaks down, sobbing quietly into the phone.

I take down the names they give me. One name I recognize, though it takes me a few minutes to remember why. He's dead. His body turned up on a golf course almost three months ago, and still his daughter tells me with conviction that three days ago he raped and killed a young girl. "I know it," she says tightly. "I just know it."

I don't think any of these women know what happened to Allison Avery. All they can tell me is what has happened to themselves.

After I hang up with the last woman, I rest my forehead on my desk and close my eyes. I keep thinking about things Carl Fitzner said to me. When he told me about Allison's fast crowd, her low-cut shirts, her short skirts, he meant the same thing Janice Smith meant. Just a matter of when.

The phone rings right by my ear, making me jump. "Olivia Dale," I say into the receiver, my voice sharp, annoyed.

There's a silence. Then, "It's Peter Avery."

I sit up straight. "Hello, Peter. What can I do for you?"

"Do you know anything?" He sounds businesslike, abrupt, not the lost boy from yesterday.

"There's been no news," I say carefully. "Have you talked to the police?"

"Why bother," he says bitterly. Then he lapses into silence. I wait it out. After a moment he says, "My mother asked me to call you. She's going to offer a reward."

I reach for my notebook. *For information leading to an arrest in the murder of.* "How much?"

"Ten thousand."

"That's a lot," I say before I think.

"Yes," he says slowly, scornfully. "It is."

I'm picturing a headline: VICTIM'S FRIENDS, RELATIVES SAY SHE 'DIDN'T DESERVE TO DIE THIS WAY,' or something better, depending on what the mother says. Subhead: Distraught parents offer reward. "Peter," I say. "I can run this information, but it would help if I could speak to your parents. A personal appeal is always—"

"No," he cuts me off. "They're not ready. My mother is . . . my mother is very private."

I consider pushing it further. "All right," I say finally. "When they are ready, I want you to know I'd do it right."

"You'll be the one they call, don't worry," he says. "We don't want to deal with television."

"Okay," I say, letting it go. I soften my voice. "How are you?"

He swallows hard. "I don't know."

"You don't know?" I say gently.

"I've gone running a lot, and I, uh . . . I just . . ." He trails off, then says, his voice very small, "I don't know."

"How are your parents?"

"My mother just sits in Allison's room. I tell her that I'm going outside and she says, 'Please don't leave,' and it's like she thinks if I step outside the house . . . but she's not talking to me. She's not talking to my father. She's just sitting on the edge of the bed. This morning I walked by there and she was curled up around Allison's pillow. Not crying. Her feet were hanging off the end of the bed." He swallows again and stops talking.

I wonder if, lying there with her knees to her chest, the mother knew she was mimicking her daughter's death pose.

"You have a brother, right?" Peter asks me. "Are you close?"

"Not really, no."

"How come?"

"My family's very religious," I say. "I'm not."

"What's your mother like?"

For a moment, I'm at a loss. Then I say, "She's nice. She does a lot of charity work."

"Charity work?" he says, and I think I hear in his voice that I should be able to say more than that about my own mother. "Do you see her much?"

I find myself telling him about the last time I saw my mother, for dinner at my brother's house. How they asked me about my job, and I answered with the truth. How my brother, Rob, took me aside afterward and hissed at me through his teeth, saying I wasn't to talk about such things in front of his kids and for God's sake didn't I know it wasn't normal? How my mother said she couldn't understand why I had to intrude on other people's tragedies, though I know she scours the papers for them. How all my life she has read to me about the carjackers who would box me in on a dark road, the men who would drag me from my car at stoplights, the rapists who would come upon me walking alone through the park and force me into the bushes.

"She doesn't have to read me those stories anymore. Now I write them."

"Now I am one of those stories," the boy on the phone says. "Or my sister is."

I wince. "Oh God, I'm sorry. How thoughtless of me."

"That's okay." There's another silence. Then he says, abruptly, "I think you're a good person."

Tears spring into my eyes. *How odd,* I think, blinking them away. "Thank you."

"I have to go," he says. "I'll talk to you again."

"I hope so," I say.

I hang up the phone and sit for a little while, staring at the wall. Then I pull his sister's picture closer to me. I trace the curve of her face with the end of my pen. *Who are you?* I think. *Tell me.* Some superstitious impulse makes me close my eyes and wait for the answer. The only voice inside my head is my own.

"Olivia?"

I open my eyes. Evan is looking at me, his head cocked quizzically. He says, "Me and Bishop are going to get a drink. Want to come?"

The M&O is Bishop's favorite hangout, close and dark, with a pool table in the back and city politicians and eccentrics caricatured in bright colors on the walls and the ceiling. We come here after work two or three times a week to have a beer or two and ease into going home. Bishop likes to ask questions—what's the most pain you've ever been in, what's the craziest thing you've done for love— and after Evan and I tell our stories, he looks into his beer mug like it's a crystal ball until one of us asks him the same question. Then, no matter how good our stories were, he tops them.

Tonight, Bishop buys a pitcher of beer and says, "What's the worst story you've ever had to write?"

"How do you mean, worst?" I say. "I can tell you the stupidest story I ever had to write."

Bishop nods at me, filling my mug.

"When Charles and Di first hit the rocks," I say, "I was working for the Nashville paper, and they asked me to call marriage coun- selors and ask them if the marriage could be saved."

"You're kidding," Evan says.

"I called one guy, who was horrified by the question, and wouldn't talk to me. I was so embarrassed, I lied to my editor and said I had called seven people and none of them would talk to me. She said, 'You'd think people would have more of a sense of humor,' but she didn't make me do the story."

"Okay," Bishop says, unimpressed. He nods at Evan. "What's yours?"

"It would have to be one of those man-on-the-street stories," Evan says. He acts it out. "Excuse me, sir, what do you think about the situation in Bosnia?" Then he says, in a redneck drawl, "Kill 'em all, let God sort 'em out."

"Ah," Bishop says. He takes a swig of his beer, sets it down slowly, and gazes deeply into it.

"Okay, I give," I say. "What's yours?"

"Well, my children," he says. "You may recall that kid who got killed in DeSoto County. Yours truly was assigned to go talk to the parents, never an enviable task. When the photog and I got to the parents' house, the lawn was packed with reporters, photographers, TV cameras, everything. And the father was standing there, drinking a beer, wearing a T-shirt." He forms a square with his hands, like a director sizing up a shot. "Now picture this," he says. "The shirt has a bottle of Jack Daniel's on it, and there's this hand wrapped around the neck of the bottle. Across the top it said 'Jack-off Daniel's.' And everybody's snapping this guy's picture."

Evan roars, slapping the table. "You're shitting me," he says.

"You're changing the rules," I say. "What's that got to do with the worst story you had to write?"

"That was a pretty bad case," he says. "That murder." I can see him withdrawing into himself—his head down, his shoulders pulled in.

"If that's what you mean," I say, "the story I just wrote is the worst. The dead girl." I reach in my pocket and find the picture Angela gave me. "Let me show you guys something." I put the photo on the table. They lean in close to see.

"Is one of them her?" Evan asks.

"Yeah," Bishop answers for me. "The one on the left." Then he looks at me. "What about it?"

"Look at her," I say, and obediently they fix their gazes on her face. "You don't think I look like her, do you?"

"Why?" Evan says.

"People keep telling me I do," I say. "I don't believe it."

Bishop sits back in his chair. "Hate to tell you, but they're right," he says. "There's a slight resemblance."

Evan is nodding, looking from the picture to my face and back again. "Definitely," he says. "Around the eyes."

"Sergeant Morris said it was the shape of my face," I say. "You guys wouldn't have noticed if I hadn't asked."

"I noticed earlier," Bishop says.

"And you didn't say anything?"

"I don't say everything I think," he says, turning his gaze back to his beer mug.

"Forget it," I say, reaching for the picture and slipping it back in my pocket. "It's no big deal." Then I reach for the pitcher and top off our mugs.

Bishop appraises us. He says, "How about this: What's the farthest you've ever gone for a story?"

"Into a Dumpster," Evan says, and laughs. "I ruined my shoes."

"Did you find anything?" I ask.

"I showed you," he says. "That witchcraft magazine." He lifts his glass and says, "Front page!" We clink our glasses against his.

Bishop nods at me. "Come back to me," I say. "I have to think. You answer."

Bishop tells us about the time he was trying to get a quote from a state senator suspected of tax fraud. While he's talking, I signal the waitress and order a bourbon, straight up. I watch her walk across the bar and bring the drink back, the little glass in the center of her large round tray.

Bishop tells us he followed the guy to a four-star restaurant, where he had his terrible car valet-parked, borrowed a jacket and tie from the maître d', and sat down to a five-course meal, keeping his eye on the senator while he ate his Cornish game hen. When the senator got up to go to the bathroom, Bishop followed. He sallied up to the urinal next to his. "So we're standing there pissing, right," Bishop says, "and I zip up and turn to the guy, who's still going, and I stick out my hand to shake and say, 'Hello, Senator, I'm Martin Bishop from the paper. What can you tell me about the charges made against you?'"

"What did he do?" Evan says.

"He shook my hand," Bishop says. Evan bursts out laughing. "I guess it was a reflex," Bishop says.

"I hope you washed your hands," I say.

"Of course," Bishop says. "With soap and hot water."

"Did he give you a quote?" Evan asks.

"He said, 'They're absolutely false, son. I'm guilty of nothing. Now pardon me while I zip my pants.'"

"You're making that up," I say.

Bishop holds his hands in the air, palms out. "Would I do such a thing?" He nods at me. "Now you."

"I'm thinking, I'm thinking," I say.

"Time's up," Evan says.

"I don't know," I say. "I don't think I've done it yet."

The waitress passes by and leans down to pick up my glass. "You want another, honey?" she says.

"Sure," I say. "Why not." Evan raises his eyebrows at me. "What?" I say.

"You drank that fast," he says.

"I'm a reporter," I say. "I'm supposed to drink hard." When the waitress brings my drink, I pick it up and throw it back in one motion. It burns going down but I don't flinch. I smile at Evan and turn the glass upside down on the table. He shakes his head. Bishop laughs. "Go easy, cowgirl." He winks at me. Then he says, "Why did you become a reporter?" and looks from one to the other of us before he fixes his eyes on Evan.

"Because I wanted to be like Woodward and Bernstein in *All the President's Men*," Evan says. "I wanted to be the person who found the truth and made sure others were held accountable for their actions. It sounds silly . . ." He trails off.

"Go on," Bishop says.

"I felt like I had a mission."

Bishop nods and turns to me. "Why did you become a reporter?"

I spin my empty glass on the table. "The same reasons as Evan."

Bishop smiles and shakes his head. "Why did you become a reporter?"

"I just told you."

"If you ask a cop why he became a cop, what do you think he'll say?"

"Because he wanted to protect and serve," I say, looking around for the waitress.

"And why do you think he really became a cop?"

"Power. A gun at his side and a siren so that he could go flying past everybody else on the road."

"Right," Bishop says.

"That's not fair," Evan protests. "Some cops do want to protect and serve."

Bishop ignores him, keeping his eyes on me. "Why did you become a reporter?"

"Why don't you ask Evan again?" I say, signaling the waitress to bring me one more drink.

"Evan told the truth," he says. "I want to know what about you makes you do this job. Are you curious? Are you a thrill seeker? Do you find it easier to examine others' lives than to live your own? Why did you become a reporter?"

I look hard at him. "I just did." Sometimes it doesn't feel like something I chose. It's just what I became, the way I grew a few inches every year until I was five feet two.

"It's never that simple and you know it," Bishop says. "You'd never take that answer from someone you were interviewing."

The other day I said to Sergeant Morris, "I need to know," and he didn't ask me why. It never occurs to anyone to ask me why. That's my job. "Okay, how about this," I say. "My mother says I always wanted to watch people. She says I would cry if someone held me so that I couldn't see the rest of the room."

"So you were born for it?" Bishop asks me, turning the words over in his mouth like they taste bad.

"I guess," I say. "Why did *you* become a reporter?"

"I'm curious," he says. "I'm a thrill seeker. I find it easier to examine others' lives than to live my own." He grins at me and lifts his glass as though in a toast. "Don't worry," he says gently. "I've been at this longer than you."

I have another drink while they make their way through the pitcher. When the beer is gone, Evan says it's time to go. "One more drink," I say. "Come on."

He stands up. "You've had enough," he says. "I'll drive you home."

"No thanks," I say. "I want another." I turn to Bishop and smile. "Bishop? One more drink?"

"Can't turn down a lady," he says, deepening his southern accent. "I'll have a whiskey."

Evan leaves, saying again that I shouldn't drive home. Bishop and I sit and order drinks and he tells me stories, some of them terrible, all of them funny. He imitates a drunk who was arrested taking pot-shots at neighborhood pets in the street, weaving a little as he sights down an imaginary gun, loading on the accent as he calls, "Here, kitty, kitty, kitty." He tells the "Jack-off Daniel's" story again.

"That's terrible," I say, over and over, laughing helplessly. "That's terrible."

"Let me tell you, kid," Bishop says. "That's not the half of it."

There is nothing Bishop doesn't know about this city. Everywhere he goes he sees a story he wrote.

If I go to the music festival next May, I'll watch crowds of people walk right over the spot where that car crushed Allison Avery's skull. I'll watch them: the dreadlocked white kids in hemp necklaces, the cowboys in tight Wranglers and sharp-pointed boots, the middle-aged couples in denim jackets, the frat boys in khakis and baseball caps, the girls with too much makeup, breasts swelling out of tank tops. The guys squeezing the girls' butts, the people huddling under umbrellas as their feet sink into the mud, the enormous bouncers glaring with their backs to the stage, the screaming women, grabbing at the air when Al Green throws down a rose. Plastic beer cups and candy wrappers will litter the ground, churned to mud by the rain and the thousands of moving feet. There will be no sign it ever happened. But I'll know. I'll know exactly where.

I have to call Hannah to come pick me up. "You're wasted," she says accusingly as soon as I get in the car. "You're not walking straight."

"Well, hello to you too," I say. This is a bad drunk. When I finally get in my bed, I'm going to have to keep one foot on the ground to stop the room from spinning. We pull over three times so I can lean out the door to vomit.

Our neighbor Denise's car is blocking the driveway, so Hannah drops me in front of our duplex and goes to find a parking place on the street . . . I'm on my hands and knees at the edge of the curb, my whole body swaying. I get up and go to sit in a dignified manner on the front steps.

I wake up. There are steps beneath my back, and the porch light shines right in my eyes. I turn my head from side to side and see that my arms are spread out above my head. I lift my head a little and look down. My legs are spread as wide as my arms, and my skirt is hiked up around my waist. I can see my underwear. Blue stripes. I hear footsteps. "Hannah?" I call out, but no one answers, and when I raise my head again, a man is just passing me. He turns to look at me, and the thought of what I must look like hits me so hard I almost feel sober. "Hey," he says. "Are you okay?"

"I'm fine," I say. I sit up and yank my skirt down.

He takes a step toward me. "I'm fine," I say again, but my voice wobbles, and he takes another step toward me and starts to reach out his hand. I squawk, and he jerks his hand back. "Go away," I shout.

He takes a step backward, hesitating. He is not tall, but thick and powerful through the shoulders, his features indistinct in the darkness beyond the porch. The porch light flickers. My thighs, pressed together, are sticky with sweat. No one else is on the street. When I turn my head I see nothing but darkness, houses where everyone sleeps behind locked doors.

I stare at him. He stares at me. If he moves in my direction I'll scream. "What do you want?" I say. My voice comes out terrified.

I think I see him smile, a ferocious appraising smile, and panic bubbles up in my throat. "Look, miss," he says. "I'm just being nice. I'm just a Good Samaritan." His voice drips with scorn. "Take a look at yourself, why don't you. Ask yourself what *you* want. You're the one sprawled out half-naked on the street." Then he rotates on his heel and stalks away.

I bite my fingers to stop my hands from shaking. I was passed out on the front porch, arms and legs out, spread out like a starfish just waiting to be slipped in someone's pocket. "Where are you, Hannah," I say. "Where are you, where are you."

Then I'm halfway across the porch, half falling, half leaning on Hannah. "Did I pass out again?"

"Yes," Hannah says.

"Where are we going?"

"To bed."

"Hannah," I say. "I feel awful."

"Okay," she says, propping me against the wall so she can unlock the front door. She looks at me. "You're going to have a bad headache."

In my bedroom, she eases me onto the bed and goes out of the room. When I close my eyes I see red, blood red. Everything spins together like clothes in a drier, the dead girl, the man on the street, my messy room. Hannah is standing there. I prop myself up on one elbow and catch her wrist with my other hand. "You have to be careful," I tell her. "The world is filled with danger." I shake her arm. "Promise me you'll be careful."

"You're just drunk." She extracts her wrist from my grasp.

"Oh. Okay." I lie back down. My throat fills with the urge to cry. "A lump of sorrow," I say, stupidly, trying not to weep.

"Open your mouth," Hannah says. She puts two aspirin on my tongue and hands me a glass of water.

Then it is so quiet I think Hannah has gone until I feel her taking off my shoes. She comes to the head of the bed and holds out my contact case. "Here," she says. "Pop them out." The small effort of sitting up makes me nauseous.

"This is going to be really bad," I say.

"When I drove by, after I dropped you off, you were spread-eagled on the front steps, right under the light. It was like you were in a spotlight," Hannah says. "It scared me. I ran home. What if you had passed out like that, on the street outside the bar?"

"I was sitting up properly," I lie. "I was careful."

"You were passed out, Olivia," she says. "After all those lectures you've given me. All that talk about inviting it. You idiot."

"I don't want to talk about it anymore, okay? Please?"

Hannah slips my earrings out of my ears. She says nothing. I know she won't say anything tomorrow, and if I'm lucky I won't even remember just how bad and scared and stupid I feel right now. Hannah runs her hand across my hair. She shuts out the light.

7

Tiny black and white kittens live underneath the porch of the house next door. One day I spent an hour trying to entice them closer by waving a stick, clicking my tongue. One came within inches of me before bounding away. It was sunny, the kind of sunny when patches of grass seem spotlit, and the hairs on my arm were golden in the light. Across the street a man and his two daughters were washing their car, and the light bounced off the car and off the water that pooled in the street. The houses here are all the same, one brick level, hunkered down low to the ground. I don't know any of my neighbors. I wanted to follow those kittens onto their own lawn but I didn't want their owner to come out and yell at me.

I don't see the kittens now. I'm sitting on our front porch drinking a glass of water. The sun beats down like noon, though it's only 8:30. Today is Allison Avery's funeral, and I am so hungover I can barely stand. I can't stop picturing myself, sprawled here like a dead thing, like a careless, stupid girl. This morning I pulled off my clothes before the mirror, searching my body for signs that someone had touched me, that someone else had pulled up my skirt. There was nothing, only the red marks my own fingers left where I pressed them hard against my skin.

My body feels like it's trying to turn itself inside out. If I call in sick they'll think I don't want to go to the funeral. I'll get assigned a new beat, or even fired. I'll be known as the one who didn't have the stomach, for alcohol, for blood, for death.

So I have to get up now, and go stand in the shower, and try to keep from vomiting when I bend over to shave my legs. I have to put on a black dress and find my notebook and have Hannah take me to my car, because the funeral is this morning and I have to be there. I have to get up now.

I have to go.

At funerals I try to stay away from the immediate family, and in that way try to make a bad thing better. I don't care what Peggy says about quotes. I get what I get. At first it looks like I'm going to get nothing, because when I try to walk into the funeral home, an undertaker comes up on quiet feet and asks me to leave. So I wait, leaning against my car in the hot parking lot, trying not to throw up. I flip open my notebook and scan my notes. *Drank too much*, it says across the top of one page. I shut the notebook. When everyone emerges, blinking into the sunlight, I follow them, over the arch of the Dudley Street Bridge, under the intricate wrought iron sign for the Elmwood Cemetery.

I once wrote a story about this cemetery and the eighty thousand corpses I called "inhabitants" in the paper. Annie Cook, a madam who opened her bordello to the sick during the yellow fever epidemic in 1878. Robert Church, the city's first black millionaire. Dorothea Henry Winston, daughter of Patrick Henry. Fifteen hundred yellow fever victims tumbled together in mass graves called No Man's Land. This is a beautiful place, bursting with greenery, and narrow winding roads take you past ornate statues of angels and the dead. As I get out of the car, through the damp still air comes the sound of a bell.

At the graveside, I see the brother, Peter, with his parents, two people of whom I can only say: moderate height, dressed in black. It's not a good day for black, my dress clinging to my skin. The newspaper photographer, Bryce, snaps a picture and the father shoots an angry look in his direction. I keep my distance from Bryce, standing on the other side of the crowd. I fan my face with my hand. My stomach lurches.

I don't know how I'm going to write this story, because I can't keep my mind on anything. I keep reaching down to smooth my black skirt, as though I'm going to walk up to someone asking for a quote and discover it hiked up around my waist. I snap to attention after a few minutes, and I don't remember what I've been thinking about. I scan the crowd. Peter's mouth is set in a straight thin line, his eyes fixed on some point in the distance. The mother has an almost identical expression on her tight face. The father's shoulders shake as he reaches in his pocket for a handkerchief. Angela is demure in a tailored black dress. Her hair is up, tendrils sticking to the back of her wet neck. With her head bowed she stares resolutely into the grave, lifting her hand from time to time to wipe her eyes with a crumpled tissue. She seems to have learned a lesson—no mascara runs down her cheeks.

Carl stands right behind Allison's mother. The material of his jacket strains as he raises an arm to squeeze the mother's shoulder. He leaves his hand there a moment and she reciprocates, holding his thick fingers in her own slender ones. He sees me and gives me one of his tentative smiles. I lift my hand in a greeting, then look away. Toward the back is the dead girl's neighbor, the young woman from Mississippi, without her children. She is openly weeping, her hands cupped around her face. The only other face I recognize is the doctor's. A pretty blond woman leans against him, her features arranged in an expression of polite sorrow.

Near the grave of Allison Avery stands a tall stone angel with spread wings, her face a picture of heavenly rapture, her eyes uplifted. This is a tribute to Mattie Stephenson, a girl who came to Memphis after her fiancé married another and broke her heart. I remember her story. The audiotape guide I rented at the cemetery office said she "gave her life" nursing victims of the yellow fever epidemic. Imagine a time when so many people died in this city that bodies were piled in the streets, so numerous that no one could identify their faces before they were hauled away. I doubt it was possible, then, to care when one more person died.

There will be no statue, no angel, to mark Allison Avery's grave, just a plain granite block engraved with her name, the dates of birth and death, the words "Beloved Daughter." People who come here won't notice the headstone, except perhaps to note the shortness of her life. She won't be mentioned on the next audiotape, though like Mattie Stephenson she was young, and this city took her life. What could they say Allison Avery gave her life for?

I manage to stand for fifteen more minutes before a wave of nausea hits me so hard I feel like I might faint. As fast as I can I walk away, trying to step lightly on the gravel path, and then when I can't go any farther I duck behind a bush and throw up. I'm on my hands and knees on the ground, beside the flat tablet engraved with the score to "Dixie." After I stop shaking I crawl backward, retreating from the mess I've just made, and put my head down on the ground between my elbows.

"Miss?" a woman's voice says from behind me. I turn my head a little and catch a glimpse of an older woman in church clothes. "Are you all right?"

"Fine," I whisper. She hesitates for a moment before she walks away, leaving me alone, she thinks, with my grief.

I don't see Peter when the burial is over, so I go looking for him, walking off between the headstones. I'm holding on to my bag with both hands like it can keep me standing up straight.

I turn a corner, and there he is, lying lengthwise on a bench with his feet still on the ground, as though he had been sitting but couldn't support his own weight anymore. His open black jacket hangs off either side of the bench; his white shirt is untucked and pushed up, his hands resting on his bare stomach. He hasn't seen me, and I watch as his fingers explore the bottom of his rib cage, pushing on the bone as though he's surprised to find something that substantial inside his own body. He lifts his hand to his face and runs a finger around an eye socket.

When he sees me, he turns his head and frowns, his hands going quickly to pull down his shirt. "What do you want?" he says. "Leave me alone." He wants to sound angry and dismissive but his voice cracks over the words. He closes his eyes, the simplest way to make me disappear. This seems to happen very slowly—I can see his eyelashes tremble—and then he starts to cry.

"Oh," I say, and approach him, taking his hand. His hand doesn't move so I close it in both of mine and rub his fingers as though to warm them, though they're as hot as my own. My face is so close to his I can feel his breath. He opens his eyes, squinting up at me. "You're that reporter," he says, trying to steady his voice. "What are you doing here?"

"I was sent here," I say. I wonder if he thinks the photographer is right behind me, ready to snap this picture, if he thinks I'm already writing the caption—"Boy, 17, mourns his sister's murder. The killer is still at large." And then I can't stop writing captions in my head— "Peter Avery, 17, brother to the dead girl." "Brother, 17, lets reporter hold his hand." I picture this photograph in the paper—me, all in black, crouched over his body, shadowing his face. I sit on the far edge of the bench, still holding his hand. His whole body shudders. Then there is a whispering sound, and after a moment I realize that it's him, saying something under his breath. "Oh God," he says, "oh God oh God oh God," until it's not even like words anymore, just breath, just painful breathing. I am not good at this. Questions cluster in my throat. *Who's the boyfriend? When's your mother going to talk to me?* It would be heartless to ask these things now. I think, *Win his trust.* I consider touching his soft cheek, splotched red with crying. If I were another sort of person, I would take him in my arms but I just hold his hand until he stops crying, with a deep breath that he holds for a long time.

He sits up and says, "I've got to find my parents." He's still holding my hand, and in this moment I realize that he is holding it, it's not just me hanging on.

I squeeze his hand again and he gives me a terrible smile. "It's just me now, you know," he says. He's not crying anymore, but I can see the film of water balanced on the skin that rims his eyes. Then he stands, taking his hand from mine, and pulls himself up tall. He tucks his shirt back in, straightens his jacket, and rubs his eyes hard. "Do I look like I've been crying?" he says, turning to show me his face. His nose is red, his eyes pink and watery.

"No," I lie.

"Good," he says. He nods once, sharply. I watch him walk away.

For a long time I sit there with one hand pressed to my wretched stomach, the other flat on the bench where the stone is still warm from his body. I don't know what it's going to say underneath my byline in tomorrow's paper. All I can picture is a big blank space, two columns of nothing under my name.

It takes me all afternoon to write the funeral story, fifteen inches I would normally pound out in less than an hour. My mind feels as wrung out as my body. When I'm finally done I send it to Peggy and leave, telling her I don't feel well. I'm halfway to David's house before I remember the Reverend James Freeland's anticrime meeting. "I'm not going," I say out loud, even as I'm turning the car around.

Half an hour later I am sitting in the basement of the Brighter Day Baptist Church. One of the long fluorescent lights flickers—brighter, dimmer—above my head while the Reverend James Freeland describes "why we're all here tonight." I'm not sure why I'm here tonight, as this story is probably destined for the weekly Neighbors section unless somebody with a gun shows up to mug us all right now.

I shift in my metal folding chair, slowly unsticking one thigh, then the other, knowing from experience they'll just get stuck again. I glance up at the reverend's face, heavy with sincerity, and back down at my feet tapping lightly on the slick gray floor. The long tables, the low ceiling, and the metal and plastic decor, the lingering smells of cooked meat and disinfectant—I could be sixteen again, sitting in a prayer circle at my parents' church, head bowed, looking at my pink flowered dress, my hands in my lap. Here is the church, here is the steeple, open the doors . . .

". . . Olivia Dale," the reverend booms out. I jerk my head up to see everyone half turned and smiling in my direction. "I want y'all to tell her how the crime in this city has touched your lives and your neighborhoods, and how we're going to fight back. We're going to send out a message today."

Of the twenty people in this room, all but four are women, one a young man who looks to be about my age. He's slouched low in his chair, his arms crossed over his chest, and doesn't turn his face toward me. Everyone else looks at me expectantly. I lift my hand in a tiny wave. "Hi," I say. "Thank you so much for asking me here. I just want to listen, and then if it's all right I'll ask you some questions at the end."

Clothes rustle and chairs creak as they turn their attention back to the front. One woman keeps her eyes trained on me. She is a heavy dark-skinned woman with darker shadows under her eyes. I smile and nod at her. She nods back, but does not smile. Then slowly she turns herself back around.

They talk for a while about the drugs infiltrating their quiet, middle-class neighborhood, where many of them have lived for twenty years or more. A sixty-something woman named Katie Mae Olson remembers sleeping on her porch without a worry. Someone else describes hearing gunshots in the distance, seeing people she's certain are drug dealers pacing on corners, watching strange cars prowl her street. "We've got to unite," she says. "We've got to give them someone to answer to."

"Amen," the reverend says. "When I see a strange car I walk past it so they know I'm watching. They'll get the picture they're not wanted and leave. It's a prime fact," he says, leaning forward in his chair, "if we sit back and do nothing, our quiet community can change overnight."

I take notes while they talk about the need for increased police presence in South Memphis, about long waits for officers to respond to 911 calls. I make a note to myself: *check average response time*. Someone mentions the possibility of a petition calling for increased manpower. One man talks about starting a Neighborhood Watch.

Then the heavyset woman pushes up onto her feet. "My daughter Tamara was eighteen years old when somebody shot her dead on the sidewalk near our house," she says. "Eighteen." She grips the back of the chair for support, though when she speaks her voice is slow and even. "The police came, but they never found out a thing, and the monster who did that to my baby is still out there. That was last year, a year ago May fourteenth. You think anybody cares about that now? There's been a hundred murders since."

I copy her words into my notebook, thinking it's probably closer to 130, 140, thinking *this is good, I'll probably use this*. I write down: *Check stats. Get her name.*

"Nobody cares," she says. "Nobody's got the time to care."

A murmur goes up of "we care" and "we love you." She turns her head toward me, her eyes trained on my face. "And that white girl," she says. For a moment I think she means me, and I work to keep her gaze, resisting the urge to sink down in my chair. "She's all over the front page. When my Tamara died, not one reporter came to ask me anything. Not one. What's the difference between Tamara and that girl but that she's white? Both young. Both gone. Both dead and gone."

I drop my eyes to my notebook. I write it down: *nobody cares*.

Katie Mae Olson has risen from her chair to put her arm around the woman. "We care about your Tamara," she says, her voice rising with indignation, "and we're going to fight. This used to be a nice place to raise your children, and we're going to make it that way again. We're not going to stand for crime anymore." She turns to me. "You put that in the paper," she says. "We're tired. And we're not going to stand it. Not anymore."

They all turn to me now, so I ask, "Do you think you can make this neighborhood as safe as it used to be?"

"I hope so," Reverend Freeland says. "Residents used to be able to sleep out in their backyards at night without fear of some maniac running and raping and cutting somebody's throat. I don't know that we'll ever again be able to sleep in our homes and not worry about whether or not we've locked our doors."

Katie Mae Olson tightens her grip on Tamara's mother, who sags a little against her. "I'm sixty-eight years old, and I've lived in this city all my life," she says. "I'll tell you one thing, it's not what it used to be." She looks around the room, taking in the upturned faces of her neighbors. "But I'll live here till I die, and I'm damned if I'll give up until then. This is my city." Her voice rises as she leans toward me. "You tell everybody that. This is my city too."

I write that down and circle it. I can already tell her quote will be my last graf. It's the perfect way to end.

I'm walking through the dark parking lot toward my car, the fat yellow moon hanging low in the sky. I can feel the humidity settling into my hair, the temperature probably only ten degrees lower than it was before sunset. When I get home I'm going to strip naked and stand in front of the air conditioner until it goes away, the stickiness in my hair, between my breasts, at the backs of my knees.

Somewhere behind me a man calls out, "Hey." Without stopping, I glance back over my shoulder. The young man from inside is walking toward me, one hand lifted in my direction. "Hey, wait," he calls out again. I turn to face him, taking a couple of steps backward. He ducks his head and jogs toward me.

"Thanks," he says when he comes to a stop in front of me. He exhales hard. I say nothing, waiting for him to speak. He extends his hand, and I take it. It's warm and dry. "I'm Russell Freeland," he says.

"Olivia Dale," I say automatically.

The corners of his mouth lift a little. "I know," he says. "I was inside." He lets go of my damp hand and wipes his palm on his jeans. Then he sees me watching him and stops.

"Are you related?" I say, nodding toward the church behind me.

He turns to look back at the church. "Yeah," he says. "He's my dad."

I wait for a moment. He just stands, rubbing his fingers hard on the back of his neck. "Okay," I say, the heat making me impatient, "nice to meet you."

"Wait, please," he says. He shifts from foot to foot. "I need to talk to you."

Over his shoulder I see the church door start to open. A man's voice calls, "Russell?"

His body tenses, as though bracing for a punch to the gut. "It's my dad," he says. His voice goes low, urgent. "I've got to talk to you. Can we meet somewhere?"

"What's this about?"

"Allison Avery," he says, taking a step back.

"Allison . . . ," I repeat. Without thinking, I put my hand in my bag, searching for my notebook. "What about her?"

"I know her," he says. He presses his lips together and blinks rapidly. He takes another step back.

I put my hand on his forearm to stop him. "Do you have something to tell me?"

"Russell?" his father calls again. "You out there?"

"Coming," he yells. Then to me he says, "I've got to go. Can I talk to you?"

"Give me your number, tell me how to reach you."

"I'll call you," he says. He spins on one foot and starts jogging back toward the church.

"When?" I call after him. He doesn't answer. I stand and watch as he reaches his father, who puts his arm around his shoulders and leads him back inside the church. The heavy door eases shut behind them.

I let myself into David's house with the key he leaves inside the mailbox. Lou greets me at the door, woofing mightily and rearing up on his hind legs. I shout no at him until he drops to all fours, and then I pat him once or twice and he licks my hand. "Where's your daddy?" I ask him, wiping my hand on my pants. He lets his tongue dangle out, looking up at me with his droopy eyes.

I like being at David's when he's not home. Lou follows on my heels as I wander from room to room, looking in cabinets. Everything is in order. I open a drawer and run my hand over his neatly folded boxers. A white T-shirt lying on the bed has the scent of him still.

On his desk is a shoe box labeled "Demo Tapes," with two neat rows of cassettes in plastic cases. He's even alphabetized them. I run my finger up to the As, and there it is. Allison Avery. He told me he'd never heard of her. I pull the tape out and stand for a moment with it in my hand.

I put the tape in my pocket and start searching his desk, going through drawers, rifling through stacks of papers, looking for something else marked with her name. Lou paws at my leg. "What do you want?" I ask him. He cocks his head. Then I look at what I've done to the desk. The drawers are all open. The papers are splashed across the desktop. Some tapes have fallen to the floor.

Hurrying now, because he might come home at any minute, I start cleaning up the mess I've made, shutting the drawers and stacking the papers. The phone rings, and I pick it up, thinking it might be David.

"Hey," Hannah says. "I thought you might be there."

"Didn't I tell you I would be?"

"What are you doing?"

"Cleaning up some papers I knocked over," I say. I step back and look at the desk. It looks neat and organized, and I don't think he'll notice I touched it. I take the tape with her name on it out of my pocket and look at it again. He gets a lot of these tapes. He probably just forgot her name.

"Why so quiet?" Hannah says.

"You know the dead girl?" I say. "I found one of her demo tapes on David's desk."

"Creepy," Hannah says. "Did you listen to it?"

"Not yet. I wonder why he didn't tell me he had it."

"Did you ask him?"

"I asked him if he knew her. He said no."

"He probably forgot," Hannah says. She pauses. "Unless of course, he's the murderer."

"That's not funny, Hannah."

"Oh come on," she says. "It is, too. Jesus, you're paranoid."

"What do you mean?"

"How many years have you been with this boy?" Hannah says. "Don't you think he would have told you if he remembered the girl's name?"

"She was very pretty. Maybe he had an affair with her and he doesn't want to tell me," I say, only half joking. I turn the tape over in my hand. "Maybe I don't know him as well as I think."

"He tells you he loves you, right?" she says. "What else do you want?" She laughs. She thinks that's funny.

"I want everything," I say.

"I don't think you do," she says.

For a moment I say nothing. I listen to her breathing. "What are you doing now?" I ask.

"Listening to Denise have sex. It's so loud today."

Denise lives in the other half of our duplex, which does not have thick walls. We know a lot about her life considering how rarely we actually talk to her, because she lives it at a very high volume. She has a crazy boyfriend, who, she screams, does *not* treat her *right*. From time to time, judging from the sounds she makes, he treats her very right.

Hannah wants to know if I'm spending the night here, and I tell her yes, that I'll see her after work tomorrow. We hang up the phone. I turn on a TV movie, and Lou flops down at my feet. He keeps his eyes trained on my face, his anxious eyebrows dancing. On the television, a man searches frantically for the woman he loves. She's been in an accident. She lies in her hospital bed, doing nothing but breathing, and he waits all night for her eyes to open. In the morning they tell him to go home and get some sleep, and when he gets home he can't be strong anymore and he just sinks to the floor and cries.

So what I want to know is, if David came home and I wasn't there, if I were dead, missing, lying in the hospital, unconscious, beyond the reach of anything he could do, what would he do? Would he sink to the floor, slide down the wall to his knees, would his breathing turn jagged, gasping, would he make any sound, would he sob, cry out, would he hold his hands out in front of him like this man, down on his knees, his hands spread, impotent, powerless, in love? Or would he hang up his jacket and go to bed, and come visit me in the hospital early in the morning, bringing flowers? Would it be tulips, because they're my favorite, or roses, because they're his?

A hand brushes against my thigh. I sit bolt upright in the armchair, blinking. It's dark. "Allison," I say. My outstretched fingers touch skin.

"Who?" David says. He is leaning over me, smiling with gentle amusement.

"Oh." I sink back into the chair. "What's going on?"

David settles on the arm and strokes my hair back from my face. "You were sleeping." He holds something up. "What's this?"

It takes me a moment to understand, as though I'm translating from a dimly understood language into my own. I want to ask David, "Who *are* you?"

"It's a tape," I say.

He laughs softly, his fingers still in my hair. "I know. Why were you sleeping with it? You had it clutched in your hand."

"I was looking at your demo tapes. This tape, it's Allison Avery."

"So? Who's that?"

"Jesus, David, don't you listen to me? Don't you read my stories? It's the dead girl. The one I asked you about."

"Don't shout, Olivia," he says evenly. "I haven't had time to read the paper lately. I didn't remember her name."

"Did you listen to it?"

He shakes his head. "I just brought that box home from work yesterday. She must have sent it to me right before she died."

He pushes up off the chair and goes in the direction of the stereo. I close my eyes. In a moment Allison Avery's voice fills the room.

"How old was this girl?" David asks, whispering so his own voice won't drown out the sound of hers.

I tell him she was twenty-four. I know why he asked. It's not the voice of a girl. If I didn't know better I'd imagine a much older woman, someone who's known twenty years of loss and heartbreak.

"Gorgeous voice," David says in the space before the next song begins. "What a waste."

"Would you have called her?" I ask.

"Definitely."

We listen in silence, her voice with us like a ghost in the room.

Neither of us moves to pop the tape out when it's over, listening without speaking to the whirring of empty ribbon through the speakers. David turns off the stereo and finally it's quiet. Then he comes back to me, and I'm surprised to see that his eyes are filled with tears. "It's terrible," he says.

I don't say anything. "What happened to her?" he says.

"I told you. Somebody grabbed her outside her apartment. They beat her, raped her, killed her."

David shakes his head like he can't believe it.

"I told you this before," I say.

He reaches for me and pulls me into a hug. "Now it seems real," he says, his breath warm against my ear. He tightens his arms around me.

I close my eyes. I stood over her body in the dirt. It always seemed real to me.

"I love you," he whispers.

I want to say it back but I don't. How can I, when I know he's only saying it because he's imagining me dead?

David is beside me when I wake up in the morning before the alarm goes off. I put a hand on his cheek, soft from sleeping. He sighs when I kiss him and then opens his eyes and smiles. "Good morning," he says.

"We'll see," I say.

We make love without kissing. No matter how long or tightly I hold him, he is never close enough. He gets out of bed and goes to shower. I lie there, sweating, stupid with desire.

8

At my desk, I read my story about the funeral over a cup of coffee. From the story, someone who wasn't there could learn what the minister said about faith and comfort, what expressions the family members wore, what flower—a lily—the mother carried. My lead begins, "Like the lily her mother laid on her coffin, Allison Avery was . . ." I skip ahead, already embarrassed by something I wrote only yesterday, its slick sentimentality. I quoted Allison's employer saying how much she will be missed, Angela saying what a wonderful friend she was, and some Avery cousin saying the family has faith in the police to bring about a swift resolution to the case. Someone who wasn't there wouldn't know how hot it was in the sun-baked black clothes we wore, how quiet it was in the moments after the minister stopped speaking, how that boy's hand felt inside my own. Next to the copy is a photo of Allison's mother, leaning forward with the flower in her hand. Her husband stands behind her, his head bowed. Half of Peter's body appears at one edge. Some careless person cropped out the rest.

I put down the paper and check the phone book for James Freeland. There are two J. Freelands. I call the first number and a querulous old woman complains that she's never heard of Russell Freeland. When I call the second, I get a machine. A girl's voice recites the phone number but no names. I hang up before the beep. If you leave a message, you can't call back.

I check my E-mail. One from Bishop. "I'm bored already," it says. "Any news on your dead girl?" I write back, tell him I'm shit out of luck with the cops and not sure what to do next. A few minutes later he appears at my desk. "Let's take a ride to the station," he says. "I'll try one of my guys for you."

As we pass a cheap motel on the way, Bishop says, "Guy killed his wife there."

"Oh yeah?" I turn to watch it go past. "How?"

"Strangled her."

"See that corner?" I say, pointing. "That's where that professor got busted picking up a twelve-year-old prostitute."

Bishop says, "What happened to him?"

"Still teaching literature to freshmen," I say, and laugh.

At the police station I sit on a bench and wait while Bishop goes into homicide. After a few minutes Sergeant Morris comes out. I stand up.

"Got nothing to tell you," Morris says as soon as he sees me. He walks toward the water fountain, and I trail after.

"Does that mean there's nothing going on, or there's nothing you can tell me?"

"Can't really answer that, can I?" he says. "Just write the same thing: police still following up leads." He bends over the water fountain. I can't tell how old he is. He looks as old as sixty to me, but police work seems like the type of thing that could age you early.

"Come on," I say. "How many times can I write that story?"

"I read your piece on the funeral," he says, wiping water from his mouth. "You're holding off on this one, aren't you. No quotes from the immediate family."

"Give me something," I say. "Anything."

He holds his hands out toward me. "I got nothing, Olivia. Nothing. Now I'm going in the bathroom, so quit following me, okay, sweetie?"

"Will you let me know . . ."

He cuts me off. "You just keep asking," he says. "Sooner or later I'll have something to tell."

I go back down the hall and take my place on the bench again. A woman sits next to me, hitting the bench hard. She's about fifty, white, with gray-blond hair to her shoulders and a face creased as crumpled paper. She's wearing green polyester pants, a yellow shirt tucked into them. A worn and enormous purse balances on her lap. She clutches white-knuckled at the handles.

I ask her how she is, and when she says not too good I tell her I'm sorry and ask her what's wrong. To her it seems like I'm just being polite.

"It's my brother," she says. "The cops called him in for an interview."

I tell her I know how that is and watch her twist her wedding band round and round her finger.

"He's not even a suspect," she sighs. "I hope not, anyway. He's got a history."

"He's got a record?"

She pops open her purse, searching through it for something. Bottles of medication rattle. She pulls one out, empties a pink pill into her hand and swallows it without water, tossing her head back. Then she says, "He's a sexual predator. They're talking to him about that girl."

"What girl?"

"That one got raped and killed at the park," she says. "Don't you read the papers?"

"Do you think your brother's involved?"

"He's no killer," she says.

"But he's a rapist?" I look hard at her. Her face is set, nothing in it to show what her brother is to her, except maybe those deep lines in her skin.

She starts rummaging through her purse again. "He is what he is. Nothing you can do."

I watch her going through her purse, looking for something in it to tell me how it is to live this woman's life. I see crumpled tissue, lipstick, a wallet bulging with change, a comb full of gray-blond hairs. She pulls out a roll of mints and offers me one. I take it. My mouth is dry. I get up and go to the bathroom, where I stand inside a stall and write down everything the woman said. When I get back to the bench, she's gone.

After a while Bishop comes back out, shaking his head, and says, "Let's go home," and by the head shake he means he got nothing from his source, and by home he means back to the paper. When we get in the car he throws his notebook in my lap and I see that he's written *"Nada"* across the page and circled it. It's funny how you get in the habit of writing down everything, even when it's nothing. In the car I tell him what I wrote down: that the police are interviewing blind, groping in the dark, that that woman's brother, he is what he is.

"That's more than I got," he says. "At least we know something."

I know something. I know what it says in my notebook: *nothing you can do.*

On the drive back I write the word *"nada"* over and over down the side of the page. "How can I get something in the paper on this?" I ask Bishop.

Bishop shrugs. "Not much to say, is there," he says.

"I want to keep it out there. What do you think it would take to sell Peggy on it?"

"Get confirmation they've got no leads, that they're interviewing," he says. "Maybe call the family. Get some quotes from them."

"They've been uncooperative," I say.

"Get them to cooperate." He glances at me. "That's your job."

Back at the newsroom, I call the Averys' house. The machine picks up. "This is Olivia Dale from the newspaper," I say. "I know you don't want to talk to me, but I want to write a story about Allison, what she was like. I need to keep this in the news. You don't want people to forget about it. The police . . ."

"Hello," a woman's voice says. Then a squeal of feedback comes through the phone. "Hold on," she says, and then she goes to turn off the machine.

"Okay," she says when she picks it back up. "I'll talk to you."

"Now?" I can't believe my luck. I wasn't even expecting her to answer the phone.

"You can come to my house at three," she says. Then she hangs up.

Evan is watching me. "She said yes?"

I nod.

"That's great."

"It's incredible," I say. "A few days ago this woman thought I was the devil incarnate."

"People change their minds," Evan says.

"Or maybe now there's something she wants printed."

"Jesus, Olivia." Evan shakes his head, grinning. "You have such a suspicious nature. She's probably just ready to talk about the girl."

"I'm going at three," I say. I look at my watch. It's quarter to twelve.

"What are you doing now?" Evan says. "I was going to go for a drive. Want to come?"

Evan likes to take these tours of the city, because, he says, it reminds him where he is. In his car we pull out of the parking lot onto Beale, driving past low-income housing and into the commercial area. Slowly we cruise past the bars. Without the crowds milling about and the darkness to make their neon signs bright, they lose their garish charm. It's so much quieter here in the day, the whole street just waiting for night to begin.

We drive down the bluff and stop at Wolf River Harbor. This is where the riverboats dock, and the tourists board for their slow trips down the Mississippi. From here down to the water the street is made of uneven cobblestones. Evan turns off the car, and the heat rushes in. I roll down my window, though it doesn't help. Evan's brought me here before. He likes to sit and watch the river go by.

Out on the water in front of us are the boats, a floating restaurant, and Mud Island, where David lives. To the south is the Arkansas-Tennessee bridge, which I last remember crossing two months ago, when that ten-year-old got killed, though I must have been over it since. To the north is the Hernando DeSoto bridge, which is big and new and shaped like an M. At night they light it with a multitude of tiny white bulbs. Their reflections shimmer in the moving water below.

When the river's high these cobblestones, and the south end of Mud Island, are underwater, and then the river rushes along so fast and hard whole trees uproot and go with it. Even now if you look at the water you can see how quickly the current's moving, fast enough to suck a body under before you could blink. We sit and watch what look like little whirlpools forming, the water whipping itself into circles. An enormous branch floats by. "Look at it go," Evan says softly. "Fast as you please."

Then he shifts in his seat like he's coming out of some kind of trance and says in a louder voice, "When we canoed in there—I told you about that, right?—I looked up and there was a tree coming right at us. We were both going along with the current. It was just going a lot faster than we were."

"What did you do?" I watch the branch spin slowly to the right, then back again.

Evan laughs. "We got out of the way quick." He turns his gaze back to the river. "Whoosh," he says.

I look past him and out his window to the left. Going that way on Riverside you come to Tom Lee Park, where Allison died.

"You hungry?" Evan asks. He reaches in the backseat for a paper bag and pulls out two cheese sandwiches and a little carton of chocolate milk. He pops the milk open ceremoniously and hands it to me. I laugh. "I love you, Evan," I say.

"I know," he says, unwrapping the sandwiches. "But you can never have me."

Evan is gay, but I am one of the few people who knows that. It's not easy to be a gay man in Memphis, Tennessee, and even harder in small-town South Carolina, where Evan is from. His parents are starting to wonder when he's going to meet that nice girl they're hoping for, but homosexuality is so far from their realm of experience that it never crosses their mind that Evan is gay. I think that his sister Kate suspects. She came up to visit and when he was out of the room she said, "Evan certainly is *outgoing,* isn't he."

Sometimes I think about Evan's parents, how they must believe they know exactly who he is, and all the time they have no idea what really happens in his life.

"Don't hog that milk," Evan says, handing me a sandwich.

I ring the Averys' doorbell promptly at three. There's a long silence. I listen for footsteps and hear nothing. Then I lean forward to ring the bell again and Cynthia Avery opens the door. I jump like a startled cat. She is taller than I am, wearing a sleeveless white shirt tucked into black linen pants. Her hair is the shade of bleached blond I particularly associate with upper-class southern women. She squints into the sunlight, her gaze fixed on a point somewhere above my head. "Come in," she says, and then she turns and walks slowly down the hall.

I follow, closing the door with great care behind me. This is a woman who would turn and frown—a slow half turn, a quizzical frown—if I let the door bang shut. I step as quietly as I can on the tile floor. The living room is all done in white—thick white carpet, white couch with some sort of shiny pattern barely visible in it. I stand until she tells me to have a seat, and then I perch on the edge of an embroidered white armchair. There's a kind of insanity to this room, so single-minded, all of these white things so clean. Cynthia Avery eases down onto the couch and lets her head fall back like she's getting her hair washed at the salon. Over the fireplace are two enormous framed photos of Peter and Allison. Allison is wearing white.

Speaking to the ceiling, their mother says, "Peter told me you talked to him at the funeral. And then I saw in the paper that you didn't quote him or say anything about it. So that's why I'm talking to you. Because if this has to be done I want it done in the best possible way."

"I understand."

Abruptly, she stands. Without a glance in my direction she glides from the room. I wait. I'm not sure where to turn my eyes. I feel as though I should let my gaze linger respectfully on the floor, as if she were in the room, trying not to let me see her cry. When she comes back, there is no trace of tears on her face, and she says nothing about her sudden departure. She walks right up to me, so that I have to turn my face up to hers like a child. She reaches down to lift my hand from my lap, pressing it between both of hers. "This is *your* story," she says. "I'm not going to talk to anyone from television. When they ask, I'll tell them I'm only talking to you."

I nod.

"I wouldn't even talk to you, but they tell me keeping it in the papers means public interest, means pressure on the police. It may help ensure that my daughter's killer is caught."

I nod again. This is usually my speech. She's stealing my lines.

"That's your responsibility, as a journalist. It's my responsibility to help you." Her face looms even larger as she says, "Together, we'll make sure no one gives up on this."

Her grip on my hand tightens, her eyes fixed on mine, until I say, "Yes, we will." My voice comes out smaller than I meant it to. Finally she drops my hand and goes back to her own chair. I sit up straight, swallowing. I feel as though I've pledged allegiance to the memory of Allison Avery, as though her mother and I have signed a pact. It makes me wonder why she thinks we need one.

"I'm going to turn on the tape recorder now," I say. "This is so I can be sure and get what you say right."

Dr. Avery waves her hand in assent.

"I'd like to know more about Allison," I say. "What was she like?"

"She was . . ." She pauses, and then suddenly lifts her head and looks me in the face. I hold her gaze, and we sit staring at one another. Everything about this woman is careful, the hair-sprayed perfection of her blond chin-length hair, the muted blush applied precisely to the apples of her cheeks, the way her gold locket nestles into the hollow of her throat, circled with the faintest lines of age. She is the type of person who puts layers between what she means and what she says, the way she puts layers of makeup between her face and the world.

I blink first. She lays one slender hand over the other in her lap. "She was perfect," she says. She presses her lips together. When I don't say anything, she raises her eyebrows to prompt me.

"Perfect?" I say.

"Look at her," she says. I turn my head obediently toward the photo of the dead girl. She looks about seventeen, her cheeks soft and lightly powdered. Wearing a short-sleeved white dress with lace across the bodice, she sits with her body at an angle, her face turned back over her shoulder to look at the camera, her eyes lifted up, one hand curved over the other in her lap. Her nails are painted a pale pink, her dark hair curled into loose ringlets over her shoulders. Her pink shiny lips curve in a faint smile. When I look at her, the perfect stillness of her face, her hands, the line of her body, I know she could have held that pose for hours, like a mannequin. "Look at that sweet face," her mother says dreamily. "Look at that sweet smile."

To me, that smile is sly, those eyes hide a laugh bubbling up inside. Her mother says, "I couldn't have asked for a better girl."

"I'm told she was a gifted singer," I say.

She lifts a hand to push her hair behind an ear and then responds as though I'd asked another question. "I remember when we took her to her first movie—*Dumbo*, I think it was. She cried and cried when Dumbo was taken from his mother. She was always like that— she really felt for people. She used to get teary-eyed at those UNICEF commercials. Or the ones, you know, where the son has been away and he comes home unexpectedly, and the mother is so happy to see him, and then they make coffee together." She plucks at her pants with one hand and flicks her fingers, ridding herself of lint. "I used to laugh at her," she says quietly. "But once, I remember, we were watching the news, and the pope was visiting America and a very large crowd had come to see him. He got all choked up, and then so did I, and Allison looked like she was about to cry, too, and then we just burst out laughing, that we were both sitting there with tears in our eyes. We're not even Catholic." She turns her head toward the picture again. "She had a sensitive soul."

Allison Avery, Perfect Doll. I let a moment pass before I ask, "And her singing?"

"She had a lovely voice. She sang in the church choir," her mother says. "But she didn't want to sing professionally. She wanted to follow in my footsteps."

I know this isn't true. I'm not sure if she knows it. "Is that why Allison worked in health care?"

She nods. "I wanted her to go to medical school right away, but she wanted a break from school first. She said she had a lot of time ahead of her." As she says this, her voice breaks for the first time, and she presses a finger against the bottom of her eye.

When she recovers, we talk about Allison's friends. She tells me Carl is a sweet boy who had been a good friend to Allison. She hesitates when I ask her about Angela, just enough to let her displeasure show, and then she says that Angela is a nice enough girl but perhaps not the best influence on her daughter. She won't elaborate. When I press her, she just waves her hand to indicate the usual teenage highjinks, things I should already know.

I flip through my notes, then remember to ask about Russell Freeland. "Russell Freeland," she says slowly. "Yes, I think he and my daughter were friends in college. I met him only once or twice." She leans forward. Her eyes narrow, her mouth tightens, and then she seems to think better of whatever she was going to say. She smiles. "Why do you ask?" she says pleasantly. "Have you spoken with him?"

"I met him. He mentioned that he knew your daughter."

She nods slowly. "Why do you ask about him?"

"I'm interested in all your daughter's friends."

"But why him, in particular?" Irritation sharpens her voice. "He must have said something to you that made him worth asking about. What was it?"

I frown, pretending to think. She's the one making me think he's important.

"What did he say to you?" She stretches over the coffee table to lay her cool hand on my arm. "Tell me dear. Is he the one who . . ."

"Is he the one who what, ma'am?"

She shakes her head, drawing herself up tall. "What did he say to you?"

"I don't really recall," I say. I can keep secrets, too, small as mine are. We sit for a moment in brittle silence. I'm formulating another question when she says, "I don't believe in capital punishment, but I want whoever did it to die. When they catch them, I want them to die. Do you know what they did to her?"

"Yes," I say. I know exactly what they did.

"I wish I didn't know," she says. "I can't stop . . ." She shakes her head. "I can't stop thinking about it."

"Will you feel any better once they catch them?"

"I don't know," she says. "I hope so. It's terrible to feel like I do now. I don't know what could be worse. It just doesn't . . ." She shakes her head again, and reaches forward to pluck a white tissue from the white box on the coffee table and wipe her eyes. "It doesn't make any sense, what they did to her. There's no reason, there's no . . . my God. There's just no reason."

Against my will my own eyes are filling. I start blinking furiously. "How is Peter doing?" I ask her.

"Peter?" she says. "I hear him crying at night sometimes. I stand outside his door. I don't know whether to go in or not. Last night I went in, and he cried in my lap, like he hasn't since he was a baby. He cried until he wasn't even making tears anymore." She stops, and looks at me sharply, like she's just remembered who she's talking to. It's a look I'm familiar with. "Please don't put that in the paper."

"I won't."

"It's paralyzing," she says. "All this sadness."

"I'm so sorry," I say. I write it down: *all this sadness.*

Typing up my notes in the newsroom, I think that Cynthia Avery told me only what she meant to tell me, that she knew what she was going to reveal before I even walked in the door. I see her again, the way she smiled sadly and pressed my hand when she said good-bye, the way she thanked me for being so circumspect and said I was different, I wasn't like most reporters, and that that was why she had chosen me. It makes me angry to remember that I was gratified.

I write the story the way she wanted it, the tale of a tenderhearted young woman brutally killed, leaving her mother to drown in grief, praying for the police to do their job. Lucky for me it's a slow news day. Peggy's not too thrilled about it, but the story runs.

After work, I go to the Four Corners for dinner. Peter's not there. I sit alone at a table by the window and order banana pudding from a slim, rosy-cheeked blonde. When she brings it over, I ask her if she knows Peter.

She nods, rocking back and forth on her heels. "Isn't it awful about his sister?" she says. "Poor Pete. He's a sweetie."

"Did you know his sister?"

She shakes her head, then leans in and lowers her voice. "From the way Pete talks it sounds like she was a wild one," she says. She straightens up, and speaks at a normal volume. "It's terrible, isn't it?"

"Yes," I say. "It is terrible."

She nods, looking down at her hands. Then she lifts her head and smiles. "Can I get you anything else right now?" When I shake my head she says, "Enjoy your dinner," and walks away, swinging her arms.

I stare at the plate, my appetite gone. I see Allison Avery in her mother's picture again, her perfect smile, her gently clasped hands. I see her hands the way I first saw them, rigid and bloody, grasping at the air.

9

Saturday morning I wake up slow, sweating and heavy as a dead thing in my bed. My arm is so numb from lying on it all night that in the first groggy moments I think that limb beneath me isn't mine. I reach a hand out for David and find only bedsheet, damp to the touch. I open my eyes. The first thing I see is the dead girl's face, grinning at me from the bedside table, where I must have propped it last night. I swipe at it with my hand and it flutters to the top of a pile of papers and notebooks on the floor. It lands faceup, still grinning. Sitting up, I rub my numb arm until sensation returns with a painful tingling. "Hannah?" I call. "Are you up?"

She appears at the doorway to my room in shorts and a jogging bra, her hair held back with a barrette, her face red and shiny. "Am I up?" she repeats. "I just ran five miles." She flops down across the bottom of my bed and pulls her knee toward her forehead, stretching. "I tried to wake you," she says. "You mumbled something and rolled over."

"What did I say?"

She lets one leg drop to the bed and grabs the other one. "I think it was *nada*," she says. "*Nada, nada, nada.*"

For some reason, I'm relieved. "Bishop wrote that in my notebook."

"Still seeing words in your dreams?" she says. "That's so weird."

I put on my glasses. "Did you bring in the paper?"

"In the kitchen." Suddenly she jumps up and stands, legs apart, her hands in loose fists at her sides. "I'll race you."

I fling back the covers and she dashes out of the room and ahead of me down the hall, her laughter trailing behind her.

In the kitchen I make coffee while she reads the arts section. "That guy Carl," she says, rustling the pages. "He works for Black Horse Theater, right? They've got an ad in here. They're doing Macbeth."

"Let me see that." She hands me the page.

"There's a performance this afternoon," I say. "Let's go." She raises her eyebrows. "Seriously, let's go."

"Why not," she says.

The Black Horse Theater Company is located on top of a pizza place. To get to it, we climb metal fire-escape stairs up the side of the building. The stairs tremble beneath us and I cling to the railing. Inside it's dark and the smell of fresh dough mingles with dust and disinfectant. A cheerful girl wearing stage makeup sells us our tickets, hand-printed on white paper. "Can I ask how you heard about us?" she says, handing us programs.

"We know Carl Fitzner." I watch her face for reaction. Her lips shade an "oh." "You're in luck," she says. "Carl's in the play today. Bob's out with the flu."

"Was Carl his understudy?" I ask.

"Not exactly," she says. "Carl just always knows everyone's lines, even mine." She laughs. "I think if I were sick he'd put on a dress and go on for me."

"Shakespeare plays started that way, after all," Hannah says. The girl looks at her blankly. "With men in drag," Hannah says. The girl nods as though she still doesn't understand, turning away toward an older couple behind us. "What are we doing here again?" Hannah asks me as we make our way to our seats.

"Research," I say, searching for Carl's name in the program. I find it on the back, beneath the lighting guy and the costume designer. Hannah takes what I said as a joke and laughs.

An older man passes by, heading up the aisle, then turns back and stops beside me. "Excuse me, young lady," he says. "Have we met?"

I look up at his face. He's smiling hopefully at me, laugh lines around his eyes. "Yes, hello, sir," I say, rising to my feet. "I'm Olivia Dale." I offer him my hand.

He takes it, squeezing it in one hand and giving it a grandfatherly pat with the other. "I knew I recognized you. How did we meet? Are you a friend of my granddaughter's?"

"Yes, sir," I say. "Please tell her hello."

"I will." He pats my hand again. "So nice to see you."

"You too, sir," I say, and when he lets go of my hand I sit back down. He smiles at Hannah, who is watching him with open curiosity, and then moves up the aisle.

"Nice man," Hannah says. "Who's his granddaughter? Do I know her?"

"No idea. Never met her," I say. "He's a city councilman. I did a story on him two years ago."

"Why didn't you just tell him that?"

"Because the story was not flattering," I say. "He got caught with a hooker."

"That cute old man?" she says, astonished.

"Yes, ma'am," I say. "The very same."

"Jesus," Hannah says. She cranes her head to look back at the old man, as though now she'll see a lustful old goat in boxer shorts instead of the sweet grandfather who was there just moments before. She turns back to me and shakes her head. I have to laugh at her openmouthed astonishment. "Damn," she says. "It makes me wonder what my own grandfather is up to."

It's not long before the lights dim and then come up on the three witches. Macbeth himself strides out of the wings. It takes a moment before I recognize Carl. Most of the actors are absurdly bad, intoning their lines without the slightest idea of what they mean.

Carl is the exception. He doesn't even look the same. He seems taller, thinner, his jaw set, his mouth firm. When he turns murderous, I look at his face and believe he's capable of anything. Maybe the sad and lonely man I met the other day was only another role.

After the play, we hang around until Carl emerges from backstage to receive praise. His cheeks are flushed, his eyes lighting restlessly on one face, then another. We wait behind four or five other people to congratulate him on his performance. He catches my eye over another woman's shoulder and grins at me, all his teeth showing. I smile back, just as though we were friends.

"Carl, that was wonderful," Hannah says when we reach him, patting his arm. I nod. He puts one hand on each of our shoulders. "Thank you for coming," he says. Through my shirt I feel the warm dampness of his palm. It makes me feel dirty, dirty and hot. I resist the urge to step away. Lined with black, his eyes seem huge. His lips are chapped and shiny. There's a smudge of tan foundation in his goatee.

"We enjoyed it," Hannah says. "You were great."

"Thanks," he says again, nodding and nodding. "Thanks a lot." He squeezes my shoulder. I try to relax the muscles beneath his hand, to imagine what it would be like to want this boy to touch me. He looks into my face and I smile and lower my eyes. "You really were great," I say. He lifts his hand from Hannah's shoulder and wipes his mouth with the back of it, leaving pink streaks across his skin. The hand on my shoulder stays.

"Listen," he says. "What are you girls doing now? I've got an evening performance, too. I was going to grab a bite to eat first. Do you want to come?"

Hannah looks at me. I nod. "Sure," she says, and I say okay. Carl squeezes my shoulder again before he finally lifts his hand. I can't resist the urge to brush off my shoulder, as though to wipe his fingerprints away.

❧

We go to The Pie Lady, a restaurant run by a woman who started selling pies to raise funds for her daughter, paralyzed by a robber's bullet to the head when she was only eighteen. Glory Hallelujah is her most famous pie. As I step into the restaurant, Carl touches the small of my back. I move away, then force myself to turn and smile at him. There's no one in the place except the Pie Lady herself, on a stool behind the counter. As Carl speaks to her, Hannah whispers, "Are you flirting with him?"

I shrug, studying the pies inside the glass case. Hannah raises her eyebrows.

Carl turns to us. "The lunch buffet is over, but she says she'll fix us something."

"What would you girls like?" she asks, showing us to a table. "I could do fish sandwiches or maybe fried chicken."

Hannah and I order the fish, Carl the chicken, and the Pie Lady wipes her hands on her apron and bustles off into the kitchen. I've interviewed her before. I don't think she remembers me, and yet I know so much about her. "So you really thought I was good," Carl says after she's gone.

"Of course," I say. "You were the best one onstage."

He smiles at me, then his expression grows serious. "How's your story going?" he says. "Have they found out anything?" He picks up his knife. I watch him turn it over and over in his hands.

"About Allison?" I say, just to see his face when he hears her name. He keeps his eyes on the knife in his hand and nods. "I haven't learned much. Just that her mother thought she was perfect."

"She was," Carl says. "In a way." He sets the knife down and sighs. "For her mother, she was perfect."

"And for you?"

He turns his eyes to me. "She wasn't perfect," he says. "But I loved her for a long time anyway." He holds my gaze, his eyes filling with tears. "I wish she could have seen me in the play today," he says, his voice trembling over the last words. For a moment I believe that his heart is breaking. Then I remember what a good actor he is. "I'm sorry," I say. "I'm doing my best to find out what happened." I reach out and squeeze his fingers and he smiles gratefully at me. "I'm glad you were there," he says.

For the rest of the meal I am quiet, watching him as he rips the chicken off the bone. He's laughing, telling Hannah a story about a set that fell over, eating the Glory Hallelujah pie he ordered. I shake my head when he offers me a bite of pears and crumb topping, holding his fork toward my mouth. Across from me is a set of untouched silverware, an empty chair. I imagine that Allison Avery sits in that chair, her dark hair falling forward across her shoulders. She looks right at me and smiles, that mischievous, mysterious smile. Hold my gaze, that smile says. I dare you.

As we get up to go, Hannah slips off to use the bathroom. Carl and I stand in the doorway. I pick up a matchbook and open and close it, reading some of the articles the Pie Lady has taped to the wall. I don't see mine. Carl's sucking on a mint and playing with his fat silver lighter, turning it over and over in his fingers, opening it to watch the flame catch and then closing it again. I'm rocking back and forth on my heels, staring at the ceiling, because every time I look at him I discover that he's looking at me. I glance his way again and find his eyes on my face. "Listen," Carl says. "I was wondering if you'd maybe like to go out some time, um, you know."

I start to tell him that I have a boyfriend. I can feel the color rising in my cheeks. He's watching me, and now his eyes are big and sad. The motherless boy. "Sure," I say. I'll gamble that he has something more to tell me. "Give me a call."

Hannah comes back and says, "Ready?"

"Bye now," the Pie Lady calls.

❧

Five hours later I'm crammed inside a crowd, so stoned I can't tell whether I'm swaying or standing still. David brought me to this club to hear some new band, because, he says, "there's a good buzz on them." Every relationship I've had has been a course in something. My high school boyfriend was an expert on the Bible. I fell asleep trying to read Deuteronomy. He also tried to teach me how to sing—from the *diaphragm,* from the *diaphragm*—but my voice always came croaking out my throat. When David and I first started dating he went through my CD collection and separated them into two shelves. "This is the cool shelf," he said. "These are . . . not so good."

"Not so good" meant Elton John, Lynyrd Skynryd, much of the country I'd collected as a college freshman. I resented his condescension then. But I just can't help it, I don't listen to those CDs anymore. I'm embarrassed to admit I ever owned them. He's right. They're not good. Everything changes when you know what you're looking for.

Right now I'm looking at David, wondering how long I can stare at him before he'll glance my way. He is standing perfectly still, his arms crossed over his chest, his neck craned to watch the band onstage. The club is a long and narrow room with the stage at the front and the bar and tables at the back. Around us, kids in tight T-shirts are dancing, moving by inches, shoulders against shoulders, hips against hips, a hand brushing the side of a breast. Their faces are the faces of addicts and zealots, glazed and ecstatic. A tall boy dances wildly beside me, his head down, his dark hair flinging sweat. He throws himself in my direction and I fall hard against David. I turn back toward the boy, my fist raised, and David grabs the back of my shirt. The boy flails off in the other direction. The crowd parts and then re-forms, absorbing him. David asks me if I'm all right and squeezes my shoulder. "Maybe we should sit," I say to him.

"I want to stand," he says.

"Well, I'm going to go sit."

"Okay." He keeps his eyes on the singer. "I'll come find you in a little while."

I stand there for a minute, looking at his profile, the clean strong lines of his jaw, his perfect nose. "I might go out with this guy Carl some time," I say. He can't hear me over the music so I lean in close and repeat it in his ear.

"You mean like a date?"

"Not exactly," I say. "He's a source. He might think it's a date."

"I don't know if I like that, Olivia," he says. He's staring at me now, frowning. "I don't like that at all."

"It wouldn't really be a date," I say. "I wouldn't kiss him or anything."

He makes an incredulous face. "What's going on with you? You've never needed to date your sources before."

"It's not a date," I say. "Really." He's still staring at me. "Don't worry," I say. I lean in and brush his lips with mine. He looks at me hard. I want him to pull me close, to tilt back my head with a kiss. "All right," he says. "You be careful." He turns his attention back to the band.

"I wish we had gone to a movie," I say.

"I wanted to hear this band," he says irritably. "You can see a movie anytime. I thought you were going to go sit."

I can't find a table so I just lean against the bar. The bartender comes over and I order a beer that I don't want, though it's cold and feels good going down my throat. This is what I love about being stoned—the pleasure of small physical sensations, liquid on your dry throat, air in your lungs, lips pressed against your lips. Someone leans in beside me to signal the bartender. His arm is warm against my shoulder. His thigh brushes my hip.

Evan told me that he was once in a "grope room" in a gay club in New York. The lights are out, and the room is filled with men, and they just touch each other, and sometimes one man will take his clothes off, and a crowd will gather around him. I can imagine the freedom of it—no faces, no expectations, just body to body. Skin to skin. Evan kissed one man and left. It was too much for him, he said. Too anonymous. Too animal.

When Evan told me this I recognized it as a fantasy I had as an adolescent, before I had ever been kissed, when my whole idea of sex came from novels I hid under my bed when my mother came in the room. Now it seems like a strange fantasy for a young girl to have. Because women are supposed to want intimacy. Women are supposed to want love. Anonymous sex is supposed to be the province of men.

"Excuse me," the man next to me says. "Did I bump you?"

"It's okay," I say.

"You like this band?"

"Never heard them before," I say. The man props himself on the bar like he's going to stay and talk awhile. All I want is for him to go away as soon as possible. Look at me, thinking about anonymous sex, and then as soon as any possibility arises I'm as nervous as a cat in a car. If Allison Avery were the one leaning against this bar, I imagine she would cock her head and smile as automatically as I turn my face away.

"I think they're pretty good," the man says.

I tilt my head in his direction and try a smile. I can feel how awkward it looks, my lips stretched over my teeth. He smiles back uncertainly, then turns toward the bartender, who hands him his change. The man lifts his beer in my direction. "See you," he says, and walks away. I put my hand to my mouth.

Over the bobbing heads of the crowd I can just see the faces of the band, three men and one woman frowning seriously into their microphones. The bass is so loud I can feel it in my breastbone like a second painful heartbeat, and the smoke from a hundred cigarettes settles into my hair, my clothes, my skin.

The line of people in front of me parts to let a jostling group through. "Let's get out of here," one of them says. She doesn't look more than sixteen, in tight black pants and a tank top, her blond hair grazing her bare shoulders. "I'm bored," she whines. "This place is lame." Her friends, all male, ignore her, so drunk they're weaving on their feet, laughing with wide-open mouths. "Y'all," she says, drawing the word out into two long syllables. One of the guys turns to her. He looks about my age, and he's sweating profusely, his face red and his eyes huge and wild. I recognize him. He's the one who slammed into me earlier. Now he scoops the girl up into a dancing position and whirls her around, his laughter loud and manic. She's insisting he let her go. Instead he hugs her tighter and tighter while her voice rises toward a scream. The other boys laugh, except for one. He stands, staring at the floor, rolling a bottle of beer between his palms. He lifts his head, and I see that he is Peter.

I look away before my eyes meet his. The girl's voice rises and rises, louder than the band. The guy spinning her seems lost in the motion, his forearms flexed with the effort of holding her tight. I go toward them. "Hey," I call out. "Hey, put her down." The guy stops spinning, glaring at me over the girl's shoulder. For a moment I could swear his eyes are whirling in his head, like pinwheels. "Let me go, Steve," the girl says. "Please."

"No problem," he says. He loosens his grip and the girl slides down his body until her feet touch the floor. "Who the fuck are you?" he says to me.

I ignore him, touching the girl on the arm. "Are you all right?" She glances at me, then looks away. "Fine," she mutters. "I'm fine."

"She's fine," Peter says, stepping forward. "Everybody's fine." The bottle falls from his hand to the floor. He stares at me, his lovely face flushed. "Are you following me?"

"You know this girl, Pete?" Steve says. He's looking at me as though he'd like to hit me.

"We've met," he says. "I don't *know* her." He looks at me again, that appraising gaze. "She's a friend of Allison's," he says suddenly, his eyes on my face. "But I don't like her." I raise my eyebrows and say nothing. He's beginning to make me angry.

At the mention of her name the rest of the group falls silent. I wonder if they're the "fast crowd" Carl told me about. Only the girl looks young enough to be a friend of Peter's.

"We were all friends of Allison's," one of the guys says quietly. He wears a concert T-shirt and army pants, and he looks stoned, his eyes small and red. He lifts a hand as though to touch Peter's back, but lets it fall away before it reaches him.

"That's right," Peter says under his breath. "That's right."

"Let's go, Pete," the girl says. She lays a hand on his arm, but he shakes it off with a quick, impatient movement. "Go ahead," he says. She hesitates, uncertain, and then she turns and disappears into the crowd. The guys follow her, the one who last spoke offering me his hand to shake before he goes. His palm is sweaty and hot.

Peter stays a moment, still looking at me. I meet his gaze. "You know what?" I say. "You're an asshole."

He doesn't laugh, or call me a bitch, or any of the things I expect. Instead he blanches, his eyes going wide, as though I've hurt his feelings. "I'm sorry," he whispers, his face a map of confusion. He stands there, weaving on his feet, and presses both hands to his forehead. Poor kid. He looks sick, and like the girl, he's much too young to be here. Then he drops his hands and takes a few steps toward me. In the half-light I can barely make out his features. "Olivia." He smiles grimly. "I've been reading your stories." He sways, and I put a hand on his arm to steady him.

"What are you doing here anyway?" I say. "How did you get in?"

He reaches into his back pocket, moving with the extreme precision of the very drunk. "You want to card me?" he says, handing me his wallet.

I pull out a driver's license. "Voilà!" he says. "I'm twenty-two." He leans over my shoulder, looking at the license. "He looks like me, don't you think?"

"You're drunk." I hand the wallet back.

"Allison got it for me," he says. "She got me this wallet, too. She said it was time I had a grown-up wallet."

"It's nice."

"Yes," he says. He shakes his head, as though to clear it. "I'm very drunk. It has me worried."

"Why?"

He sighs. All the bravado is gone, and he looks like a child. "You met my mother," he says. "I have to go home sometime."

"Better sober up first then," I say.

He laughs. "That could take a while."

"Where did your friends go?"

"My friends," he repeats. "My *friends*. They're around here somewhere." He takes the beer from my hand and drinks. "You're stoned, aren't you?"

"How did you know?"

"Your eyes," he says, gesturing with the beer. "All red and squinty." He grins. The discovery seems to please him. "Are reporters supposed to be potheads?"

"Are teenagers supposed to hang out in bars?" I take the bottle from his hand. "You should probably go home."

"You're right," he says, turning away from me. "I should find my friends."

"Peter," I say, stepping toward him. He turns, and I touch his arm, lightly, with just my fingertips. "Please be careful." I don't know where that came from, the urgency in my voice.

Peter raises his eyebrows in a question and then smiles. Then he lifts his hand and tousles my hair, as though he were the adult and I the scared and reckless kid.

He disappears into the crowd, and I go back to the bar and climb onto a stool, turned out so that I can watch the room, thinking about that hand in my hair. That boy has a car crash feeling about him. I wonder if he learned it from his sister, how to live your life like a rock and roll song. Everyone but me has a reckless youth to look back on, even my brother, Rob, telling tales of redemption for his church youth group. I've never slept around or danced on tables. I've never jerked my car over the railroad tracks just in time to miss the train. There is nothing I can claim to have survived. I'm just growing older with my same cautious self, like settling into marriage without ever feeling that first wild flush of love.

Next to me a big-breasted girl bounces up and down on her toes, trying to get the bartender's attention. Her breasts jostle against my arm. "Hey," she keeps saying, her voice pitched high. A man leans over and asks me for a light so I pull matches from my pocket and strike one. I love the way that flame appears, something from nothing.

Peter comes weaving back toward me. It seems hours since he left me. I look at my watch. It's been five minutes.

"I can't find my friends," he says. "I think I'm going to be sick."

"Hold on to me," I say. "I'll take you outside." He takes my hand, and I lead him through the crowd to the side door. Faces, confused and laughing, bob before me and disappear. I'm looking for David, but I can't see him. I tighten my grip on Peter's hand. We go through a heavy metal door into the alley, and Peter drops to his knees at the side of the building. I crouch beside him. His head is swaying back and forth. "Fuck, fuck," he mutters. "I'm going to die."

"You'll be okay. What did you drink?"

"Everything," he says.

"I know you feel awful," I say. "Just try to be calm." I put a hand on his back and rub it in small, slow circles. "You'll be okay," I say over and over, I don't know how many times, until the voice saying those words doesn't even seem to be mine. He vomits, more than once, and I try not to pay attention because it makes me nauseous. I'm focused on the circles my palm is making against his back, I'm watching the way the T-shirt wrinkles and smoothes as my hand goes round and round.

After a while I notice he's quiet. "Are you okay?" I ask. "Peter?"

"I don't know," he says. "I don't think I'm going to throw up any-more."

Pulling on his arm I manage to get him to a sitting position. He leans his head back against the wall. His throat is smooth, a perfect curve. I lift my hand and let my fingers brush it. He doesn't seem to notice.

"We need to find your friends," I say. I take my hand away, embarrassed by the impulse that led me to touch him.

"I can't go back in there," he says. "Please don't make me go back in there."

"Stay here," I say. "I'll be back." The metal door is locked from this side, so I go around the club and show my hand, smeared with a blurry stamp, to the skeptical bouncer. He looks from my hand to my face, my hand to my face, before finally stepping aside. Down the dark hall, and the music roars up and hits me in the chest again, the woman singer wailing while the bass drum plays a heavy thudding beat. I push my way between warm sweaty bodies, muttering "Excuse me." A girl's cigarette stings my arm, a fat man steps on my foot, a woman pushes back against me so that I almost fall. I keep pushing and pushing. All of the faces wear the same oblivious expression, shifted by degrees like pictures in a flipbook. I'm not even sure where I've been or where I'm going anymore, like I'm a child lost at the swimming pool without my glasses. Then hands are reaching out and grabbing me. It's David. He lifts me off my feet and then lowers me down so I'm leaning against his chest.

"Hey," he says. "I was just about to come find you."

"I've got to go somewhere," I say, breathing hard against his shirt. "I'll be back in half an hour."

"Where are you going?"

"To give someone a ride home."

"Someone you know?"

"This girl Hannah knows," I say. "Kathleen. She's wasted, so I think I should get her home as quickly as possible." The lie just slips out. I want to correct it, but there's no way to explain why I lied in the first place.

"That's nice of you," he says. "Do you want me to come with you?"

I shake my head.

"Are you okay to drive?"

"Yes, David."

"All right," he says. He pulls me to him and kisses me quickly. His lips are warm. "Be careful." I go back through the crowd with my hand pressed to my mouth. When I push that metal door open I find myself gasping in the air outside.

In the alley, Peter sits with his eyes closed, his legs sprawled out in front of him. I'm relieved that he opens his eyes when I say his name. I don't know how I would've gotten him to the car if he'd passed out. It's hard enough with him conscious. Somehow I get him standing and then I walk behind him with my hands on his waist, steering him toward the parking lot. My palms and his shirt are damp with sweat. "Where are we going?" he says.

"I'm taking you home," I say.

He weaves abruptly to the right, almost falling, almost knocking me down. "Careful," I say.

"I can't go home like this," he says.

"I don't know what else to do with you," I say.

"Allison used to drive me around first. We used to go get coffee." He stops walking, leaning back against me. "I should go get coffee."

I hesitate, bracing myself against his weight, and think of David waiting for me in the club. "Not this time," I say.

"Allison used to drive me around first," he says again.

"I'm not Allison," I say sharply, pushing him to start walking again.

"I know." His voice catches, and I am ashamed. "You'll be okay," I say. "Here's the car." I prop him up against the car and open the door. He gets in, and I go around to the other side. He has his head back at an impossible angle, his eyes closed. "Put on your seat belt," I say.

"I can't," he says. I feel a flash of irritation, and then I look at him and see that tears are slipping out from underneath his lids. I sit for a moment and watch. He turns his head from me and lifts his hand to his face, trying to sniff quietly.

I reach across him and pull the seat belt down past his chest, over his thighs, to snap into place with more force than was probably necessary, my hand brushing against his soft flat stomach, over his long thighs. The sensation lingers on my skin. I shake my hand to get rid of it. His house is less than ten minutes from here. Neither of us speaks on the way.

When we pull into his driveway, he opens his eyes and looks around as though he's never seen this house, this yard before.

"You're home," I say.

He turns toward me, his eyes wide, appealing. "Come in with me," he says. "I don't want to go in there alone."

"You know I can't do that," I say. I hand him a piece of gum. "Just go in, take some aspirin, and go straight to bed."

He opens the car door. "Listen," he says. He's not looking at me. "I'm sorry I was such a prick before."

"It's okay."

He takes a shaky breath. "Can I call you again? At home?"

"What for?" I say. I think of Carl, flipping his lighter, the way I smiled when I told him he could call me. It seems like days ago. I'm so tired, I could curl up and go to sleep right here, where Peter's parents would find me when they came out for their paper in the morning.

"I'm not hitting on you," he says. "Jesus. I guess you think I'm stupid. I probably wouldn't ask you if I weren't drunk. It's just, I miss . . . I feel like I can talk to you."

"Why?"

He shrugs. "You saw me cry."

"How do you know I won't put it in the paper?"

"Why would you say that?" He looks hurt.

"I'm sorry," I say. I take the gum wrapper and write my home number on it. When I hold it out to him, he takes it, and then touches my fingers. I'm looking down at his bent head, the brown curls, the curve of his slender neck. He turns my hand over in his like a palm reader and runs his fingertips over the lines in my skin. Then he raises his head, searching my face. I don't know what he sees there, but something makes him smile. He leans forward. Without thinking I close my eyes, as though I were back in high school and this were the end of a date, sitting in the car outside his parents' house. He kisses me, his lips slightly parted, tugging gently at mine. Then I remember where I am and who I'm with, and I open my eyes and pull away.

With a confident touch he tucks a strand of hair behind my ear, lets his hand run down the side of my neck to my shoulder. Like a well-stroked cat, I want to lean into that hand. Instead I frown at him. I can feel the color rising in my cheeks. "You should go in," I say, trying to make my voice sound firm and adult.

He nods, his expression serious. "Thanks," he says. He squeezes my shoulder gently before letting go. As he gets out of the car he says, "I'll call you," and then he stands in the driveway, his hand lifted, as I back out onto the street. I can see him in my rearview mirror, still watching me, until I turn the corner and he is gone.

When I pull into the club's parking lot, I can see David waiting, his tall figure spotlit beneath the streetlight, his face creased with worry. When he sees me, his mouth relaxes into a smile. He lifts a hand in greeting and starts toward the car.

As we drive back to Mud Island, David says, "I've been thinking about that dead girl. Allison, right?"

"What about her?"

"The tape she sent me," he says. "Do you think her family would be interested in us putting it out? We could even give a portion of the profits to some charity, victims' rights or something. What do you think? Should I talk to them?"

I don't say anything for a moment, asking myself why I want to tell him no. Finally I say, "If you want."

"I just think people would buy it. Pretty girl, tragic story. And that voice. It's a shame to let it go to waste," he says. "Can you give me their number?"

"Sure," I say. "Remind me." I picture him listening over and over to her tape, talking in a low, sympathetic voice to Cynthia Avery, shaking Peter's hand.

"It'd be a good story for you, don't you think?" he asks. "Human interest?"

"Sure," I say, although he should know by now that that's not the kind of story I write. Soon he'll be sitting in that white living room, staring at her perfect picture. Even David, coming under her spell.

10

Monday morning and Angela is late. I pace in front of Allison Avery's building, walking the path the dead girl must have taken from the front door to her car. I stand on the doorstep and look at the street. This is what she saw in the moments before her life turned upside down—trees, thick with summer leaves, grass in need of mowing, a patch of pink and yellow tulips, her car, waiting, only a few feet away. Or maybe she saw none of that, hurrying, her mind on the rest of the evening, searching in her purse for her keys.

A car pulls up and parks, and Angela steps out. She lifts a hand in greeting and bends to retrieve her bag. Then she walks quickly toward me, traveling that same path. She looks demure in a blue linen sundress over a T-shirt, her hair pinned up behind her head. "Sorry I'm late," she says. "Thank you so much for coming." She touches my arm and leads the way inside.

The entryway to the girl's apartment is a jumble of shoes—sandals, running shoes, cowboy boots, elegant black high heels, tall silver boots designed to hug a slender calf. "She likes shoes," Angela says. "She spends half her paycheck on them."

I notice she's using the present tense. She stands staring down at the profusion of sandals, boots, and sneakers. Maybe she imagines that Allison is in her room, taking too long to get ready for a night out, that she'll call out any minute, asking her what shoes she should wear. Or maybe she's picking out the pairs she wants to keep.

"Come on," she says after a minute. She reaches out toward me, and I take her hand and squeeze before letting it go.

"You can do it," I say, and she moves on down the hall, turning on lights. In the living room, cassette tapes and CD cases litter the floor near the stereo. Videotapes are piled on the television. I pick one up. It's labeled: Allison 5, May 9, 1992. The rest of the tapes are labeled, too: Allison 1, Allison 2, up to 11. Angela has wandered into the kitchen. I put the tape in my bag, meaning to ask her about it later. Stacks of magazines cover the coffee table. A half-full coffee cup sits on one stack, with the pink lipstick print of Allison's lower lip visible at the rim. I notice a bottle of moisturizer smashed beneath the table, shards of glass glinting in the yellow stain on the floor. I check the answering machine. The tape is missing. I wonder if the police have taken it.

In the kitchen, pots and Tupperware spill out of cabinets. There's a pile of laundry on the table, more magazines spread across the long counter. Angela is staring into the sink.

I wander over to the refrigerator and open the door. A gallon of skim milk, not even opened. A bottle of diet Coke, a few eggs, a carton of sugar-free strawberry yogurt, half an apple, browning. Not much food for someone who had just gone to the grocery store. Angela says my name. I turn my head; she's staring right at me, a little frown creasing her forehead. I shut the door and go to stand beside her. She says, "There's still food in here," and points at the sink. She looks at me with tears in her eyes. "SpaghettiOs. She never could cook."

Some last meal, I think. I say, "I wondered why there weren't more groceries."

"Did you look in the freezer?" Angela says. "It's probably full of frozen stuff. I used to cook for her sometimes. I should have done that more often."

"Why aren't you two roommates?" I ask. I'm careful to use the present tense, like Angela, although in my own voice I hear the falseness of it, the lie.

"She's too messy," she says with a wave of her hand. "Just look at this room." She turns on the water and uses her hand to scoop the noodles into the garbage disposal. When she switches it on, the dishes on the counter rattle and shake.

I open the freezer. The walls are packed thick with ice. There's an open box of Popsicles, something wrapped in tin foil, a bag of frozen french fries. Nothing else but empty ice cube trays. "I don't think she went to the grocery store," I say.

Angela turns and stares into the freezer. "Where the hell was she then?"

"I don't know. With a guy?"

Angela lowers her head, shoulders tensed, and says nothing. I spot something tucked into a corner of the freezer, behind the ice cube trays, and reach in to find a fat bag of dope. I show it to Angela. "You might want to take this out of here before her mother sees it," I say.

She takes it and turns it over in her hands. "Do you want to smoke some?" she says. "It's good stuff."

It's eight o'clock in the morning, and I have to be at work at ten. "All right," I say.

"There might be rolling papers in that drawer," she says, indicating where with a nod of her head.

I open it and start rummaging through expired coupons, rubber bands, scissors, and tools to find the papers. When I reach for the papers I prick my finger on something. I snatch my hand back, then reach in carefully again. It's a hypodermic needle.

I find a cap for the needle in the drawer and put it on. Angela is standing with her back to me, looking at the photos on the refrigerator. I grab the papers and call her name. When she turns she sees me holding the needle in the air, like my mother used to hold up a lighter when she found one in my brother's drawer.

"What's this?" I ask.

She comes over and takes it from me. "It's a hypodermic needle," she says, handing it back.

"Why would Allison have this?" I set it on the counter and roll it back and forth with one finger.

"I don't know. Maybe she brought it home from work. Maybe her mother left it here." She plucks the papers from my hand. Sitting on a stool at the kitchen counter she begins to roll an expert joint.

"Do you bring needles home?" I ask.

She shakes her head, her eyes fixed on the counter, where her fingers delicately slide each leaf into the crease she's made in the paper.

"Why would Allison do that? Was she diabetic?" I swallow. "She didn't have AIDS."

Angela shoots me a look. "Of course not."

"I pricked my finger on it," I say, sitting on the other stool.

"Even if she had it, you couldn't get it from that. The virus would be dead by now," Angela says. She finishes the joint and pulls matches from her pocket. "I don't know why she had that. I'm sure it's nothing." She lights the joint and takes a drag, then offers it to me.

"Angela," I say, taking the joint from her hand, "was Allison into anything more than dope?"

"Like what? Heroin?" She shakes her head, frowning. "We draw the line at dope. Never even shroomed or dropped acid. I had a friend who dropped acid in college. She said she thought the walls were bleeding. Doesn't sound like any fun to me." She watches me take a drag, a smile playing over her lips. "Allison's a pack rat," she says. "You should see the shit she kept. Clothes she hasn't worn since tenth grade. You saw all those shoes in the hall. I don't know what the needle was for, but I know it wasn't heroin." She leans in close. "I knew everything about her," she says. "You can bet I would've known that."

I hand her the joint. She believes what she's saying, but I might tell someone I knew everything about Hannah, and I didn't know she had ever done cocaine. "Can I ask you something?" I say. "Why did you want me to come with you?"

"I like you, Olivia," she says. She inhales and lets it out slow. "You want to know what she was like."

"Yes," I say. *Was,* she said, the truth slipping through her unwillingness to believe it. "What was she like?"

"She was fun. She was . . . generous. She . . ." She gestures helplessly with the joint, trailing smoke.

"Yes," I say. "But what was she *like?*"

"We were closer than sisters," she says, her eyes watery and bright. "I loved her."

Later I sit on the bed, the needle in my pocket, and watch as Angela rummages through the dead girl's bureau. "I've never seen this before," she says, holding out a pink sweater.

"Can I see that?" I ask.

Angela hands it to me and I check the tag. It's angora, a petite small. Joan Bracken's sweater. "I think this belongs to Joan Bracken," I say.

"Who?"

"The skinny woman down the hall."

"That figures," Angela says. "It's ugly as shit."

Angela says Allison just borrowed the sweater, and keeps saying it, until I've told her three or four times that Joan Bracken said it was stolen. Then she says maybe Allison did it on impulse, maybe she did it to fuck with that anorexic bitch, maybe she didn't do it at all and Joan Bracken is lying. "At any rate," she says, "it doesn't matter now." She takes the sweater from me and stuffs it back in the drawer, then slams the drawer shut and stalks out of the room.

I sit for a few minutes, bouncing on what feels like a brand-new mattress. This apartment has central air, like David's, and I think how nice it would be to sleep on a firm new mattress and wake up cool every morning, instead of glued to the sheets by the sweltering heat. Allison's bedroom is even messier than mine, clothes draped everywhere, an ashtray trailing ash onto the dresser. The trash can beside the bed nearly bursts with her garbage. I lean forward to peer into it. Tissues. A broken eyeshadow, powdering everything around it a glittery bronze. I think of Evan and his front-page Satanist magazine, and gingerly lift away the tissues that form the top layer of trash.

Below I see balled-up notes, an empty toilet paper roll, a box the right size for jewelry. I plunge my hand into the trash, turning over more papers, more soft, damp tissues, the crinkly foil wrapper of a chocolate bar, until my hand meets something sticky and slick. I jump back as though stung. It's a used condom.

In the bathroom I wash my hands five or six times. I don't want to think about what I just touched, the queasy intimacy of it. I wonder if that happens to Evan in his rummaging through people's garbage, if he puts his hands on used tampons, dirty diapers, wet pieces of dental floss that cling to his fingers like cobwebs, and if, when he does, he shrugs it off as part of the job and goes on digging.

I dry my hands on one of Allison's towels. Reaching for the doorknob, I hesitate. I go back and wash my hands again, my fingers turning a faint red from the hot water, and then I wipe them on my shirt. I'm thinking about my options. I could confront Angela with this evidence and ask her again who Allison's lover was. I could take it to the police. Surely they'd want to analyze it, compare whatever they found to the result of the rape kit. To do that, though, I'd have to touch it again. I look at myself in the mirror. I look harried and pale. My mouth is dry from smoking. I put two fingers to the pulse in my neck and feel how quickly my heart is beating.

I go to the door of the bedroom and listen for Angela. I can hear her moving around in the living room, picking things up and setting them down, talking to herself in a low, bewildered murmur. Satisfied that she's not about to catch me rifling the room, I start with the desk by the window.

A "to do" list, dated the day of her death. *Get groceries* is at the top of it, and then a list of other things she'll never do: *Mail demos. Call Grandma. Return videos.* Allison had that curlicue handwriting girls perfect in elementary school. My handwriting used to look like that too, before I grew up.

Underneath the list is a letter from someone at a record company, saying he found her demo tape "promising" and that he would like to hear more. David might have written her a similar letter; his address could be somewhere in her desk, one more possibility for a future of lights and smoke and crowds. In the moments before she died, I wonder if she thought about all these things she would leave unaccomplished, or if the pain and terror drove everything else from her mind.

The top right drawer is a jumble of letters and postcards, birthday cards from Allison's mother—To a Special Daughter. I pick up a postcard of Memphis at night, lights shimmering in the dark river below. I turn it over "Allison," it says, in careful childish print, "I hate the Boy Scouts. Today they made me eat powdered eggs. I miss you. It makes my stomach hurt. Your brother, Peter."

I set that on the desk and keep looking.

A letter from Carl, dated last October. "You are the most precious person to me. Why are you building a wall between us? You say I seem like a completely different person, but you go out of your way to treat me like I'm not the Carl you've always known. Don't shut me out. If you love me like a friend, like you said, then I can handle that. As long as you love me. Please, Allison."

A piece of paper folded into a tiny rectangle with a pull tab, the way we used to fold notes in high school. "PRIVATE!!!," it says. "DO NOT READ." I open it. It's from Angela. "A, I don't know what to do about Bryant. Help. Tell me what to do. A."

Two sentences on the back of a receipt. "Where are you? I'm out looking for you. R."

I look at these letters and notes, spread out across the desk. *I miss you. Tell me what to do. Where are you? Love me. Please.* I imagine them, still writing these letters, putting them in a drawer because there's no one to read them now. All these people adrift without her, like planets that once circled a star.

❖

I take a quick glance in the closet, running my hand down the long row of brightly colored shirts and dresses, silk and cotton and slick polyester. I hold one of her dresses up to myself. The skirt wouldn't even reach halfway down my thighs. The shiny black material gives off a faint odor of smoke and sweat. Strange that I can still smell her, days after she has gone.

Hanging up the dress, I move on to the bureau. I'm hurrying now, thinking Angela's going to wonder what I've been doing in here so long. I open the drawer where Angela found the sweater and run my hands over the cotton and wool and linen jumbled inside. The angora is soft beneath my hand. I shove that drawer closed and open the one above it. Allison Avery was one of those girls who wear matching bra and panty sets. The drawer is a mess of lacy pink and purple and red things. I pick up a black satin bra and put my fist in one of the cups. Then I realize what I'm doing and drop it back in the drawer. I wonder what color set she was wearing the night she died, if the panties the killer kept look like any of these.

What am I going to do with all this, the matching underwear, the letters, the condom, the detritus of this girl's life. I sit on the bed, imagining the girl's mother discovering the bag of dope in the refrigerator, the condom in the trash, confronted with this fact of life none of us can get used to, that everyone we know has a world we can't enter.

I run my hand across the smooth wood of her headboard. Some instinct makes me rise up on my knees to peer down into the space between the headboard and the wall. Sure enough, there's something wedged there. By forcing my arm down until it feels like my shoulder is going to wrench out of the socket, I'm able to reach it, sliding it up the wall until I can hold it in both my hands.

It's a rectangular box, about six inches long, and the lid is painted with a silvery-blue fish. I open it.

A large metal spoon. Another needle. A tiny foil package, which, unwrapped, reveals a white pellet, about the size of an aspirin.

I close the foil back around the pellet. Then I close the lid and stand for a moment weighing the box in my hand.

Angela calls my name. "Coming," I shout back. I wedge the box back into that space and leave it there. When I find Angela in the kitchen, she hands me another joint and leans forward to light it for me.

We are sitting on the floor in the living room, near the stereo. Being stoned makes everything around me look sharp and bright, and I feel I'm coming close to understanding something. Maybe the girl's death had nothing to do with Carl or the condom in that trash can and everything to do with that box and the needle inside my pocket. Maybe she did know the people who killed her. Maybe they sold her drugs. I touch the needle through the fabric of my pants. Right here in my pocket I could have the explanation for everything.

"Listen," Angela says. She pops a tape in the cassette player and hits play. There is a click and a whirring sound, and then a female voice says, "April 24, 1997." Her voice is husky, lightly flavored with a southern accent. I hear an intake of breath, and then she begins to sing, a John Prine song called "The Speed of the Sound of Loneliness." I try to imagine what Angela is feeling right now, as the disembodied voice fills the room. A cough cuts short the last note. "Ah shit," the voice says. There is a loud click, and then the whirring again. Angela removes the tape and holds it in her hand. She strokes the tape with one finger as though the plastic were the dead girl's skin. Then she folds in on herself. Her back shakes with sobs. She barely makes a sound, rapid breathing, a gasp, an almost inaudible moan.

There is not a foot between us but I don't reach to touch her. One thing I know is how to hold myself apart. I know how to absorb another's life until it's as familiar as my own and when the story is over I know how to put that life away with my clip file. What I don't know is how to feel what she feels, the hot unbearable rush of it.

I watch, as always. Then I reach out and pull her to me. With my arms around her I rock us back and forth. Her tears are hot and wet against my neck. "Allison," she says. "Allison."

On the way to work I stop for coffee and a doughnut. I'm taking deep breaths, blowing out hard as though I could expel the dope from my system with the air from my lungs. I'll just spend the morning at my desk until the high wears off.

Walking through the newsroom, I keep telling myself no one knows, no one is staring at me. When I checked my eyes in the rearview mirror they were big as ever and clear of any red. "Good morning," Evan says when I sit at my desk.

"Good morning," I say brightly. "How are you?"

"Tired," he says, and yawns to demonstrate. "I was here late last night finishing up my story."

"Which story?" I pick up today's paper and scan the front page.

"That story," he says, pointing. "Haven't you seen the paper yet?" I read the headline: SUSPECT INVOLVED IN CULT ACTIVITIES, NEIGHBORS SAY. Evan says, "The Satanist kid who killed that ten-year-old. *Allegedly* killed."

I skim the story. A plastic skull in his locker. The witchcraft magazine Evan found in his trash. An upside-down cross a teacher thinks she remembers him wearing on a chain around his neck. "Well," I say. "I guess he did it."

"Are you being sarcastic?" Evan taps his pen on my hand.

"No," I say. "He probably did do it."

"These things add up," he says. "They might seem small, by themselves. But two and two equals four, you know. It always does."

"You don't have to tell me," I say. "I believe it."

After Evan turns back to his computer I pull the needle from my pocket and study it, holding it out of sight beneath my desk. I grab a notebook and write: *Heroin. Where did she get it? Who did she do it with?* I don't imagine she had a solitary habit. Someone had to introduce her to the drug. Someone had to sell it to her. I think of Carl, telling me Allison Avery lived dangerously. There are only so many ways to live dangerously if you're a middle-class girl. I write them down: *1. Sex. 2. Alcohol. 3. Drugs.* "Whatcha got there?" I hear Evan say.

I turn and see him leaning over his desk, peering under mine. "Doing a story on me now?"

He winks. "Better be careful what you put in your trash."

"I've got nothing to hide," I say, curling the needle inside my palm. I don't want him to see it. It's my story, my secret for now.

He sinks back down in his chair. "Seriously, what's in your hand?"

"Nothing," I say. I drop the needle on the floor and hold up my hand, "See?"

He studies my face. His eyes are a warm brown, and he has the long eyelashes mascara is supposed to give you. "What's wrong?" he asks me.

"Nothing." I'm fighting an urge to put two fingers to the pulse in my neck, my heart beating double-time with marijuana and caffeine. "What makes you think something's wrong?"

"I know you, Olivia," he says. "You're not yourself. Is it this story? Is it getting to you?"

I meet his gaze, looking right into those pretty eyes. For a moment I know how good it would feel to curl up inside his arms and let him rock me until I fell asleep, nowhere safer than in his embrace. I look away. "Evan, I'm fine," I say. "Nothing gets to me. I'm one tough bitch, remember?" As I say it, I believe it. A feeling passes through me, almost like elation. I say, "I can handle anything," and grin at him until he smiles back, relieved.

❧

I spend the rest of the morning in the paper's library, looking at clippings on heroin use in the city. The library is shelf upon shelf of boxes filled with envelopes filled with cut-out articles. My fingertips turn black as I go through them. The clippings are flimsy between my fingers, their brittle paper easily torn. I learn that heroin is now so pure it can be snorted or smoked, that the emerging junkie demographic is young, twenty-something hipsters, often from middle- or upper-class backgrounds, that heroin-related arrests in the city are on the rise. I get this last piece of information from an article on crime statistics with my byline above it. I sit staring at the letters spelling out my name. I have no recollection of writing this, no memory of making the phone call to Lieutenant Nash, who's quoted here. I look up at all the shelves of boxes and think how many other stories I must have forgotten, how many facts and opinions have passed through me and out into the world, gone now, as if I had never known them at all.

I put the clipping away and lift another one from its envelope. It's a story by Peggy, about three years old, on drug use among middle-class kids. I skim it. Most of the kids Peggy quoted were using pot and cocaine. There are a few quotes from a junkie named Paula, who says she grew up in a normal family, making A's in math and science, before she found heroin. "Even though it's screwed up my life," she says, "nothing is better than getting high. It's the best feeling in the world."

Carefully I fold the clipping along its creases and put it back in the envelope. I'm having visions of dark houses with bad green carpeting, Allison Avery passed out on the floor. In Peggy's article, Paula says she knows about thirty users. There can't be too many sources for heroin in this city. Maybe Peggy can put me in touch with Paula, with someone who can tell me about what Allison Avery was putting in her veins.

Back in the newsroom, I see Peggy walking in my direction, reading something and frowning. I stop her and ask if I can talk to her about an old story.

She leans in toward me, still frowning. "You've got newsprint all over your face. Hold still." She takes a tissue out of her pocket and wipes the side of my nose. "Hazard of the job," she says, and laughs. Then she turns back to the papers in her hand and starts walking.

"Peggy," I say to her back. "Can I talk to you about this? It's important."

"Catch me later, kid," she says. "I've got a meeting."

When I get back to my desk, I remember the needle and bend down to retrieve it. It's not there. I straighten up so fast I crack my head on the desk, and I'm sitting there cursing, pressing my hand to the bump forming on my head when I notice the needle off to the side, next to my trash can. I must have kicked it over there when I got out of my chair. I take a quick glance around. Evan is gone. Everyone else is on the phone or frowning at their computer screens, fingers flying over the keyboards. I grab the needle and drop it inside my bag.

I call my house to check my messages, wondering if Carl has called, if Peter has called. My head aches. I count four rings and then a woman answers. "Hannah?" I say, though it doesn't sound like her voice. The person hangs up, so I dial again.

"Hello?" the same woman says. Hannah sometimes brings a co-worker home for lunch. I rack my brain for the woman's name.

"Hi, is this Alice?"

"Who?"

"Sorry," I say, thinking that's the wrong name. "Is Hannah there?"

"Who?" she says.

"I must have the wrong number."

"Okay," she says.

I dial again.

"Hello?" It's the same voice.

"Is this 555-5999?"

"Uh . . . hold on," she says. There's a silence. "I don't know. The number's not on the phone. Who are you looking for?"

"Hannah."

"She's not here, but you can come over if you want," the woman says.

"Who is this?" I ask.

"Who is *this*?" she says.

"This is Hannah's roommate."

"Oh shit," the woman says, and drops the phone. I hear her shout something, then there's a crash, followed by a click and a dial tone.

I pick up the phone to call the police, then hang it up again. It occurs to me that our neighbor Denise could be in our side of the house. Or she might have heard something. So I dial her number instead.

"What are you talking about?" she says. "You know I don't have a key. No way was I in your side of the house."

"Have you noticed anything?"

"Everything seems peaceful," she says. "Maybe you dialed the wrong number."

"I know my own number."

"Well maybe the wires got crossed," she says. "These things do happen."

I ask her to call me if she hears anything, and then I hang up. If I call the police and it was just a wrong number I'm going to feel like an idiot, like when I make a doctor's appointment and complain of symptoms and the doctor says, "Can't find anything wrong with you." On the other hand I should know my own number. I dial it again. The answering machine picks up, and I listen to Hannah's voice calmly saying that we're not home. "Hello?" I say after the beep. "If anyone's there you better leave because I'm calling the police. Do you hear me? I'm hanging up and calling the police right now."

I hang up, and stare at the phone. Then I call Hannah.

"It probably *was* Denise, making long-distance calls on our phone or something," Hannah says. "That woman's crazy."

"That makes sense," I say.

"Think about it. Why would a burglar answer the phone? And why would Denise get so snippy about it if it wasn't her? And, if it wasn't her, wouldn't she have heard people breaking in? We can hear her having sex and someone breaking our door down would surely be louder than that. You know what else? She lied—she does have a copy of our key. We traded keys a long time ago in case we ever locked ourselves out."

"I forgot about that," I say.

"Let's check our phone bill for calls to Cookeville."

"Why Cookeville?"

"That's where she's from."

"Who?"

"Denise," Hannah says. "What's the matter with you?"

"I'm a little jumpy," I say. "So you don't think I should call the police?"

"No," Hannah says. "I'm sure it's fine."

I don't want to tell her that I'm scared, that I want to call the police. I don't want to be a child imagining a bogeyman in the closet, screaming at nothing.

Peggy appears at my desk and motions for me to hang up the phone. When I do, she says, "An abandoned building's collapsed downtown. Get on it, kid."

I'm out the door in less than five minutes.

I spend the afternoon studying rubble. The story runs front page, with color art of the building, caved in like something in a war zone. When I get home at six-thirty, all the lights are on, but Hannah's car is not parked anywhere on the street. I sit in the car a few minutes, staring at the front door. It looks untouched. Maybe Denise left the lights on. Just to be sure, I walk around to the back. The storm door is hanging open, but that's nothing unusual—it's broken. I'm feeling silly for even worrying about this now, but when I get closer I can see that the main door is cracked open, and the light picks up broken glass all over the kitchen floor. "Fuck me," I say.

I bang the door open and jump to the side of it like someone in a cop show. I fumble in my bag for something heavy, cursing myself for not thinking of this before I opened the door. I grab and drop a roll of Tums, a pen, and my notebook before I find my makeup bag, heavy with lipstick and bottles of moisturizer. With this in my hand, I swing around the door, crouching low.

Glass is all over the floor. The window on the kitchen door has been shattered and the lock is smashed. I step on a cockroach. It crunches horribly and I gasp, then clamp my hand over my mouth. Giant moths are flitting insanely around the kitchen light. It looks like a camping trip in here. I drop the bag on the table and grab an empty champagne bottle. The weight of it feels good in my hand.

I ease down the hall toward the living room, sliding my back along the wall. There is no sound but the swishing of my shirt against the wall, the whisper of my breathing. I clutch the bottle with both hands. Soon I can see the television. The VCR is still on top of it. I step into the room, letting the bottle dangle at my side. I take a quick inventory—stereo, CDs, answering machine, telephone, Hannah's computer. The living room looks undisturbed.

I tiptoe back down the hall to the bathroom, even while I'm thinking, *No, you idiot, don't go in there,* and with the bottle raised in my hand I whip back the shower curtain. Nothing. In the bedrooms, I peer under the beds, check the closets, my heart pounding inside my ears. Nobody.

Then I sit on Hannah's bed and stare at the wall, rolling the champagne bottle between my hands. The adrenaline is fading, and I'm stunned by my own stupidity. There could have been someone in here with a gun. There could have been a man waiting in the living room to rape me and beat me, turn me into a police photograph Sergeant Morris would hand to Bishop in the morning.

The front door slams shut, and I jump up. I consider hiding in the closet, and then I think that it could be Hannah. But I can't call out, because if it isn't her, I don't want to give away where I am, so I stand out of sight just inside her door, with the champagne bottle raised, and when she walks in the room, she sees me and screams.

I drop the bottle on the floor. "It's just me," I say.

"What the hell," Hannah says, breathing hard. "You gave me a heart attack."

"Someone broke in here. Go look in the kitchen."

I listen to her footsteps go down the hall, stop, and then come back. "What a mess," she says. "Did you call the police yet?"

While we wait for the police, I tell Hannah what I did when I got home. I can't be still; I pace around the room while Hannah sits on the couch. Caught up in my own story I'm starting to believe I could have handled it. If I'd found people here I would have knocked them out with the bottle, stood over them until the police arrived. "I felt like a Charlie's Angel," I say. "I didn't stop to think. I was hardly even scared."

"But why did you take out your makeup bag?" Hannah says. "Wouldn't it have made more sense to hit them with your whole bag?"

I stare at her. "Jesus Christ, Hannah," I say. "I'm a fucking idiot, okay?"

"I just wondered," she says.

"Next time I'll remember that." I pretend to take notes. "Hit them with your whole bag."

"Fuck you," she says.

"No, fuck *you*," I say. Then to my embarrassment I burst into tears.

"My hero," she says, but nicely.

"Shut up," I say. "Don't you ever shut up?"

She stands up and puts her arms around me. "You were very brave," she says. "I mean it."

At first we thought nothing was missing. They went through my jewelry box and tossed things aside—real pearl earrings, savings bonds, my passport—but took none of them. Then we realized they'd taken a gold necklace of mine, some earrings of Hannah's, a case full of my mixed tapes and an old Walkman, two pairs of cheap sunglasses and some loose change that was on Hannah's dresser. They also took a bag of shake from Hannah's room. We didn't tell the cops about that. "Probably high school kids or junkies," one of the cops said. "Looking for quick cash, stuff they could stick in their pockets. It was probably an impulse break-in, too stupid or too high to plan it better. You said they answered your phone?"

"You got lucky," the other one said, looking around at our TV, our VCR. "You got the stupidest burglars in the state of Tennessee."

After the cops left I called David, and he came right over. Now he's fast asleep on his side, facing away from me. With one finger I write my name on his back. I've been awake half the night, thinking about what was on those mixed tapes, especially a particular one I made in college. I don't think I can re-create it. I know it was the greatest mixed tape I've ever made, but even so I can remember only half of the songs. To make the tape I borrowed some CDs from my roommates, and the sad fact is I don't even like those people anymore.

I get out of bed and go through my bag looking for the needle I found at Allison's. Sitting on the edge of the bed, holding the needle in one hand, I watch David sleep. I take the cap off and press the point of it with one finger, gently, not enough to break the skin. David rolls over toward me, murmuring something, and in that moment I accidentally press too hard. A drop of blood bubbles out. I rub it round and round between my finger and my thumb. I don't know what any of this means.

I'm going to find out.

11

In the morning David leaves before I'm fully awake, heading home to shower and let out the dog. He says in passing that he's going to call Allison's parents today, and I tell him not to say he knows me.

"Why not?" he asks, pausing at my bedroom door.

"I'm a reporter," I say. "They don't like me."

He nods. "I'll just say she sent me a tape." Then he's gone, a man with a mission.

Hannah calls our landlord to tell him he'll have to fix the back door, and I go into the kitchen to see what's left of the monster bugs. I spot some moths high up on the wall, near the ceiling, and my impulse is just to let them be, but I make myself climb up on the counter to catch them in my hands, one by one, so I can let them go outside. If I think too hard about their little wings beating against my palms it makes me shudder but as long as I keep my mind on the job I'm fine. I'm listening to the murmur of Hannah's voice in the other room, the gentle rhythm of the southern accent I almost never notice anymore. She laughs. I've known her so long, I could recognize her just by that sound.

Hannah comes in and watches me, leaning against the opposite counter. I'm trying to catch the last moth in my palm, it keeps fluttering away, and having an audience is making the muscles in my back tense up.

"Oooh, almost," Hannah says as I miss the moth again.

"What do you want, Hannah?" I say.

"Rude," she says, and crosses her arms across her chest.

"Sorry," I say. "This is frustrating." I get a wing between my thumb and forefinger. The moth flaps furiously, in a panic, and I'm trying as best I can to cup it gently in my hand without pulling its wing off.

"You got it," she says. I hold the moth between my hands and step backward, carefully, off the counter and onto a chair. Hannah opens the door for me and I open my hands to let the moth go. It just sits in my palm. "Go on," I say, shaking my hand out the door. It holds on. Finally I toss up my hand like I'm serving a tennis ball and the moth flies away.

"It liked you," Hannah says, and laughs.

I brush my hands together. "I wasn't so crazy about it." With the glass off the floor and the bugs gone, the kitchen almost looks normal. Hannah follows me out and down the hall into my bedroom. She sits in my desk chair and watches while I get dressed. She says, "What are you doing tonight?"

"I'll probably have a drink with the guys after work," I say, pulling my shirt over my head.

"Want to do something after that? I feel like I've hardly seen you lately."

"Sure," I say. "I'll call you."

She smiles at me and stands up. "Good," she says. At the door she pauses, holding on to the door frame. "Listen, you really were brave yesterday. I was impressed."

I pull a pair of pants off a hanger. "Thanks," I say, but she's already gone.

In the newsroom I'm a celebrity, everyone lingering at my desk to hear the story. After an hour, I'm making it funny, acting out the way I jumped to the side of the door, pretending that I brought my fingers up and together like a gun before I rotated into the room.

Peggy laughs and laughs, and then stops and looks serious. "Don't do that again," she says. "Next time call the police."

"Next time call me. I'll come right over," Bishop says. "I'll rescue you."

"That's okay. I'd rather be a Charlie's Angel than a damsel in distress," I say. "Next time I'll just get a real gun."

"You're not serious," Peggy says.

"Of course not," I say, though I can imagine how that would feel, the cold weight of a gun in your hand. "Anyway, I'm hoping there won't be a next time."

"Amen to that," Bishop says. He puts his hand on my shoulder and squeezes it before he ambles away.

"I'm glad you're okay," Peggy says. "Be more careful next time, okay, kid?" She grins. "I mean, there won't be a next time. Just be more careful."

As she turns to go, I remember the story I wanted to ask her about. "Wait, Peggy," I say. "I want to talk to you about a story you did on drug use."

She laughs. "You'll have to be more specific."

"It was about three years ago. You talked to a junkie named Paula."

She frowns, and when she speaks her voice is chilly. "What about it?"

"I was wondering if you could put me in touch with Paula, or if you know of any other sources. I'm looking for some background on heroin use in the city." The whole time I'm talking, Peggy's shaking her head.

"That was a while ago," she says. "I don't think I can help you. That culture, it changes by the minute."

"Anything you could tell me would be more than I've got now," I say. "It's important."

She sighs and leans forward against my desk. "There's a bar called the Lizard Lounge. That's where Paula made her connections."

That's where Allison Avery was supposed to be the night she died.

I write *Lizard Lounge* in my notebook. "I know the place," I say. "Thanks a lot."

She looks at me and nods slowly, not saying anything, a faint hint of a frown between her eyes. After she goes back to her desk, I sit and try to make notes. *AA was a junkie? Why wouldn't Angela know?* I chew on my pen for a minute, then write: *Why doesn't P want to talk about it?* The whole time I just keep thinking, *Next time, next time, next time.* I look at the page and see I've written that down. *Next time.* I drop my hands hard on the desk and push myself up. My chair rolls back, clattering into Evan's desk. The impact sends a stack of papers sliding. I stand perfectly still, realizing that everyone in the newsroom has turned to look at me. For a moment, I am at the center of a waiting silence, the eyes of all these curious people on me, watching, judging. Then I hear voices and the clicking of keyboards and I let out my breath.

Peggy is beside me. "Are you okay?" she says, her voice low with motherly concern.

I look around. Evan immediately begins gathering his papers. Bishop catches my eye and looks away.

"I'm fine," I say. "Why?"

"No reason," Peggy says.

"I'm fine," I say again, laughing a little. "I'm just going to the bathroom. I didn't mean to be so loud."

"Okay," she says, nodding at me. "Okay."

In the bathroom I lean in close to the mirror and look myself in the eye. I hold my gaze steady. Once again, I have newsprint on my face. I wet a paper towel and wipe it off.

Outside it's raining, beating faster and harder against the roof. I'm glad I'm in here, where it's cool and dry and nothing can touch me.

At lunchtime I head home for an hour, telling Evan that I just want to make sure no one's having a party in my living room. I say it like

I'm joking and he smiles. When I get home, I sit in the car for a few minutes, wishing I had one of David's cigarettes. I've been smoking too much lately. It's not raining anymore, and the street is quiet, the noon sun beating down on silent houses, toys abandoned in patches of unmowed grass.

I get out of the car and walk up to the house carefully, like it's an animal I don't want to startle. The front door is shut. I walk around to the back to see if the house looks secure. The screen door hangs open a little. I push it closed. It won't stay so I find a rock to prop against it. I walk back around to the front door, grab the doorknob and turn. It's locked. I throw my shoulder against the door. It doesn't move.

I step off the porch and cup my hands around my face to peer in the living room window. Nothing moves inside except the dust that floats in the sunlight. I pretend that I don't know the people who live here, moving my gaze over their ratty furniture, their piles of clothes and books and magazines, the CDs scattered across the floor. These people are young and messy and careless, the whole living room like the jumbled inside of somebody's junk drawer.

A car passes by, slowly, and I turn. How strange I must look to the neighbors, standing in the bushes with my heels sinking into the mud, a voyeur outside my own home.

Inside, I glance in all the rooms, holding my bag tight against my side. No one. In my own room, I peer into the corners of my closet. Nothing but a row of work clothes, suit jackets and blouses in muted colors. At the back I find a skimpy black cocktail dress I don't even remember buying. I've never worn it, the price tag still attached.

Under the bed there's a jumble of newspaper and, back by the wall, a shoe I thought was missing. On the desk, more newspaper. When I open the drawers I find old notebooks, a postcard from David saying he likes Paris though his parents dragged him to the Eiffel Tower, a letter from my mother asking if I ever think about rejoining the church. I run my finger down the line of books on my shelves: college textbooks, a few novels, the AP style manual. If I were writing about the girl who lives in this room, I'd say she thinks about nothing but her work.

I open my dresser drawers. In here the clothes are younger, brighter, tumbled together. Beneath a sweater I find my old pipe, a small gray one with the cold smooth feel of marble, a little ash still in the bowl. I turn it over in my hands. My mother, at least, would find this shocking, though I think if I were dead Hannah would get rid of it before my mother came to the apartment. If I were dead. I look around the room. What would be left in here to tell anyone who I was?

In the living room I sit on the couch, my bag in my lap. The weight of it reminds me of the videotape I borrowed from Allison's apartment. I pull it out. Allison 5, May 9, 1992.

I pop the tape in the VCR and rewind it to the beginning. When I press play, the TV fills with static, and then there's a click and a face appears, filling up the screen, so close I can tell only that the person is white. Then the face pulls back, features emerging. It's Allison. She is biting her lip, concentrating, while the camera moves up and down. Then she disappears to the side. The camera moves again, fitting a tall stool into the frame, and she is back. She walks backward, leans over to pick up a guitar, and perches herself on the stool.

Allison lifts her head and smiles at the camera. "May ninth, nineteen ninety-two," she says. "I'm Allison Avery." Her voice curls around the words, as though her name were part of the song. "Allison," she says again, her lips slowly shaping each syllable. "Avery." She laughs, a deep-throated, husky laugh, and then she begins to play. She lowers her head over the guitar, cradled against her stomach, her hair falling forward to hide half her face. Her body moves to the rhythm of the song, and she is beautiful. Then she begins to sing, and the room is full of that voice. I think of Angela playing the cassette for me and wonder why she didn't choose a video. Maybe she thought it would be too much, that the sight of Allison, her chest rising and falling with breath, her fingers flickering over the guitar strings, would shake her apart.

This is the first time I've seen the girl alive. I can't stop thinking of what awaits that lovely body, the way it will be broken and abandoned, emptied out.

Allison slips off the stool and walks toward the camera until her torso fills the frame. She bends down sideways, so that her face is visible, her long hair draped across her cheek, and then she says, "See you later." The screen goes blank.

I stand up and go over to the television, rewind the tape a little and press pause as Allison's tilted face fills the screen. She looks mischievous, as though she made this tape for someone who wanted her, someone she wanted to tease. A piece of her hair sticks to the corner of her mouth. Her lips curve in a half smile, the point of her tongue showing through her teeth. She is heavy-lidded, her lashes thick with mascara, her eyelids glittering with bronze shadow. It's an expression that suggests more to come, mysteries to uncover.

It's a face with secrets.

At the police station, I flip through the day's reports, almost shivering in the air-conditioned chill. Here are the things that happen in a day in the city. A hit-and-run. Two burglaries. The murder of a woman whose boyfriend shot her, then himself, while her five-year-old watched. The boyfriend is still alive.

I walk down the hall in a daze, writing leads in my head. "Five-year-old Sergio Davis . . . Lucille Davis, 29 . . . Bullet to the temple . . ." I don't even see Sergeant Morris until he speaks. "You heard?" he says.

"Yeah," I say. I have no idea what he is talking about. I know it's probably good. I flip open my notebook. "What happened?"

"A Mississippi state trooper found it abandoned off Highway Sixty-one." He leans in close, almost whispering.

"You're talking about the car," I say. "The dead girl's car."

"What else?" he says. He tells me they found the girl's missing shoe in the trunk of the car. Her purse was on the backseat. The wallet was gone, and her underwear was not in the car, which might mean the killer still has it. "Souvenir," Morris says grimly.

I take a stab. "Any drugs or paraphernalia in the car?"

He looks surprised.

"Heroin?" I say.

Morris shakes his head. "Morphine. How did you . . ." He stiffens, looking past me down the hall. I don't turn my head, just lower my notebook so that whoever is passing by won't see it. "Lieutenant," Morris says.

Lieutenant Nash passes us. He frowns, trying to place me. "Sergeant," he says, and keeps walking. I'll have to call him later to get confirmation and hope he doesn't make the connection to Morris. Morris makes as if to go in the opposite direction. I touch his arm. He turns, a look of warning on his face. He almost looks angry. I hesitate, a drug question dying on my tongue. "What kind of shoe was it?" I ask.

He frowns and takes another step away from me. "What's that got to do with anything?"

"It could be useful," I say, standing with my pen poised to write down his answer. He says, "If you say so." I can see him telling his buddies about this later. "Only a woman," he'll say, and they'll all laugh.

"What kind of shoe was it?" Bishop says. He snorts into his beer. "What the hell you ask that for?"

"That's the point," I say. "That's what I'm saying."

"She doesn't know why she said it," Evan says.

"What kind of shoe did you think it was?" Bishop says.

"A black sandal," I say. "I was picturing it, this one shoe sitting there when they opened the trunk. I bet she pulled up her foot and unbuckled it and took it off to bang on the roof, for all the good it did her."

Evan looks under the table. "You're wearing black sandals," he says.

"Don't psychoanalyze me," I say. "Half this town is wearing black sandals."

"Not me," says Bishop. "You, Evan?"

"Sneakers," he says. "White."

"Don't forget I saw the body," I say. "That's probably how I knew. Because it *was* a sandal. He told me."

"What color?" Bishop says.

"I didn't ask." I drain the rest of my beer. It's flat, acrid. "Her toenails were pink, if you want to know." In my head I see a foot, small, with toenails painted a shade called Innocence. I don't know if I'm remembering that color or making it up, but I know that shade of nail polish exists—my mother put a bottle in my stocking last Christmas. It's the color of Pepto-Bismol. I've never used it. Pink, the color of girls. Some women never stop being girls. I never wanted to be one in the first place.

"What else have you got?" Bishop asks.

"I'm running down a couple of leads," I say. "I found some interesting stuff at her apartment."

"Her apartment?" Bishop says. "How did you get in there?"

"Her friend Angela took me," I say. "She seems to think we're friends."

"That's a little weird," Evan says.

"I guess," I say. "She wanted someone to go with her."

"Hanging out with her friends," Bishop says. "It's above and beyond the call."

"What, you don't spend time with the people you're interviewing? When you're trying to get something from them?"

"It's different," Bishop says. "What are you trying to get? It's a stranger killing."

"You don't know that," I say.

"I befriend people while I'm interviewing them," Evan says. "It's over when I walk out the door. I don't call them up later and ask them to the movies."

"She asked me," I say. "And I learned something in that apartment."

"Like what?" Bishop says.

"Yeah, what?" Evan repeats.

They're both leaning in now, eager for the scoop. I realize I don't want to tell them yet. This is still my story. "She stole," I say. "She stole a sweater from her neighbor."

Bishops snorts. "I don't think *that* got her killed." He leans back in his chair, losing interest. "What else did you learn? The girl's shoe size?"

"Her taste in couches?" Evan says. "Whether she made her bed?"

"You," I say, pointing at Evan, "dig through people's trash." To Bishop I say, "You hung around a trailer park peering in windows."

"The suspect's windows," Evan says. "The suspect's trash."

Bishop says seriously, "It's a stranger killing. What do you think you're going to learn from the victim?"

"Why are you two turning on me?" I say. "You're the ones who taught me everything I know. You're the ones who showed me how to lie and cheat and steal."

"I could teach you to shoot a gun," Bishop says. "It's not my fault if you blow off a man's head." He points his finger at me and pretends to shoot.

We go outside, and it's only a moment before a sheen of sweat covers my skin. "Damn," Bishop sighs. "I'm moving to Alaska." He pulls his button-down shirt loose from his pants and fans his stomach with it.

"Send me a postcard when you get there," I say. "I'm going home." I pull my hair up into a ponytail and start walking back to the newspaper to get my car.

"Do you need a ride?" Evan calls after me. I shake my head and keep walking. Evan calls, "See you."

When I pass a pay phone two blocks later, I stop and dial into my voice mail. Three messages from Peter. I hunt in my pocket for more change and call him back. "Olivia," he says in a rush, when I'm only halfway through identifying myself. "My parents aren't here. Can you come?"

I park down the street and walk up to the Averys' house. Peter said he didn't want the neighbors to see my car in the driveway. "I know they're watching me," he said. "I heard my mother talking to Mrs. McAndrews on the phone." I'm not sure why I have to be a secret, but I oblige him. I have a strong feeling that there's something he can tell me, and I want to know.

When Peter opens the door, cool air touches my skin. He is wearing a white T-shirt and a pair of jeans, and he smiles when he sees me. "Come in," he says, and steps back inside. In silence, I trail behind him into the kitchen. "I just made coffee," he says. "You want some?" I nod and he takes two matching blue mugs from the cabinet and fills them. All of his movements seem slow, precise, as though he's drunk again and aware of how careful he has to be not to spill. I sit down at the kitchen table and he sets the mugs down in front of me. A few drops of liquid slosh out of one. "Shit," he says under his breath, and turns slowly to the counter for a paper towel. I watch him lay the towel flat on the table and press his hand against it. When the brown stain has soaked into the paper, I look up at his face. He's staring at his hand on the towel but he's not seeing it.

I touch his hand with a finger, and he starts.

"Sit down," I say. "I'll get it."

He eases into a chair. I move briskly, keeping my voice matter-of-fact while I ask him where the sugar is, opening and closing cabinets. I set everything on the table, pushing his mug toward him, dropping a spoon beside it, opening the carton of milk. The coffee is strong and bitter. "Good coffee," I say, nodding at him over my mug.

"What?" he says. He hasn't touched his.

"Good coffee," I say again. "Thanks."

Finally he picks up his spoon, adds sugar. "I'm glad you came," he says.

"Well," I say. I reach in my bag, fingering the metal rings of my notebook. "How are you?"

He meets my eyes and smiles. He actually looks grateful. "I'm okay," he says. He lifts his mug.

He tells me that he's been trying to keep busy. He hasn't wanted to see his friends much, they're nervous around him, he feels them watching him like he's become someone different, someone unpredictable and strange. They're afraid to laugh around him, afraid to talk about anything but Allison, and there's only so many times, he says, that he can listen to them say they're sorry. He tried going to work. Two women sat at one of his tables before he was finished clearing it, and he was awkward, trying to clear the dishes from the small table around them, their elbows and purses. As he walked away, he heard one of the women say, "I certainly hope the food is better than the service," and rage flooded his body. He dropped the bus tray to the ground where it crashed, silencing the restaurant, and then he turned toward that woman with his fists clenched. He got out, "If you think . . ." between his teeth before the manager grabbed him and hustled him into the kitchen, where she told him in a low, sympathetic voice that it would be better if he took a few days off. He's been watching a lot of television, he says. He's been working in his greenhouse. Even his parents are hard to talk to now, caught up in their own anger and grief.

"I feel like a crazy person," he says. "At least everyone treats me like a crazy person."

"People are afraid of you, because something terrible has happened to you." I stand up and go to the counter for the coffeepot. Leaning over him, I pour him another cup. For a moment I rest my hand on his shoulder.

"I guess you've been around a lot of people who've had something terrible happen to them," he says.

"Yes. A lot of people."

"And what about you?" he says. "Has anything terrible happened to you?"

"No," I say. I don't say that I wonder whether, when it does, I'll feel it like he feels this. Maybe I'll be one step removed, as though even my life were only another story I'm writing.

"You're lucky," he says. Then he takes the coffeepot from me and sets it on the table. "Do you want to see my greenhouse?" he asks. "It's in the backyard. I'd like to show you."

When he said "greenhouse," I pictured a lush jungle of tropical flowers and creeping plants, so many that they would block the cloudy glass walls, making it impossible to see in. But here are only neat rows of tiny trees, and the setting sun shines right in through.

"This one," he says, "is a maple grove. Forty years old." At first they look to me like leafy sticks planted upright in a pot, but then my vision swings around and I can see that they have the grace of whole trees. For a moment I feel that I am the one who is wrong, out of proportion, monstrously large. "Aren't you going to say how small they are? Some girls say"—his voice goes high in imitation—"'Oh, how cute! They're so tiny!'"

"I'm not a girl," I say.

He looks confused. "What do you mean?"

"I'm twenty-five. That's hardly a girl."

He grins, that mischievous grin, and throws his arm around me. "Come on," he says. "I'll give you the tour."

I try to ignore the weight of that arm on my shoulders. "This tree here is in the informal upright style," he says.

"What does that mean?"

"See, bonsai trees are sculpted into one of several different shapes. I forced this one to grow this way," he says. "Though it didn't take a lot of forcing. It's the most basic design because it follows the natural shape of the trunk." He draws a line in the air with his hand. "You want to develop a single line of the trunk, from the roots to the top, and you want the branch structure to look natural. The branches start about a third of the way up. But right here, see? I screwed up. Because there's not supposed to be any empty spaces."

"I bet you bring a lot of girls here," I tease. This is the first time I've seen his mood lighten. I move forward, out from under his arm, and run my fingers over the top of the tree.

"Of course I do, darling," he says, affecting a British accent. "But in the end there's only you."

"Of course," I say.

"Of course," he says.

I can't think of a joke to make. Against the tiny leaves, my fingers are clumsy as logs. When I look at him next he's not smiling anymore, and I know he's thinking about his sister. His sister. When I'm with him I find it difficult to think of her by name. Allison. He's thinking of Allison. He keeps his eyes on the tree while his hand finds a pair of tiny scissors on the counter, and then he snips off a miniature branch. "I have to keep them pruned," he says before he moves on down the row of trees.

I follow, watching him roll the branch between his fingers. "Can I have that?" I ask.

He looks surprised. "What for?"

"Because it's so small," I say. I think he'll take this as a reason; he can file it under the category of "girl."

He hands it to me. I drop it in my bag. "Maybe I should go," I say.

Chewing on his lower lip, Peter says nothing, and I wonder if he heard me. "Maybe I should go," I say again.

"You haven't asked me anything," Peter says. "About Allison."

"Another time," I say, taking a step backward.

He watches my face, considering something. Then he says, "Do you want to see her old bedroom?"

Yes. Of course I do.

Upstairs in her bedroom the shades are drawn and half-dead plants are clustered on the windowsills. I don't know if I'm imagining the smell of some musky perfume. It must be her mother's scent, because it seems impossible that hers could linger so long. In the center of the room, I turn around and around. Peter watches me from the doorway. "She just moved out a year ago," he says. "I come in here sometimes, and it's almost like she's just left the room."

I have a feeling that he expects me to put on her clothes, curl up on her bed, go to sleep, maybe, with her pillow beneath my cheek. The thought doesn't frighten me as much as it should. I want to know her, the dead girl. I could learn so much about what happened to her, if just for a moment I could slip inside her skin.

I remind myself that this wasn't the room she lived in anymore, and that that explains the little-girl furniture—wood painted white, with tiny yellow and pink flowers—and the framed cross-stitchings on the walls. One is a sloppy picture of a house with a fence and purple flowers around it. "Bless This House" it says across the top in red, and at the bottom her initials "AMA" and the date. On the desk is another list of "things to do." *Pay credit card bill. Write Aunt Lucy. Make doctor's appt. B-day present for Pete.*

"When's your birthday?" I ask, and from behind me he says, "Valentine's Day." I turn, and he's standing close enough to kiss. Here in his dead sister's bedroom, he leans toward me like he's going to press his lips to mine. I start to step back, but all he does is hug me, bending down so that his head rests on my shoulder. "I miss her so much," he says, and we stand like this, my hands resting gently on his back. More than anyone I've met, this boy clouds my mind, leaves me hovering between the professional and the personal, sympathy and desire. I think, *I'm holding him like this so he'll tell me what I want to know.* But he's right—I haven't asked him anything since I walked in the door. "Just come in the room. Just fucking come in the room," he whispers, and I know he's not talking to me.

"You poor baby," I say, and I reach up a hand to stroke the back of his head. His hair is slightly damp with sweat. His head is heavy on my shoulder. "Allison," he says. I try not to stiffen. This is the second time someone has murmured that name into my skin.

"I want her back," he says. "I just want her back." He steps back and stares at me hard, as though he's searching for her in my face. "Nothing can make it better," he says. "I've never wanted anything so much that I couldn't have. Do you know what that's like?"

"What if they catch them? The guys who did it."

"I don't know if that will make me feel better," he says, his voice weary and adult. Then he asks, "Will it?" and now his voice is like a child's, like he really thinks I know the answer.

"I hope so," I say. "I'll do my best to help."

"Why are you so nice to me?" he says. I touch his cheek with my fingertips. "You haven't asked me anything about her," he says again. "Why did you really come here? Was it to see me?"

"You asked me to come." I lift my hand from his face.

He fingers a strand of my hair. "Why don't you wear your hair long, like you used to?" he says. "It looked good on you."

"You remember what I looked like?"

"Of course," he says. "I never forget a pretty girl." His hand slides to my shoulder and tightens there. "I really want to kiss you," he says, and his voice cracks, so that I can hear how much he wants it. "Is that okay?" Over his shoulder as he leans in toward me I see his sister's pink-and-white bed, and then I close my eyes and he slips his tongue inside my mouth. He tastes of coffee and faintly of cigarettes. Downstairs, the front door slams. Peter jerks away. "Shit, my mother," he says. He looks both frightened and defiant. "She's early." He goes to the door and looks down the hallway. "Stay here."

He slips out of the room. I hear his feet on the stairs and then voices below. In his sister's mirror I see my face. My cheeks and neck are flushed, my lips red.

Die FART HeAD BASTARD   STeVe VAneK

Something pink is wedged behind the mirror where it's propped on the dresser. I pull it out. It's a wig—a bob, with bangs, in a brilliant pink. In the mirror I slip it on and tuck my hair beneath it. It looks good on me, though I feel distant from the image in the glass, like a cat thinking she sees another cat instead of her own reflection.

Someone is coming up the stairs. I yank off the wig and shove it in my bag, and when Peter comes through the door it's too late to change my mind.

"Come on," he whispers. "I'm going to sneak you out off the deck."

"Are you crazy?"

"Do you want my mother to see you up here?"

He hustles me down the hall into the upstairs den, out through the sliding glass doors onto the wooden deck. I let him help me up and over the railing, but when he tells me to reach for the thick branch of the tree that grows less than a foot away, I shake my head. "I can't."

"I've done this a million times," he says. "Allison showed me. You can do it." Then he wraps his arm around my waist and holds me, the muscles of his arm tense and hard against my stomach. He kisses my cheek. "Reach for the branch," he says, his breath warm against my ear. "I've got you."

"I must be crazy," I say, I reach out and wrap both hands around the branch like a gymnast on the parallel bars.

"Now swing," he says, and letting go, he gives me a little push. For a moment I'm just dangling, my throat full of a scream I can't let out, and then my frantic feet find the branch and I'm standing. My heart is jumping, and it's not with fear, it's with exhilaration. I look back at Peter leaning against the rail, his hair a golden brown in the setting sun. "I knew you could do it," he says. "It's all easy now."

Half-falling, half-climbing, I make it down the tree. I jump from a low branch and fall to my knees. When I'm standing, Peter leans over the deck railing and sails my bag down to me. A pink strand flutters out the side. I grab the bag and push the wig to the bottom.

"Cut through the neighbors' yard," he says in a stage whisper. "I'll meet you at your car."

The neighbors' dog barks at me from behind their screen door as I pass through the yard. I hear a voice ask the dog, "What is it, Apollo?" but no one comes to the door. I want to laugh at the idea of a dog named Apollo, and then just as suddenly I feel like crying. I break into a run, and reach my car sweaty and panting. The air inside the car is thick with heat, and my thighs stick to the vinyl seat. In the rearview mirror I pull my hair up into a tight bun, trying to breathe evenly. I fan the back of my neck with my notebook and wait for Peter.

When he comes, he opens the passenger door and sits in the car. "So Allison taught you that?" I say. "Was she a gymnast?"

"No, she was just brave. If she wanted something, she got it."

"Like what?"

He tells me that Allison had heard that a boy at her college was the son of a Nashville music executive. She found out what classes he took and went to one of them—it was something like advanced calculus, he says—and sat beside him and took notes. Then she asked if he wanted to study together. For two weeks she studied for a class she wasn't even taking, and then one night she put one of her own tapes in the stereo and waited until he asked who it was to tell him that it was her voice coming out of the speakers. He told her he would play the tape for his father. "I don't know if he did," Peter says. "I guess it doesn't matter now."

He tells the story in praise of his dead sister. I'm thinking about that poor kid, the way she manipulated and used him. Then I picture Carl, leaning in close across the table, the way I smiled as though I wanted him to touch me. I'm no better than Allison Avery. I'm just not as good at it as she was.

"You know a guy called today who wants to put out her CD?" Peter says. "I guess she'll finally get what she wanted."

"Your parents said yes, then?"

"I think so. He told my mother it would be tastefully done. A tribute."

"I know that guy," I say. "He'll do a good job."

"You know him?" Peter turns to look at me. "He sounded real interested in my sister. Did he know her?"

"I don't think so," I say. I should have just said no, but maybe David did meet her. Maybe he just didn't remember it until he heard her gorgeous voice, saw her pretty face. "If Allison always got what she wanted," I say, "why was she going to med school when she wanted to be a singer?"

"Did my mother tell you that?" I nod. He says, "She was never going to go to med school. It doesn't hurt for my mother to believe it. None of it matters now." He is quiet for a minute, and then he reaches over and punches in the cigarette lighter. "Do you mind?" he asks, pulling a pack from his pocket.

I tell him I don't mind and watch him take out the last cigarette, hold it in his mouth and reach for the lighter. These things seem to take a long long time. He inhales deeply, as though it's been a while since he's had a smoke.

"Can I have a drag?" I say. When he passes me the cigarette, his fingers touch mine. I inhale and pass it back. He has one arm folded across his stomach. The other lifts and lowers, lifts and lowers as he smokes.

This is what it's come to. I ask for another drag. His fingers touch mine. When he finishes the cigarette, he starts to talk. He tells me that he loved his sister, that she was pretty and brave and wonderful. The light outside fades while he remembers. He tells me that she got him through algebra, that she taught him to drive, that whatever he did, she had already done, and come back to show him the way. She always took care of him, no matter what.

"You sound like your mother," I say. "She tells me your sister was perfect."

"She wasn't perfect." He sighs. "But my mom refuses to admit it."

Peter says he's not even supposed to mention that she smoked, al-most a pack a day, for a while, though she was trying to quit. He says, "She got me that fake ID, you know. She used to take me out sometimes." He shakes his head and says bitterly, "My mother never really knew her at all." He falls silent, staring out the wind-shield at nothing.

This is the moment.

"Peter," I say softly. "Tell me about the morphine."

His jaw tightens. He doesn't look at me. "So you know," he says flatly. "I should've known you'd find out." His voice grows sharp. "The medical examiner said only the cops and the family would know, but I guess nothing is sacred to a reporter. Who told you, anyway?"

What I say next has to be perfect, enough to make him go on. To ask him directly what he means would be to reveal I don't know. Medical examiner, he said. That means he's talking about autopsy results, the tox screen, maybe drugs in her system. "Sometimes we have a source," I say carefully.

"Well, that's vague." He shakes his head angrily. "They told my parents the media would never know."

"I was only told about the morphine. Nothing else."

"That's enough, isn't it?" He turns to look at me. In the fading light he looks years older than he is, his mouth strained, dark circles under his eyes. "It was a lot of morphine," he says. "Enough to kill her, maybe, if someone else hadn't."

"I'm surprised your parents told you," I say.

"They wanted to know if I knew why she had it."

"Did you?" I ask. "Did you know she was a user?"

His eyes widen and he laughs, a short, astonished laugh. "But she wasn't, that's what's crazy. That's what doesn't make sense."

"You don't have to lie to me, Peter." I put my hand on his thigh and give it a gentle squeeze. "It happens to a lot of people in medicine."

He stares at me, then speaks very slowly, as though to a child. "What does?"

"Painkiller addiction." I'm weighing whether to tell him about the heroin. Maybe she was trying to move down the ladder, one rung at a time. Why else would she be using morphine when she still had heroin in her room?

"Olivia . . . ," he starts, then subsides. He returns his gaze to the windshield, his whole body gone oddly wooden. He doesn't move, doesn't speak. I can't even hear him breathe.

"Peter?" I reach out to touch his shoulder. With a sudden movement, like a cat pouncing, he grabs my hand and squeezes it. "Please don't print it, Olivia." His voice shakes, though he's trying to sound calm, reasonable. "It's not fair."

"Why not?" I say.

"It has nothing to do with . . . It doesn't even make sense."

I say gently, "If Allison was buying or selling drugs, it could have a lot to do with what happened."

"But she wasn't," he says, his voice rising with frustration. He snatches his hand from mine. "She wasn't. I know it."

"It's not just the morphine." I hesitate. He's staring at me now, so intently that I almost feel frightened. "I found heroin in her apartment."

"You found . . ." He looks away and for a long moment says nothing. When he speaks again his voice is calm. "How did the police miss it?"

"It was well hidden. I'm not even sure what made me look."

"Where was it?"

"In her bedroom."

"What did you do with it?"

"I left it there."

"I don't want my mother to find it."

"It's well hidden," I say again, reluctant to tell him where.

"This is hard enough already."

"I know."

"You won't print it, will you?"

"I can't promise that." He turns to look at me, his expression pleading. "I won't print it now," I say.

"People should be talking about what happened to my sister," he says bitterly. "Not about the things she did."

We sit without talking for a moment, the only sound the crinkle of cellophane as Peter unwraps a new pack of cigarettes. He slaps the pack hard against his hand. I watch him from the corner of my eye. He keeps his eyes down. He told me a secret. I told him one. Why do I feel like he came out ahead?

"When can I see you again?" he says abruptly.

"Peter," I say, "I know that you miss your sister . . ." I'm not sure how to finish the sentence.

"I want to see you," he says. "You don't believe that? Or you don't want to see me."

"I don't know what I want." My head is floating above my body like a balloon on a string, a cocktail of caffeine and nicotine and adrenaline pounding through my bloodstream. I'm tired of testing the water, trying not to scare him off. What I want is to ask him "What else can you give me?"

Peter lights another cigarette, his hand shaking. "You're the only person I can talk to," he says, not looking at me, his voice flat. "Nobody else understands."

"All right," I say. "All right."

He turns to me quickly. "When?"

"Friday," I say. "If we talk about your sister. I'd like you to take me to the places she used to take you. I want to meet the people she knew."

A smile breaks across his face. He nods. "Friday." He leans forward as though to kiss me, but I turn my face away and his lips meet my cheek. "Friday," he says again, and swings his long legs out of the car. He shuts the door gently and steps away.

I grip the steering wheel hard and pull away. He stands smoking, watching me go, and I know what I want. I want to stop the car and hold my hand out for that cigarette, just to feel him touch me again.

One thing I know, if you get what you want, the only thing that happens is you want something else.

❁

When I turn the key in my front door, I remember my plans with Hannah. The apartment is dark, and there's a note from her on the coffee table. "Waited for you until nine," it says. "Went to the movies with Linda from work. See you. P.S. Carl called."

I sit down heavy on the couch, fold the note into a square like the ones we used to pass each other in school. Then I unfold it again, turn it over and write on the back. "Hannah, I'm so sorry. I got hung up with work stuff. Wake me when you get in. Love, Olivia."

The sun wakes me in the morning. Hannah never did.

12

I'm in my car, strained forward over the steering wheel as though the movement of my body could translate to the line of traffic in front of us. Beside me Bryce mutters a steady stream of invective, most of it directed at the cop up ahead who just waved a Channel 5 van on through. The sun through the windshield pricks at my eyes, making them water. "Goddamnit," Bryce says. "God fucking damnit. Holy fucking shit. He's not going to let us through."

There's an accident on the interstate—a tractor trailer and at least three cars. We're trying to reach it.

Bryce rolls down the window and sticks his head out. "Officer," he says. "We're reporters, too. Newspaper." The cop just looks at him and doesn't say a word. "Come on, you let them through," Bryce says, and when the cop still doesn't answer, he says, "What's the deal, you like the way you look on TV?" The line starts moving. Bryce shouts out the window, "I could take your picture. You could get it framed."

"Forget it," I say. "We'll find another way."

Darting in and out of slow lanes of traffic, I get us onto the overpass that rises above the accident scene. I pull onto the shoulder and we get out. A line of people has already formed, leaning over the railing and shaking their heads or pointing. Newcomers slow their cars, pull over and get out, their faces eager with the question "What happened?" Bryce shoulders his way up to the railing, saying,

"Excuse me, media," and holding his camera before him as proof. Once up there he digs film out of one of the innumerable pockets on his photographer's vest and starts shooting pictures. The scene spreads out before us, an overturned tractor trailer in the middle of the road, one car in the ditch beside it, two more spun out away from it, one half crushed. Ambulances and cop cars with their lights going, cameramen readying their equipment. I can just make out Lydia McKenzie, combing her bleached-blond hair.

I lean way out over the railing. A few feet down is a grassy hill that slopes down to the interstate below. You have to be brave, I think, to get what you want. "Bryce," I say, "I'm going over."

He lowers his camera and leans out to look. "It's too far to jump," he says.

"That's why you're going to lower me," I say. I look around at the crowd. "Excuse me," I say, raising my voice. "Can someone help lower me down to the hill?"

A large black man steps forward, lifting his arm. "I'll help," he says. A slow grin spreads across his face.

"You picked the wrong day to wear a skirt," Bryce says as I hike my skirt up and clamber up and over the metal railing. I turn around, slowly, slowly, on the concrete until I am standing on the other side of the railing and gripping it with both hands. Then Bryce holds one of my hands, the man holds the other, and in unison they lean their bodies over while I push off with my feet. No one is watching the accident anymore, all their shiny faces turned down to look at me. Behind me an ambulance siren wails. I am dangling. The two men grunt, their hands gripping mine slick with perspiration, as they lean more and more forward, inching me toward the ground.

"That's as far as we can get you," Bryce says. He draws a deep breath. A drop of sweat falls from his forehead onto my face, and since I can't lift my hand to wipe it, it makes its way down my cheek.

"Okay," I say. "Let go." Bryce drops my hand immediately, and then I am dangling by one arm, the other man grabbing my hand with both of his. "It's too far," he says. "You'll get hurt."

My arm begins to ache. "Let go," I say. "It's okay. Let go."

He looks at me, frowning with effort and worry.

"Let go," I say. "Please."

He takes his hands away, and in that split second as his face rises up, up, I am afraid. Then I hit the ground, landing hard on my side, and start to roll. One of my shoes comes off, making its way down ahead of me. I keep rolling, closing my eyes like I did when I was a child so I wouldn't have to watch the green-blue whirl of sky and ground. I can feel myself collecting cuts and bruises, a rock thumps my shoulder, a stick scrapes my thigh. Then I stop rolling and open my eyes to the hot blue sky. I stand, brushing grass off my skirt, probing the tender place on my shoulder with my finger, and then I hear it.

Applause.

I look back up at the overpass, and see a blur of motion all along the railing, that long line of people clapping. I raise my arms like a gymnast dismounting and listen to someone cheer.

Behind me another siren starts up, and I turn, startled by the reminder. I find my shoe and put it back on. Then I clamber, half sliding, the rest of the way down to the interstate. The accident is on the other side of the concrete divider in the middle of the road. When I reach the pavement I see that the cops, too, are watching me, laughing and nudging each other and shaking their heads. I have to hike up my skirt to climb over the divider, and one of them whistles like a construction worker.

I straighten my skirt, smooth my hair behind my ears and walk up to the cops, grinning. An older man claps me on the back, still laughing. "Anything for a story, eh, little gal?"

"Just doing my job, sir," I say. The cops tell me two people were killed, three severely injured, including one pregnant woman. All have been rushed to the hospital. They say it looks like the truck driver was drunk, though I'm going to have to get confirmation before I can print that.

When I'm through I have to scramble back up the hill like a monkey on all fours. More people hold on to Bryce and the other man so they can lean way over to grab my hands, and then the people pull, and Bryce and the man pull, and I leave the ground. It's almost like flying.

When my feet are back on the concrete people gather around, patting my shoulder and shaking my hand. One woman says, "Honey, you still got grass on your back," and brushes it off with quick, firm strokes.

"You are crazy," Bryce says with admiration as we walk away. He holds up his camera. "Wait until you see the pictures. We should put you on the front page."

I imagine the cutline: "Anything for a story, reporter says." I turn and wave good-bye to the crowd. They wave back, smiles on all their shiny faces.

I'm just finishing the story when the phone rings. I pick it up and tuck it under my chin, still typing, and a male voice says, "Hi. I saw your stories today." I don't answer for a moment, and then I identify the voice as Peter's.

"Hey," I say, making my voice gentle. The story about his sister's car can't have been easy to read. "Had you already heard?"

"Heard what?" he says.

"About the car."

"No, no," he says. "Just what I read in the paper."

"I'm sorry," I say. There's a silence. I say, "Are you okay?"

He expels a heavy breath. "I guess." Then his voice brightens. "It was good to see you the other day."

"It was good to see you too." Then I laugh. "You wouldn't believe what I did today. I think swinging off your deck inspired me."

There's another silence, and the voice is different when he speaks again, puzzled, suspicious. "What are you talking about?"

I don't say anything for a minute. "Who is this?"

"This is Carl. Carl Fitzner," he says. "Who did you think it was?"

For a minute I just sit there with my mouth hanging open. Then I take a breath. "Hi, Carl," I say brightly. "Sorry about that. How are you?"

"I'm okay," he says, sounding irritated. "I wanted to know if you would meet me for lunch."

"Well—" I start.

He cuts me off, saying again, "Who did you think I was?"

"Sure," I say. "Where do you want to eat?"

When I get to the restaurant, Carl's at an outside table sipping a frozen margarita. He stands when he sees me, and leans forward to give me an awkward half hug. I sit down facing the sun and leave my sunglasses on. "Margarita?" Carl asks, waving the waitress over.

"I don't know," I say. "I have to go back to work." I flash him a smile.

"You should definitely have one then." He smiles back. "All the more reason."

I nod, and when the waitress comes I order one. "I'm sorry I didn't get back to you earlier," I say to Carl. "It's been a busy week."

"I've seen your byline a few times."

"You saw the story about Allison's car."

"Yes." Carl's face seems to sag. He looks down at his hands on the table.

"So how are you?" I say brightly. "How's the play going?"

"Good, good," he says, nodding. "Bob decided not to come back, so I've taken over his part permanently."

"You were the best actor there." I lean forward and touch the back of his hand.

He blushes.

When the waitress comes I pick up the margarita and hold the cool glass to my cheek before I take a sip. We order and while we wait for our food I tell him stories about the newspaper. I tell him about rolling down to the interstate this morning. I tell him Bishop's

Jack-off Daniel's story and pretend it's my own. Listening to me, he finishes his drink, and when the waitress brings our food he orders another. By the time we finish dessert he's on his third. I'm still nursing the first.

"You know what I really love about acting?" he is saying. "It's getting to be all those different people." He waves his arm expansively. "I've gotten to be a drug addict, a priest, a soldier . . . It'd be so boring just being Carl Fitzner, some guy. Every time I take a role, I'm someone else." He says it like he's amazed. "You must know what that's like a little," he says. "You're always finding out about something else, right?" His face is flushed with drink and the pleasure of having an audience. His grin is wide and sloppy. He's eager to listen to me. He's eager to talk.

"I'm having trouble finding out what I'd really like to know," I say.

"What's that?"

"What really happened to Allison. Who could have done this to her. What she was really like. I've heard a lot of conflicting stories."

"Like what?" he says, frowning.

"That she was a churchgoer," I say, watching his face. "That she was a heroin addict."

He laughs, a short, astonished bark, then frowns reproachfully. "That's not true," he says. "Who told you that?"

"Well . . . ," I say. I'm trying to decide how much I want to tell him. I put my bag on the table and pull out my notebook, pretending that I'm paging through it to see who said what. He's watching me intently, leaning forward as though to read what I've written, and his elbow knocks into my bag. It spills sideways onto the table and the empty chair below.

"Shit, I'm sorry," he says. I reach under the table to gather up pens and pieces of crumpled paper. When I sit up again he's clutching that pink wig, staring at it with a face as white as if Allison had just come walking onto the porch. "Where did you get this?" he says.

"It was Allison's," I say, too flustered to lie.

He turns his stricken gaze to me. "She used to wear this onstage sometimes," he says. "She said it helped her become a different person."

"I can imagine that."

He keeps staring at me, turning his eyes from my face to the wig and back again. "Did you steal this?"

I shake my head. "Someone gave it to me."

"Who?"

"Peter," I say, and wish I hadn't.

He frowns. "Why?"

"I don't know." I can't imagine why he would.

He nods to himself, running his fingers over the slick bright strands. "Maybe because you look a little like her," he says. He thrusts it at me suddenly. "Will you put it on?"

"Oh no," I say, leaning back in my chair and holding my hands out to stop him. He shakes it at me like a pom-pom. "I can't, Carl. It's too strange."

"Please," he says. He makes a choked attempt at a laugh. "Please put it on. I want to see what you look like." His voice is rising, and I glance around and catch the eye of an older woman. She's openly staring at us, her forkful of enchilada suspended in the air. I frown at her and she looks away. "Please," Carl says.

"All right," I mutter, snatching it from his hand. He's breathing so loudly I can hear the way the air shakes as he lets it out. I bend over and adjust the wig on my head. When I sit up, I flip my head back and lift my hands. "Ta da," I say, trying to make a joke of it. "It's a whole new me."

He stares at me. His face goes pale. His lips twitch. Then the color rises quickly back into his cheeks. He reaches for his glass and lets the margarita slide down his throat. "I'm sorry," he says, setting the glass down. "In those sunglasses, and that wig . . ." He swallows, his Adam's apple bouncing inside his throat. He's staring at his glass, turning it in his hands. He can't lift his eyes to mine.

I feel slightly sick, the way I did when I was ten after playing doctor with the neighborhood kids, wondering what inside me could make me do such things, knowing how my mother's eyes would widen, then narrow, if she caught me at it. I pull the wig from my head and put it back inside my bag.

"I'm sorry," he keeps saying, his voice wobbling on the edge of tears. "I know I asked you to do it. I don't know why . . ."

"It's all right," I murmur. "I know you were very close."

Finally he lifts his head to look at me, opening his eyes. "Oh," he says, a sound of surprise and disappointment. "You took it off."

I let a heartbeat pass. "You had been fighting when she died. That must be hard."

He nods. He's so shaken up he doesn't even ask me how I know about the fighting. "I'm so sorry," he says.

"Why are you sorry?" I say gently. "Tell me."

I watch his throat working. He begins to tell me about Allison's carelessness, how he saw her go home with one guy from a gig, and just a week later saw her with another guy, a black guy. "She said she was seeing this guy and she was going to keep seeing him." He presses the heel of his hand into his forehead, rocking a little in his chair. "She never knew how to keep herself safe. I wanted to protect her." His voice cracks over the word "protect."

"Carl," I say. "These men she was seeing? What were their names?"

"Names?"

"You never heard her mention them?"

He puts his hand on the table, and I take it. "Let me think, let me think." He squeezes my fingers. "One was white, one was black, that's all I know."

I think, *Russell Freeland.* I think of the note I found in her desk: *Where are you? I'm out looking for you. R.* "Was one of them Russell Freeland?"

"Russell? How do you know him?" he asks, his voice edgy with suspicion.

"I met him covering a story. How do you?"

"I never met him, but I remember her dating him in college," he says slowly. "I bet that's who it was." He moves his hand to grip my wrist. "You know what," he says. "I'm going to the police."

"Wait a minute, Carl," I say. He's hurting me. He's threatening to pull my story out from under me. I peel his fingers from my wrist. "What makes you think there's any reason to?"

"If he was seeing her, why hasn't he said anything? I think that's suspicious."

"We don't even know it was him."

"It's him all right. And I bet he knows something."

"Just let me find him first. Okay, Carl? Just let me find out."

He stares angrily past me, saying nothing. I take his hand again, rubbing one of his fingers with my thumb. "Please? Just give me a couple of days."

He nods. His face melts from anger back into sorrow and with his free hand he clutches at mine. "Thank you," he says.

"You're welcome," I say, though I'm not entirely sure what he's thanking me for.

For the next fifteen minutes I try to extricate myself, making half-hearted attempts to restart the conversation. All I can think about is letting Russell Freeland walk away across that parking lot. Carl doesn't want to let me go, and he doesn't want to talk. He just sits there nodding to himself, saying, "What?" whenever I ask him a question, and then, "I'm sorry," as though he's apologizing for something much greater than his inattention. At this moment, I don't even care what else he has to say. Like someone waking up after a drunken one-night stand, all I want to know now is how soon I can leave.

The phone is in my hand before I sit down. The girl who answers at the Freeland home says, "Russell? He's at work."

"That's right," I say. "I'll call him there."

"Okay."

"You know what?" I say. "I'm looking, and I don't have that number after all."

"Hang on," she says. "I'll get it for you."

I call the number she gives me, and a man's voice answers the phone with the name of a local law firm. I ask for Russell and wait while the man transfers me, drawing jagged lines across the page of my notebook, like bolts of lightning.

"Hello?" He sounds like he's speaking from inside a tunnel.

"Russell." I caress the name. *Russell.* Please be the one. "This is Olivia Dale."

Silence. "Hi."

"You said you wanted to talk to me about Allison Avery?"

"I did. But I've been reading your stories. I'm not sure there's anything I can tell you you haven't already printed."

"I'd like to talk to you, anyway. I think you might know her better than others." I wait a beat. "She is your girlfriend, isn't she?"

A long, long silence. I drum my fingers on the desk. I want to shout into the phone: "Tell me!" "Was," he says. "She *was* my girlfriend."

I can't keep the disappointment out of my voice. "You broke up?"

"No." His voice catches on a humorless laugh. "She died."

I can't help myself. My heart lifts at those words.

It's five-thirty, and two long hours remain before I'm to meet Russell Freeland at his father's church. I'm trying to pass the time reading the AP wire when I hear Evan shout my name. I look around. He's standing in the doorway to the TV room. "Hurry, hurry," he says. I half jog over there, Bishop and Peggy and two other reporters falling in behind me. Evan steps out of the way and I stand in front of the television. "Holy shit," Bishop says. "That's you."

On-screen, I'm dangling off the overpass, kicking my feet like I'm treading water, and then the hands holding mine let go and I'm falling. Watching my body drop, my stomach lurches and I feel the heat rising in my cheeks. The me on television hits the ground and starts rolling toward the interstate. Then she stops, and stands, stumbling a little, and straightens her skirt, and I hear the applause. The woman on-screen turns her back to the camera and throws out her arms, and the film freezes that way, in that moment of victory. I can't believe that's me, that woman with her body drawn up tight, her hands reaching up for the sky.

"There's a woman with real commitment to her job, Ted," Lydia McKenzie says, turning to her co-anchor. He chuckles. "Talk about persistence," he says. "She gets an A for effort." Lydia McKenzie giggles, and then they shuffle their papers and look seriously into the camera and say good night.

"Damn," Bishop says. He slaps me on the back. "You're a celebrity." I smile at him.

Peggy's shaking her head, grinning. "You're getting to be quite a daredevil," she says. She points her finger at me. "You be more careful from now on, kid. You're supposed to cover the news, not make it." She's still grinning.

"Just trying to do my job, Peggy," I say.

Evan says, "Remember when Bishop asked you how far you'd go for a story? I guess now you know."

"That? That was nothing," I say, laughing. "Just you wait."

When I get back to my desk, the phone rings. It's David. "Did you see me on TV?" I ask.

"What?" he says. "No. You were on TV?"

"On the local news. At an accident scene. You should watch tonight. Maybe they'll show it again."

"Can you tape it for me?" he says. "I might be busy."

"Sure," I say. "Okay."

"I called to tell you Allison's parents okayed the CD. Her mother's really nice, by the way. She's going to sort through her tapes and bring me some so I can figure out what should be on it."

"That's great, David."

"Yeah," he says. "I'm really excited. I can't wait to hear the other stuff, because if it's half as good as what she sent me, the only hard part will be figuring out what to drop." There's a pause. Then he says, "If this works, maybe I can do more than one."

"Maybe," I say.

"God," he says quietly. "What a voice."

Back in the basement of the Brighter Day Baptist Church, I sit with Russell Freeland in a pool of flickering fluorescent light, the room outside it a waiting darkness. I'm perched on the edge of my metal folding chair, my notebook on the seat behind me. We've been talking about how much he misses her, about the difficulty of his position, because to come forward would be to reveal the secret of their relationship and more than likely bring suspicion on himself. I'm trying to ease him into the more difficult questions, going as slow as I can stand, keeping my body still. I feel like a lit match.

Russell Freeland sits hunched over, his elbows resting on his knees, his clasped hands dangling between his legs, a reverse prayer. "We had issues," he says.

"Racial?" I prompt, and he flashes his eyes up at me. "No." It's a reproach. "I mean, yes, that was true for our parents. We had other issues."

He falls silent.

I take a guess. "She wasn't faithful?"

He smiles without humor. "Does everyone know about it?"

"It was something Angela said, about her wanting to touch the whole world."

"I guess you could put it that way," he says dryly. He drops his gaze to his hands. "Have you ever been around someone who was so . . . charismatic . . . I was just so happy when she was around, I tried not to think about what she did when she wasn't." He takes a few shaky breaths. I watch a tear run down the length of his nose and hang there. He knocks it off. "I don't know how to make you understand." He looks up at me and holds out his hand to me. I take it.

"I remember the first time I met her. She looks you in the eye like she *knows* you." He drops my hand.

I notice this is the first time he's used the present tense. "How did you know she was unfaithful?"

"She told me." I must look surprised, because he says, "Oh, she never lied. It was more like, this is me. Take it or leave it."

"Must be nice to have that kind of confidence." I didn't mean to say that out loud, but, when he answers, I know he must have thought about it too.

He says, "Some girls take it as a matter of course that every guy they meet will fall in love with them."

I'm trying to decide if that edge in his voice is bitterness. I say, "And that gives them power."

"Yes." He lets out a long breath. "I let her get away with . . ." He swallows the word. Murder.

I let Russell talk, about how he and Allison broke up in college over her infidelities, about how they met again last Christmas, when he came home on break from law school in Knoxville. These are the words he keeps using: *charisma, talent, electric, magnetic.* But he can't make me feel what it was like to be with her, any more than I can make him feel what it was like to see her dead, no matter how well I might describe her broken body in the dirt.

"Did your parents know about you?" I ask him.

"They knew we had seen each other before, you know, in college. But this time we decided to lay low until we were sure, because, why cause trouble. The mother . . . They ran these ads in the newspaper for the children's hospital? She was cradling this black child in her arms, looking all tender. But you think she wanted me in her white house? And my father . . . to him it's like abandoning everything he fights for."

I lean in close. "Is that why you didn't come forward before?"

"That, and . . ." He takes a breath. "I loved her."

He doesn't go on. I know what he means. To come forward will not be to assume his proper place as the grieving boyfriend. It will mean recriminations from his parents, most likely denials from Allison's mother, questions from the police. For a while this will be the lens through which everyone sees Russell Freeland, his image shimmery and distorted on the other side of his love for her, her terrible death.

He tells me she was beautiful, which she wasn't.

He tells me again that she was not a liar, which perhaps she wasn't. There's a difference between lying and not telling the truth.

He tells me she was a little bit wild, which she was, and I feel the moment has arrived.

"So you know about the drug use?" I study his face. He frowns.

"You mean like weed?"

I shake my head. "I mean the heroin."

His face is a picture of disbelief. "What are you talking about?"

I let a long beat pass. "Look, Russell, Peter told me about the morphine."

"Morphine?" he says. "Peter? I don't understand."

"The autopsy showed morphine in her bloodstream. Peter told me."

He jumps to his feet. Coming in and out of shadow, he paces behind his chair. "First of all, that kid is fucked up. I wouldn't believe a word he says. I don't know what his motivation could possibly be for telling you that, even if it were true, but I don't believe it."

"I got confirmation," I say quietly as he snaps, "What? What?" over the words. "I got confirmation," I say again calmly. "Morphine. Heroin."

He sinks back into his chair. "Maybe the guys who did this . . ." He swallows. "Maybe they gave it to her."

"Why?"

"I don't know," he shouts. He jumps to his feet again. "Jesus, why did they do any of it?" He presses his fingers hard into his eyes. "Peter." He shakes his head. "Why would he tell you that?"

"I don't know. He needs someone to talk to."

Russell laughs bitterly. "And he picked a reporter?"

Yes, I think. *And so did you.*

"Let me tell you something about Peter. The way he felt about his sister, it wasn't normal."

I frown. "What do you mean?"

"You know what I mean. He looked at her sometimes, and it wasn't like a brother. It was like a man."

This lodges like a rock in my throat. "You said she had that effect on men."

"He was her brother!" he bursts out. He sets to pacing again.

"Did he know about you?"

"I don't know. She could keep a secret when she wanted to, but they were close. She used to say he was like a part of herself. But for her, it was just sisterly. I don't know if she knew . . . the way he was about her. She never felt like her parents were really there for him, so she thought she had to be. She protected him. When he was little, she did his homework."

"When he got older . . . ," I prompt.

"I don't know. She introduced him to her friends. She loaned him her car." The mention of the car is a reminder; he stops talking, staring at the wall.

"Russell . . . those hours between when Allison left work, and when . . ." I stop and word it carefully. "When the neighbors say she got home. Do you know where she was?"

He shakes his head. "She was supposed to meet me for dinner. She never showed up. I called. She didn't answer."

"Did you leave a message?"

"Yeah, I . . ." He stares at me. "That means they know about me, doesn't it."

"What did you say?"

"Something like, I'm at the restaurant. Where the hell are you?" He grips the back of his chair. "I was pissed. I think I said, 'Who are you with?'" Swallowing, he closes his eyes. "Oh God. I said, 'Who the fuck are you with?'"

"You called from the restaurant. Did you say your name?"

"I don't think so. So they don't know who it is . . ."

"But they know you exist." I go over to him and lay my hand gently on his arm. "I think it's time you talked to the police."

"I know," he says. "I'm not looking forward to it."

"They're trying to figure out where she was those missing hours. It could be important."

"All I can tell them is she wasn't with me. So where was she?" We stare at each other. "You know where I'd start, if I were the one asking? I'd start with Peter."

I look away. He sounds jealous of Peter. I'm starting with the morphine in her bloodstream. I'm starting with the heroin nestled behind her bed.

"All right." He sighs. "You know these guys, the cops, right? Will you come with me?"

I hesitate. I have no idea whether my presence will help or harm him. I think, *It's the story. Follow the story.* "Sure," I say. "I'd be happy to." I think of what Morris said the first day, that they'd be looking for the boyfriend. Here he is, making this story so easy for me, a present in my lap.

One thing I know, for Russell Freeland, it only gets harder from here.

While Russell is with the cops, I make phone calls. First the newsroom to prepare them. Then the family. The mother leaves me in silence a few moments after I tell her. "All right," she says finally. "Here's what I want you to say. Are you ready to take it down?"

"Ready." I tuck the phone under my chin and prop my notebook on the metal box.

She speaks slowly, letting me get every word. "While we have no reason to consider this young man a suspect, we have confidence that the police . . ." She pauses. "What do you think? Something general like, police are doing everything they can? Or something focused on him. Police will . . . no. How about, we're sure he'll help the police in any way he can."

"Do you consider him a suspect?"

She sighs. "Don't write this down, Olivia, but I'll tell you. It makes me suspicious that he waited so long to say something. But if I accuse him, I might sound racist."

"Yes."

"And there's really no reason, other than his silence, to think he could have done it."

"Yes."

"So let's go with the general statement for now, don't you think?"

I nod into the phone, taking it all down.

"And could you add something about how we're sorry they felt they had to keep this relationship a secret?"

"Yes, ma'am," I say. "I'll put that in."

"Thanks, dear," she says.

After I hang up, I read over my notes. Tailor-made quotes, coming right up. There's a quality to that woman that I admire, even as I begin to despise her.

I'm sitting on the bench outside homicide, idly paging through my notebook, my eyelids heavy with exhaustion. The story is written, except for a comment from the police, which I'm unlikely to get at this hour. They cleared space for me on the front page by cutting one of Evan's Satanist stories.

Sergeant Morris comes out and crooks his finger at me. I follow him a little ways down the hall, and he puts his arm around my shoulders. We keep walking toward the exit. "Thanks for bringing him in," he says. "You can go home now."

"I'm waiting for a comment from you guys."

"It's too late for that," he says. "Tomorrow."

"Tomorrow it'll be all over the TV." I plant my feet, and he turns to face me.

"You don't have to say it," he says. "We owe you one. So we'll talk to you first."

"Promise?"

He laughs. "Promise."

"How long are you keeping him?"

He shrugs. "We're not charging him or anything. Just talking."

"Is he a suspect?"

He sighs, rolling his eyes up to the ceiling as he recites, "We're following all possible leads."

"Off the record. Is Russell a suspect?"

"Olivia . . ."

"Is he a suspect?"

He looks at me hard. I open my mouth. Nothing comes out. "What do *you* think?" he says. Then he turns and begins his slow progression back down the hall. "He's no murderer!" I want to shout after him. I don't. I picture Russell Freeland waiting by the phone, heart in his throat, asking himself where she was, who it was this time. Everyone keeps telling me any woman could be a victim. What does it take to make a murderer of any man?

13

Last night when I got home, Hannah was asleep on the couch in front of the television. The light on the answering machine was blinking and when I played it I heard David, Carl, and Peter one by one asking me to call them back. Carl mentioned he'd seen me on television, his voice warm with admiration. I didn't call any of them. I covered Hannah with a blanket and put the tape of Allison Avery in the VCR. With the sound turned down low I watched it over and over, pausing at various points to examine her expressions, as though each smile, each frown, were a possible answer to all the questions I wanted to ask.

When Hannah stirred and said my name I turned the tape off and we both went to bed. I don't know what Hannah dreamed about. All night I kept waking up in the dark hot room with no idea where I was, my heart racing, my body as heavy against my damp sheet as if I'd been drugged.

This morning I drank two cups of coffee and stood in the shower for twenty minutes. Despite my three trips to the newsroom coffeepot my head still buzzes with exhaustion. I've called Peter and David. I'm meeting Peter Friday night. I'm seeing David Saturday. I'm putting off returning the call from Carl.

The police, of course, aren't holding Russell, and all Lieutenant Nash will give me is that he isn't, at this time, considered a suspect. I write that down: *at this time*. I couldn't find Morris. Russell isn't at work, and when I call the Freeland house I get his father. "Already," he tells me. "Already we're getting the calls."

"I'm so sorry."

"Stick to your own kind. And that's the mildest of it."

"I'm sorry," I say. "Is Russell there?"

"My son has spoken to you enough already, Miss Dale. He has nothing further to impart."

"But he came to me in the first place," I say. "Are you sure he doesn't . . ."

"He has nothing more to say," the Reverend Freeland says. "Not even to you. I realize that this is your story, but Russell, Miss Dale, is *my* son."

I write those words in my notebook. *Your* story. *My* son. I'd like to hurl the notebook across the room, watch it slap against the wall, all the heads in the newsroom turning to look in my direction with the same motion, the same curious eyes. Russell Freeland is starting to look like a dead end. I need something more. I am starved for information.

I keep thinking about all those tapes in the dead girl's apartment, stacked precariously on the table and the floor. I need to see more of them.

Angela is not at work when I call, so I try her apartment, hoping that she's home. She answers on the fourth ring. I ask her how she is, and murmur sympathetically when she says in a small voice that she guesses she's okay. Then I tell her that I hate to bother her, but I think I lost an earring at Allison's apartment. There is a silence when I'm through speaking. Then Angela says, "I don't think I can go back there today."

"That's fine," I say. "That's . . ." Perfect. "Can I just come and get the key from you? I'll bring it back. I'm sorry to bother you about this, but my mother gave me the earrings, so . . ."

"No, that's fine," she says. "Come on over."

Angela comes to the door in a terry cloth bathrobe. She's been in the shower recently, and her hair clings damply to her head. Her eyes are swollen, the skin beneath her nose chapped and red. She invites me in. When the door is shut I open my arms and she lays her head on my shoulder and lets out a long, shuddering breath. Over her shoulder I look around the living room. A pizza box is on the floor, dirty dishes stacked beside it. Papers and envelopes spill from the couch to the floor, and open photo albums lay on top of each other on the coffee table. Newspapers are strewn everywhere. The one on the couch is turned to the page with my story about the car. I can't quite read my byline from here, but I can recognize the shape of my name.

I pat her warm, damp back and she takes a deep breath. "I'm sorry I lied to you about Russell. I had promised her, and a promise is a promise."

"I understand."

She steps away and studies my face. "Do they think he did it?"

"Do you?"

She shakes her head decisively. "He loved her."

Yes, and isn't that his motive? I say, "I know. He's not a suspect."

"Good." She looks vaguely around the room. "I found some letters," she says, waving a crumpled tissue in the direction of the couch. "From when she went away to camp." I think she's telling me this to explain her emotional state. I wonder how many days she's spent like this. Her apartment, so neat when I first saw it, is starting to resemble mine in messiness. It's starting to resemble Allison's.

Angela drifts over to the couch and picks up one of the letters. "'There's a really cool girl in my cabin named Susie,'" she reads. "'She says she's already French-kissed three boys. She says it just takes practice.'" She laughs and folds the letter in half, then sinks down onto the couch. "She wrote, 'P.S. She's not as cool as you.' I guess she thought I'd be jealous."

If I could I would gather those letters up, take them home and pore over them at my desk. I'd like to put them in chronological order, use them to chart Allison's childhood, add them to the map I'm making of her life. This led to this led to this and that is why. Angela folds the letter again and presses it to her chest. I can't think of a way to take it from her.

"I saw your story about the car," she says. "Does it mean they're getting closer to finding them?"

"It helps," I say. "When they find them, the evidence in the car will help get a conviction."

"The cops think they still have her underwear," she says, her voice flat. "As a souvenir."

"They might have her wallet, too," I say. "If we're lucky it will get them caught."

Angela turns her face to me. "You're doing everything you can, aren't you?" she says. Her eyes well up.

I nod. A lump rises in my throat. I take a tissue from the coffee table and hand it to her. I ask her, as gently as I can, if I can have the key.

Alone in Allison's apartment, I move from room to room, turning on lights. Someone has been here and cleaned up. The furniture has been dusted, clothes and dishes put away, even the shoes in the foyer lined up in neat rows. I picture her mother here, kneeling on the floor putting pairs together. Silver boots. Pink sneakers. Red high-heeled sandals. It seems wrong that these things go on existing without her, as though all evidence of her life should have disappeared when she did. Now everything she owned is neat and organized, and the apartment feels like a museum, a historic home. I should be standing behind a red velvet rope, looking at a pair of glasses on the desk, slippers beside the bed, all those careful, eerie touches meant to suggest the person who lives here has only just stepped out of the room.

I walk in the bedroom and stop, clutching at the doorknob. Someone has cleaned it, just like the other rooms, but someone else has come after them and rifled through it. The dresser drawers are wedged open with bright pieces of fabric, as though the person were in too much of a hurry to fit the clothes back in. The bedclothes are rumpled, the mattress slightly askew, and a box of trinkets protrudes from underneath the bed. The wastebasket is empty. The papers on the desk have obviously been shifted since they were first stacked. The searcher didn't line them up properly before putting them back down. I don't know who it was—maybe the cops. Maybe Angela, Peter, Russell, or someone else, looking for some remembrance of Allison, looking for evidence of her misdeeds or theirs.

I check behind the headboard for the box. It's untouched. I pull it out and open it, touching the spoon, the needle, the foil with my fingertip. Then I close it and drop it inside my bag.

In the living room I find the videotapes stacked against the wall beside the television. Someone has put them in order, one through eleven. I run my finger down the stack. Two are missing. Five, the one I took, and nine. For a moment there is nothing I want more in the world than to know what is on that tape. I take number one off the top and put it in the VCR. For the next hour I sit watching tape after tape, the moments jumbling together in my mind.

Allison, wearing the pink wig and a short black dress, singing. She throws her head back and opens her arms wide to make room for the last enormous note, and then when she lifts her head again I can see it in her eyes, the triumph, the way her body tingles with the knowledge of her own power.

Allison and Angela sitting at the kitchen counter, smoking a joint and talking, with the long pauses and low voices of the very stoned. "I just have to be myself," Allison is saying. "I don't know how to be anything else."

Allison, onstage, beating out a rhythm with her hand on her guitar.

Allison, running her fingers through her hair.

Allison, laughing.

Allison. Allison. Allison.

The camera zooms in on Peter's face. He rolls his eyes, then puts a cigarette in his mouth and leans forward to light it.

Allison's voice says, "This is my baby brother, Peter. Isn't he adorable?" Peter's face fills the frame. He crosses his eyes and sticks out his tongue.

The camera shakes with Allison's laughter. "I'm teaching Peter to dance," her voice says. The picture bobbles as she sets the camera on the tripod and then she appears in the frame, holding out her hand to Peter. Peter shakes his head. "Come on," she says. "If you're going to the prom, you have to learn to dance."

"I do not," he says. "People don't dance this way at the prom."

"Come on," she says. "It'll be fun."

Peter sighs, and puts his hand in hers. I watch them dance, Allison leading, Allison singing, dee da da dee da da as they spin around the room. Peter joins in. Dee da da dee da da. They start spinning faster and faster, a blur of dark hair and smiling faces, until finally Allison collapses laughing on the couch, saying he's worn her out. He stands grinning at the camera. Then he holds out his hand to her. "One more dance?" he says.

She shakes her head.

"Please?" he says.

"All right," she says, and bounds up and into his arms. I watch them dance. I look at her hands clasped behind his neck, his hands on the small of her back. I see the way he's looking at her, and I know what it means. Russell was right. He whirls her around, and when they come to a stop he keeps on holding her. She laughs, and tries to step away, but he just tightens his arms around her waist. "Let go," she says, still laughing. She beats lightly on his shoulders with her fists. "Let me go, little brother."

He shakes his head and says nothing.

"Come on, Peter." She's not laughing anymore. "Let go of me. I know you're stronger than me. It's not funny."

He still doesn't speak, a strange smile frozen on his face. Allison begins to push as hard as she can against his shoulders. "Goddamnit," she says, breathing faster now with the effort. "Let go!" She throws all of her weight against the arms around her waist and in that moment he lets go of her and she stumbles back against the couch. I can't see her face anymore, just her torso and her thighs. "Jesus," she says. "Grow up."

Peter is still in the frame. He says nothing. A slow flush creeps up his neck and into his face, and he turns away like he's ashamed to look at her. "What is wrong with you?" she says, moving out of the frame so no part of her is visible anymore. Then the camera shuts off.

I sit for a moment watching the static on the screen. Whether he admitted it to himself I don't know, the desire that drove him to hold her like that. I don't know if now his sorrow is shaded with guilt. I don't know if the faint resemblance between me and that dead girl explains why he let me hold his hand at the funeral, why he kissed me that first night in the car.

There's one thing I do know.

I'm jealous.

I find Evan eating his lunch in front of the twelve o'clock news. When I walk in, Lydia McKenzie is promising surprising new developments in the Allison Avery murder case. "She's a little late, don't you think?" Evan nods at her serious face, his mouth full of sandwich.

"Unless they've got something else." A sick feeling rises in my stomach.

"What could they have that you don't have?" He pushes a bag of chips toward me.

"Nothing." I take a chip. "Sorry your story got bumped."

He shrugs. "Bishop wants us to go out with him after work." He glances at me, then looks back at the television. "To celebrate your big stories."

I watch him, trying to read in his face whether he's angry or jealous or mocking. His tone was neutral.

"It's coming on," he says.

We watch as one of the correspondents stands in front of 201 Poplar and relates the things everyone has already read in the paper. Cut to the Averys exiting the police station. Dr. Avery stops. A slight breeze lifts her blond hair away from her head like wings. Around her the shouted questions intensify. She calmly says, "I've given my statement to Olivia Dale. You can read it in the newspaper. That's all I'm going to say."

"Wow," Evan says, as we watch her walk away. "You're really the anointed one."

"Strange isn't it," I say. On-screen the correspondent's lines are almost word for word from the article I wrote. "She has a way of making me feel like we're in league together."

"For what?" Evan asks.

"I don't know," I say. "I'm trying to figure that out."

I find Dr. Gregerson standing in the hall outside his office, hands in his pockets. His mouth open a little, he's staring at nothing, and for a few moments I don't register in his view. Then he blinks, straightens up, and says, "Miss Dale? How can I help you?"

We sit in an exam room, the tools for a pelvic laid out on the table beside us. He tells me what he's already told the police, that Allison could somehow have gotten the keys to the med cart and stolen the morphine herself. Or Allison could have persuaded one of the nurses to do it for her. "We're forced to give everyone a lie detector test now," he says. "It's a real shame."

I think of Angela. She must top the list of suspects. I hope she passes that test.

The doctor says he never saw any signs that Allison was using. He says that it never occurred to him to wonder. Then he asks me, "If you already know all this, why hasn't it been in the paper?"

"I've had it in bits and pieces," I say vaguely. "I'm waiting."

He nods as though that makes sense. "I hope there's an explanation."

"So do I," I say.

Out in the hall, I put my notebook in my bag and shake his hand. Then I frown, as though a thought has just occurred to me. "Doctor," I say, "were you and Allison ever involved?"

He blanches. "What kind of question is that?"

"I'm sorry." I turn to go.

He touches my arm. "No," he says. "But I was very . . ." He searches for the word. "I was very fond . . ."

"I'm sorry," I say again.

When I was younger, scraggly-haired strangers with tattoos came to our church youth group to tell us they had had wild sex and done drugs and now they were reborn and sorry and here to tell us to keep going straight and true, take a bypass around that city of sin. They had done those things, though, tasted sin and survived to set it aside, and didn't that make them some kind of heroes?

If Allison Avery had lived, some day she might have had a husband who grinned when he said to the children, "Your mama had a wild youth." And she would have smiled and kept her secrets. But she died, and so in one version of her story she is stupid and reckless, she is a warning, a bad example.

I haven't written that version, and this is what I could have answered when the doctor asked me why.

This is America, land of rebels, land of puritans, land of hypocrites. I print that she did drugs, and Allison Avery is a bad girl come to a bad end.

I don't, and she stays what she is now. The perfect victim.

Bishop and Evan and I walk three abreast up the sidewalk to the M&O. I'm in the middle, my arms linked with theirs, and we're laughing. Bishop keeps calling me his "little girl," talking about how far I've come since the days when it made me nervous to approach somebody on the street with a question. At one point he bursts into a chorus of "Sunrise, Sunset."

Inside they insist on buying me a beer, and then Evan proposes a toast to the overpass, and then we toast Bryce for being so willing to let go of my hand. For the next two hours I rehearse my stories, my reaction to the break-in, my roll down the hill, my trip with Russell to the police station. I let them admire me. I don't tell them about swinging off the Averys' deck on a tree branch, Peter's arm around my waist. I don't tell them I'm thinking about going to the Lizard Lounge to talk to the people who might have known Allison, who sold her drugs or know who did.

When we say good night outside, Bishop hugs me and kisses me on the cheek. "You're a damn fine reporter," he says, his eyes a little misty. "I'm very proud."

Over his shoulder Evan rolls his eyes and grins. "Me too," he says. I hug him. "Just don't break your neck," he says, his breath warm against my ear.

I head back to my car, twirling my key chain on my finger and humming to myself. I'm as awake as if I had consumed an entire pot of coffee, my head buzzing and my cheeks flushed. I feel like I'm about to burst out of my skin. "Allison, Allison," I say under my breath. I'm going to go back to that bar, and maybe the people there will tell me what turn in her life took her to the place where I first saw her.

I'll tell them I'm looking for the best feeling in the world, and see what I can find.

Before I get out of the car I glance at myself in the mirror. My own face shocks me, it's so at odds with the way I feel. I look haggard— pale and plain. There are dark circles under my eyes, and my hair is limp against my cheek. In my button-down shirt and knee-length skirt I look nothing like the sort of girl a guy would walk up to in a bar. I look nothing like Allison Avery.

I dump my bag out on the passenger seat. The pink wig is a splash of brilliant color against the beige upholstery. I pick it up and turn it over, running my fingers over the slick strands. Then I put the wig on, looking in the rearview mirror to adjust it on my head. I open one more button on my shirt and pull off my dark panty hose. In my bag I find a never-opened tube of red lipstick. I run it over my lips, paint my lashes with mascara. "Hello," I say to the unfamiliar girl in the mirror.

Inside the bar it's almost as dark as outside, and I stand in the doorway for a minute while my eyes adjust. Cigarette smoke sits in the air. I glance into the side room, where the pool table is. A guy with long hair tucked behind his ears is lining up a shot. His opponent stands with his hands folded around the top of the cue. I can see how thick the muscles of his arms are beneath his skin. He glances at me and lets his gaze linger, looking at the wig. Immediately I duck my head and look away. Then I force myself to stand up straight, to turn and look right back at him. He's not watching me anymore. He's watching the other guy sink a perfect shot.

There's no band tonight and the place is not crowded. A couple sits at the bar, a group of college-age guys in baseball caps spills out from two tables. As I walk past them I watch them from the corner of my eye. They're drinking beer, smoking Marlboros, and paying no attention to me. One of them tells a dirty joke and the rest laugh uproariously, smacking the table with their open palms.

At the bar I swing myself onto a stool and order a bourbon on the rocks. With the cold drink in my hand I turn from side to side. A big-haired girl sits at the side of the bar next to a boy whose curly hair is damp against the back of his neck. He leans in close to her and she laughs, spluttering into her beer. He puts his hand on her shoulder. Her whole body inclines toward him, her eyes raised to his.

Behind the bar the bartender washes glasses, his face set and businesslike. "Excuse me," I say, leaning on the bar. He comes toward me, wiping his hands on a rag. "Can I get you something else?" he says.

"Actually," I say, "I was just wondering if you knew Allison Avery."

"Allison Avery," he repeats, slowly. "Sounds familiar. What's she look like?"

"She's about my height," I say. "Dark hair. She might've worn a wig like this one."

For a moment he stares at me. Then he says, "I think I know who you mean. Singer, right? Real sexy voice?"

"That's her. Does she come here much?"

"Look." He lowers his voice. "Maybe you don't know this. She's dead." He takes my silence as shock and says, "I'm sorry. It's been all over the news."

I lower my voice to a conspiratorial murmur. "I know she's dead. I'm looking into it."

He raises his eyebrows. "You a cop?" He sounds skeptical.

I look at him, saying nothing. "Can you just tell me if anyone else in here would know her?"

Studying the faces, he says he's not sure. "I don't think she's friends with any of these guys," he says. "They might know who she is."

I thank him and he goes back to washing glasses. I turn on my stool and lean back on the bar with my elbows, scanning the room. The stage is empty except for a tall stool and a microphone stand. She could have been there, propped on the stool, laughing into the microphone she held close to her lips. I look at the guys playing pool, the guys getting louder and louder at the table. Any of them could have sold her drugs. Maybe the long-haired guy leaning down to sink the eight ball had a crush on her and she turned him down. Maybe his friend thought she was a rich girl and he could scare her into paying him more, came up behind her and wrapped that big bicep around her throat. Maybe he knocked her to the ground with one of those powerful hands. The guys laughing at the table look like harmless college kids. They could have meant to play a prank on her. She could have gotten frightened and scratched one of them, and he hit her, and the whole thing turned on that moment, a second blow following that first the way one drink leads to another. As

I watch them now they urge each other on, one of them shouting, "One more round!"

Even the couple at the bar could be the ones. Out of the corner of my eye I watch them come together to kiss, opening their mouths wide, his hand sliding up her side to the curve of her breast.

"You look kinda familiar," a male voice says. "Do I know you?"

I turn to see the man from the pool table beside me, one of his thick arms resting on the bar. He has small eyes under bushy black eyebrows, a nose that looks like it's been broken. "Maybe," I say. "You might." I take a sip of my drink. The bourbon is warm in my throat.

"I think I do," he says. "I think I've seen you here before." He snaps his fingers and points one at me. "I danced with you once."

I look him up and down. It's dark in here and the wig hangs over my eyes. I think it's the wig he recognizes, that he danced with Allison, held her close. He might be the one who knows. "That's right," I say.

"I'm Vance," he says. "I like that wig. It's different."

"Thanks," I say. I set my glass down on the bar, letting my fingers hover just above his arm. "I remember those biceps," I say.

He grins and flexes his arm for me. The muscle pops out obediently. "Go ahead and touch it," he says. "Girls always want to."

I lift my hand and run my fingers along the muscle. It's firm, and his skin is taut and warm. It doesn't give beneath the pressure from my fingers. I wrap my whole hand around it and squeeze.

"Hard as a rock," he says, and I let go. He raises his hand to signal the bartender. "Can I get you another drink?"

"I was hoping for something a little stronger." I raise my eyebrows and smile at him.

"Ah," he says, nodding. "I know just what you mean." He leans in close and lowers his voice. "Let's take a trip to the parking lot," he says. "I've got just the thing in my truck."

As we walk through the bar, past the college boys, he puts his hand in the small of my back. "Jerome," he says to his buddy, who's playing pool with one of the boys now. "I'll be right back." Jerome lifts his head, looks me up and down, and grins. "Sure you will," he says.

He drives a truck with an oversized cab, jacked up on huge tires. He walks with me around to the passenger side and holds the door open for me. I stare up at the black leather seat, thinking maybe this isn't such a good idea. "Go on," he says. "Climb in."

When I'm sitting, he shuts the door, and goes around to his side. He's got a cross hanging off the rearview mirror. The cab is immaculate, no trash on the floor and just a baseball cap sitting on the seat. He swings himself in and shuts the door. Then he sinks back into the seat. "Like my truck?" he asks.

I nod, staring out the windshield at the dark parking lot. I glance at my door to make sure it's still unlocked. Casually, I rest my hand on the door handle.

"Let's see," he says under his breath. "'Scuse me." He leans across me to open the glove compartment. His arm brushes against my knee. His head is inches from my breast. I press my body back into the seat. He's whistling through his teeth, searching through the compartment. Now his arm is almost resting on my thigh. "It's in here somewhere," he says. I don't know what he's going to pull out of there. If I'm lucky it will be a small foil package. If I'm unlucky, it will be a knife, or a gun. I'm trying to breathe normally, keep my body from touching his.

"Here we go," he says. He straightens up. In his hand is a slender white joint.

"Marijuana?" I say. My voice is heavy with disappointment. "Don't you have anything else?"

He lowers his hand, frowning. "Like what?"

"Like heroin," I say.

He laughs. "Oh, girl, I don't do that stuff."

"I was just hoping."

"You don't look like a junkie," he says.

"I'm not." I turn my face to look out the window.

"What are you then, a cop or something?"

"No," I say. I must not sound convincing. He turns on the light and takes my chin in his hand, studying my face. "I don't think I know you after all," he says finally. "I thought you were a different girl."

"I'm sorry," I say. I push open the heavy door and jump down from the cab. Walking away, I pull the wig from my head and run my hand through my own damp hair. "A totally different girl," he yells after me. I don't turn around. I wipe the lipstick off with the back of my hand.

In my car I sit and watch him climb out of his truck and walk back to the bar, shaking his head. His hands are jammed down into the pockets of his jeans, and even from here I can see the outline of his triceps. When he opens the door to the bar a burst of laughter explodes into the parking lot, cut off sharp when the door shuts again behind him. Every turn I take just brings me to a dead end. It's like I'm traveling through a maze, the place where she died both the beginning and the end. She runs ahead of me, calling catch me if you can.

David finds me sexy in the wig. When I walk in his front door carrying it in my hand, he looks me up and down and says, "Have you been to a costume party?"

"I was undercover," I say in a teasing tone so he'll think I'm joking. I put the wig back on to show him, and he walks around me like I'm a car he's thinking of buying, running his fingers lightly across the middle of my back. "I like it," he says in my ear, then wraps his arms tightly around me. "Hey you," he murmurs. "Looking for a good time?"

"I don't even know you," I say.

"Want to?" he asks.

He leads me into the bedroom, where he takes everything off me but the wig.

❧

In the middle of the night, I wake up. The place is quiet, and when the air conditioner starts up it seems to roar like a jet engine. Even David's breathing seems too loud. I can't sleep anymore and I wonder what I've been dreaming. A faint light comes in the window, and I can make out that the closet door is open. When I look at it, my conviction that someone is in it is as strong as it ever was when I was a child. I sit up and stare at it, telling myself that it's empty. I crawl to the edge of the bed, trying not to disturb David, and reach out to push some shirts aside. Nothing but swaying clothes, shoes in a neat row. I ease back under the covers and pull the sheets to my nose, but my stomach still burns with stupid fear.

I get out of bed, and go to the closet, throwing the clothes to either side. I see nothing, but it's a walk-in closet, and someone could still be standing behind the coats all the way at the back. On hands and knees I crawl to the back of the closet, the heavy coats draped around my head. My hands find a stray belt, a pair of running shoes, then the back wall. The wall is cool and I press my face against it, remembering when I thought if I went into the back of my closet enough times I might eventually find a door. I always went looking for a way out when something frightened me. One night when I was nine and home alone, the phone rang and a man's deep voice asked for my mother. I said, as I had been taught, that she was in the shower. "Go get her, then," the man said, and when I said I didn't want to bother her and asked if I could take a message, he took a deep breath and said, "Do you want me to rape your mother?"

"No," I whispered. I was shot through with terror, the kind that turns your body cold.

He laughed and said, "I know where you live."

I dropped the phone and ran. When my mother came home she found me shaking at the back of the closet.

I can still hear it, the arrow in that disembodied voice, how much he hated me.

I close my eyes, and the thought flashes through my head: *The only thing we have to fear is fear itself.* It almost makes me laugh.

A hand touches my back.

I scream and scream. Arms wrap around my waist and haul me backward, and I fall against a body, still screaming. "Olivia, for God's sake," David shouts. "It's me. It's me."

I sit up. My pulse is pounding so hard inside my neck I can feel the skin above it is moving. "You scared me," I say.

"No shit," he says, running his hand up my arm. "What's the matter with you?"

"I don't know," I say. "I'm an idiot."

"Poor baby," he says. "Did you have a bad dream?" He takes me in his arms—and I have to put it that way, because when he wraps his six-foot-three self around my five-foot-two body, that's how I feel—taken, enclosed, held somewhere between security and fear.

14

For the thirty-fifth day in a row the temperature was above ninety degrees. Two old ladies were found dead in their apartments yesterday. I wrote the story this morning. Already this summer six people have died from the heat.

I'm waiting for Peter outside the Four Corners, fanning my face with my hand. It's been a long and frustrating day. I can't keep Allison on the front page. Forensic evidence has all but eliminated Russell Freeland as a suspect. I couldn't reach him for a quote and space was tight, so a small story is running on an inside page. Only suspects and murderers get front-page coverage, and often even murder's not enough.

Peter emerges from the restaurant, saying good-bye over his shoulder to someone inside. He's wearing his busboy outfit, a white button-down shirt tucked into black pants. He's got the sleeves rolled up to his elbows and his hair is mussed, his eyes are heavy-lidded with exhaustion. "I can't believe how hot it is," he says when he sees me waiting on the sidewalk. "It makes me want to lie down where I am and go to sleep. I read in the paper today some old lady died."

"There's been a couple," I say. "Old people with no air-conditioning."

"You wrote that story," he says. "It's weird to see your name in the paper."

"Wasn't much to it. I just talked to the cop on the phone." He's not really listening, pulling his shirt out of his pants and unbuttoning it. Underneath he's wearing a white T-shirt.

"Where are we going?" I ask him.

"Where my sister went. Isn't that what you said you wanted?" He shrugs out of the button-down and balls it up in his hand. "My car's just up the street."

When we get to his car, Peter opens the passenger-side door for me and grins, as though this is a trick he's just learned. His car smells of smoke and faintly of sweat. I glance in the back. The seat is covered with cassette tapes. Ratty gym shorts and a pair of old running shoes are on the floor. He gets in. "Sorry about the mess," he says. When he starts the car, the radio blares. "Shit," he says, switching it off quickly. "Sorry."

He pulls the car out onto the road. "So why do you want to do this?"

"I want to talk to people who knew her," I say. "I'm hoping someone can help us find a connection the police might have missed."

"You mean like someone who knows who killed her?" He swallows. "I thought the cops said it was a stranger killing."

"It probably was, Peter," I say. "I just want to check it out."

"I guess that can't hurt," he says as we come to a stop at a red light. "The police haven't found a goddamn thing." His voice fills with fury and he says again, "Not a goddamn thing," and drives his fist into the steering wheel.

I don't say anything. He lets out a long breath. Then the light changes and we pull on through. I watch the streetlights go by outside the window, wondering if anyone loves me as much as Peter loves his dead and buried sister.

"Are we going to the Lizard Lounge?" I ask, and when he nods I say, "I've heard a lot of drugs move through there."

He gives me a wary glance. "Are you still thinking about that?"

I reach inside my bag and pull out the box, holding it out to him in my palm. He looks down at it, then back at the road, gripping the steering wheel hard. "Where did you get that?"

"You recognize it?" He gives me a tight nod. All he says is, "It's Allison's," but something about his face tells me he knows what's inside. "You lied to me before about the heroin, didn't you?" I say.

"It's weird the way you say 'heroin,'" he says. "Her-o-in. So formal. Say junk. Smack."

"Junk," I say. "Smack. You lied to me."

"Yeah," he says, his voice heavy with sarcasm. "How'd you know?"

I open the box to show him the needle, the spoon and the tiny foil package nestled inside. He takes it from me and touches the needle with one finger, his face gone pale. "You know what this is, don't you?" I say.

"Of course," he mutters. He doesn't look at me. "Where was it?"

"Your sister's apartment," I say. "I told you."

I nod, and he lets out an aggrieved sigh. "Where?"

"That was you, wasn't it? You searched her room."

He doesn't answer. He runs his finger over the spoon and I wonder what he's thinking, if he ever saw his sister use it. "Why did you take it?"

I hesitate. "I didn't think your mom should be the one to find it."

"Thanks." He shoots me a grateful smile.

It gives me a pang of guilt, the way he believes whatever I say. "What can you tell me about it?" I ask him gently.

Shrugging, he lifts the foil package from the box and then drops it back in again. "Whatever you want to know," he says. "I'll tell you whatever you want to know."

"Can you show me where this came from?" I ask. "I want to meet the people you and your sister knew."

He stares at me as though this is not what he expected me to say. Then he nods, slowly. He smiles his transforming smile at me, and I wonder if I'm ever going to see it when his eyes aren't wet with tears. He stops the car at another light, and with his free hand he reaches for the back of my head and pulls me to him to press his lips hard to mine. "Thank you," he says, kissing me again and again. "Thank you."

I'm almost laughing, trying to say "You're welcome," though I'm not sure what he's thanking me for. Maybe for keeping his sister's secrets. Maybe for wanting to know what they were. By the time he lets me go I'm dizzy. My hand shakes when I reach for the box. Peter doesn't let go. "Maybe I should keep this," he says.

"I don't think so," I say. "What if your mother catches you with it?"

"I guess you're right." He lets me lift it out of his hand. "She sometimes searches my room," he says, and laughs without humor. "I even have to hide my cigarettes." While I tuck the box back inside my bag he lights a cigarette. I notice his hands are shaking, too.

The light turns to green, and Peter whips a U-turn in front of the oncoming cars. "Where are we going?" I say, bracing myself against the dash.

"You don't want to go to the Lizard Lounge," Peter says. "I'll take you where you really want to go."

A guy opens the door wearing nothing but a pair of shorts. He's pale and so thin that his ribs protrude. I have an urge to run my fingers along the first ridge of bone. He looks at me and his face is blank with confusion, his eyes small and rimmed with red. "Hi," he says. His face is familiar. He was there the night I took Peter home from that bar.

"Hi, Nate," Peter says, stepping up beside me.

Nate's face clears. "Mr. Avery," he says, offering him his hand. "How are ya, sir? Come in, come in." He moves aside so we can step into the apartment. We're standing in an entryway, carpeted in brown, with an open litter box in one corner. Ahead of us a long hall stretches away. When the door is closed Nate looks us up and down, smiling. "Hey," he says, pointing at me. "Friend of Allison's?" As her name leaves his mouth, he shoots a worried look at Peter.

"Olivia," I say to Nate, holding out my hand. Instead of shaking it he lifts it to his lips and leaves a wet kiss on my skin.

"Charmed," he says. Then he throws his arm around Peter's shoulders, still holding my fingers loosely in his other hand. "Pete, my good man," he crows. "Why haven't you brought this lovely young lady around before?" Peter's not looking at Nate, but staring down the hall. Inside his pockets his hands are balled into fists. "I know this little boy has a way with the ladies," Nate says to me in a confidential tone. "But wouldn't you prefer a man?"

I shrug. "I don't know any," I say. Nate throws back his head and roars with approving laughter. "Let's go in," he says. "The rest of the gang is in the living room."

We walk down the long empty hall to a nearly silent room. Six or seven people recline against cushions on the floor. I recognize two others from that night—Steve, who hails Peter, and the girl he was tormenting. She's sitting in a corner, her head back against the wall and her eyes closed. Every face in the room is flushed an unhealthy red, and then I notice that even the walls are glowing that same color. At first I think this is a trick my eyes are playing. Then Nate says, "You like my new bulbs?" and points at a lamp in the corner. It's a relief to see that the red light is real, and not some fever vision.

There are only three pieces of furniture, an armchair, a tiny sagging sofa, and a rickety coffee table. On the tiny couch is an electric guitar, a four-track on the coffee table. Nate sees me looking at it. "I just recorded something," he says, "Y'all want to hear it?"

"Sure." I stand looking around while Nate busies himself hooking the four-track up to his stereo. His walls are hung with rock and roll posters and glossy ads he's cut from magazines, most of them featuring the same thin, stringy-haired model. Peter sits on the couch. I perch on the edge of the ratty armchair and look around. There's a reddish-brown stain toward the bottom of one wall. "What is that?" I point at it.

"Puke," Nate says. "I don't clean if off as a reminder not to do speedballs."

"What's a speedball?" I wrap my arms around my stomach and lean forward, trying not to look at the stain. I wonder how much time Allison spent in this apartment, if she laughed or looked away when she first saw that mark on the wall.

"Cocaine and heroin," Peter says. I shoot him a look. He's staring at a Rolling Stones poster, his face a blank.

Nate nods. "Almost killed me," he says, and laughs. "It's ready." He sits on the couch beside Peter and presses play.

For a moment there's no sound but the faint whirring of tape casters. Nate closes his eyes, settling back against the couch. A guitar starts up, playing chords with the distortion turned up high, and then Nate's voice comes in, droning lyrics I can't make out. What seems to be the chorus starts, and Nate sings along with himself: "Oh, baby, I've been livin' on the edge, drivin' all night just to see you." Then the voice stops, and I hear the unmistakable gurgle of a bong hit.

Nate opens his eyes. "Isn't that cool?" he says. "I got the idea right before you came." He nods at me. He nods all the time, like a doll whose head is loose in its socket.

"It's really cool," I say. A pleased smile spreads across his face. It makes me sad. The sound of another bong hit comes out of the speakers, and he points at the stereo, grinning at me.

"Are you playing that shit again?" Steve groans from the floor. He clambers to his feet and comes over to stand behind my chair, leaning so heavily against it that I tilt backward, looking up into his face. His features are thick and droopy, as though the pull of gravity is stronger on him than the rest of us. "I know you," he says to me. "You knew . . ." He shoots a look at Peter and doesn't finish the sentence.

"Allison," Peter says sharply. "You can say it."

"How did you know her?" I ask, looking at Nate.

"College," Nate says. "We had a couple classes together. Chemistry." He gives a barking laugh. "I sucked at it. She let me copy her notes. She's cool." He frowns. "She was cool," he says softly. Then he touches Peter's arm. "I'm sorry."

"Goddamnit," Peter bursts out, jumping to his feet. "Stop fucking apologizing."

"I'm . . . ," Nate starts. He stops, uncertain. Peter strides out of the room. I hear a door slam.

"Shit," Steve says under his breath.

With some effort, because Steve's weight is still pulling the chair backward, I slide forward and get to my feet. Nate watches me, saying nothing, and I head to the back of the room and into the kitchen, looking for a closed door. When I see it, I go to it and knock. There's no response. "Peter, it's me," I say. "Can I come in?" I hear his voice on the other side, though I don't know what he's said. I open the door.

It's the bathroom, and Peter is sitting on the closed toilet, his arms wrapped around his stomach, rocking back and forth.

"Are you okay?" I say, because that's what you ask, even when you know the answer is no.

"I need something," he whispers. "I need something bad."

I go in and crouch beside him, my hand on his warm thigh. "What do you need?"

He runs his hand over my head, smoothing back my hair. Then he brings his hand around to my face, cupping my cheek. He's staring into my face like he's going to learn something there, and then in one motion he brings his other hand to my other cheek and slides forward off the toilet so that he's kneeling with me on the floor. Before I can think, he's kissing me, his hands are inside my shirt, and there's such urgency in him I can't help but feel it too, like an ache in the pit of my stomach, a buzzing in my skin.

"You'll do it, won't you?" he murmurs in my ear, and I lean back, frowning. His hand still cups my breast. "Won't you?" he asks, his voice imploring, and I don't say anything because I'm not sure what the answer is. Then he says, "I want you to do it too," and I realize he's not talking about sex.

"Do what?" I say. I pull on his arm to slide his hand out from under my shirt.

"Her-o-in," he says in a voice that suggests I should have known exactly what he meant.

"You want me to do heroin?" I say. I put my hand on his shoulder and push myself up to a standing position.

"Yeah," he says, standing too. "What else did we come here for?" We stand in this dirty bathroom staring at each other, and I wonder if this is like the first time he kissed me, if he sees something in my face I didn't even know was there. "What else?" I repeat stupidly.

"Don't you know?" he says, and then there's a knock at the door. "Peter?" Nate's voice says. "Olivia? Are you guys okay in there?"

Peter steps around me and whips open the door. Nate is standing there, his hand raised to knock again, his mouth a perfect O of surprise. "Listen, Nate," Peter says. "We'll be okay. But we'd like something to take our minds off it, you know?"

"I've got nothing, man," Nate says, spreading his fingers wide.

"We have some," Peter says. "Can you do the honors?"

"Yeah, sure, of course. Anything I can do to help," Nate says. "Jesus. All you gotta do is ask, you know that."

Nate and Peter leave the room, and I follow, because I don't know what else to do. I feel responsible for what he's about to do. I'm the one who showed him Allison's stash. I'm the one who asked him to bring me here to see her friends. Maybe he thinks when that heroin hits his brain he won't even remember her, and he can imagine nothing better than to forget her now.

Nate leads us into his bedroom, away, he says, "from the rest of those greedy fuckers." This room too is hung with posters and almost bare of furniture, just a little table next to a double bed in a surprisingly ornate wooden frame. Peter reaches for my bag and I let him have it. From the box he takes a small foil package.

Peter looks at me, hesitating.

"If this is the same stuff I had," Nate says. "It's pristine."

I rock back and forth a little on the bed. I keep swallowing, as though something is lodged in my throat. Unsure where to fix my gaze, I let my eyes drift from poster to poster. Only one is in a frame. I keep reading it over and over. Syd Barrett. The Madcap Laughs. Is this what I came here for, to find out what it feels like, to know what the dead girl knew? Being here is beginning to feel like a dream, like I can do anything because in the morning I'll blink myself awake and none of this will matter.

Nate puts some of the heroin in a metal spoon and heats it over a candle flame. I watch it turn to liquid amber. I watch him draw the liquid into a syringe and turn to Peter. Nate is smiling, heavy-lidded with desire and anticipation. "You want to go first?" he asks Peter.

Peter shakes his head. "Her first," he says. He fixes his gaze on me.

"Which arm?" Nate asks me, like a nurse giving a vaccine. I extend my right, then change my mind and hold out my left. I look down at my arm and imagine that I can see the pulse fluttering wildly inside my wrist, like a trapped moth. I resist the urge to switch arms again. Carefully, Nate sets the syringe down on the bedside table and wraps a black belt around my upper arm. He pulls it, tighter than any blood pressure cuff, and I watch a large vein rise to the surface of my skin. Nausea rises in my throat, and I look up to see Peter staring at my arm, his face white and sick.

Nate leans over and picks up the syringe, then crouches down in front of me, balanced on his toes. A little frown of concentration appears between his eyes. He starts to bring the needle to my arm, then hesitates, looking up at me. "First time?" he asks, and I nod. "This is going to feel like nothing you've felt before," he says in a teacher's calm and patient tone. "The important thing is to relax and enjoy it. It's the greatest feeling in the world." He turns his eyes to my arm again. "Like nothing you've felt before."

My heart pounds inside my ears. I think of Allison's face, her laugh, her enormous, aching voice. When I do this, in at least one way we will be the same.

"Clench your fist," Nate says. "That's right." Slowly he moves the syringe closer to my arm. I close my eyes and feel the prick of the needle entering my vein. I gasp. I think I feel my whole body melting. I see Allison again, not her face, but her body, her body like a broken doll.

I jerk my arm away, clamping my mouth shut to keep in a scream.

Nate rocks back on his heels. "Shit," he says calmly. "I didn't even touch you yet."

There is a silence. I stare at my unmarked arm, the purple vein plump and ready. "I . . . I," I say. I feel the blood rushing to my face, flushing my cheeks.

"It's natural to be nervous," Nate says. "I'll try again." He leans toward me. I take a deep breath, trying to calm myself. The needle comes closer. I watch, and I know I won't be able to let him put it in my vein.

I am a coward, and that is why I never get what I want.

"You know what?" I say. With my right hand, I pull at the belt, trying to undo it. It just gets tighter. I keep my eyes on my arm, afraid to look at Peter, afraid I'll see disappointment in his eyes. "I changed my mind."

"Oh," Nate says. He looks confused.

"So you go ahead," I say.

"But . . . ," he says.

"You go ahead," I say again firmly. I hold out my arm. "Take this off."

"All right." He seems cheerful again. He undoes the belt. I rub at the red mark left around my arm. Then I turn my eyes to Peter. His face is drawn. He closes his eyes and I notice that his hands are shaking. "Nate," he says, keeping his eyes closed. "I'm next."

Nate sighs. "I know it," he says. He lifts the belt to Peter's arm.

"Peter, don't." It's out before I meant to say it. He looks at me, his eyes gone dead. "We can't. This is stupid. I've got to tell the cops."

"Jesus," Nate says.

"Don't do it," I say, staring at Peter, and this time it sounds like a threat. "I mean it. I'll call your mother."

Peter closes his eyes. He looks beaten. "Fuck," he says under his breath.

"Look, this is too much controversy for me," Nate says. "I've got a joint you can smoke." He fishes a plastic bag out of his pocket and pulls a joint from it. "Wouldn't want you guys to feel left out."

Peter says nothing else to me. We sit pressed together on the bed, passing the joint back and forth, while Nate tightens the belt around his own arm. We watch Nate slip the needle under his skin. After a moment, Nate gets up and stumbles out of the room. We are silent. Nate returns, holding a clear plastic bowl. He sits, then calmly vomits into the bowl and sets it on the ground. I try not to look, feeling my throat constrict. "How's it feel?" Peter asks him.

Nate smiles, his head nodding gently. When he speaks, it's with a wheeze. Inside his blue eyes his pupils are tiny black dots. "Sorry," he says. "Just really high."

I keep my eyes trained on him, as though if I look at him hard enough I will catch some edge of the sensation he feels. I meant to feel it myself. Here I am again, just looking on.

We watch Nate float there for a while, then I take Peter's hand and stand up, and he stands too. Quietly, we file past the silent people in the red living room and let ourselves out.

Outside the apartment building the air is still and warm. A couple passes us, holding hands, the girl talking brightly about something, waving her free hand. Peter leans down and kisses me on the cheek. His cool lips feel good against my flushed skin. "What was that for?" I ask. "I thought you were angry."

"I was," he says. "But I know you were trying to look out for me. Allison was the same."

"She wouldn't let you?"

He shakes his head ruefully. "No one wants me to have any fun."

"I'm sorry."

"I wish everyone would stop saying that," he says. "Don't apologize to me again." He opens the car door. "You don't want to go home yet, do you? I feel like going for a ride."

The tension rushes from my body. I lean against the car for support. I am weak and frightened, and I'm glad he doesn't know it. "A ride sounds good," I say, and get in.

In the car, I'm half asleep, not paying attention to where we're going. When the car stops, I open my eyes. He's taken us to the crime scene. It seems inevitable that we should be here. Peter turns off the car and we sit and listen to the silence. He gets out, and after a moment I get out too. He's leaning against the front bumper, his arms folded across his chest. I walk over and lean back with him, his shoulder pressed to mine. "I know it's morbid to come here," he says. "I just keep thinking, this is the last place she was alive." He waves his hand. "Something here was the last thing she saw."

I can't think of anything to say. The image of her face on the television screen returns to me. Her dark hair slips across her cheek. Her lips move.

Peter turns toward me. I can feel him studying the side of my face. I don't move. "Olivia?" he says. He turns my name into a question.

I turn toward him. He searches my face, then reaches a hand up slow and brushes his fingers across my cheek. I'm holding my breath. "Eyelash," he says, and holds his fingers close to show me the lash resting there. "Make a wish." I close my eyes and blow the lash from his fingers. With my eyes still closed, I hear him say, "Your life stops." I open my eyes and watch him snap his fingers. "Just like that."

He looks terrified. I take his hand, locking my fingers with his. I want to throw myself open, feel everything as intensely as I can, the stars so bright out here where there are no lights, the air warm on my skin, the pressure of each of his fingers against mine. I could tell him the best you can hope for is these moments when you know it is you inside your skin. Your heart beats. You take a breath and warm air rushes into your lungs. There is no space your body cannot fill.

"Look how bright the stars are," I say.

He leans his head back. We are quiet. "Yes," he says. "Yes."

15

It's Saturday and I'm not supposed to be working. I snuck into the newsroom through the back door, because I knew if Peggy were here and she saw me she would turn me around and send me home. Luckily for me, another editor is on the desk. When I came in the room, he lifted his head from his computer screen just long enough to nod hello.

I feel sick to my stomach when I think about last night. Sitting at my computer, making phone calls, taking notes—these are balms to the painful memory of my own stupidity, these are the route back to control of my story and myself.

How Allison got the morphine is still a minor mystery. The lie detector tests are scheduled for next week. I've learned that the vial and the hypodermic were found in the trunk of the dead girl's car. Morris thinks that Allison gave herself a shot while she was locked in the trunk, knowing that pain was coming. I'm reluctant to accept this. She would have known that a high dose of morphine would impair her ability to fight. She would have known that it might kill her if her captors didn't. She would have been giving up.

Angela still claims to know nothing about the drugs, and though I couldn't say why, I believe her. I called Russell's house again, and to my surprise he called back to tell me he wasn't going to tell me anything more. He sounded weary, making a sad joke about going back to law school with firsthand experience with the law. They don't answer the phone anymore, he said, because of the media, but mainly because of the obscene phone calls, the threats. "I'm sorry," I said, for the thousandth time.

"I'm sorry too," he said.

I haven't called the Averys' house again. I don't want to talk to Peter, though I can't stop myself thinking about him.

Peter. I know him to be a strange and unstable person, too afraid of his mother, too much in love with his sister. Last night probably wasn't his first experience with heroin; he may not only have known about Allison's drug use all along, but have shared it with her. I don't want to believe it. I recognize my weakness when it comes to that boy. If I could find the root of it, I would pull it out and cut it into tiny pieces.

Perhaps they felt that way about Allison, the men who loved her. I write down their names. *Russell Freeland. Carl Fitzner. Peter Avery.* I add *Antonio Roberts.* This is the name of the man who tried to shoot his wife while I watched through the window. I add *Kenneth Obie.* This is the name of the man who put a bullet in his girlfriend Lucille Davis's head. I leave a blank line for the name of the unknown man who killed the prostitute Bernadette Smith.

I think about David, what he might do if he knew that I'd let Peter kiss me, that I'd let him touch my breast, that I'd not only let him but wanted him to.

One thing I know. Nothing kills like a man's love.

David stands in the center of the roof of the Peabody Hotel, calling after me, while I run laughing around the perimeter, as close to the edge as possible. "Why don't you catch me," I say, stopping in front of him, breathing hard. He looks like he doesn't want to play, but then he grins and lunges at me, arms out. I jump aside and dash back to the wall around the edge of the roof, leaning way out over it, just to see his eyes widen with fear for me.

"Come over here," I say. "It's a great view."

"I can see just fine from here," he says. "Please don't lean over the rail. You know it makes me nervous."

David is afraid of heights.

We've been to dinner downtown, where he told me all about his plans for the Allison Avery CD. "Gorgeous voice," he said over and over. "Such a pretty girl. So tragic. I wonder if I ever did meet her," he said. "You would think I would remember."

"Yes," I said. "Yes, you're right."

After dinner I coaxed him up here, which I can every once in a while, because I love the view, I love the little duck house, I love the way the air is thinner up here, breathable. Sometimes there are tourists up here, couples holding hands, loud clusters of drunken college kids. Tonight it's only me and David. I turn toward him and pose against the wall, arms out, head tilted. It's one of those nights when my whole body feels tingly, like there's magic in my fingertips and I could light the sky with one touch. "Come here," I say.

He shakes his head. "You come here."

"I want to kiss you under the stars."

"There's stars right here," he says, and folds his arms across his chest.

"Come on, David," I say. "You've got to confront your fears. Come to the edge and look over."

He shakes his head. I walk slowly toward him and he watches me warily. When I reach him I grab one arm and pull. His arms unfold, but he doesn't budge, bracing his weight against me. "No," he says.

I put my whole weight into pulling on his arm. He snatches his arm free and I fall, hard, on my tailbone. Sitting on the ground, my feet sprawled in front of me, I look up at him frowning over me. "You always do shit like this," he says. Then he launches into a recitation of my crimes, the time when I leaned so far over the railing in a movie theater balcony that he grabbed me, certain I would fall. The time I let my father bully him into hiking up to a cliff, where his knees locked and my father and I had to half carry him back down. There's more, but I stop listening, focusing my gaze on his legs, the soft brown hairs on his knees. "You're not even listening to me," he says. He sounds tired. "Olivia," he says. "Are you even listening to me?"

The thought of continuing this conversation exhausts me. I wish I could be transported out of here, that I could click my heels like Dorothy and find myself somewhere else.

"What are you hoping to accomplish?" he says. "Are you trying to make me mad? Are you trying to give me a heart attack? It would be easier to just break up with me, you know." He nudges me with his foot. "Olivia? Are you okay?"

I look up at him. His face is in shadow. "I'm just trying to have a little fun," I say.

"Well, I've had enough fun. I'm going home. Are you coming?"

"Don't go home. I'm not ready."

"You can come or not," he says. "I'm leaving."

We are both silent. From the duck house comes the sound of rustling feathers, the contented quacking of one of the ducks. On the street below the cars whoosh past. Someone laughs. A sweet smell, like flowers, rises on the air. David holds out his hand to me and when I take it he pulls me up to standing. He drops my hand then, and we look at each other, inches apart. "I'm not going home," I say.

"Suit yourself," he says. We both turn. He walks away. I walk to the railing and lean on it. There is the city, like any city, beautiful on a summer night with the lights shining through the warm air and the people moving languorously on the streets below, calling out to one another, extending their hands. An urge to jump runs through me, a sensation so physical it's hard not to let my body move. I feel as though jumping from this roof would not be suicide, but entering the city like a diver enters a pool, a fast and clean arrival in the center.

The door to the roof slams. David is gone, and it's a relief to me. He makes me feel guilty, and I'm tired of it, tired of my uncertainty and fear. I'm tired of myself. I tighten my grip on the metal rail. Somewhere down there is the woman who broke into my house, the man who killed Bernadette Smith, the person who left Allison Avery dead on the ground. The summer's murderers hide their darkness inside them as they walk outside with their neighbors, looking up at the stars.

Inside the hotel I go to the bathroom and pull Allison Avery's wig from my bag. I couldn't bring myself to let Nate slip that needle in my vein, but at least in this small way I can be, if not who she was, at least someone different from myself. In the mirror I adjust the wig on my head, tucking the strands of my own hair away. Then I call Evan on the pay phone. He'll meet me on Beale Street, he says, in half an hour.

In the daiquiri bar at the end of Beale I order a strawberry daiquiri that comes in a child's sand bucket with a green plastic shovel. I offer Evan a shovel full. He shakes his head. He can't stop frowning at my wig. "You're in a weird mood," he says.

"I'm in a good mood," I say. I lean in and kiss him on the cheek.

"Your mouth is so cold," he says.

I kiss him on the other cheek, warm as the air. Then I kiss him on the forehead.

"What's with all this kissing?" Evan says. "Somebody might get the wrong idea."

"Or the right idea," I say, and wink at him. What I like about Evan is I can touch him all night and we will both know it doesn't mean a thing.

"You're on fire tonight," Evan says. "I'm getting nervous. Where's David?"

"He went home," I say. "It's just you and me." I take his hand and we step off the curb and enter the crowd moving along the middle of the street. We pass two men wearing dusters, the long coats of cowboys, their faces reflections of each other. I turn to look at them. They walk on by in perfect unison, matching each other stride for stride, the hair on each head parted at exactly the same point. "Did you see that?"

"I know them," Evan says. "They're identical twins, but they tell people they're cousins."

I stop and look hard at him. "You're full of shit."

He holds up his hands. "I swear," he says, laughing. "It's the God's honest truth."

"Why would they do that?"

"Why do people do anything?" he says. "To fuck with other people."

"You can't trust anybody," I say. I hold up my shovel full of daiquiri and this time Evan leans in and slides some into his mouth. He straightens up, his mouth stained pink, and I reach out to wipe the syrup from his lips.

"Allison?" a voice says behind me.

I turn, feeling like I'm moving in slow motion, like this is a scene in a movie, and there is a man behind me who starts when he sees my face. "I'm sorry," he says. "I thought you were . . ."

"Allison Avery?"

"You know her?" he says. He's a tall man in a T-shirt and jeans tight enough to show the long muscles of his thighs.

"I know her," I say. Evan frowns. He digs through people's trash, but he doesn't like to lie. "How do you know her?"

"I took her out a few times," he says. "Once she showed up in a wig just like that one. Did you buy them together?"

I tell him yes. I tell him Allison called us the pink ladies.

He says Allison turned to him in a bar and asked if he knew the difference between Ring-Dings and Ding Dongs and that when he explained she hugged him and said he had won her a bet and gave him her phone number. He said she dragged him to a ballroom dance place, he and she were the only couple under fifty and she didn't know the dances but she worked up a sweat trying and let a couple of the old men lead her through the twists and turns of the rumba. Allison told him she'd once waded into the Mississippi, fully dressed, on a hot day. "Bet she just dipped her foot in, and even that's dangerous. That girl," he says, shaking his head. "She couldn't stop moving. At a restaurant once, I bet her twenty bucks she couldn't sit absolutely still for ten minutes. She tried sitting there with her feet planted, her hands folded on the table. Her eyes were darting around, her lips twitching. She started chewing the side of her mouth."

Without my noticing, Evan has moved a few steps away. He stands at an angle from me, looking hard into the crowd as though to pick out a face he knows.

The man is looking around, too. I know he's looking for Allison and I imagine that she walks up behind me, complaining about the line at the bathroom. "Is she with you?" he asks.

"No," I say. And then I blurt out, "She's dead."

His face registers horror, disbelief. "My God," he says. "How?"

I shake my head, pressing my lips together like I'm trying not to cry. Tears burn beneath my eyelids; who am I fooling, this man or myself? "Somebody abducted her, killed her," I say. "Didn't you see it in the paper?"

Aren't you reading my stories?

"I heard a woman was dead," he says. "Never heard the name." He sounds so earnest when he says he's sorry. He fumbles in his pocket and hands me a handkerchief. I'm surprised. Not many men still carry them, especially not men his age. It's soft, white cotton.

"I don't need this," I say.

"You're crying," he says.

"I am not," I start to say before I decide it's better just to dab at my eyes. "Thank you."

"Keep it," he says. He looks so helpless, sagging like an unstuffed scarecrow, all useless, dangling limbs.

I look at the handkerchief. "You're right," I say. "I am crying."

At Evan's side I turn back and look at the man, slumping like a broken thing inside the moving crowd. His lips shape the words *my God my God,* still moving as we slip into the crowd and walk away.

"What was that all about?" Evan says, jamming his hands in the pockets of his jeans. "Did you get anything?"

"Just character stuff. Nice enough guy. He gave me his handkerchief." I wave it in the air as proof.

"Why did you say you knew her?"

"It just popped out," I say. "At any rate, it got him talking."

"I don't know," he says.

"You don't know what?"

"I don't know," he says, not looking at me. "I don't know."

"You never know what might be helpful," I say. I throw my hands in the air. "Who can understand that, if not you?"

Music bursts from the club next to us when someone opens the door. Inside the people bob and dip, holding each other close. "Let's go in," I say, taking Evan's hand and pulling. "I feel like dancing."

"No more talking to strangers?" Evan says, hanging back.

"You know me," I say. "I never talk to strangers." I bat my eyes. "I'm very shy."

He grins. "All right, then."

Inside we sit at the bar and order two bourbons. "On the rocks," Evan says.

"Straight up," I say, and Evan shoots me a look, eyebrows raised. When the drinks come Evan says, "To the news," and we clink our glasses together. I watch the dancers out of the corner of my eye while Evan talks about the story he's working on. I catch a few words, "terrible . . . dead . . . police . . . scoop." I lift my glass and realize it's empty. The bartender brings me another and I smile at him and tip him two dollars. Then I glance across the bar and see a woman staring at me. I look away, trying to listen to Evan talking. "You know?" he says. "You know what I mean?"

"Yeah," I say. "Sure." A few minutes later I look sidelong to see if she's still watching me. She stares right at me. This time I meet her gaze. She just keeps watching. In the darkness I can barely make out her face, but I see her eyes. I feel them on me. Evan is saying, "Are you listening to me?" Everyone keeps asking me that.

"Excuse me," I say, slipping off the barstool and taking a step in her direction, my pulse pounding inside my ears. She is standing too, her fists clenched at her sides, ready to accuse me of something. She's looking right at me. She knows me. I take another step toward her and then I realize.

She is me. It's a mirror.

The room whirls around me and I put a hand on the stool for support. "Are you okay?" Evan says.

"Oh yeah." I flash him a smile. "Just going to the bathroom." I lift my hand from the stool and squeeze his arm. "Be right back." It's a long trip through the crowd. Inside I lean against the counter and splash cold water on my face, avoiding the sight of myself in the mirror.

Head down, I come barreling out of the bathroom and smack up against a man's chest. "Sorry," I say. I look up, and see Carl's face, flushed red. "Oh," I blurt.

He cups my shoulder in his hand. "Are you all right?" he says, his voice gentle.

"Fine," I say, taking a deep breath and stepping back away from him. He leaves his hand on my shoulder. "I didn't see you."

"I know," Carl says. He lifts his hand from my shoulder and rubs the hairs on the wig between his fingers. "You look beautiful," he says. His voice is still soft and sweet when he says, "Who are you here with?"

"My friend Evan," I say. "He's at the bar."

"Would he mind if we had a dance?" He smiles at me and holds out his hand.

"Of course not." I put my hand in his and let him pull me out to the dance floor. As we reach the center the song comes to an end. We stand for a moment, smiling awkwardly at each other, and then a slow song begins. Blushing, Carl shrugs and reaches for me, his large nervous hands on the small of my back. I rest my hands on his shoulders. I don't know where to look. Carl keeps his eyes fixed on mine, a tiny smile playing over his lips. I smile back, and he takes that as an invitation to pull me closer, so that I'm pressed against his chest and there's nothing to do but rest my cheek against his shoulder. He's humming along with the song, one of his hands making slow circles on my back.

"Was Allison a good dancer?" I ask, and the hand stills. "You miss her, don't you," I say, leaning back so I can see his face. He nods, his mouth twisting like he's fighting back tears, and I sound as sympathetic as I can when I say, "I know it makes it worse that you can't apologize about your fight."

He nods and lets out a shuddering breath.

"What did you say to her that night?" I say. "I think you'll feel better if you tell me."

He shakes his head, pressing his lips together.

"Pretend I'm her," I say. "You can apologize to me." I wrap my arms around his neck and press my cheek against his shoulder. For a few moments we sway gently together, and I think it's not going to work, and then he begins to talk.

"When we were in high school," he says, "Allison got pregnant. It wasn't mine, but I asked her to marry me. She laughed. I asked her to marry me and she laughed." His hands tense against my back. "She had an abortion."

"But that's not what you were fighting about now," I say.

"No," he says. "It's just that sometimes it comes back to me, you know? What our lives could have been." Then he says, so softly I feel it more than hear it, a rumble in his throat, "She never even gave me a chance."

The song comes to an end, but I let him keep holding me. As a fast song starts and people split apart and begin to move, I take his hand and pull him to the side of the dance floor. "What happened that night?" I ask, keeping my eyes fixed on his face. He's looking at the floor.

"Think how different our lives would have been if she would have just let me take care of her," he says. "We'd have a baby, and she'd still be alive."

I imagine the two of them fighting, and in my imagination he calls her a whore, a baby killer, and then maybe he slaps her. I imagine Allison's face, flushing red with anger and hurt, the white mark of his hand across her cheek. She grabs Carl by the arm and pushes him to her door, and even once he is on the other side, shouting her name, she still wants to hit him so badly that she picks up a bottle of moisturizer and smashes it, listening to his heavy foot thud against her door, asking herself how he could call this love.

"She would still be alive," he says again, rubbing his fingers across his eyes. He sniffs, wiping his nose with the back of his hand.

"What's going on?" a voice says. I turn and see Evan standing beside me, an uncertain smile on his lips.

"Who's this?" Carl says, his voice sharp. "Your boyfriend?"

"This is my friend Evan," I say. "I told you, Carl."

"And who are you?" Evan says, irritation in his voice. He frowns at Carl.

Carl doesn't even look at him. He pulls me closer, lowering his voice. "I thought you said this guy wasn't a date."

"I'm not," Evan says.

"Then what do you want?" Carl says sharply.

"Jesus Christ," Evan says. "Who is this asshole?"

"Evan . . . ," I say, putting my free hand on his arm.

"Hey, Evan," Carl says, suddenly turning toward him. He drops my hand and squares his shoulders. "Back off."

Evan makes an incredulous face, looking at me. "Are you ready to go?" he says.

"No, she's not," Carl says. "We were talking." He looks at me. "Tell him."

Evan puts his hand on my arm. "Let's go, Olivia," he says. "I'm taking you home." With a quick motion, Carl knocks his hand away. "Are you her boyfriend?"

"No," Evan says. "Jesus."

"Don't touch her then," Carl says.

Evan shakes his head. He looks at me. "Are you coming?"

I don't say anything.

"Damnit, Olivia," Evan says. "What is going on here?"

Carl pushes Evan's shoulder with his hand. "Don't talk to her like that," he says.

"Fuck you," Evan says, his face turning red. He pushes Carl back.

Carl grabs Evan's shoulders in his hands and leans in close to his face. "Back off," he says.

"Olivia," Evan says, pushing Carl away, "will you tell this asshole to get lost?"

I don't say anything. Evan gives me a disgusted look and stalks off. Carl smiles and reaches for me. I step away. "I'll be right back," I say. I turn to go after Evan, pushing my way through the dancers. When I catch him, he stops and says, "What the fuck was that?"

"I'm sorry," I say. "I didn't want to piss him off. He's important to the story. I need to talk to him."

"I'm your friend, Olivia," he says. "Sometimes that has to come before the story." He looks up over my shoulder. "Here he comes," he says. "We're getting out of here." He wraps his fingers around my wrist and begins to pull me from the bar.

"Evan." I'm trying to speak calmly. "Evan. Let go of me. I've got to talk to him. I'm not ready to go home."

"I don't give a goddamn what you're ready for," he hisses. "You're drunk and we're leaving." He's pulling me through the crowd. I bump against an older woman in a halter top, knocking into one of her enormous breasts. "Sorry," I mutter.

"That's okay, sugar," she says. Her eyes follow me. She feels sorry for me, she wonders what I did to make my boyfriend, my husband, drag me out of the bar this way. She hopes he won't hit me when he gets me home, or maybe she thinks, from the wig and my short skirt, that I might deserve it.

I try to wrench my wrist from Evan's grasp, stumbling into a group of dancing college kids, who part around me and don't look me in the face. Evan tightens his grip and pulls harder. "Let go of me," I say.

"Keep your voice down," he says. He presses his lips together. No one wants to look me in the eye. He stares ahead. The crowd looks away.

"Look at me, Evan," I say. He keeps walking. "Look at me," I call, trying to plant my weight so he can't pull me through the door. He gives a final yank, and we're out in the hazy night, forcing the sidewalk traffic to diverge around us. I'm asking Evan to stop, to let go, to please turn around, but he just keeps walking, not saying a word to me, not even acknowledging that it's me he's got in tow. I see a headline: REPORTER HUMILIATED ON BEALE STREET. I'm staring at the back of his head, the muscles tight in the back of his neck, and then he yanks me around a group of people, so I stumble and almost fall and suddenly I hate him. "Let go of me," I shout. "Let go of me, you fucking faggot." As soon as the words are out of my mouth I feel sick.

Evan drops my wrist.

"Evan," I say, reaching for him. "My God, I'm so sorry." He says nothing. He stands for a minute with his back to me, clenching his fists at his side. Then he stalks off through the crowd.

"Fine," I shout after him. "Fuck you too." Above my head a blue neon guitar blinks on and off. A woman beside me takes off her tank top and runs laughing down the street in her bra. Her boyfriend picks up her top and goes after her. I pull my shirt away from my skin, sticky with sweat and the alcohol I can feel coming out my pores.

From behind me, Carl says, "Is he gone?"

"Yes, he's gone," I say, spinning around. I'd like to sink my fist into his pudgy stomach. "You shouldn't have talked to him like that."

"I was jealous," Carl says plaintively, reaching for me. "I'm sorry."

"He's not my boyfriend, Carl," I say. I step backward, leaving his grasping hands dangling awkwardly in the air. "He's not even my date."

"If he's not a date," Carl says, "why have you been with him all night? I saw you sharing your daiquiri with him. I saw how angry he looked when you were talking to that other guy."

"What other guy?" I ask, and then I realize he means the one who knew Allison. I take another step back. "Have you been following me?"

"I told you," Carl says. He catches my hand and holds it tight. "I'm watching out for you. Just like I did for Allison." He tightens his grip on my hand, pulling me toward him. He looks at me like he means to kiss me, inclining his face toward mine.

"You know what, Carl?" I say, panic rising in my throat. "I've got to go. I'll talk to you later." I pull my hand away.

"What do you mean?" he says. "We . . ." I don't stay to hear the rest. I turn and push into the moving crowd, almost running in the direction Evan went. I go until I reach the statue of Elvis at the end of the street. Evan is gone. Carl hasn't followed me. I stand there breathing hard. A man leaning against Elvis winks at me as he lights his cigarette. I stare at him. "All alone?" he says. He's got a tattoo of a dragon on his shoulder. I've never touched tattooed skin. He gestures at me with the cigarette hand. "Who are you supposed to be?" he says.

I've got the strangest sensation, like I'm running a fever, like this heat has slipped its way inside my head. The man's voice seems to come from very far away. "What?" I say.

"The hair," he says, gesturing again. "What's with the pink hair?"

I reach up and touch the wig. It feels slick between my fingers, not like real hair. "I don't know," I say.

"I like it," he says. He holds the cigarette in his mouth and talks around it. "Sexy."

I look back down Beale. I don't see Carl. The lights blink on and off. Crowds of people seem to be crossing and recrossing the street. A woman's voice rises from among them. "Can you believe it?" she is saying. "Can you believe it?"

"Hey," the man is saying, "Hey, pink girl."

I put my hands on my hips. "What do you want?"

He looks me up and down. "What do you got?"

"You can see what I got," I say.

"I sure can," he says. He grins and takes a step toward me. "I sure as hell can." He holds out a cigarette. "You want?"

I lean way forward and take it. "I don't smoke," I say, even as I'm putting the cigarette in my mouth.

"I can see that," he says, laughing. He strikes a match and lights my cigarette. "What are you doing here all alone?"

I take a step back and inhale. "I'm not alone," I say. He takes another step toward me. Panic flutters up in my chest. "Don't come any closer," I say.

"What's the matter, pink girl?" he says. "I just want to get to know you better."

"There's nothing to know." I take another step backward, then another. Then I drop the cigarette on the ground and step on it hard. When it's out, I spin on my heel and start walking as fast as I can back down the street. "Don't go, sugar," he calls after me. "I was just starting to like you."

A voice in my head is saying, *What are you doing? What are you doing?* and I don't know what to tell it. I'm moving through groups of college boys, couples, tourists, even a few children. They part around me, talking over my head, the same fixed grins on their faces. I am invisible.

In front of the bar where Evan left me, I sit on the curb and pull off the wig. My own hair is wet, plastered to my skin, and I run my fingers through it trying to shake out the sweat, trying to sober up and come back to myself. I've been down here talking to people for stories before. Once it was because a street artist who used to paint sidewalk portraits of tourists had died of AIDS. Every Christmas he decorated all the windows of the bars and souvenir shops with pictures of Santa and elaborate, writhing ivy. I put on my reporter voice and I went from place to place and told these bar people that their friend was dead. Whatever they said to that, I wrote it in my notebook. I typed it in my computer. I saw it under my byline the next day in three neat columns of text.

I can imagine myself in a story right now. I can hear these people saying to a reporter, to someone like me, "I saw her, wearing that pink wig. She was out of control, drunk, shouting on the street. I saw her talking to some strange guy. I don't know what happened to her after that."

I get up and start walking. Two blocks from Beale it's so quiet my footsteps on the pavement pop like gunshots. A police cruiser flies by, sirens wailing. Up ahead a tall figure crosses under a streetlight and disappears around a corner. I keep walking. A man comes toward me, watching his feet, his hands in his pockets. When he passes me he looks up. I force myself to look into his face. He raises his eyebrows and drops his head again. For another block I hear no one, passing in and out of patches of light, past storefronts with dark corners, past the mansion the Union Army used as its headquarters when they took this city whole. Now it costs $8.50 to go inside.

I come upon a man sleeping in a doorway and stifle a gasp. Somewhere off to the right, car brakes squeal and I jump. When a car turns down the street, I step out of the way of the headlights like a fugitive. Up ahead a woman walks quickly across the street, glances over her shoulder, and disappears. I have the feeling that if I turned my head just right I'd catch a glimpse of Allison Avery, wearing her pink wig, a short dress, her silver boots, hurrying in the opposite direction, turning her head back to look at me.

I turn in a wide circle. I am alone. Everyone on these streets is alone, strangers clutching their fear and loneliness to them like a purse they think someone wants to steal, hurrying home to lock themselves away.

It takes me ten minutes to reach the newspaper building. A security guard lets me in the back. She looks at my outfit when I show her my press pass. "Late night," she says.

"Left my wallet here," I say cheerfully. "Pretty stupid." I hit the up button on the elevator.

"Someone waiting for you in the car?" she asks, and I nod. The elevator arrives. "You gotta be careful," she says, as I step in. "Did you hear what happened last night?"

"No," I say, holding the door open. "What happened?"

She nods out at the parking lot. "Woman from Circulation was held up in the lot," she says. "Guy made her perform oral sex on him."

"That's awful," I say. "Did they catch him?"

"Not yet," she says. "They've got a description. It's posted all over the building. From now on you should get one of us to walk you to your car when you're in the building late. Gotta be careful."

I nod at her. The doors close on her worried face.

On the way down the hall I pass the windows that look down into the production room. The presses are still. The building seems to vibrate with a high electric hum. In the newsroom I turn on all the lights and walk down the aisles, running my fingers along the sharp edges of the metal desks. I don't know what I came here to do. I feel in this moment that I am capable of almost anything, flying off a deck, rolling down to an interstate, running down Beale Street with my breasts exposed. Making the news, instead of just covering it.

I come to a stop at the wall. In front of me is a blue flier. I lean in to read it.

ATTENTION, it says. A WOMAN WAS SEXUALLY ASSAULTED IN THE PARKING LOT LAST NIGHT. PLEASE BE ALERT. DON'T WALK ALONE.

I go back to my desk. I pick up the phone and call a cab.

When I open my eyes, a figure is leaning over my bed. I take a breath to scream and Hannah says, "It's me." She's wearing a cardigan over a long T-shirt and she's holding that pink wig out over my face like she's going to smother me with it.

"Jesus, Hannah." I press my hand to my heart. "What time is it?"

"Four-fifteen," she says. "I woke up and I was worried you hadn't come home." She holds up the wig. "What is this?"

"A wig," I say. "A pink wig." Just the thought of explaining myself to her exhausts me. I know what's she's going to say, where did you get it, where have you been, what have you been doing, how much did you have to drink.

"I can see that," she says. "Where did you get it?"

"Somebody gave it to me," I say.

"Who?"

"Somebody I know from work," I say. "Why are you wearing that cardigan?" Her T-shirt says NO ONE CAN MAKE YOU FEEL INFE-RIOR WITHOUT YOUR CONSENT.

"I woke up cold," she says, sitting down on the edge of my bed and frowning at me. I can't understand how she could be cold. My skin, my sheets, are so wet with sweat it seems likely that I'm melting. I turn off the window unit at night because it makes a rattling sound that keeps me from sleeping.

Hannah turns toward the mirror and holds the wig up over her head to see what it would look like on her. In the half-light, without my glasses, it could be anyone's face reflected in that mirror, framed by that bright pink hair, and for a sharp and terrible moment I believe that it's Allison's. I have a vision of us all in pink wigs and cardigans, reflected side by side, the brilliance of the wigs washing out our faces until each pale circle is just an image of the others.

"Put it on," I say, though I don't want her to.

"No thanks," she says, still frowning. She lowers her arms and turns the wig round and round in her hands. "What . . . ," she starts.

I hold up my hand to stop her there. I say, "No comment."

She closes her mouth tight and drops the wig on the floor. For a long moment she stares at herself in the mirror, as though she's con-

ferring with her reflection about her next move. She says, "I was going to say, what do you think this is made of, but I guess that's too
painful to discuss."

Then she gets up to go, and I say, "I'm sorry, Hannah. I just want
to forget this evening ever happened, okay?"

"You don't have to tell me anything you don't want to," she says
before she shuts the door. "I'm not a fucking reporter."

16

Someone is ringing the doorbell. I come awake slowly and lie there listening for the sound of Hannah's footsteps. The house is silent, and then the sound of the doorbell comes again. I sit up and call Hannah's name. No answer. Pain pulses through my head. Every morning, lately, is worse than the one before. I swing my feet onto the floor and call Hannah again. When she still doesn't answer I get up and go down the hall. The place has a messy, abandoned look this morning, like a trashed motel room. The person is ringing the doorbell constantly now, not even pausing to give me time to answer.

I reach the door and look through the peephole. An enormous eye stares back at me through the hole. I jump back, knocking some shoes against the wall, and, hearing the noise, the person starts knocking on the door. I look through the peephole again and this time see a face. It's Carl.

I glance down at the deadbolt lock. It's open. I put my hand on the lever and click the lock into place as quietly as I can. Then I stand there, watching him through the peephole, trying not to make a sound. He turns away from the door, then back. "Shit," I hear him say.

I realize I've been holding my breath and let it out. It's quiet. I look through the peephole. No Carl.

Staying close to the wall, I creep over to the window and stand behind one of the open curtains. Slowly, I lean over just enough to look out. Inches from me, on the other side of the glass, I see his face. He's got his forehead pressed to the window, his hands cupped around his eyes. I jerk back behind the curtain. I don't think he saw me.

He knocks on the window with his fist. I press myself as far as I can into the corner. Every time I see a horror movie, every time I write a story about a woman assaulted in her home, I wonder what I would do in a situation like this. The truth is I'm terrified, my heart inside my throat, my hands shaking. The truth is I don't want to know what I'll do if he breaks that window open. All I want is for him to go away.

I hear his voice, muffled by the glass, as though he's underwater. He's calling my name. "Olivia," he says. "Are you in there? I want to talk to you. Olivia!"

I look around me for a weapon I could reach. There's a small lamp on the end table by the couch. I need something heavy in my hand. I dart toward the end table, and in that moment he sees me.

"Olivia!" he says. "I'm sorry about last night! I'm so sorry."

I look at him, his eyes wide, his forehead flattened by the glass, his lips shaping over and over the word *sorry*. I take a step toward the window, the lamp in my hand. "Get out of here," I say.

"What?" he shouts.

"Get out of here," I shout back. "Get the hell out of here."

For a moment he says nothing. He lets his hand slide down the window. It makes a squeaking sound. Then his face crumples and he starts to cry. His shoulders shake. His forehead bumps against the glass. "I'm sorry," he chokes out. It's not loud enough for me to hear, but I can read it on his lips. Finally he pushes himself away from the window and turns to go. I watch him walk to his car, his shoulders hunched in a position of defeat. He gets in the car and sits staring at my house for a moment and though I don't think he can see me now I take a step back.

Not until his car disappears up my street do I put the lamp back down on the table. Then I close the curtains on the living room window and go around the house making sure the doors and windows are locked, the blinds lowered. I go back in my room and get in the bed, shaking with nausea. I don't know how long I lie there, drifting in and out of sleep. When I finally sit up again my hair is plastered to my forehead with sweat.

I think about Carl's face, pressed up against my window. I pick up the phone and call Sergeant Morris. He answers on the first ring.

"Sergeant, it's Olivia Dale."

"Hello there, honey," he says. "What can I do for you?" He sounds like he's in a good mood.

"I wondered if you have any new leads on the Avery girl."

"Nothing I can tell you."

"What about the men she knew?" I ask. "Have you talked to Carl Fitzner?"

"I think Baker did," he says. "Friend of hers, right? Why do you ask?"

"I just thought maybe you should check him out," I say.

"Why?"

"He was in love with her," I say. "He never forgave her for rejecting him."

"That may be," Morris says. "But he didn't kill her, I'll tell you that much."

"Does that mean you have a suspect?"

"Ah, now, girl," Morris says, a laugh rumbling in his voice. "Are you asking me about Fitzner to trick me into telling what I know? You're a smart one."

"That's not it," I say. "I think there's something about him."

"Olivia, honey," he says. "Do me a favor. Leave the police work to the police."

"So you won't talk to him," I say.

"I don't need to," he says. "Don't worry about it. Everything's under control."

"Does that mean you have a suspect?" I ask again.

"Oh ho." He laughs. "Don't try that again. I got nothing to tell you." In the background I hear a low male voice say, "Morris, you got a minute?"

"You betcha," Morris says. Then to me, "Gotta go, honey." He hangs up the phone.

I'm still sitting there, staring at the phone, when it starts to ring again. I reach for it, then just let my hand dangle. The machine answers and the person hangs up. After a moment I pick up the phone, dial *69, and listen to the phone ring three times before a cheerful female voice says, "Black Horse Theater Company."

"Hello," I say. "May I speak to Carl Fitzner?"

"Sure," she says. "Hang on." I hear her sing out, "Carl, telephone."

I wait. Then he picks up. "Hello?" he says.

I hang up the phone and get out of bed. If Morris won't check Carl out, I will.

I'm driving into the sun, so bright through my windshield that it's hard to see anything else. I hope the stoplight I just drove through was still green. In ten minutes I'll be at Carl Fitzner's apartment building. I'm not sure what I'm going to do once I get there. I just want to take another look at the place where he lives. If he can come peer in my windows, I can go look in his.

The first time I looked at Carl Fitzner I thought I knew who he was, a lonely young man living in a basement apartment with failure wrapped around him like a blanket, angry with people like Allison for shining brighter, for being what he couldn't be and couldn't have. Then I saw him onstage, and he was the kind of actor so talented he didn't even seem to be acting, and now I wonder if he could be a murderer, someone for whom rage overcame everything else.

People are like those nested Russian dolls. There's always someone else hiding inside the person you think you know, layer after layer, each with the same painted face. I want to open someone up and hold that last solid little doll in my hand. I know all of Allison Avery's disguises, femme fatale, loyal friend, maternal and corrupting sister, virginal obedient daughter, performer, alive with the magic of her own touch. But who was she at the center? I don't know if I believe in the soul. I'm afraid of the darkness I see in all of us, every one of us a mystery.

I have looked in the mirror and not been certain that I saw myself. And what separates me from Allison Avery, from Carl Fitzner, but the features of my face?

When I get to Carl's building, I park my car in the farthest corner of the lot and walk back in the direction of the building. Heat rises off the asphalt in waves; I swear I can almost smell it, feel it filling my nostrils like steam from a kettle. I approach Carl's window from the side, staying close to the wall, and then I crouch near the living room window so I can look in. I've decided if anyone asks I'm going to say I think I dropped an earring here. I could even tell this story to Carl and be believed. I see only the living room I remember, spare and ratty.

Five minutes go by with no sign of Carl. My legs start to cramp from my crouched position. I study the room, trying to determine whether anything has been changed since I last saw it. On the bookshelf is a large framed photograph I don't remember seeing before. I lean in until I can feel the cool glass against my forehead, trying to make out the face in the picture. The long full hair indicates a woman, the face is pale—a white woman. I think it's Allison. I'm almost certain. I've come to know that face well.

A window around the corner opens into Carl's bedroom. He's not in there. The bedroom, too, is sparsely furnished. He has a twin bed covered with a blue blanket, tucked neatly under the mattress and pulled so tight it could be in a military barracks. The closet door is closed. There's a little loose change and a shoe box on top of the old white dresser, but nothing else to indicate anyone has ever lived in this room. I lean in, trying to peer into the corners of the room, and then I notice something. The window is unlocked.

I rock back on my heels. It would be so easy to slip inside. *Breaking and entering*, I imagine Evan saying. *Are you insane?* I picture Hannah's eyebrows raised, that look of contemptuous disbelief she perfected a long time ago. I shouldn't do it. I know that.

The window slides up without a sound. The screen squeaks, a small, barely audible noise. The frame is just large enough for my shoulders but with my torso half in I see that there's nothing to break my fall if I slide through headfirst. I wiggle back out and look around for any curious passersby. Nothing moves but the heat waves rising from the parking lot. I grab my bag and toss it through the window, aiming for the bed. It slips off and lands on the floor, pens and a notebook spilling out. Then I turn around and start easing my feet through, like I'm going cautiously down a slide. When my legs are all the way through, I take a breath and push off hard against the ground. My shoulder scrapes the metal frame and I land hard, wrenching my left knee. I crouch there until my heart rate slows. The air in here is still and heavy.

The room is just as monastic as it looked from outside. There's a television and VCR on a rolling cart at the foot of the bed. There's a desk and chair in the corner. I drag the chair over to the wall and stand on it to shut the window. I'm careful to leave things the way I found them; I move the chair back so its legs fit neatly in the indentations on the carpet. I pick up my bag and smooth the blanket.

On top of the dresser I find the shoe box full of playbills and scripts. I sift through them and find a clipping from the newspaper, a review of a local production that mentions a "promising performance from Carl Fitzner." Someone has inked in a huge exclamation point at the end of the sentence. In one script, Carl has written 1,233 on the last page in pencil. I flip through, trying to figure out what the number means. On other pages he has written smaller numbers, and I realize he was going through his lines, counting every word.

The dresser drawers are a turmoil of underwear and single socks, jeans and crumpled T-shirts. Underneath a sweater I find a book of monologues checked out from the library three months ago. I turn to a dog-eared page. It's one of Hamlet's. "O that this too too sullied flesh would melt . . ." I shake the book and a snapshot falls out— Carl in a black turtleneck, grinning into a dressing room mirror, his hand raised to apply foundation to his cheek, his eyes outlined in black. The reflection of the camera flash in the mirror beside him hides the photographer. On the back it says *Hamlet,* 1993 in neat print. I slip the picture into my pocket. In another drawer I find a wooden box. Inside is a jumble of high school yearbook photos. I sort through them, looking for Allison's face. They're all of girls, all with faces that seem plump and shiny with newness, emerging from clouds of glossy hair. I turn some over and read their curlicue hand-writing: "To Carl, a sweet guy." "Carl, maybe I'll see you around this summer." "Dear Carl, it was fun being in French with you. Au revoir!"

I wonder if he sits here, reading these over and over, hoping to find more in these words. At the bottom I find Allison's picture, the same one we ran in the paper. I turn it over. "Carl, we've had our problems but I'm glad we worked them out cuz you're a nice guy. Wasn't driver's ed fun? I'll never forget how Coach Murdock screamed when I ran that stoplight! Oops! Love, Allison." I slip that in my pocket too.

On top of the television is an empty tape case. I push open the VCR with my finger, just enough so I can read the label on the tape inside. Allison 9, it says. I take my finger away and let the slot swing shut. Carl stole a tape from her apartment. I shudder, and then I think, *And so did I.*

I walk into the living room, and stop. The floor in front of the couch is littered with snapshots of Allison Avery. You could walk across them like a rug.

The picture on the bookshelf I saw from outside is also of Allison. It looks like a snapshot blown up to eight by ten. Allison is smiling, outside somewhere. Wearing a red shirt, she stands out in sharp focus from the trees behind her, their deep green leaves. Tucked inside the frame is a notecard. I open it. It reads "Dear Carl, I thought you might like to have this. Thank you for your thoughtfulness. Take care, Cynthia Avery."

I walk over to the couch and stand looking at all those faces on the floor. Then I drop to my knees and pick one up. It's Allison and Carl at a high school dance. Carl is thin and almost handsome. Allison is laughing, an enormous corsage at her wrist, her hair bountiful and stiff with hair spray. The picture is so soft to the touch I can only imagine he holds it in his hands every night.

I keep picking up pictures. Allison onstage in tight black pants and a tank top. Allison in a Betty Boop T-shirt, leaning forward and pursing her lips. Allison outside wearing a backpack and walking somewhere in a hurry, frowning at the ground. Allison as a little girl at the beach, her hair in pigtails. The little boy just behind her could very well be Carl. I hold on to that one for a moment, looking at their soft round cheeks, their brown legs coated with sand.

Some of the photos are as recent as a month ago, the date printed in the corner in blocky yellow figures. One of them, a picture of Allison curled up on her couch, frowning hard, is dated two days before she died. Her mouth is open, like she's telling him to get out, to go away, to stop.

I slide the pictures around with my hands. A foot away I spot one of Allison wearing that pink wig. I pick it up and bring it close to me, and my heart jumps.

The face in this picture isn't Allison's. It's mine.

I don't know how long I've been sitting here, surrounded by Allison, holding that picture in my hand. There's a sound—footsteps, the jingle of keys. I jump to my feet, scattering the pictures. Without thinking, I bolt back into the bedroom, where there's nowhere to go except the closet. As the front door opens, I pull the closet door closed. It clicks, too loud, and I hold my breath. I still have the picture in my hand. I shove it in my pocket. A long minute goes by. I'm imagining the door swinging open, Carl's shocked face, me blinking helplessly as the light rushes in. Nothing happens. I push through the clothes to the back of the closet, where there is barely enough space between the clothes and the wall for me to stand.

Footsteps approach, stop, approach. A light shines in through the crack at the bottom of the door. I clutch at his shirts and feel polyester, slick inside my hand. Then there's the sound of the bed creaking. Two thumps could be his shoes hitting the floor. I strain for more but hear nothing. The hot, close air inside the closet makes me want to gasp for breath. The line of light at the bottom of the door disappears.

Then I hear the sound of Carl's sock feet, padding across the carpet. The television goes on, a loud blare of sitcom laughter, and then a few clicks and silence. Then I hear a voice I recognize. "Hi," it says. "I'm Allison Avery. Thanks for coming."

Inside the closet I listen to Allison sing, and rub impatiently at the tears that come to my eyes at the sound of her voice. Then I listen to what must be the few moments after she comes offstage, the voices of her friends' congratulating her, her own giddy voice rising above the rest. I hear a male voice, murmuring something, and then Allison says clearly, "Well, thanks, Carl. Thanks for coming." Then she laughs. "Don't just stand there," she says. "Give me a hug."

The tape goes silent. I press my ear to the door. There's a faint whirring, and then I hear it again. "Thanks, Carl. Thanks for coming."

Three more times Carl rewinds the tape and plays those few words again. Then there's silence again and I wonder if he's paused the tape on her face, shaping her lips around his name.

What seems like a long time goes by before it begins, a sound I can't identify. It stops and starts, stops and starts. I push as quietly as

I can through the clothes and press my ear to the closet door. It's quiet, and then I hear the sound again.

Carl is sobbing.

He takes a ragged breath so loud I can hear it on the other side of this door and then he wails. The cry goes on and on, rising and falling. It chokes down into silence, then hiccups out again like the sputter of a motor. I sink down until I'm crouched on the floor of the closet, my ear tight against the door, and I listen to him cry. I notice everything about it—the high-pitched whimpers at the end of a long wail, the rapid exhalations that signal the start of another, even the tiny moans between those outward breaths—as though the quality of his crying can tell me whether this is the sound of sorrow or remorse. He sobs with abandonment, not even muffling the sound with his pillow, and I think the neighbors must be able to hear him, if they're home and listening.

I listen to him until he stops, trailing off into a series of sniffs and whimpers. I think I hear him whispering something to himself. Then he blows his nose, once, twice, and is silent.

I can just make out the face of my watch. I wait for half an hour. My knee aches where I wrenched it dropping through the window. I long to straighten out my legs. I recite lines of poems in my head—"In Xanadu did Kubla Khan/A stately pleasure dome decree:/Where Alph, the sacred river, ran/Through caverns measureless to man/Down to a sunless sea." I say the alphabet, shaping my lips in silence around each letter. Something in my bag jabs me in the breast. I change my position with tiny, cautious movements.

When half an hour has passed I wrap my hand around the doorknob and turn it slowly, slowly, and with a tiny click the lock springs back and the door opens. I lean out into the dark room, bracing myself on the door knob, until I can see the bed, and Carl's figure on it. He is fully clothed, but stretched out, and his chest rises and falls with a sleeper's slow breathing. I straighten up. My knee cracks painfully. Carefully I close the closet door. For a moment something keeps me there, watching Carl, trying to see in his puffy red face, his curled-up body, the shape of a murderer. Instead what I notice is the place where his black shirt has pulled loose from his belt, the soft white roll of belly slipping out.

I let myself out the front door.

At home I sit on my bed, looking at that picture of myself. Hannah is still not here. Twice the phone rings but I don't want to answer it. The third time I hesitate for four rings, then snatch the phone off the receiver, but the person has hung up. I stare for a moment at the phone in my hand. Then I dial Angela's number.

She answers, and we talk for a moment about how she is. I bring the conversation around to Carl, and her voice tightens while she tells me again what a creep he is. "Angela," I say, "do you think there's any reason to consider Carl a suspect?"

There's a silence. I'm holding my breath. I'm hoping for a yes, because I need to know, because I want it to end. I'm hoping for a no, because Carl knows where I live, and I'm afraid.

"I don't think so," she says finally. "I think he was there the whole time."

"Where?"

"At the bar," she says. "Sitting at a table in the corner, pretending it was just a coincidence. He knew we used to go there and sometimes he would show up, looking for Allison. Sometimes he wouldn't even talk to her, just watch her from the corner. God, it was creepy. They'd even had a fight a few nights before about him following her around. But he didn't kill her. He was there all night, pretending not to wait for her." She sighs. "Sometimes I almost feel sorry for him."

"You do?"

She pauses. "No," she says, and her voice is sharp with hatred. "I don't."

17

The surface of my desk is an Allison Avery collage. Her high school picture in blurred newsprint. The back of the photo I took from Carl's, that looped handwriting, that girlish tone. Carl's face, grinning in theatrical makeup. The girl's dead body, curled up and smashed. The branch from Peter's bonsai tree. My notes. *Nice girl. Lilies. Rock and Roll. Wild. Sexy. Slut. Pothead. Junkie. Thief.* The picture of me, looking like her.

I'm picking up the phone to call the police station when I hear Peggy say my name. I look up, and she is standing beside my desk. "Can you come into my office?" she says. "I want to talk to you."

"I'll be right there," I say. "I need to make a phone call."

She shakes her head. "Make your phone call afterward," she says. She waits there until I stand up, and then we walk together across the newsroom into her office, my body jumping with impatience.

I sit down on the other side of her desk. "I'm going to get some coffee," she says. "Want some?" I nod, and she leaves the room. Peggy almost never uses this office; it's pristine compared to her desk in the newsroom. Framed articles circle the walls, one on political corruption that put her in the running for the Pulitzer fifteen years ago. I haven't been in here since I was first hired.

She comes back in and hands me a cup of coffee, saying it's hot. I sit and blow on it, waiting for her to talk. She seems uncharacteristically nervous, pretending to straighten papers on her desk, taking long sips of her coffee. Then she sets the cup down and leans forward, putting her hands palm down on her desk. "Look," she says. "I'm not going to pussyfoot around this. I need to know—are you using drugs?"

I just stare at her. Did someone know I was stoned that day in the office? It's not possible. "No," I say. "What are you talking about?"

"I'm talking about heroin," she says. "Are you using? Are you experimenting? Tell me the truth. I'll get you help."

I shake my head, flooded with relief. "I swear to you, Peggy. I don't know what you're talking about."

She sits back in her chair. "I can have you tested, Olivia. It's in the union contract. But I'd rather you just told me."

"Peggy, please tell me where you got this idea."

"Evan came to me," she says. She holds up a hand. "Now, don't be angry at him. He was worried about you, said you wouldn't talk to him, that you'd been strange lately." She sighs. "He saw you with needles. You've been so jumpy."

"My house got broken into!"

"I know. But one day, there was something about your eyes . . . I'm trying to give you the benefit of the doubt, but I have to agree that you just haven't been yourself."

"My God," I say. "Is everyone insane? The needle came from the story I'm working on. It came from Allison Avery's trash."

Peggy watches my face. "Why wouldn't you have told Evan that?"

I shrug. "I didn't want to talk about it until I was sure." Even to my own ears, that sounds like a lie. "Look at my arms," I say, leaning over the desk and extending my arms, palms up. She runs her fingers down my arms, then tilts her head up and looks into my eyes. "Pupils look normal," she murmurs. I straighten up. "You believe me now?"

She waves a hand. "It can be snorted now," she says. "It can be smoked. In the early stages of addiction, injection sites might not even be visible." She sounds as though she's quoting from one of her own articles. Then she says, "I'm going to tell you something." She takes a deep breath. "Paula, in the story. Her real name was Vivian, and she was my niece." She reaches a hand out toward me. "I've seen this thing drag people down. I don't want to watch it happen to you."

"It won't," I say. "I promise I'm clean. You've got nothing to worry about."

Peggy lets her hand fall on the desk. She says, "I want to believe you. So I'm not going to have you tested now. But I'll be keeping an eye on you, Olivia. One slipup and I'll have you peeing in that cup."

"I swear," I say again, standing up to go. "I'm clean."

She nods, her head bowed.

"What happened to your niece?" I ask her at the door.

She doesn't look up. "She's dead."

I stand in front of Evan's desk. I've never noticed before that bald spot forming at the crown of his head. "Can I speak to you?" I ask. He stands up and we walk in silence down the hall to stand near the window overlooking the presses. They're silent now, still waiting for the day's news.

"Peggy talked to you," Evan says, not even making it a question.

"Are you trying to get me fired?" I say. "Are you that angry about the other night? I know it was terrible, what I said to you, and I'm sorry."

"I didn't do it because I was angry. I did it because it was so unlike you. I was worried." He folds his arms across his chest. "You were out of control. The way you've been about this story, I thought you were crossing the line."

"It's a story," I say. "I'm covering it the best I know how."

"It's not about the story, Olivia," he says. "Admit that it's not about the story anymore."

"What's it about then, Evan? What's it about, if it's not about covering my beat?"

"I don't know," he says. "The way you told that guy on Beale that you knew her, that crazy lie you told him about the wig, you sounded like you believed it. You sounded like you thought she was your friend."

"The needle came from her," I say. "It came from Allison Avery. Are you happy now?"

"Did you tell Peggy that?"

"Of course," I say. "She might have me tested anyway."

"Well, if she does you'll come up clean," he says. "And everything will be fine."

"You idiot, I'm going to test positive for marijuana," I say. "You think they'll just let that slide? Remember Bob Anderson in Sports? He got fired for smoking dope."

Evan reaches out a hand toward me. I step back. "I'm sorry," he says.

"Maybe I should tell them to test you too," I say. I hear how my voice comes out, cold and sharp.

Evan recoils as though I'd struck him. "You were acting crazy, and I had seen the needles," he whispers. "I just wanted to help."

"Needle," I say. "One needle."

"I'm sorry," Evan says again. "It's just, in my experience, where there's one there's more."

"Two and two equals four," I say. "That rhymed. Did you notice?"

"Don't make jokes." He reaches for me again, and again I step away. "Please, Olivia."

I take a few steps backward, watching his face, those big brown eyes gone shiny with tears. He says, "You've been crazy lately. I just want to know what's wrong. Hannah says . . ."

"You've talked to Hannah?" I imagine the two of them, their heads together, whispering my name. "Are you checking all your sources? Have you talked to David? I bet he'd give you some good quotes. Maybe he already has."

"You know that's not fair." I take another step backward, then turn on my heel. He grabs my arm. "Don't go," he says. "We need to talk."

"We've talked enough," I say, wrenching my arm free. "I don't feel like being interviewed." I walk away. He calls my name. I don't look back.

Allison Avery is disappearing. Nothing I can come up with will put us back on the front page. I'm at the police station, paging through the day's reports without reading them. Morris isn't here, and Nash will only say that he has nothing to say. There was no mention of the girl on the twelve o'clock news. Things change. More people die, get raped, get shot, get robbed. It's the rare murder that lasts. I try to focus on the names in the stack of papers in my lap. The latest victims, the most recent offenders.

"Olivia Dale," a deep voice says. I look up and see Officer Smiley standing over me.

"Officer," I say. "How's it going?"

"Not bad." He grins. "I saw your story."

It takes me a moment to realize that of course he means the one about him. "Oh yeah? What happened with that? Is he in jail?"

"You didn't hear?" He shakes his head, eyes narrowed. "I thought you'd have followed up."

I feel stung. "I got busy."

"With that doctor's kid, right?" When I nod, he says under his breath, "Yeah," and that one soft word feels like an indictment.

"What happened?"

He shrugs. "She came in and paid his bail. I'm waiting to get the call that he's shot her."

"I'm going to do a series on domestic violence," I offer. I'd nearly forgotten that idea.

"Great," he says, his voice neutral. "I'm sure that'll help." He touches my shoulder gently. "See you around."

I watch Officer Smiley walk away down the hall, his powerful stride, his gun tight against his hip, his air of authority and purpose. I feel like a child, small and afraid.

❧

I spend the afternoon trying to let it go. I don't make a single phone call regarding the Avery investigation. Instead, I call David for the first time since Saturday night, and apologize like a good girl. He's not angry. He, too, sighs and talks about his worry for me. Then I write the stories I'm supposed to write. A two-year-old child run over by a truck. A liquor store holdup. I call the highway patrol to check fatalities. I am distant but polite with Evan. Maybe we're even now, depending on how you weigh our crimes.

At 5:35 my phone rings and before I touch the receiver I know it's Peter. "Can you come see me?" he asks as soon as I say hello.

"I'm really busy, Peter."

"I need to talk to you."

"We're talking."

There's silence. "Why are you being this way?" He sounds hurt. "Why would you be angry with me?"

I sigh. "I'm not angry. I've had a shitty day."

"Every day is a shitty day," he says. "I just want to see you."

I give in. I tell him I'll stop by on my way home.

No one answers the door at the Averys' white house. I walk around the house, looking up at the windows, searching for movement. No lights are on, no figures pass behind the windows. In the backyard I pull a leaf off a tree and shred it, tearing along the veins. I reach for another, and hear movement inside the greenhouse.

Inside, Peter stands with his back to me, running his fingers over one of his trees. His T-shirt clings to him, wet with sweat, and I watch the muscles in his back contract when he bends to clip a branch. *Ten minutes,* I think. *Then I'll go.* He turns, scissors in hand. "Olivia," he says. "You came."

"What did you need?" I ask, trying to sound brusque.

He smiles. "Let me just finish this," he says, and bends back to his tree.

My heart jumps wildly inside my throat. In this moment there is nothing but my desire, as though everything I am has contracted to a point. I could cross over to him, drop my bag on the floor, and lay both hands, fingers spread, on the small of his back, which would be hot and damp and tense with surprise beneath my palms. Then slowly, slowly, I could slide my hands around to his stomach, slip them up inside his T-shirt and touch his soft belly, skin against skin.

I cross my arms over my chest. "I've got to go home, Peter. What did you want?"

He turns, frowning, the sharp edge of his scissors pointed at me. "Why are you being such a bitch?"

What can I say? Because I'm worried I can't control myself? I say, "I'm in a hurry."

"Just get the fuck out, then, if it's so goddamn difficult to give me five minutes of your time."

"Fuck you," I say, suddenly blinking back tears. "You called me and I came. What do you want?"

He comes toward me now, waving those scissors. "The story's over, is that it? So I'm of no use to you now?"

"That's not . . ."

"What about all that *concern* for me?" He's right in front of me now. I keep my eye on the moving point of the scissors. "Was that faked?"

"My concern was real," I say slowly. At least it became real, and that's what matters now.

He mimics me. "My concern was real. Oh, Peter, how *are* you? I'm *so* sorry about your poor dead sister, at least as long as she sells papers."

"Listen to me." I reach for him but he steps back.

"I don't have to listen to you. I'm nothing more than a story to you, am I." He leans in again, bringing the scissors an inch from my hand. One quick jab and he could sink the point into my skin. "Fuck you," he says. "Fuck you."

Carefully I reach out my hand. I close my fingers around the scissors, and when I feel his grip slacken I take them from his hand. He stares at me. "Did you think I was going to hurt you?" He sounds as though he's going to cry.

"Of course not," I say, though for a moment anything seemed possible. Slowly I set the scissors down.

"I would never hurt you," he says. His eyes are filling with tears. He bites his lip. "I'm sorry," he says. "I don't know what's the matter with me."

"It's okay," I say. I pull him to me, his head against my shoulder, and he begins to shake. I hold him as tight as I can.

"Olivia," he says. "I think I love you."

"Oh, honey," I say. I think, *My God, he's seventeen,* as though I've only now learned it.

He lifts his head to look at me. "I mean it," he says. "I love you." His eyes keep searching my face, his hand clutching at my arm. The need is so naked in him, I can't help but say it. "I love you, too." He presses his lips against mine, hard, urgent, then leans back. That smile of his lights up his face, beautiful.

I feel about a million years old.

18

I leave Peter with promises that I'll see him again soon. He stands in the driveway and watches me go, his body leaning after my car. I drive all the way home with a lump in my throat and when I get there I go straight into my bedroom and curl up in a fetal position on the bed. I'd like to hold myself and sob, like I watched Carl do, but no tears come. This day has left me hollow.

The phone wakes me early in the morning. I lie there for a moment, my skirt twisted up around my waist. The ringing stops. I undo my bra and run my fingers over the painful red ridges it's left in my skin. I hear Hannah shout, "Wake up, Olivia. It's for you."

"Good morning, gal. Up and at 'em. It's gonna be a long day for you." It's Sergeant Morris and he sounds happy.

"What time is it?" I squint at my clock.

"Early. But you'll be glad I woke you." He pauses, letting the suspense build. "It's the Avery case. There's been an arrest."

I'm stunned.

"Olivia? Are you still there?"

"Who?" I say.

"Three kids in Bolivar," he says. "They tried to use her credit card at the gas station there. The Mississippi cops called us." His voice turns hard. "We've got them cold," he says. "We found her underwear in one of their bedrooms. The ringleader. Jared Gillespie."

"My God," I say under my breath.

"There's going to be a press conference this afternoon," he says.

"Did they know her?"

"Doesn't look like it," he says. "Stranger killing, just like we thought."

"But why did they do it?" I say. "It doesn't make sense."

"Lord, I don't know," he says. "Thirty years I've been doing this, and I can tell you—it never makes sense."

When I'm off the phone, I run to the bathroom. For several minutes I kneel on the floor beside the toilet bowl. I feel like I'm going to be sick. Instead what comes out is a rush of tears. My whole body shaking, I put my face in my hands and sob, and that is how Hannah finds me, half-naked over the toilet bowl, my face a sticky mess.

She kneels beside me and holds me against her, and when she asks me what's wrong her voice trembles like she's going to cry too. I can't tell her. I just keep shaking. Hannah helps me stand. She helps me undress and turns on the shower. Underneath the stream of water I stand with my eyes closed, my face in my hands, until my body stills.

On the other side of the curtain, Hannah is asking me if I'm all right.

I open my eyes. There are the same blue tiles, the same green shower curtain I see every morning before I go to work. If this were any other day I'd be hurrying through this shower, singing while I washed my hair, anxious to follow up on the big break I'd just gotten. The scoop. So today I will finish this shower and get dressed and call Peggy and drive to Bolivar, Mississippi, in search of Jared Gillespie. I will find out how old he and his friends are and whether they have criminal records. I'll ask anyone who might know when they did it, and how, and where, and why.

This is my job. This is just my job.

The last time I was in Bolivar, it was to cover a story about the Board of Aldermen's attempt to get a local monument repaired. It was a memorial for the town's Confederate dead, and the problem was that in the forty years since its building, it had begun to lean. When two aldermen went out and took measurements, they confirmed what everyone had feared: the monument leaned, six inches to the North. At the meeting, an old man with a beard stood up and said, his voice breaking, "It's a mockery to the boys that gave their lives fighting the Yankees. Our monument should be straight. Upright," and he snapped his legs together like a soldier coming to attention.

In this town there are three places of business, a general store, a diner, and a gas station. When I pull into the gas station, a boy about Peter's age comes out and motions for me to roll down my window. He squints in at me. "What'll it be, ma'am?"

"Regular, please," I say. He starts the pump running and leans over my windshield with a squeegee, methodically running it in neat lines across the glass. I watch his face. He is whistling, eyes focused on the water running down the windshield, never glancing at me on the other side of the glass. I get out of the car. "Been a lot of excitement around here," I say, leaning against the door.

"Oh yeah," he says. He straightens up, puts the squeegee away, and heads toward me. "'Scuse me, ma'am," he says, and I press up against the door so he can get by. He whips the pump out of the car and screws on the gas cap with a practiced air.

"You know those boys?" I let my voice slide into a drawl.

"Could you pop the hood?"

I lean inside the car and pull the lever. When I straighten up he is under the hood of my car. His voice emerges, muffled. "The ones killed that girl in the city, you mean?"

"Yeah," I say. "You know them?"

"I seen 'em around," he says. "This is a little town." He comes out from under the hood, holding the dipstick. "You need oil."

I nod, and he goes about adding the oil. "You know where Jared lives, then?"

"Oh yeah, I know," he says. He straightens up and lets the hood drop, gently, then gives it a quick slam into locked position. "It's hard to find." He wipes his hands on a rag. "I could take you." He doesn't look at me, pretending nonchalance as he runs the rag over each finger. His body is drawn up straight while he waits for me to answer. He wants to go. He's curious.

"Okay," I say. "Let's go." I get back in the car. He goes around to the passenger side and vaults into the seat. Then he holds out his hand to me. "Name's Mike."

"Olivia," I say, giving his hand a hard squeeze. He's covered in a fine layer of dust and his blond-brown hair falls in his eyes. He reminds me of my high school boyfriend, coming to my house after driving a tractor on his father's farm, his skin powdered with dirt and hot to the touch.

"What you want at Jared's house anyway?" Mike asks. "You don't look like a cop."

"I'm a reporter," I say. "I want to talk to his family."

"To get some insight and all?"

I nod, turning the key in the ignition.

"That's cool," he says.

He directs me off the main road down a series of dirt roads until we crunch over gravel and pull up to the house. It's a tiny house, no better than a shack, really, with nothing around but tall grass and weeds and the requisite auto parts piled to the side. A black dog sleeping inside a pen lifts its head to look at the car but doesn't bark. It yawns hugely and drops its head again. "They're not home," Mike says. "Car's not here."

For the first time it occurs to me that coming here alone with this boy was not the smartest thing to do. For all I know this isn't even the right house. I sit for a minute with the car running. Mike swings open the door and vaults out. He disappears from view around the side of the house and then reappears, leaning in my car window. His face shines with excitement. "I scouted it out," he says. "No one's here for sure."

Mike follows me around the yard as I circle the house. In the back, we press our faces to a window and peer inside at the living room. A few battered plastic toys lie in front of the television, which is the only thing in the room that looks new. "A kid lives here?" I say.

"Yeah," Mike says. "Jared's kid. A little girl." Then he disappears. I stand with my hands cupped around my face, looking for details. The ironing board in the corner, a child's pink dress waiting to be pressed. A ragged pair of women's slippers beside the sofa, which is orange and velour and shredded on the sides, probably by the tabby cat now watching me from the back of the couch. Even the cat looks battered and used, one ear bitten jagged, burrs caught in its fur. I tap on the glass and the cat's body stiffens. It leaps from the couch and disappears from view, then reappears suddenly on the windowsill, its nose working as though it can smell me through the glass. I scratch on the window with my finger and the cat puts its paw there, then looks at me, its eyes wide with curiosity, and meows. "What do you know about it?" I say, and it meows again.

"Hey!" Mike whoops from the side of the house. "Come here! I found something!"

Following his voice, I run around the house and smack into him. Together we stumble a step or two and then he puts his hands on my arms and steadies me, laughing. "Slow down, girl," he says.

I step back out of his grasp. "What did you find?"

He gestures at the ground. "This is where they burn their trash." The grass doesn't grow inside this circle, which is littered with scraps and bits of wood and plastic. I grab a stick and poke at it. The wind catches a piece of paper and it flutters away.

A car approaches, bumping down the dirt road. "It's them," Mike says softly, and I drop the stick and move to the front of the house, standing with my hands clasped in front of me as the car turns up the hill and comes to a stop next to mine. I feel myself growing calmer. I know my part now. When the car door swings open and a woman gets out with a bag of groceries I go toward her with a sympathetic smile. "You look like you could use a hand," I say, and wordlessly she hands me the bag. I balance it on one hip and extend my right hand. "Olivia Dale," I say, and when she takes my hand and gives it a limp squeeze, I say, "So nice to meet you, Mrs. Gillespie."

She nods, a sharp worry line appearing in her forehead. She is probably not long past forty, but she looks like an old woman. Her thin brown hair is pulled back into a ponytail, which she tugs on as she looks at me. Her pale flesh sags on her small frame—her breasts huge and ponderous inside her tank top, her legs lined with blue veins, her face puffy and pasty white. "Can I get another bag for you?" I say, and finally she finds her voice.

"That's all right," she says. "Only got a couple more."

I wait while she opens the back door and heaves out two more straining bags. From behind the windshield, a little girl watches me, her features small and sharp beneath a mass of curly hair. When I catch her eye, she looks away, and then she swings the passenger door open and gets out. When she stands, I see that she is not a little girl, but a teenager, in a T-shirt and a tight pair of cutoffs. Her face is heavily made up, and from beneath her purple eyelids she watches me for a minute, before she opens the back door and leans in. She stands up slow, a child of about four clinging to her neck, almost as big as she is. Under all this weight the two women move toward the house, and I follow. Mike appears at my side when I reach the front door. I had forgotten all about him. "You don't need to come in," I whisper.

He looks astonished. "But I want to," he says, and shuts the door behind us. The air inside the house is hot and close, and it's dark where we're standing. I follow Mrs. Gillespie into the kitchen and set the bag on the counter. She is putting her groceries away, milk and eggs in the ancient refrigerator, canned corn on the shelf on the wall. "Mrs. Gillespie," I say. "I'm so sorry to trouble you at a time like this. I wondered if I could talk to you for just a few minutes, about what your family is going through. About what they're doing to your boy."

"Jared's a good boy," she bursts out. She takes a paper towel and wipes her forehead. "They've got him locked up."

"I know," I say, moving in closer to lay a gentle hand on her shoulder. "I know how hard it is to see your boy locked up in that tiny cell. I'm sorry this has happened to you. You seem like a good woman."

She stares at me. "Who did you say you were?"

"Olivia Dale," I say. "From the newspaper. I won't take but a few minutes of your time. I want you to tell your side of the story." I squeeze her fleshy shoulder. "Jared's side."

"All right," she says, nodding. She waves her hand in the direction of the living room. "You just go ahead and sit down. I want to freshen up." She pulls her sticky tank top away from her breasts. "I won't be but a minute."

In the living room, Mike leans against the wall, hands in his pockets, talking to the girl. She sits with her feet up under her on the couch, absently petting the tabby cat. Mike turns his head when I walk in. "Teresa and I went to junior high together," he says. "She was a year behind me."

"I had to drop out in the ninth grade," Teresa says, her voice high and heavily accented. She's talking to Mike, but her eyes are fixed on me. "I got pregnant. I stayed until I couldn't fit inside the desks no more, then I had to drop out. I was fixing to graduate, too."

"How old is your daughter?" I ask.

"Almost four," Teresa says. "Her name's Annabelle."

"That's a pretty name," I say, easing down onto the couch. I touch the cat's tail, and it twitches away. I snap my fingers and hold my hand out, and the cat leans in to sniff me, then rubs its face against my hand and begins to purr.

"She likes you," Teresa says. "She's Jared's cat. She's been lonely without him. Haven't you, kitty?" she says to the cat. "Haven't you?"

"Jared's your boyfriend?" I guess.

"He's my fiancé," she says. "We've been engaged two years." She shows me her ring, a tiny gold band with a diamond—or imitation diamond—so small it's hardly even there. "It's real," she says, as though she knows I've been wondering, and then she strokes it with the tip of her finger. "We're supposed to get married in September," she says, her voice breaking. She lifts her head, gulping for air, and then she stares at me angrily while tears roll down her cheeks.

"I'm so sorry," I say. I reach out, slowly, and lay my hand on the back of hers where it rests on the couch. She stiffens. I keep my hand pressed on hers, and after a moment she relaxes. "Mike," I say, "can you find Teresa a tissue?"

"In the bathroom," she says, pointing. When Mike is gone, I say, "How can they think Jared did this awful thing?"

She shrugs, wiping at her face with her free hand. "I guess it's because he was gone those days."

"He was gone?" I say, trying to keep my hand relaxed on hers.

"Yeah," she says. "He wasn't at work, and couldn't nobody find him." Mike comes back in, holding a wad of toilet paper. She thanks him, and slides her hand out from under mine to blow her nose.

"You didn't know where he was?"

She shakes her head, dabbing the tissue carefully beneath her eyes. "He left for work Friday morning like always, but then I guess he never got there, 'cause his boss called here to see where he was. He didn't come back until Saturday night."

"Why would he disappear like that?"

She shrugs again. "Sometimes he does," she says. "When he's been drinking and whatnot."

"Whatnot?"

"Well, you know," she says, leaning forward conspiratorially. "Sometimes . . ." Mrs. Gillespie's heavy footsteps sound in the hall, and Teresa shuts her mouth and sits up straight. She blows her nose again, then raises her eyes to Mrs. Gillespie's face. They stare at each other for a moment, and I wonder what there is between them. Then Mrs. Gillespie nods, once, as though she's decided something, and sits down in the tattered plaid armchair next to the couch. She has changed into a flowered dress with a wide neck and a short skirt that strains over her knees. No one speaks.

I lean forward, my elbows on my knees, and turn my head so I can look into the woman's downturned face. "Mrs. Gillespie," I say softly. "I'd like you to tell me about your son. I'd like to know what kind of person he is."

Mrs. Gillespie starts talking, telling me stories about Jared as a little boy, about the troubles that started when he was eleven. I don't even have my notebook out. I'm just nodding as she talks, and when she pauses, I say, "How awful," or "And then what?" or "I understand." I glance at Mike and see that he's closed his eyes, slumped back against the wall. Teresa stares out the window, petting the cat robotically until it gets up, shakes itself and jumps down from the couch. We all start when we hear a car motor, the crunch of tires on gravel.

"Are you expecting someone?" I say, standing, and Mrs. Gillespie shakes her head. I go to the door and open it a crack. Outside, Teresa's little girl, Annabelle, is standing, her feet apart, her hands clenched at her sides, watching a van with Channel 5 emblazoned across its side pull up. The van comes to a stop, and as the door opens and a high-heeled shoe appears at the bottom, Annabelle pulls her hands back and lets fly with a rock that thuds against the windshield. I hear a high-pitched "Oh!" and see the man behind the wheel instinctively duck his head. I open the front door all the way as Mrs. Gillespie and Teresa come to stand on either side of me. The van's back door opens and a young man in jeans and a baseball cap steps out. "It's Joe," Teresa says.

"Who's Joe?"

"He works at the diner," she says.

"Mrs. Gillespie?" Joe calls. "I've brought the TV reporters to talk to you."

Annabelle lets fly with another rock. Joe jumps to the side, and says, "Now, now, Annabelle." She says nothing, just bends and picks up another rock. Then Lydia McKenzie steps out, smiling, her hands up and palms out like she wants to show she's unarmed. Her camera man is right behind her. "Mrs. Gillespie," she calls. "I'm

Lydia McKenzie from Channel Five." She takes a step toward us. Annabelle's next rock strikes her foot. Lydia squeals and bends to rub her foot. Annabelle takes aim at the camera and comes within inches of hitting it. The camera man hustles his expensive equipment back into the van while Lydia hops out of the way of another flying rock. "Damnit," Lydia splutters. Then I hear a strange sound and look around to identify its source. It's Mrs. Gillespie. She's laughing, her face turning red, making a sound that's closer to choking. Teresa lets loose with a high-pitched giggle as Annabelle throws a shower of gravel in the direction of the van.

I stand at the door, waving good-bye, as Lydia McKenzie drives away. Annabelle keeps throwing rocks, watching them thud with a puff of dust into the place where the van used to be. Mrs. Gillespie touches my arm. "Come back inside," she says. "Can I get you some iced tea?"

The truth is, Mrs. Gillespie knows her son carries a darkness inside him. She knows he is sullen, and violent, and careless, that he can't hold down a job and doesn't always seem sober. With a hopeless look in her eyes, she keeps insisting that he's a good boy. It's too late to stop loving him now.

I ask her about the underwear found in his room and she says that they're probably Teresa's. I ask about the credit card and she says the real murderer left the wallet where Jared and his friends found it, that's all. I ask her about the DNA testing, and she draws herself up, and says, her voice shaking, that she knows it will prove her boy's not guilty. What I would really like to ask her is what it's like to love a monster. What is it like, Mrs. Gillespie, to carry a killer in your womb?

When we say good-bye at the door, she presses my hand and tells me she's praying for the poor girl's family. "I don't know what I'd do if something like that happened to my Jared," she says. "I hope they catch the real killers. I'm praying that they do."

❖

By the time I reach the afternoon press conference I've already learned more about Jared Gillespie than the police are going to tell us. I've learned, for instance, that since turning eighteen he's been picked up twice for drug possession. I take notes while the captain announces what I already know, that there's been an arrest, that the evidence is good. Flipping through my notebook I see Teresa's phrase "drinking and whatnot," and I can't stop thinking about that moment, the secretive look on her sharp face, the way she shut her mouth when Mrs. Gillespie came back in the room. I raise my hand and ask the captain about Jared's record. "Was it heroin?" I ask. "Was he dealing?"

The captain says it was heroin, but as far as he knows that has no relevance to this case.

This story will run front-page lead. THREE TEENAGERS AR-RESTED IN BRUTAL RAPE, MURDER. Back at the newsroom I type their names into my computer and stare at them, the ordinary names of these young boys. Robby Shavers, 16. Cody Parker, 17. Jared Gillespie, 19. The last people to see her breathing, the boys who took her life.

At the end of the day I go down to watch the presses roll. I lean my forehead against the glass and watch those pages fly by. When I leave here, I'm going to go find Nate and ask him if he knows Jared Gillespie. It's my last possible answer to the question of why. When I close my eyes, I don't see the white pages or the neat type of my story. I see the needle in Nate's hand.

By now Allison's family has gotten the news about Jared Gillespie and his friends. I imagine her mother talking calmly about the death penalty while Peter slams his fist into the wall, picturing their faces. I wonder if he's thought of me at all today, if he knows I'm the one who wrote the story. What would he have thought if he could have seen me sitting in Jared Gillespie's living room, holding his mother's hand?

❧

I knock sharply on Nate's door. From the other side of the door I can hear music, but Nate doesn't appear. I lean in close and shout, "Nate, it's Olivia. Peter's friend," and then I hear him shout, "Come in."

Nate is sprawled out on his tiny couch. Again he's wearing nothing but a pair of gym shorts, his skin so pale it's almost translucent. "Hey," he hails me. "What's goin' on?"

"I wanted to ask you something." I stand over him.

"Shoot," he says genially.

"Do you know a guy named Jared Gillespie?"

He frowns. "The one who . . ." He lowers his voice, glancing behind him. I follow his gaze. There's no one there. "The one who killed Allison?"

"You know about it?"

He points with his chin in the direction of the kitchen. "Pete's here," he says as Peter emerges through the door. He stares at me like he's never seen me before, then moves slowly to the armchair and sits down, looking at the floor.

" 'Scuse me a moment," Nate says, slipping off to the bathroom.

I go to Peter and graze the back of his neck with my fingers. "What are you doing here?" I say.

He reaches up and grabs my hand. "What are *you* doing here? Looking for me?"

"What did you do today?" I ask. "After you heard?"

He is silent for a moment, playing with my fingers. Then he says, "For a while we sat around, my parents and me, and my mother talked about what will happen now, how there will be a trial and lots of media attention and how we need to stay calm and do everything we can to make sure these people get what they deserve. Then she and my father decided to go back to work. My mother said we have to keep doing what we do, and that she had patients to see."

"And you?"

He sighs. "After they were gone, I got in my car and drove to Mississippi. I drove around that shitty little town where they came from. I felt like I wanted to burn the whole place down."

"What did you do?"

"I found out where he lives, the one they think was the leader. I drove up and down past that house. It's a dump."

"I know. I saw it."

"You talked to those people?"

"I talked to his mother, his girlfriend," I say. "That's my job."

"I hate them," he says, his voice catching. "I know they're not the ones who killed her. But I hate them, all of them." He squeezes my hand. "When I was sitting outside their house today, I kept wishing I could make it explode, so the whole thing, all that junk in the yard, would just disappear like it was never there. I knew he wasn't there. I knew there wasn't anything I could do. But I wanted to do something. So I backed up, and then I slammed on the gas and drove my car into his mailbox." He laughs, a short, bitter laugh. "He killed my sister. I knocked down his mailbox."

"Did it make you feel any better?"

He looks up at me and shakes his head. "Now there's a big dent in my car," he says, and two fat tears spill out of his eyes. He brushes at them impatiently. "I came here to get high," he says abruptly.

"You mean to shoot up," I say.

"Yes," he says. "That's exactly what I mean." He looks at me like he's waiting for a lecture, but I don't give it.

"Olivia," he says, his voice choppy with desperation. He clutches at my hand. "Listen to me. It will make this all go away. Think about it. No pain, no anger." He presses my hand against his mouth and puts a kiss in the center of my palm.

No desire. No fear.

Nate returns before I say anything. "The thing is," he says, "I don't have any."

"Can you get some?" Peter says. "I've got money."

Nate stands up, reaching for a T-shirt crumpled in the corner of the couch. "In that case," he drawls, "I'll see what I can do." He pulls on his shirt, heading for the phone on the floor in the corner. I kiss Peter on the temple and slide my hand from his. Then I get up and go to the bathroom. It looks as though it hasn't been cleaned in months. Instead of a bath mat Nate has a crumpled towel on the floor. The bottom of the white shower curtain is stained with mildew, and some of the holes at the top have ripped, so that the curtain sags, barely holding on. The toilet seat is up and the rim of the bowl is stained yellow. With a piece of toilet paper in my hands I gingerly push it down. It lands with a clatter, and I think how ridiculous it is that I won't touch his toilet seat, but I'm considering letting him put a needle in my vein.

At the sink I wash my hands twice and splash my face with cold water. I look at myself in the mirror, letting the water drip off my face. I feel as though I should have put that pink wig on, painted my lips a deep red.

When I go back in the living room, Peter has sunk even lower into the chair, staring at the ceiling with a look that suggests he's trying not to cry. One of his legs is jiggling, the way David's does when he's itching for a cigarette. Nate is still on the phone. He has his back to me, and he's rising up and down on the balls of his feet. "Yeah, yeah, yeah," he is saying. "Tell me where?" He turns from side to side, looking lost. "Got a pen?" he says to me.

From my bag I take a notebook and pen and hand them to him. He flips to a blank page and writes something. "Take a left there?" he says, then writes something else. It's the most prosaic of conversations. "See you in half an hour," he says, and hangs up the phone. He rips out the page, folds it up and slides it in his pocket. "You ready?" he asks us, handing me the notebook and pen.

"Should we get some needles?" I don't know what the proper etiquette is, so I just ask him. "Do you have clean ones?"

"Brand-new," he says. He frowns. "I'm not stupid."

"Sorry," I say. "Just checking." I slip the notebook back in my bag.

"I've just got to find my shoes," Nate says, looking around. I follow, two feet behind him, as he hurries into the bedroom. I stand in the doorway and watch him crouch to peer under his unmade bed. His T-shirt rises, and I stare at his narrow lower back. I'm starting to feel a strange tenderness toward him, he is so thin and pale. At what moment did this become his life? I wonder if it was the first time he took a hit, or even earlier, the first time he skipped chemistry class, the first time he picked up a guitar he'll never really be able to play. "Shit," he says, straightening up. He comes out of the room so fast he almost collides with me in the doorway.

I watch him roam around the room, lifting newspapers and clothes and finding no shoes. He's chewing on his lip, and he stops and puts his hands on his hips. "Did you look under the couch?" I say. My voice booms out across the room. Nate drops to his hands and knees and peers under the couch. He gives a cry of triumph and stands up with a pair of old sneakers in his hand.

It takes him a long time to put the shoes on. I'd like to go over there and tie them myself. I just stand there, trying not to think.

"Olivia?" Peter calls from the other room. When I don't respond right away he calls my name again, his voice rising. I go back into the living room. He's sitting up straight, blinking hard, as though he's just woken up, and the look on his face is something close to panic.

"I'm here," I say, and he jumps to his feet and comes toward me. "What's the matter?"

"I didn't know where you were," he says. "I thought you might have left."

"Don't worry," I say. I give him a quick kiss. "I'm not going anywhere."

"We're doing this together," he says, sliding his fingers into mine again.

"I haven't decided yet." It's a lie. I've decided, but I don't want to think about it. I don't want to lose my nerve. I squeeze his hand.

Nate appears in the doorway and both of us turn. "You guys ready?" he says. "I'm getting antsy." He almost jogs to the door and we follow.

Outside, the night is soft and warm, like a gentle hand brushing your cheek. In the parking lot I stop and look around me like I have to memorize this scene. Peter stands here beside me. Across the street at Dolly's a giant neon doughnut blinks on and off. A girl's voice floats down the street, calling somebody's name. The moon is almost full, and in the air there's a faint electric hum.

"What are you waiting for?" Nate says. "Come on. We don't want to be late."

We take my car. I follow Nate's directions onto the interstate and outside of town. For a long time none of us speaks. I'm listening to the whirring of the tires on the road below, watching the headlights of other cars approach and recede. This is what I love about driving on the highway late at night, that you just keep moving.

I hear a faint rumbling and look at Nate in the rearview mirror. He's asleep and snoring, his head back against the seat, his mouth hanging open. I let him sleep until we reach our exit, and then I whisper his name.

He sits up with a start, blinking hard.

"We're here," I say.

He leans forward to peer out the windshield. There are not many lights off the exit ramp, no fast-food restaurants or truck stops, just an abandoned gas station with an old-fashioned pump and boards across its windows. "There it is," he says, and at the same moment I see it: a roadside motel with a blinking red vacancy sign. The place is U-shaped, with rooms that open onto the parking lot and an office at one end where, through the glass, I can see a fat woman reading a romance novel at the desk. Nate directs me to room 13, and I park in front.

"You got the money?" Nate says. I find my wallet and hand him a stack of bills. He tells us to wait in the car and gets out. I watch him knock on the door, dancing from foot to foot, until it opens and he disappears inside. Peter has his head turned out the window, his body rigid, with anticipation or anxiety, I'm not sure. I am not afraid now, because this isn't happening to me anymore. I'm watching it like a movie, and this is a movie set, this place that looks like a stopover for people on their way down. On the other side of that door is a room with bad green carpeting, and a bed too many people have slept in, and maybe a cheap TV and some indeterminate stain in the bathtub. It's number 13, just like Allison Avery's apartment, and Allison could be in there with Nate, smiling that mischievous smile as she hands some guy the money, her tongue just visible at the corner of her mouth.

I look at myself in the rearview mirror. There's that girl again, the one who is capable of anything.

Finally Nate emerges from the motel, one hand in his pocket. He flashes us a victory sign and hurries to the car. When he gets in he's as jumpy as if he'd consumed a pot of coffee inside. "Let's go, let's go," he says.

Once we're on the road he pulls his hand out of his pocket and shows us a small foil package. "Get us back as fast as you can. This is gonna be great." He slides the package back in his pocket and settles in against the seat.

"What was the guy like?" I ask. "The dealer?"

"He's just this kid from the suburbs in a baseball cap. But he gets great stuff. He doesn't cheat you like some people."

"You never said if you know Jared Gillespie."

Nate shakes his head.

"Why would he?" Peter says, his voice sharp.

"I'm just asking," I say. Then I say to Nate, "Are you sure? He's from Mississippi. He might be a dealer."

"Doesn't sound familiar."

"It's possible Allison knew him."

"She didn't *know* him," Peter says. He sounds furious. He crosses his arms over his chest and turns away from me to stare out the window.

"Sorry," Nate says, yawning. "Before today, I'd never heard of him in my life."

When we reach his apartment building, Nate takes the stairs two at a time. Peter follows him, and I bring up the rear, slowly. When I reach his living room, Nate is hunting for a candle. When he finds one and lights it, it's Peter who heats some of the heroin in a spoon over the flame. Sitting in the armchair, I watch him, humming under his breath as the little rock melts into a golden brown liquid. "Beautiful, isn't it," Peter says to me, and I nod. It is pretty, the color of amber. He draws it through a cigarette filter into a syringe.

I watch Peter slip the needle into Nate's arm like it's something he's done a thousand times before. I watch the red blood rush into the clear tube. I watch Nate's face contort in ecstasy. I watch his head drop backwards onto the floor. Peter looks down at Nate, satisfaction on his face, and then he unwinds the belt from Nate's arm and comes toward me on his knees. "Now you," he says.

These are the last moments before it happens. I think of Hannah, rocking me in her arms. David, pulling me to him through the crowded bar. Peter, telling me he loves me while his eyes fill up with tears.

Now he kneels before me, then reaches up and brushes his lips against mine. "You ready?" he says. I hold out my left arm. He leans in, the belt in his hands.

"Did you used to do this for Allison?" I say, looking down at his curly brown hair, his bent neck.

He shakes his head, tightening the belt around my arm. The vein pops out.

"Did Allison do this for you?" My voice catches over her name. I stare at the tender inside of my arm.

"What are you talking about?" He picks up the needle, touches my plump vein with a finger. "Allison and I never shot up together."

"Peter," I say, panic fluttering in my chest. "Didn't Allison do this?"

He glances up at me. "Allison?" he says. He looks down again, positioning the needle at my arm. "No, my sister was never a user."

"I don't get it," I say. My voice rises. "I found the stuff in her apartment."

"That box? That was mine," he says. "She took it from me so I wouldn't use it."

"But these were her friends."

"These are my friends," he says. "She just hung around to keep an eye on me. She pretended she was just spending time with me, but I knew what she was doing." With his free hand he reaches up and strokes the side of my face. "Don't worry," he says. "Everything will be fine." Then he plunges the needle into my vein.

I take a deep breath as he pulls the needle from my arm. He seems to be receding from me, though he is still there, kneeling at my feet and smiling.

I am warm.

I am calm.

I am sinking, heavy as a stone.

Someone is screaming my name.

I'm dreaming, and in the dream I'm cold and wet and the ground beneath me is shaking. Someone is screaming my name.

I open my eyes.

All I see is water. It's cold and it's beating down on my face.

I blink and try to lift my hand to wipe my eyes. I can't move. There's a weight on my chest, and pain. Someone is pounding on my chest so fiercely it jams my spine into the hard surface below me. I lift my head.

My skirt is bunched around my waist. A boy is straddling me, beating his hands against my chest. He is close to sobbing, calling out my name. We are in the shower. I stare at him, his red frantic face, his flying fists. He's hurting me. I think maybe this is still a dream.

"What . . . ," I try to say. My voice is so small.

The terrible pounding stops. The boy lifts his head and grabs my face between his hands. "Olivia?" he says. "Oh my God, Olivia?" I recognize him now, his face so close to mine I can see the pores in his skin. It's Peter.

"What . . . ," I say again. He clutches me to him, so hard it hurts. "I'm so sorry," he is saying, over and over, sobbing out my name. "I almost killed you." Then I turn my head and vomit over his arm. "Shit," I say. I realize that I'm crying.

"It's all right," he says. "It's my fault. Oh God, I'm so sorry." He eases back and helps me to a sitting position. He rinses his hand and arm under the water. With his other hand on my back, he holds me up. "How do you feel?"

"Terrible," I say. "I'm all wet."

"I know," he says soothingly, as though he's talking to a child. "Let's get you cleaned up." He takes off my wet, stained shirt and puts it in a ball on the edge of the tub. I can't even help him. I just sit here letting him lift and lower my arms like he's undressing a doll. I've never been so tired in my life.

Peter squirts shampoo into his hand and begins to wash the vomit from my hair. "You're all right now," he murmurs. "Everything's going to be fine." I lean forward and close my eyes. I feel as though I'm just now learning how to breathe.

"What happened?" I say.

"Your heart stopped," he says. He runs his hand through my hair to rinse it and it tilts my head back so that I'm looking him in the face, only inches from him, as though we're going to kiss.

"What do you mean, my heart stopped?"

"You died," he says. "I swear to God you died."

I shake my head. "That's impossible."

"Well, it happened," he says. "You were dead."

I try to speak but my voice lodges inside my throat.

"You were dead." He takes a choking breath. "Just like her."

I shake my head again.

He runs his hands through my hair. "Thank God you're all right. You scared the shit out of me. One minute you were fine, and then I was about to shoot up, and you just didn't look right. I could tell somehow, the life had gone out of you. I carried you in here."

"How long?" I manage to say.

"How long what?" The cold water keeps coming down, and I'm shivering.

"How long did it stop?"

"I don't know," he says. "It can't have been long, or I wouldn't have been able to start it again." He leans down and presses his ear to my chest, up against my wet skin. "It's beating now," he says. Sitting up, he takes my hand and lays it over my heart. "Feel that beating?"

I do feel it, my heart's faint rhythm against my hand.

Peter reaches over me and turns off the shower. "You're shivering." He rubs his hands rapidly up and down my arms to warm me. "Let's get out." While he climbs out of the tub I put my other hand to my neck and find that pulse with my fingers. Peter gets a towel and leans over to wrap it around me. Then he tells me to put my arms around his neck. I don't want to let go of my heart, but I do what he tells me. He half lifts me to a standing position. Leaning on him, I step out of the tub.

"Can you stand now?" he asks me, smoothing my hair back from my face. I nod. "Get out of those clothes and dry off then. I'll go get you something to wear." He leaves the room, dripping water.

Alone, I put both hands on the sink and lean in to stare at myself in the mirror. I look terrible. My shoulders are bare, my nipples showing through the wet fabric of my bra. There are dark circles under my eyes, and my pupils are enormous. My hair is wet and tangled. I run my shaking fingers through it. I see no resemblance to Allison in my face. This is just me who did this, pale lips, lank brown hair, skin drained of color.

I slip out of my wet clothes and wrap the towel around myself. I'm still shivering. A terrible sick feeling flashes through me, and I have to drop to my knees by the toilet and vomit again. This is all I can think about, each small movement I have to make. Put your hand on the sink. Pull yourself up. Turn on the water. Rinse out your mouth. Look in the mirror. This is just you, naked and afraid.

Peter comes back in with a T-shirt and a pair of boxers that must belong to Nate. "This is all I could find that's clean," he says apologetically. "Put them on and I'll make a bed for you on the couch."

"I've got to go home," I say.

He shakes his head. "You're not going anywhere. You've got to sleep this off, and I want to keep an eye on you." His tone is so firm, I don't argue. He watches me like he can't stand to move his eyes away. I drop the towel and put on the clothes. The T-shirt clings to me like a second skin. I feel like I should hang up Nate's towel. When I bend to pick it up another wave of nausea washes over me so I just leave it crumpled on the floor.

"I'm so sorry," Peter says again. He catches me up in a fierce hug. I don't have the energy to put my arms around him, so I just lean against him, like a rag doll. He helps me down the hall to the living room. He puts a pillow on the couch and hums to himself while he lays a blanket across the cushions. His fear is gone. He seems giddy with relief. All I feel is sad and tired and sick.

The couch is so small I have to curl up in a fetal position to fit, my body still shaking, with cold or fear or nausea. Nate is still spread-eagled on the floor, his eyes closed, his face a picture of bliss. Peter finds another blanket and tucks it around me. Then he kisses me on the cheek, and I close my eyes. "You didn't die," he whispers. Across my lids I see the headline: REPORTER DIES OF DRUG OVERDOSE. FRIENDS SAY DALE, 25, LED A SECRET LIFE.

I open my eyes again. Peter is sitting in the armchair, tightening the belt around his arm with his teeth. The needle is in his hand. I sit up. "What are you doing?"

He hesitates. "I don't want this to go to waste."

"I almost died," I say, my voice rising.

I almost died.

"I've done this before," he says. "It would take a much higher dose to kill me."

"You can't," I say, clutching at the blanket. "What if something happens?"

"Nothing's going to happen," he says.

"Please don't."

He sounds irritated when he says, "I know what I'm doing. Just go to sleep. It's fine." He sinks the needle into his arm. The color rises in his face and he slumps backward in his chair, nodding himself away.

I sit watching him breathe, terrified that the slow rise and fall of his chest will stop. It would break my heart if he died, because in this moment this boy feels like the only person in the world I really know. Not even Allison Avery would understand what I did tonight. All this time I never asked the right questions.

Peter is still breathing. I keep watching him, afraid to go to sleep. Later Nate rouses himself and stumbles off to bed. I stay awake, listening for the sound of my heart.

19

I have no idea where I am. It's dark in this room, and my legs are drawn up tight and cramping. There's a strange smell in here, both sharp and musty, like vinegar, and when I reach for the lamp that sits beside my bed my hand touches nothing but air. I sit up, my hands clutching at a blanket that doesn't feel like mine, and look around a large and nearly empty room with posters hanging on the walls. Then my vision clears and I know what all of these things mean. I know where I am. I remember, and the memory makes me shudder, brings back the sick feeling in the pit of my stomach.

I swing my feet onto the floor and stand up. My muscles ache as though after a hard run. My mouth is dry. Peter is sleeping on the floor beside the couch. I step over him and go down the hall to the bathroom to scoop water from the faucet into my mouth. On the floor in a pile are most of my clothes. I put on the skirt. It's still damp. The shirt, which is wet and crumpled on the bathtub, I leave behind.

Before I go I stand for a moment over Peter's body, watching him sleep. The faint sound of his snoring reassures me that he's still breathing. "Good-bye," I say out loud. I find my bag in the living room and leave.

Outside the sun is just coming up, and the sky is streaked with pink. The street is quiet. The sign over the doughnut shop is turned off. Everything is still and waiting. I put my hand over my heart and feel it beating. If my heart really stopped, shouldn't there be some kind of pain?

The drive home seems to take an hour. I listen to the radio without really hearing it. I put on my blinker and turn down streets and stop at red lights without ever thinking about where I'm going or how to get there. When I get home I let myself in as quietly as I can. It seems like a place I haven't seen in months, and I move around the room, touching the things I know to be mine, reminding myself that I live here.

In my bedroom I sit on the edge of the bed and think about going to work. I am sore and sick and dreadfully tired. I have no idea how long the signs will last, and I keep imagining Peggy peering into my eyes, noticing some mark on my left arm, and ordering me off for drug testing. The safest thing to do is call her voice mail and say I have the stomach flu and I'm not coming in. "Someone else will have to do the follow-up," I say into the phone. "I don't care who. Somebody else."

Then I take off my damp skirt and Nate's tight T-shirt and crawl into bed.

Later Hannah comes in and says I'm going to be late for work. I tell her I'm sick and she lays her hand on my forehead and says it feels like I have a fever. She brings me a glass of water and makes me sit up and take some aspirin. Then she leaves, saying she'll call later to check on me. After she is gone I sink back down into sleep. It is like going underwater, dropping like a stone to the bottom of a pool.

The sound of the doorbell ringing drags me from some terrible dream. I wake up drenched with sweat, naked and uncovered. I've kicked the bedclothes off. The doorbell rings again. I roll out of bed and find a T-shirt on the floor. Then I stumble down the hall to the front door, still half dreaming, moving on instinct. I reach the door and open it. For a moment I can see only a dark figure against the brightness outside, and in my half-dreaming state it seems like something out of a nightmare, a ghost, a visitation. Then the figure steps closer. It's Peter.

"I called the newspaper," he says. "They said you were sick." He touches my arm. "You look awful," he says, his voice colored with shock and worry. I put a hand to my cheek. I am hot to the touch. I know how I must look, damp and feverish, my hair tangled and wet. "Can I come in?" he says. I step aside. He comes in and shuts the door and the room is dark again. "Were you sleeping?"

I nod, leaning back against the wall. He shifts from foot to foot, looking around the room, the clothes draped over the couch, the magazines sliding off the coffee table onto the floor. "You're just as messy as . . . ," he says, but doesn't finish. He looks at me, biting his lip. I can't think of a thing to say. For a moment we are frozen here, staring at each other, and then he lunges at me and pulls me into a hug, holding me so tightly that for a moment I can't breathe, my face pressed against his chest. "I'm so sorry," he says. One of us is shaking.

He says that he wants to stay with me tonight, that he told his mother he was spending the night at a friend's. Then he is whispering something, that he's sorry, that he loves me, I think, and then he takes my face between his hands and kisses me, frantic, wet kisses on my forehead, my eyelids, my trembling mouth.

"Wait, wait," I say, taking my mouth from his.

"What's the matter?" he says.

I shake my head. A flush is rising through my body and I am so hot I feel as if I might faint. I clap my hand to my mouth and run down the hall to the bathroom to be sick again.

Afterwards I brush my teeth twice and stand in the shower under the cold water for five minutes. When I come out, tying my bathrobe tightly around me, Peter is waiting in the hall. "I'm so sorry," he says. "I don't know what's the matter with me."

"It's okay," I say.

"You're shivering." He rubs my arms with his hands. "You should be lying down." He puts his arm around me and we go into my bedroom.

We sit on the bed and he takes my hand. Cold water drips from my hair over my shoulders.

"Are you mad at me?" he says. I look at him, his face lined with worry as he asks the question again. He seems at once much younger than me and much older. I don't say anything. "I almost killed you," he says, his voice breaking. "I don't know what I would have done . . ."

"Why did you want me to do it?" I ask him.

"I thought that . . ." His voices trails away.

"Tell me."

"I don't know. I wanted you there." He looks at me, his eyes filling with tears, and gives me that beautiful smile, just like the first time I saw him. "I wanted you with me."

"And Allison never did it?" I say. "Never once?"

"I tried to get her to," he says. "I told her it was the only way to really be in your body. Do you know what I mean? Sometimes everything seems gray to me, the people I know, school. Like my parents, just doing what they're supposed to every day. Life shouldn't be just day after day of doing your laundry, taking the car to the shop. It should be . . ." He looks up at the ceiling, searching for the right word. "It should be fierce."

"Why wouldn't she do it?"

"She said, all of that makes no difference if you die." One corner of his mouth slides up, somewhere between a smile and a grimace. "And I said, 'I'm going to die.'"

"What did she say?"

"She said, 'And if you don't?'"

For a long moment he is silent. Then he says, "There's something I haven't told you."

"That doesn't surprise me," I say. I almost laugh.

He says he'd been mainlining about two months when Allison found his stash and took it, then gave him the option of quitting or telling his parents. She stayed with him through the worst of the withdrawal, convincing his parents he had the flu. It was almost over when he woke up alone, overwhelmed with craving. When his sister came by after work to check on him, she found him headed out the door to Nate's. When she couldn't change his mind, she persuaded him to come back to her apartment with her, saying she would go get something to make it better.

I watch him as he tells his story, feeling oddly distant from him, as though there is a pane of glass between us. It doesn't quite make sense to me, why his sister would steal morphine for him, believing that it was better than heroin. He responds with impatience when I ask. "She was worried I would OD," he says. "Because my tolerance was lower. She wanted to control the dosage."

"Why didn't she give you the heroin?"

"She wouldn't have known how much to give me," he says irritably. "And maybe she didn't want me to know she still had it."

I nod, turning that over. "Did she give you the morphine?"

He shakes his head. "I never saw her again. She took me up to her apartment and made a bed for me on the couch. She kissed me on the forehead and she said, 'I'll be right back.'"

"But she wasn't."

"I don't know," he says. "I left. I just couldn't stand it, the waiting, so I left and I went to Nate's." He finishes the story in a rush. "I've thought about this a lot. And I think when she got back to the apartment and I was gone she went racing out after me, in a panic, and that's when they got her. That's when they killed my sister. And then when she was in that trunk, alone and trapped, she must have known they were going to kill her. Maybe they told her they were going to rape her, maybe she could just tell." He turns to me. "Think of it."

I'm shivering. "I have," I say.

"So she gave herself the morphine so there wouldn't be any pain. And she couldn't tell, in the dark, how much to use, so even if they hadn't killed her, she'd be dead." He takes both my hands in his and says very slowly, as though to be sure I don't miss a word, "It's all my fault. If I hadn't told her I was going to Nate's, if I had stayed in her apartment, she wouldn't have been there when they came by. I was weak. I as good as killed her." He shakes his head. "Nate wasn't even there. I just went home."

It's easy to believe it's his fault. He's right. He could have changed her path. I don't say that. I say, "If she hadn't taken a job at the doctor's office, if she hadn't gone home to check on you, if she hadn't met Russell in college and been in a hurry to meet him, if she'd left ten minutes earlier or later . . . a thousand things took her to that moment. You can't blame yourself." It's easy to believe that, too.

He sobs, his shoulders shaking. I know he wants to believe me. I pull him toward me, so his head is on my breasts, and I rock us both from side to side. "I'll never do it again, Olivia," he whispers, "I swear." He feels so fragile to me, his bones so close to the surface of his skin. I think about Allison Avery, how she would want me to hold her baby brother like this, to tell him it's not his fault. I know her secrets, the dead girl, but that is not what I want to remember, the facts of her life stripped bare and laid on the page. I want to remember how she felt, how much she loved this boy. When he stops crying, I ease him back on the bed, and he closes his eyes as though to sleep. I curl into him, my head in the curve of his shoulder. I listen to the warm thudding of his heartbeat inside his chest. We begin to breathe in unison. I close my eyes.

When I wake, one of us has rolled away. We are lying side by side on the bed, on our backs, Peter is still sleeping. I prop myself up and watch the gentle movement of his eyes beneath his lids, the flutter of his pulse inside his throat. I don't want him anymore, but I do feel, in this moment, that I love him. He sighs and murmurs something I can't understand. I would like to remember this forever, how it felt to be here now, the stillness of the room, the softness of his face in sleep.

I am certain of one thing. It will not be like this again.

20

When Peter and I walk into the kitchen, Hannah is sitting at the table, eating a bowl of cereal. She raises her eyebrows. "Well, hello?" she says, making it a question. I say good morning and introduce them. Then I pull out two bowls and some cereal boxes. Peter shifts nervously from foot to foot and says he's not hungry. "Do you want some coffee?" I ask, then I see Hannah hasn't made it yet.

Peter says he'll make some and busies himself with filters and grounds. I go outside to get the paper. As I leave the room I hear Hannah asking, "So how do you know Olivia?"

On the porch I unfold the paper and look for the follow-up story on the front page. There it is, WITNESS HEARD SUSPECTS PLANNING ROBBERY, with Evan's byline above the copy. I read the lead: "Samuel Peterson, 18, told police last night that he heard the suspects in the Avery slaying planning to steal a car and commit robbery," and then I make myself stop and go back inside.

When I walk back in, Hannah gives me the look I'm expecting, knowing, disapproving. I ignore her, and go over to Peter, where he is leaning against the counter and watching the coffee drip into the pot with a look of desperate concentration. I touch his arm and he smiles at me. "It's almost done," he whispers. I ask Hannah if she wants some, and when she says yes I reach into the cabinet for three mugs and set them in a neat row on the counter. Then I go to the refrigerator for milk. I retrieve the sugar bowl from the top of the fridge. I open a drawer and take out three spoons. This is the strangest moment of my life. I shot heroin into my arm. I spent the night curled up with a seventeen-year-old boy with a dead sister whose wig I have been wearing on the streets around Memphis. Now I am putting one spoon in each mug so that we can all have coffee and go off to work.

In silence the three of us sit at the table and drink the coffee. I reach for the paper again and read Evan's story. Samuel Peterson claims he heard Jared Gillespie and Cody Parker planning to drive to Memphis in order to steal a car and hold up a convenience store. He says he heard Gillespie suggest taking a car from the owner at gunpoint, because that way they could get the keys. The police now think that the abduction wasn't planned, that, as Lieutenant Nash says, "the whole thing just escalated."

That should be my byline above the first column, not Evan's.

"Olivia?" Peter says.

"Yeah?" I glance up. He's leaning toward me across the table, his empty mug pushed aside. With her head bowed over her bowl, Hannah is pretending not to watch us.

"I said, 'I'm going to go home now,'" he says. "My mother will be wondering where I am."

"Okay." I put the paper down, and he stands and comes around the table toward me at the exact moment that I scoot my chair back, so the leg of the chair rams into his leg. "Oh God, I'm sorry," I say, jumping to my feet. "Are you okay?"

He gives me a smile that looks more like a wince, and nods. Then he turns to go. I follow him down the hall into the living room, and at the door, we come together and hug. He kisses my cheek. I reach up to kiss him once on the mouth. I step back. We start to speak at the same time, and then we both stop, and then he smiles and says he'll talk to me later, and I nod and say good-bye, and that is all. He is gone.

I'm standing by the front door, my hand pressed to my mouth, when I hear Hannah's voice. "The dead girl's brother, Olivia?" she says. I turn to see her standing with her arms crossed at the other end of the room. "What is going on? How old is that child?"

I shake my head and say nothing. She must see that I'm on the verge of tears because she crosses the room and touches my shoulder gently. "Okay," she says, her voice softer now. "Okay."

When I walk into the newsroom, I feel as though everyone is going to fall silent and turn to stare. I stand for a moment at the front of the room. No one looks at me. Then Peggy lifts her gaze from the newspaper on the metro desk. She calls my name. I walk over to her, resisting the urge to tug on my left sleeve. She studies my face. "How are you feeling?" she says. I'm listening for a current of suspicion in her voice. I hear only a distracted concern. Now that I'm actually guilty of the thing she suspected, her mind is on other things.

"I'm fine now," I say. "Must have been one of those twenty-four-hour bugs."

"Good, good," she says, turning her attention back to the paper. "Glad you're back."

"About the story, the dead girl," I say. "I want to stay with it."

"That's fine with me," she says. "Just mention it to Evan. He took over yesterday."

"Okay," I say. "Thanks." She's not looking at me anymore. I stand here watching her. I have an urge to confess, to tell her the story of all the stupid things I've done, to show her the tiny mark on my arm.

"Don't stand there staring," she says without lifting her gaze. "Go back to work."

I walk through the rows of desks to Evan's. He watches me approach, playing with a pen in his hand. The front page is spread out on his desk. I point at his byline. "Good story," I say.

"Thanks." He touches my hand with his pen. "How are you?"

"Okay." We both nod. He looks down at the paper, chewing on his lip.

"You know it's my story, don't you?" I say. "Because I want it back."

He looks up and gives me a weary smile. "It's yours."

As I turn toward my desk he says my name. When I look at him, he says, "I'm sorry. I don't know how I could have thought . . ." He shakes his head. "I want us to be friends again."

"Don't worry," I say. "I'm sorry too." I touch the back of his hand, and he turns it over and grasps mine. We stand there for a moment, our hands locked across his desk. Then Evan's phone rings.

When Evan hangs up, he calls me and I roll my chair over to his desk. "That was my source in the DA's office," he says. "She says one of the boys has confessed." He hands me a piece of paper with a name and number. "I told her you would call her back."

I reach for the phone, my heart rate accelerating.

The woman in the district attorney's office reads me Robby Shavers's statement over the phone. At sixteen, Robby is the youngest of the boys, and he sobbed while he told the story. He didn't mean to kill anyone, he said, he just went along with the plan to steal a car. He thought they'd just go joyriding, something they had done before. They were cruising around in Cody Parker's car, trying to pick out one to steal, when Jared Gillespie saw the girl, walking toward the street, her car keys in her hand. Jared and Cody got out, and Robby Shavers slid into the driver's seat of Cody's car. Robby watched through the window as Jared and Cody forced the girl into the trunk of her car at gunpoint. The girl was shaking her head and trying to back away. Robby rolled down the window and he heard her saying, "Just take the car. I won't tell anyone." Jared hit her across the face, and she fell against the open trunk. Jared and Cody shoved her in. Then Robby followed them out to the park.

It was never part of the plan to kill anyone, Robby said, but they had trouble getting her out of the trunk, she seemed barely conscious, and during the struggle to lift her out she scratched Jared and he hit her. Then Cody hit her, and when she fell to the ground they were on her. They tied her hands. Jared raped her, Robby said. He didn't. He hung back, listening to her scream, and then he got back in Cody's car. He didn't look until he heard the other car's engine start. When he looked back, the girl's body was disappearing beneath the wheels of her car.

I hang up the phone. I put my hands flat on my desk. My fingers tremble slightly and are still. The picture of Allison Avery is still propped against my computer. She laughs. The boy in the baseball cap kisses her cheek. All the images I have seen of this girl alive can't erase the first one, the one of her dead. One thing I know, I won't forget this. I won't get over it. Some part of me will always be afraid.

For a moment I sit looking around the newsroom. A reporter stands up, grabs his jacket, and goes striding out of the room. Two editors stand close together, talking low, showing each other the papers in their hands. A woman leans into her phone, gesturing wildly, her voice rising. "I need to know," she is saying. "I need to know." I glance over at Evan. He's frowning at his computer screen, chewing on a fingernail. Around me the noise rises and falls, the clatter of keyboards, the ringing of telephones, the buzz of all these voices. Here in the center it is quiet.

I reach out and turn on my computer. I pick up the phone and dial the police station. While I'm waiting to speak to Lieutenant Nash, Bishop goes sauntering past, hands in his pockets. He's whistling through his teeth, a notebook in his breast pocket, his glasses sliding to the end of his nose. I catch his eye and smile. He smiles back at me and winks, welcoming me home.

21

In August, Jared Gillespie's attorney calls me and asks me to come to the jail and meet him. He wants me to sit in on an attorney-client meeting. He won't tell Jared who I am, he says, and everything I hear will be off the record. He wants me to see with my own eyes that Jared Gillespie is just a scared young boy.

Both of the other boys have now confessed, each claiming that he didn't rape her, that he wasn't the one who drove the car. The DNA evidence will prove at least one of them a liar about the rape. About the driver, everyone seems to agree. Jared Gillespie, scared young boy.

I meet the attorney at the county jail, just outside of Bolivar, Mississippi. Inside it's cinder block walls, and a few men dressed like inmates, just walking around. The attorney shakes hands with one and high-fives another, a man with a mustache who gives me a slow wink. Then he walks up to the woman manning the desk. She looks up and says, "Who do you want?" Half the prison population must be his clients.

I sign my name to a list at the desk. The woman doesn't even ask me who I am. She gets on the radio and says, "Bring in Gillespie." After a few minutes a man walks through the doors, alone, wearing handcuffs. I take a quick glance at him, then look at the lawyer, who motions for us to follow him into a side conference room. The room is so small that when I reach for a chair my arm brushes Jared

Gillespie's. There is no electric shock of revulsion. It feels like nothing. It feels like skin, warm to the touch.

We sit around the little table, the three of us, and I stare at the
man across from me. Jared Gillespie is about six feet tall. He is thin
but muscular, his biceps hard little lumps inside his long, slender
arms. He sports a scraggly mustache. His stringy brown hair is long
in the back and hangs over his eyes in the front. His face is young
and round and soft. His eyes are black. He has a small mouth, lips
so thin and pale they're nearly indistinguishable from his colorless
skin. His overlapping teeth are stained a faint yellow from nicotine.
He is nineteen years old.

He does not seem evil. His face is as blank as a doll's, even when
he smiles.

The lawyer calls a guard to remove Jared's handcuffs. Jared rubs
his wrists. He takes a cigarette from a pack and lights it, inhaling
slowly. Then he pushes the pack in my direction across the table.
"Want a smoke?" he says. It's the first thing I've heard him say. His
accent is thick, lower-class southern. I nod and take a cigarette. He
leans forward and lights it for me, and I look right into those black
eyes. It's like peering through a window into a dark and empty
room.

According to his friends' accounts, Jared Gillespie is the one who
forced Allison Avery into the trunk of the car. He was the first to
rape her, and he paced back and forth punching the air while the
others took their turns. He was the one who began to hit her, and
then he kicked her, said Cody Parker, until she stopped screaming.
The other two say they started to run back to Cody's car, but Jared
wasn't with them, and when they heard a car engine start up they
turned back to see the blue Honda Civic backing away, then racing
toward the curled-up girl, Jared at the wheel. "We just stood there,"
Parker said. "We couldn't do nothin'." When Jared pulled up beside
them and ordered them to follow him, they did it, they say, because
they were afraid he would kill them too. "He kept sayin' we couldn't

let her go," Parker said. "He said she saw us and we couldn't let her go."

I can chart it out, now, exactly how it happened, who grabbed her, what they said, what they did, when they did it. I still don't know how it felt to be there, to be her, to be him, this boy who sits slouched in his chair smoking a cigarette, the picture of sullen youth. I'm watching him, trying to picture him doing the things I know he did, trying to picture his face contorted with rage, the desire to destroy. I would like him to be an evil genius out of the movies, leaning back in his chair and coolly regarding us while he explained his master plan. All I see is this blank-faced boy, and I can't feel anything about him, not fear, not even hate.

His lawyer begins to go over some of his strategy for defense, that the cops coerced the other boys into pinning the blame on Jared because he's the only one who will automatically be tried as an adult. Jared's claim is that he was there, but he didn't rape her, he didn't hit her, and in fact he got scared and took off running when the other boys climbed back in the car and gunned the engine. He says they came after him and demanded he get in the car. "I didn't want to hurt nobody," he says, his voice a monotone. "I thought we was just gonna steal the car."

"How are you feeling, Jared?" The lawyer leans forward, an expression of avuncular concern on his face. "Are you scared?"

Jared looks down at the table and shrugs. "Yeah, I'm scared, man," he says. He studies the cigarette in his hand, burned down almost to his fingers. "I'm really scared. There's no doubt about that."

"You know, Jared," his lawyer says, "that the district attorney will likely seek the death penalty."

"I know, man," Jared says, shaking his head. "I'm scared, too. Them other guys is lyin', and I'm the one who might fry for it."

The lawyer looks at me, as though to say, are you getting this? I raise my eyebrows. We stare at each other for a moment, and then he turns back to Jared. "I'm going to do everything I can to make sure that doesn't happen," he says. Then he pauses, leaning back in his chair. "Have you seen Teresa lately?"

"Yeah, she came to see me the other day."

"And how's your little girl? What's her name? Annabelle?"

"Annabelle, that's right. She's okay, I guess. I haven't seen her." He takes another cigarette from the pack.

"You miss your family, don't you?"

"Sure I do. I miss my mama, and Teresa, and my baby. What's she gonna think, her daddy locked up in a place like this?" He waves his hand to indicate the room. Then he lights his cigarette. "You want another one?" he says, looking at me. I look back at him, and he smiles, showing all his jagged yellow teeth. I shake my head, and he shrugs as if to say, your loss. He takes a drag and exhales slowly.

"You know Allison Avery's family misses her too," the lawyer says, his voice grave. He shoots me another look to see how I'm taking this.

"I do, and I feel real bad about that," Jared says. "I wish I'd never gone along with that plan. I read about her mama in the paper, and I'm real sorry for her. But she said she wanted me dead, and that's not right. I didn't kill her baby. I wasn't the one."

The righteous indignation in his voice when he says "that's not right" makes it hard to hold my tongue. Underneath the table I rub my hands up and down my thighs. Anything I could say to him would be like Peter ramming his mailbox, a useless, hopeless gesture. I want to say "You hit her. You raped her. You killed her." I want to ask him if there was any reason why.

I sit here listening to his lawyer feed him questions designed to provoke responses that will make me see him as human, as pitiable. I'd like to stop him and tell him that I've seen Jared Gillespie as human from the moment I walked into this room, and that it makes no difference. He is the reason I have to be afraid. He is death visited upon you without reason or remorse. He didn't kill her because she spurned him, because she cheated him in a drug deal, because he knew her and wanted her to die. He just killed her.

Jared Gillespie stands up to go back to his cell. His lawyer stands up, saying something I'm not even hearing anymore, and then I'm on my feet, too, and I hear myself saying, "Why did you do it?"

"Don't answer that, Jared," his lawyer says sharply. He frowns at me, his face a picture of righteous anger at my violation of the deal.

I ignore him, staring at Jared Gillespie. "Tell me why," I say. I can hear the note of pleading in my voice.

Jared looks at me for a long time. I wonder what he sees. I am the same height as Allison Avery, the same age. I have dark hair, the same shape to my face. Does he see her when he looks at me? Does he want to rape me, beat me, crush my bones? "Jared," I say, making my voice hard and sharp. "Tell me why."

"Lady," he says, finally, "I don't even know."

Epilogue

In Memphis, the end of the summer begins with Death Week. Every year thousands of people come from everywhere to line up outside the iron gates of Graceland and weep for a man they think they knew. Tonight I'm covering the candlelight vigil, moving through a crowd of solemn men and women in Elvis T-shirts, candles in their hands. Some of them are waiting to file through the gates behind the house and past the grave, strewn with flowers and love poems. Some of them have already been, and now they are just waiting with the others for the night to pass into the day that Elvis Presley died. A loudspeaker broadcasts his ballads, and some of the people sing along, tears streaming from their eyes. It's a hot, sluggish late August night.

When I'm through here, David wants me to come to Mud Island so we can talk. Two weeks ago I finally told him about the heroin, about my desire for Peter, about how completely I lost myself in the story. We were sitting on his front porch. Across the street a couple sat close on a porch swing, not talking, just watching the sun go down. Some mother's voice rose in the air after a tardy child. "I can't believe it," David kept saying over and over. "I thought I knew you. I had no idea."

"Neither did I," I said.

I don't know what else to say to him. I don't know what will happen to us. Perhaps he deserves someone more like himself, someone who takes people at their word. I'm not sure what I deserve. In the end I will probably go to my car and drive past all the yellow-painted homes, the porches, and hanging plants. A young woman riding her bike will lift her hand in a wave and I'll wave back. Then I'll drive onto the bridge off Mud Island, heading back over the river into town.

In the next week or so Peter will call to say that he's leaving for college. He'll say that he's going to write and I'll pretend to believe him. He's spent the last month in a drug-counseling program, and he'll swear to me again that he's stopped using forever. Neither of us will mention the fact that we'll both be at the trial, and most likely we won't speak there, just lift a hand in greeting from opposite sides of the room. What we have left between us now is a faint tenderness, a faint embarrassment. He seems like a dream I had, and when I remember it now it's not the words that passed between us I think of. It's the small sounds he made when I kissed him, somewhere between pleasure and pain.

As for Carl, sometimes I still catch a glimpse of him on the street or at another table in a restaurant where I'm eating lunch with Hannah. I pretend not to see him there.

I'm not going to put in the paper that Jared Gillespie doesn't know why he killed that girl. I'm going to keep reporting the things I've learned about him, that his father abused him, that he grew up poor and uneducated, that his father's departure and his own early parenthood left him blaming women for the problems in his life. I'm going to report that he was hopped up on pills and alcohol. When you read it you still won't understand how someone could do what he did, but the course of events will make a familiar, sad kind of sense, and you will know that everything happens for a reason.

I'm not going to put in the paper that I went looking for Allison Avery, that I thought I would find her in the heroin rushing through my veins. Instead I found her in the terror I felt when I woke up in the shower with a boy I didn't recognize screaming my name. I stopped my heart for her, and this is my secret, that I followed her as far as I could.

"Love Me Tender" comes over the loudspeaker, and on the chorus thirty thousand voices join in. There is no way to describe the sound except to say that it's beautiful, that it swells my heart. I look around me. A man beside me with dyed black hair and sideburns sways from side to side, his eyes closed. Two women hang on each other's necks, weeping. I am not as different from these people as I would once have thought, all of us just looking for some kind of meaning, a story to shape our lives. When I leave here I will go back to the newsroom and make these people into a story. I will describe them, and report the things they've told me here tonight. They come because Elvis helped them through some of the worst moments of their lives. They come to see how he lived and where he died. They come because he was pretty. They come because once they met him, touched his hand. They come to be swept up in emotion, to let the sound of his voice remind them what they're living for. When they see my story in the paper, when they see their names in print, they will feel a part of something so much larger than themselves.

One thing I know. I am still here. In the hot, thick night, I stand shoulder to shoulder with thirty thousand people. The tiny flames of candles flicker in their hands.